KINGDOM OF THE WICKED

Also by Kerri Maniscalco

Kingdom of the Wicked
Kingdom of the Cursed

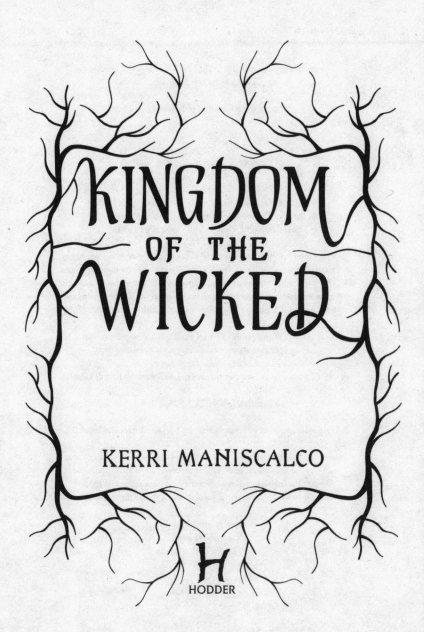

KINGDOM OF THE WICKED

KERRI MANISCALCO

HODDER

First published in Great Britain in 2020 by Hodder & Stoughton
An Hachette UK company

This paperback edition published in 2021

22

A CIP catalogue record for this title is available from the British Library

Paperback ISBN 978 1 529 35048 7

Printed and bound in Great Britain by Clays Ltd, Elcograf S.p.A.

Hodder & Stoughton policy is to use papers that are natural, renewable and recyclable products and made from wood grown in sustainable forests. The logging and manufacturing processes are expected to conform to the environmental regulations of the country of origin.

Hodder & Stoughton Ltd
Carmelite House
50 Victoria Embankment
London EC4Y 0DZ

www.hodder.co.uk

For my grandmother Victoria Marie Nucci
and my aunt Caroline Nucci.

And for my great grandparents – who immigrated
from Sciacca, Sicily to America – whose
restaurant inspired much of this story.

This may be a fantasy,
but the love of family found within its pages is very real.

Flectere si nequeo superos,
Acheronta movebo.

If I cannot bend the will of Heaven,
I shall move Hell.

Virgil, *Aeneid*

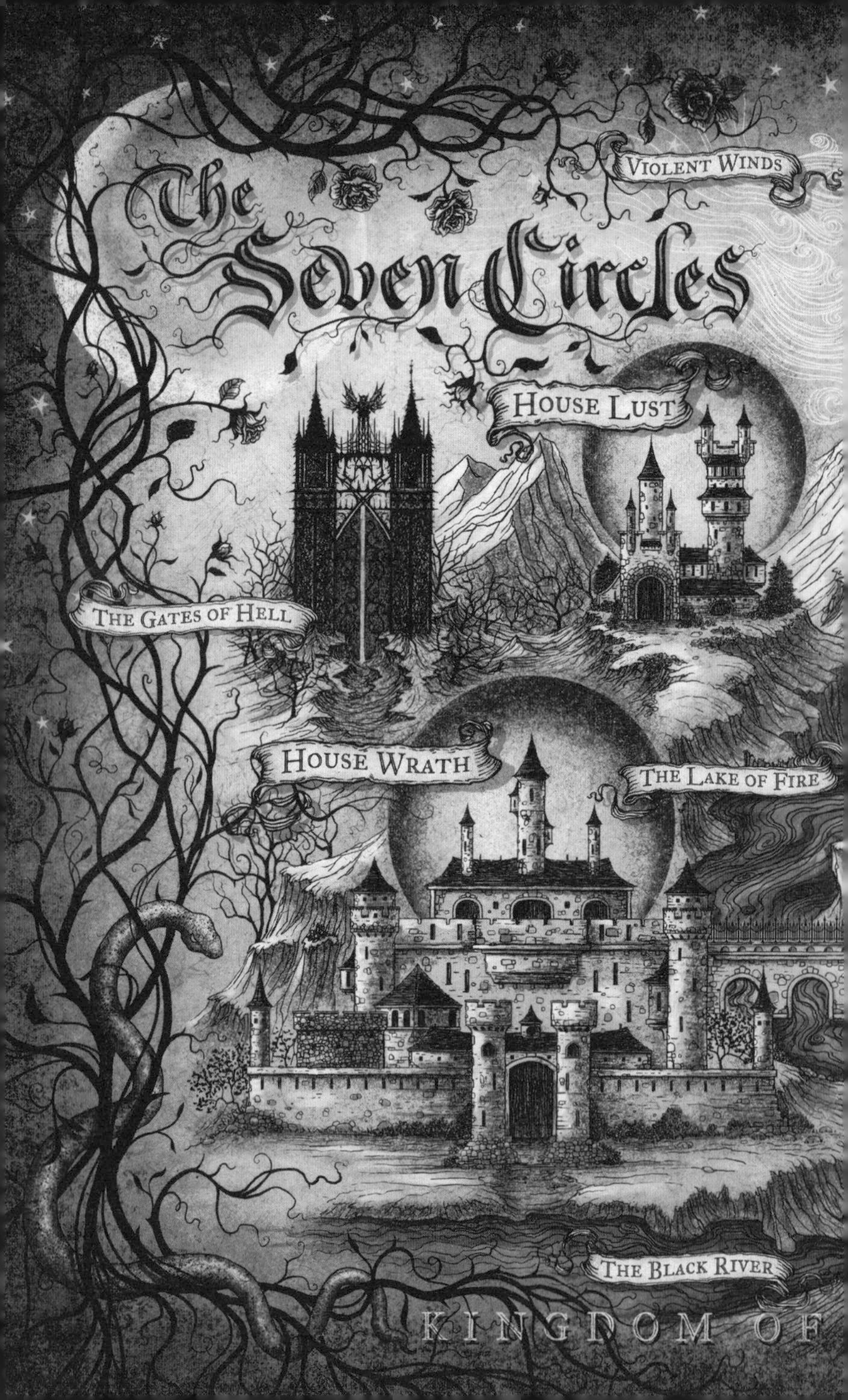
The Seven Circles
Violent Winds
House Lust
The Gates of Hell
House Wrath
The Lake of Fire
The Black River
KINGDOM OF

House Gluttony
Storm of Sins
House Sloth
House Pride
The Flaming Tombs
House Envy
House Greed
Bloodwood Forest
THE WICKED

PROLOGUE

Outside, wind rattled the wooden chimes in warning. In the distance, waves crashed against the shore; the frantic whispers of water growing louder as if the sea was a mage summoning violence. On this date—for nearly a decade now—the storm followed the same pattern. Next, thunder would roll in quicker than the tide with lightning cracking electric whips across an unforgiving sky. The devil demanded retribution. A blood sacrifice for power stolen.

It wasn't the first time he'd be cursed by witches, nor would it be the last.

From her rocking chair near the fire, Nonna Maria monitored the twins while they chanted protection charms she'd taught them, a *cornicello* clutched tightly in each of their little fists. Pushing the howling gusts from her mind, she listened closely to the words Vittoria and Emilia whispered over the horn-shaped amulets, their matching dark heads bent in concentration.

"By earth, moon, and stone, bless this hearth, bless this home."

It was the start of their eighth year and Nonna tried not to worry over how quickly they were growing. She pulled her shawl closer, unable to ward off chills in the small kitchen. It had little to do with the temperature outside. As much as she tried ignoring it, sulfur snuck in through the cracks along with the familiar plumeria-and-orange-scented breeze, raising the graying hair she'd swept up from her neck. Had she been alive, her own human grandmother would have called it an omen and spent the evening on her knees in the cathedral, rosary clutched close, praying to saints.

The devil was on the prowl. Or one of his wicked brothers was.

A sliver of worry slid in as quick and smooth as one of her paring knives, lodging itself near Nonna's heart. It had been an age since the last sighting of the Malvagi. Hardly anyone spoke of the Wicked anymore, except in stories told to frighten children into staying in their beds at night.

Now adults laughed at the old folktales, all but forgetting the seven ruling princes of Hell. Nonna Maria never would; their legends were burned into her mind, branding her with a bone-deep sense of dread. The area between her shoulders prickled as if their midnight eyes were upon her, watching from the shadows. It was only a matter of time before they came looking.

If they hadn't begun to already. One didn't steal from the devil and go unpunished.

Her focus darted back to the twins. Like the churning Tyrrhenian Sea, there was a restlessness about them tonight. One that spoke of unseen trouble to come. Vittoria's charms were rushed and Emilia stumbled over hers, trying to keep up.

A twig popped in the fire, quickly followed by another. The sound like wishbones snapping over their spell books; a warning in its own right. Nonna gripped the arms of her rocking chair, her knuckles turning the color of the blanched almonds lying on the counter.

"*Calmati!* Not so fast, Vittoria," she scolded. "You'll have to begin again if you don't do it correctly. Do you want to gather grave dirt alone in the dark?"

Much to Nonna's dismay, Vittoria didn't appear as frightened as she should have. The thought of wandering around a graveyard under the light of a full moon and an angry storm seemed appealing to the child. She pursed her lips before offering a slight shake of her head.

It was Emilia who answered, though, giving her sister a warning look. "We'll be more careful, Nonna."

To prove her point, Emilia held up the vial of holy water they'd gotten from the monastery and tipped it over their amulets, allowing one drop to sizzle over each. Silver and gold. An offering of balance between light and dark. A gift for what had been stolen all those years ago.

As above, so below.

Pacified, Nonna watched as they finished their charm, relieved when white sparks rose in the flames before burning red again. Another year, another victory. They'd tricked the devil once more. Eventually there'd come a day when the charms wouldn't work, but Nonna refused to think of that now. She glanced at the windowsill, pleased by the dried orange slices laid out in even rows.

Lavender sprigs hung to dry over the mantel, and the tiny stone island was covered with both flour and fragrant herbs waiting to be tied into neat bunches. Verbena, basil, oregano, parsley, and bay leaves. The scents mingled pleasantly. Some were for their celebratory dinner, and others for their charms. Now that the protection ritual was done, they might enjoy their meal.

Nonna looked at the clock on the mantel; her daughter and

son-in-law would arrive from the family restaurant soon, bringing with them laughter and warmth.

Storms and omens or not, all would be well in the di Carlo home.

The flames settled and Emilia sat back, biting her nails. A nasty habit Nonna was determined to break. The child spit a nail clipping out and went to toss it on the floor.

"Emilia!" Nonna's voice rang loudly in the small room. The child started, dropping her hand, and gave a sheepish look. "In the fire! You know better than to leave things for those who practice *le arti oscure*."

"Sorry, Nonna," Emilia mumbled. She chewed her lip, and her grandmother waited for the question she knew was coming. "Will you tell us about the dark arts again?"

"Or the Malvagi?" Vittoria added, always interested in stories of the Wicked. Even on nights they were forbidden from uttering such names. "Please?"

"We shouldn't speak of dark things aloud. It invites trouble."

"They're just stories, Nonna," Emilia said quietly.

If only that were true. Nonna Maria traced a protection charm over her heart, finishing it with a kiss to her fingertips, and exhaled. The twins exchanged triumphant grins. It was impossible to keep the legends from the girls, no matter if it filled their heads with dreams of the seven princes of Hell. Nonna feared they romanticized demons too much. It was best, she decided, to remind them why they should be wary of beautiful creatures without souls.

"Wash your hands and help roll the dough. I'll talk while you make the *busiate*."

Their matching smiles warmed the chills still clinging to Nonna brought on by the storm and its warning. The little corkscrew pasta served with tomato pesto was one of the girls' favorite dishes. They'd be pleased to find cassata already waiting in the ice box. Though the sweet ricotta sponge cake was an Easter specialty, the girls loved it on their birthday.

Even with all of their precautions, Nonna was unsure how much sweetness would remain in their lives, and spoiled them often. Not that she required extra incentive to do so. A grandmother's love was its own sort of powerful magic.

Emilia pulled the mortar and pestle from the shelf, face strained in concentration as she gathered up the olive oil, garlic, almonds, basil, pecorino, and cherry tomatoes for the pesto alla Trapanese. Vittoria removed the damp cloth from the mound of dough and began rolling the pasta as Nonna had taught her. Eight years old and they already knew their way around the kitchen. It was unsurprising. Between their home and the restaurant, they practically grew up in one. They both peered up from thick lashes, their expressions identical masks of anticipation.

Vittoria said impatiently, "Well? Are you going to tell us a story?"

Nonna sighed. "There are seven demon princes, but only four di Carlos should fear: Wrath, Greed, Envy, and Pride. One will crave your blood. One will capture your heart. One will steal your soul. And one will take your life."

"The Wicked," Vittoria whispered, her tone almost reverent.

"The Malvagi are demon princes who stalk the night, searching for souls to steal for their king, the devil, their hunger ravenous and unyielding, until dawn chases them away," Nonna continued, slowly rocking in her chair. The wood creaked, covering the sound of the storm. She nodded toward their tasks, making sure they held up their end of the bargain. The girls settled into their work. "The seven princes are so corrupted by sin, that when they cross into our world, they can't bear being in the light and are cursed to only venture out when it's dark. It was a punishment sent from La Prima Strega, many years ago. Well before man roamed the earth."

"Where is the First Witch now?" Emilia asked, an edge of skepticism creeping into her little voice. "Why hasn't she been seen?"

Nonna thought carefully. "She has her reasons. We must respect them."

"What do the demon princes look like?" Vittoria asked, though she must have had this part memorized by now.

"They appear human but their ebony eyes are tinged red, and their skin is hard as stone. Whatever you do, you must never speak to the Wicked. If you see them, hide. Once you've caught a demon prince's attention, he'll stop at nothing to claim you. They are midnight creatures, born of darkness and moonlight. And they seek only to destroy. Guard your hearts; if given the chance they'll rip them from your chests and guzzle your blood as it steams in the night."

No matter that they were soulless creatures who belonged to the devil, or they'd kill them on sight, the twins were enchanted by these dark and mysterious princes of Hell.

One more so than the other, as fate would have it.

"But *how* will we know when we meet one?" Vittoria asked. "What if we can't see their eyes?"

Nonna hesitated. They'd already heard so much, and if the ancient prophecy held true, she feared the worst was yet to come. "You just will."

Steeped in family tradition, Nonna Maria taught them magical ways of hiding from both humans and the midnight creatures.

Each year on their birthday, they gathered herbs from the tiny garden behind their home and made charms of protection.

They wore amulets blessed in holy water, freshly turned grave dirt, and sparkling shafts of moonlight. They recited words of protection and never spoke of the Malvagi when the moon was full. More importantly, they were never without their amulets.

Emilia's *cornicello* was made of silver, and Vittoria's gold. The girls weren't allowed to bring them together, or something terrible would happen. According to Nonna it would be like forcing the sun and moon to share the sky, bringing the world into an eternal twilight. There, the princes of Hell could escape their prison of fire for good, murdering and stealing souls of the innocent until the human world turned to ash—like their nightmare realm.

After they devoured their dinner and cake, the twins' mamma and papa kissed them good night. Tomorrow they'd begin helping in the family restaurant's busy kitchen, their first real dinner service. Too excited for sleep, Emilia and Vittoria giggled on their shared mattress, swinging their horn amulets at each other like tiny fairy swords, pretending to fight the Malvagi.

"When I grow up, I want to be a green witch," Emilia said later, cradled in the nook of her sister's arms. "I'll grow all kinds of herbs. And have my own trattoria. My menu will be crafted of magic and moonlight. Like Nonna."

"Yours will be even better." Vittoria's grip tightened in comfort. "By then I will be Queen, and I'll make sure you have whatever you like."

One night they decided to be brave. Nearly a month had passed since their eighth birthday and Nonna Maria's dire warnings seemed a lifetime ago. Vittoria thrust her amulet at her sister, her face determined. "Here," she commanded, "take it."

Emilia hesitated only a minute before clasping the golden horn in her palm.

A shimmering lavender-black light exploded from their amulets, startling Emilia enough that she dropped her sister's necklace. Vittoria swiftly fastened it back where it belonged, brown eyes wide as the glittering light abruptly faded. Both girls remained silent. Whether in fear or fascination, they couldn't be sure. Emilia flexed her hand, trying to work out the pin-prickling sensation crawling under her skin. Vittoria watched; her face hidden in shadow.

Nearby a hellhound howled up at the moon, though later they'd convince themselves it was only the wind snarling through the cramped streets of their quarter. They never told anyone what they'd done, and never spoke of the strange inky-purple light.

Not even to each other. And especially not to Nonna Maria.

Since they pretended the incident away, Emilia didn't tell her sister she'd been irrevocably changed—from that evening forward, whenever she held her *cornicello* and concentrated, she saw what she'd call *luccicare.* A faint shimmer or aura surrounding a person.

The only exceptions being herself and her twin.

If Vittoria also possessed this new talent, she never admitted so. It was the first of many secrets the twins would keep from each other. And would prove deadly for one.

ONE

Ten years later

Nonna Maria buzzed around the kitchen like she'd guzzled every drop of espresso in our restaurant. Her mood was downright frantic. My twin was late for dinner service and our grandmother saw it as a portent of doom, especially since Vittoria was out the night before a holy day. Goddess forbid.

The fact that the moon was not only full, but also a putrid shade of yellow had Nonna muttering the kind of warnings that normally made my father bolt the doors. Thankfully he and Uncle Nino were in the dining room with a frosty bottle of limoncello, pouring after-dinner drinks for our customers. No one left Sea & Vine without sipping the dessert liqueur and feeling the utter satisfaction and bliss that followed a good meal.

"Mock me all you like, but it's not safe. Demons are prowling the streets, searching for souls to steal." Nonna chopped cloves of garlic for the scampi, her knife flying across the worn cutting board. If she wasn't careful, she'd lose a finger. "Your sister is foolish to be out." She stopped, immediately shifting her attention to the little horn-shaped amulet around my neck. Worry lines carved a deep path around her eyes and mouth. "Did you see if she was wearing her *cornicello*, Emilia?"

I didn't bother responding. We never took our amulets off, not even while bathing. My sister broke every rule except that one. Especially after what happened when we were eight. . . . I briefly closed my eyes, willing the memory away. Nonna still didn't know about the *luccicare* I could see shimmering around humans while holding my amulet, and I hoped she never would.

"Mamma, please." My mother raised her gaze to the ceiling as if the goddess of sky might send an answer to her prayers in the form of a lightning bolt. I wasn't sure if the bolt was meant for Nonna, or my mother. "Let's get through dinner service before worrying about the Wicked. We have more pressing problems at the moment." She nodded to the sauté pan. "The garlic is starting to burn."

Nonna mumbled something that sounded suspiciously like "*So will their souls in Hell if we don't save them, Nicoletta,*" and I bit my lip to keep from smiling.

"Something's terribly wrong, I feel it in my bones. If Vittoria isn't home soon, I'll go looking for her myself. The Malvagi won't dare to steal her soul around me." Nonna brought her cleaver down on an unsuspecting mackerel, its head flopping to the limestone floor.

I sighed. We could've used it to make fish stock. Nonna was *really* getting herself worked up. She was the one who'd taught us the value in using every part of an animal.

Bones, however, could only be used for stock, not spells. At least those were the rules for us di Carlos. *Le arti oscure* was strictly forbidden. I scooped the fish head into a bowl to give to the alley cats later, banishing thoughts of the dark arts.

I poured some chilled wine for Nonna, adding orange slices and sugared peels to sweeten it. In moments, condensation bloomed like morning dew across the glass. It was mid-July in Palermo, which meant the air was stifling at night, even with our windows open, coaxing a breeze.

It was especially hot in the kitchen now, though during colder months I still wore my long hair up because of the soaring temperatures created by our oven fires.

Sea & Vine, the di Carlo family trattoria, was known across Sicily for our sinfully delicious food. Each evening our tables were crowded with hungry patrons, all waiting to dine on Nonna's recipes. Lines formed in the late afternoons, no matter the weather. Nonna said simple ingredients were her secret, along with a touch of magic. Both of those statements were true.

"Here, Nonna." We weren't supposed to use magic outside of our home, but I whispered a quick spell, and, using the condensation dripping onto the stone, slid the drink along the counter in front of her. She paused long enough in her worrying to sip the sweet red wine. My mother mouthed her thanks when my grandmother's back was turned, and I grinned.

I wasn't sure why Nonna was so agitated tonight. Over the last several weeks—starting around our eighteenth birthday—my twin missed quite a few dinner services, and had snuck in well past sunset, her bronze cheeks flushed and her dark eyes bright. There was something different about her. And I had a strong suspicion it was because of a certain young vendor in the market.

Domenico Nucci Junior.

I'd stolen a peek at her diary and had seen his name scribbled in the margins before guilt had overtaken me and I'd tucked it back under the floorboard where she'd hidden it. We still shared a room on the second floor of our small, crowded home, so thankfully she didn't notice my snooping.

"Vittoria is fine, Nonna." I handed her some fresh parsley to garnish the shrimp. "I told you she's been flirting with the Nucci boy who sells arancini for his family near the castle. I'm sure he's busy with all the pre-festival celebrations tonight. I bet she's passing out fried rice balls to everyone who's overindulged. They need something to soak up all that sacramental wine." I winked, but my grandmother's fear didn't abate. I set the rest of the parsley down and hugged her close. "No demon is stealing her soul, or eating her heart. I promise. She'll be here soon."

"One day I hope you'll take signs from the goddesses seriously, bambina."

Maybe one day. But I'd heard stories about red-eyed demon princes my whole life and hadn't met one yet. I wasn't too worried things would suddenly change now. Wherever the Wicked had gone, it seemed to be permanent. I feared them as much as I worried about dinosaurs suddenly returning from extinction to take over Palermo. I left Nonna to the scampi, and smiled as music filtered in between the sounds of knives chopping and spoons stirring. It was my favorite kind of symphony—one that allowed me to focus entirely on the joy of creation.

I inhaled the fragrant scent of garlic and butter.

Cooking was magic and music combined. The crack of shells, the hiss of pancetta hitting a hot pan, the metallic clang of a whisk beating the side of a bowl, even the rhythmic thwack of a cleaver against a wooden cutting board. I adored each part of being in a kitchen with my family. I couldn't imagine a more perfect way to spend an evening.

Sea & Vine was my future and it promised to be filled with love and light. Especially if I saved enough coin to purchase the building next door and expand our family business. I'd been experimenting with new flavors from across Italy and wanted to create my own menu one day.

My mother hummed along while forming marzipan into fruit shapes. "He's a nice boy. Domenico. He'd make a good match for Vittoria. His mother is always pleasant."

Nonna tossed a flour-coated hand in the air, waving it around as if the idea of an engagement with a Nucci stunk worse than the streets of the nearby fish market. "Bah! She's too young to worry about marriage. And he's not Sicilian."

My mother and I both shook our heads. I had a feeling his Tuscan roots had little to do with Nonna's disapproval. If she had it her way, we'd live in our ancestral home—in our little quarter of Palermo—until our bones turned to dust. Nonna didn't believe anyone else could watch over us as well as she could. Especially a mere human boy. Domenico wasn't witch-born like my father, and therefore Nonna didn't think he could ever fully be trusted with our secret.

"He was born here. His mother is from here. I'm fairly certain that makes him Sicilian," I said. "Stop being grumpy. It doesn't suit someone as sweet as you."

She harrumphed, ignoring my blatant attempt to charm her. Stubborn as a mule, as my grandfather would've said. She picked up her carved wooden spoon and pointed it in my direction. "Sardines washed themselves onto the shore. Gulls didn't touch them. You know what that means? It means *they're* no fools. The devil's stirring the seas, and they'll have nothing to do with his offerings."

"Mamma," my mother groaned and set the almond paste down. "A boat carrying kerosene crashed into the rocks last night. The oil killed the fish, not the devil."

Nonna shot my mother a look that would sink lesser souls to

their knees. "You know as well as I do it's a sign the Malvagi have arrived, Nicoletta. They've come to collect. You've heard of the bodies. The timing matched what was foretold. Is that a coincidence, too?"

"Bodies?" My voice shot up several octaves. "What are you talking about?"

Nonna clamped her mouth shut. My mother whipped her head around, forgetting about the marzipan again. A look passed between them, so deep and meaningful that chills crept down my spine.

"What bodies?" I prodded. "What was foretold?"

Our restaurant was busier than normal while we prepared for the influx of people attending the festival tomorrow, and it had been days since I'd listened to gossip swirling around the marketplace. I hadn't heard anything about bodies.

My mother gave my grandmother a look that said *You started this, you finish it,* and went back to her candy shaping. Nonna settled onto a chair she kept near the window, clasping her wine tightly. A breeze lifted the oppressive heat. Her eyes fluttered shut, as if soaking it in. She looked exhausted. Whatever was happening, was bad.

"Nonna? Please. What happened?"

"Two girls were murdered last week. One in Sciacca. And one here. In Palermo."

Sciacca—a port town facing the Mediterranean Sea—was almost directly south of us. It was a little jewel on an island filled with visual treasure. I couldn't imagine a murder there. Which was ridiculous since death didn't discriminate between paradise and hell.

"That's awful." I set my knife down, pulse pounding. I looked at my grandmother. "Were they . . . human?"

Nonna's sad look said it all. *Streghe.* I swallowed hard. No wonder she was carrying on about the Wicked returning. She was imagining one of us discarded in the streets, our souls being tortured by demons in Hell while our blood slipped through cracks in the stone, replenishing Earth's magic. I shuddered despite the sweat beading my brow. I didn't know what to make of the murders.

Nonna often chided me for being too skeptical, but I still wasn't convinced the Malvagi were to blame. Old legends claimed the Wicked were sent to make bargains and retrieve souls for the devil, not kill. And no one had seen them wandering our world in at least a hundred years.

Humans murdered each other all the time, though, and they definitely attacked us when they suspected what we were. Whispers of a new band of *strega* hunters reached us last week, but we'd seen no evidence of them. But now... if witches were being murdered, I was more inclined to believe human zealots were to blame. Which meant we needed to be even more careful to avoid discovery. No more simple charms where we could be seen. I tended to be overly cautious, but my sister was not. Her favorite form of hiding was not hiding at all.

Maybe Nonna was right to be worried.

"What did you mean about the Malvagi coming to collect?" I asked. "Or it being foretold?"

Nonna didn't look happy about my line of questioning, but saw the determination in my eyes and knew I'd keep asking. She sighed. "There are stories that claim the Wicked will return to Sicily every few weeks beginning now, searching for something that was stolen from the devil."

This was a new legend. "What was stolen?"

My mother stilled before shaping the marzipan again. Nonna

sipped her wine carefully, gazing into it as if she might divine the future in the pulp floating on the surface. "A blood debt."

I raised my brows. That didn't sound ominous at all. Before I could interrogate her further, someone rapped on the side door where we brought in supplies. Over the chatter in the small dining room, my father called to Uncle Nino to entertain the dinner guests. Footsteps thudded down the hall and the door creaked open.

"*Buonasera,* signore di Carlo. Is Emilia here?"

I recognized the deep voice and knew what he'd come to ask. There was only one reason Antonio Vicenzu Bernardo, the most newly appointed member of the holy brotherhood, ever called on me here. The nearby monastery relied heavily on donations and charity, so once or twice a month I made dinner for them on behalf of our family restaurant.

Nonna was already shaking her head as I wiped my hands on a towel and set my apron on the island. I smoothed down the front of my dark skirts, cringing a little at the flour splattered across my bodice. I looked like a queen of ash and probably stank like garlic.

I swallowed a sigh. Eighteen and romantically doomed forever.

"Emilia . . . please."

"Nonna, there are already plenty of people in the streets celebrating before the festival tomorrow. I promise I'll stick to the main road, make dinner quickly, and grab Vittoria on the way back. We'll both be home before you know it."

"No." Nonna was out of her chair, ushering me back like a wayward hen toward the island and my abandoned cutting board. "You mustn't leave here, Emilia. Not tonight." She clutched her own *cornicello,* her expression pleading. "Let someone else donate food instead, or you'll find yourself joining the dead in that monastery."

"Mamma!" my mother scolded. "What a thing to say!"

"Don't worry, Nonna," I said. "I don't plan on dying for a very, very long time."

I kissed my grandmother, then snatched a half-formed piece of marzipan from the plate my mother was working on and popped it into my mouth. While I chewed, I stuffed a basket with tomatoes, fresh basil, homemade mozzarella, garlic, olive oil, and a small bottle of thick balsamic Uncle Nino brought from his recent visit to Modena. It wasn't traditional, but I'd been experimenting and loved the flavor of vinegar lightly drizzled on top.

I added a jar of salt, a loaf of crusty bread we baked earlier, then quickly ducked out of the kitchen before I was wrangled into another argument.

I smiled warmly at Fratello Antonio, hoping he couldn't hear Nonna condemning him and the entire monastery in the background. He was young and handsome for a member of the brotherhood—just three years older than Vittoria and I. His eyes were the color of melted chocolate, and his lips always hinted at the sweetest smile. He'd grown up next door to us, and I used to dream about marrying him one day. Too bad he'd devoted himself to chastity; I was certain half the Kingdom of Italy wouldn't mind kissing his full mouth. Myself included.

"*Buonasera,* Fratello Antonio." I held my basket of supplies aloft, ignoring how odd it felt to call him "brother" when I had some *very* un-sisterly thoughts about him. "I've been experimenting again and am making a sort of a caprese-bruschetta combination for the brotherhood tonight. Does that sound all right?"

For his sake, I hoped so. It was quick and easy, and though the bread tasted better brushed with olive oil and lightly grilled, it didn't require a fire to make.

"It sounds heavenly, Emilia. And please, Antonio is fine. No need for old friends to stand on ceremony." He gave me a shy nod. "Your hair looks lovely."

"Grazie." I reached up and brushed my fingers against a flower. When we were younger, I began weaving orange blossoms and plumeria in my hair to set my twin and I apart. I reminded myself Antonio was involved with the Almighty Lord now and wasn't flirting with me.

No matter how much I sometimes wished otherwise.

While he studiously ignored the tinny sound of a pot hitting the stone floor, I internally cringed. I could only imagine what Nonna might toss next.

"Most of the brotherhood won't return to the monastery until later," he said, "but I can help, if you'd like."

Nonna's hysterics grew louder. He was polite enough to pretend he didn't hear her dire warnings of demons killing young women in Sicily and stealing their souls. I gave him my most winning smile, hoping it didn't look like a grimace. "I'd like that very much."

His attention slid behind me as Nonna's cries reached us, a tiny crease forming in his brow. Normally she was careful around customers, but if she started screaming about the dark arts and protection charms where he could overhear her, our bustling family restaurant would be ruined.

If there was one thing humans feared as much as the Malvagi, it was witches.

TWO

When we entered the monastery, I wasn't thinking about the devil. Or the wicked, soul-snatching demons Nonna swore were roaming the earth again. And while Antonio was undeniably pleasant to look at, I wasn't distracted by the slight curve of his mouth. Or the flop of brown hair that fell across his brow whenever he glanced at me then quickly looked away.

Of all things, I was thinking about olive oil.

For some reason the corridor smelled faintly of burnt thyme, which made me wonder what thyme-infused olive oil might taste like lightly brushed across crostini. I started daydreaming about my own restaurant again—about the menu I'd perfect. The crostini would make a fantastic antipasto. I'd top the toast off with some sliced mushrooms sautéed with a pad of butter, garlic, and a splash of white wine. Maybe I'd even sprinkle a bit of pecorino and parsley to round out the flavors...

We entered the room where kitchen supplies were kept, and I tucked those thoughts into my mental recipe folder and focused on the task at hand. I removed two cutting boards and a large bowl from the cupboard, and laid everything out on the tiny table.

"I'll dice the tomatoes, you cube the mozzarella."

"As you command, signorina." We both reached inside the basket I'd brought and Antonio's fingers brushed mine. I quickly yanked the tomatoes out and pretended a little thrill hadn't shot through me at the unexpected contact.

Cooking alone with Antonio—in a darkened chamber in a near-forgotten section of the building—was not a bad way to pass the time. If he hadn't turned his life over to the lord, this might have been the beginning of something between us.

Now, unbeknownst to him, we were enemies.

He belonged to the church and I was a witch. And not just a human *strega* using folk magic against the evil eye and praying to Catholic saints. My family was something other, something not entirely human. Our power was feared, not respected. Along with twelve other witch families living secretly in Palermo, we were true Daughters of the Moon. Descendants of an actual goddess. There were more families scattered across the island, but for everyone's safety, we didn't interact with each other.

Our magic was a peculiar thing. While it only passed down the matriarchal line, it didn't manifest in *all* women. My witch-born mother didn't possess any supernatural abilities. Unless her baking could be counted, which I fully believed it could. Only someone goddess-blessed could craft desserts the way my mother did.

At one time there'd been a council made up of the eldest member of each witch family. Nonna had been the leader in Palermo, but the coven disbanded soon after Vittoria and I were born. Stories were a little murky on the exact cause of the coven's collapse, but from what I'd gathered, old Sofia Santorini had invoked the dark arts and something went very wrong, leaving her mind fragmented. Some said she used a human skull during a scrying session. Others claimed it was a black mirror. All agreed on the end result: her mind was now trapped between realms.

Humans grew suspicious of what they deemed sudden madness. Whispers of the devil followed. Soon our world became too dangerous for real witches to meet, even secretly after that. So the thirteen families of Palermo adopted a strict code of silence and stuck to themselves.

Man had a funny way of blaming the devil for things he didn't like. It was strange that we were called evil when humans were the ones who enjoyed watching us burn.

"So aside from the demons invading our city, how are you?" Antonio didn't even try to hide his grin. "Good thing you've got a member of the holy brotherhood watching out for your trembling soul."

"You're terrible."

"True, but you don't really think so." His dark eyes glittered as I tossed a diced tomato at him, my face flaming. He dodged it with ease. "Or, at least I hope you don't."

"I'll never tell." I dropped my attention to the plump tomato I was dicing. Once, when we were younger, I'd used a truth spell on him to see if he'd returned my feelings. Much to my delight, he had and it felt like the world rejoiced with the discovery. When I told Nonna what I'd done, she made me scrub the kitchen from top to bottom by myself for a month.

It hadn't exactly been the reaction I'd expected.

Nonna said truth spells—while not explicitly part of the dark arts—should never be used on humans because they were part of *Il Proibito.* The Forbidden were few, but held severe consequences.

Free will was one of the most basic laws of nature in this world, beyond notions of light or dark magic, and should *never* be trifled with, which was why truth spells were off-limits. She used old Sofia Santorini as a cautionary tale whenever we questioned her strict rules.

Not every witch in our community shared the same views as Nonna, though. When the coven disbanded, some families—like my friend Claudia's—openly turned to the dark arts. They believed magic was magic and could—and should—be used however a witch wanted to use it. Blood, bones; practitioners of the dark arts said all were viable tools. Vittoria tried using that logic on Nonna when we were fifteen, and ended up being the toilet chambermaid for a solid week.

"Are you planning on sneaking away from the restaurant to celebrate tomorrow?" Antonio finished cubing the mozzarella and dutifully started chopping fresh basil.

"Maybe. It depends on how many customers we have and how late it gets. Honestly, I might just go home and try out some new recipes, or read."

"Ah. Such a pious young woman, reading the Good Book."

"Mmh." I smiled down at my cutting board. The novel I was in the middle of *was* a good book, it just wasn't *the* Good Book. I refrained from telling him about the last chapter I read—the one where the hero expressed his love in many colorful and physically astounding ways. I supposed, technically, his stamina *could* be considered miraculous. I'd certainly become a believer of impossible expectations. "Do you have any fun activities planned with the brotherhood?"

"Fun is subjective. We'll probably be somewhere near the float, doing very serious and holy things."

I didn't doubt that. After Antonio's mother died suddenly last summer, he'd surprised everyone when he left home and started his religious life. Focusing on strict rules helped him grieve. He was doing much better now, and I was glad for him, even if it meant we would never be.

"Here." I handed him the loaf of bread. "You slice this and I'll season the food."

I scraped the diced tomatoes into a bowl and added the mozzarella and basil. A hit of olive oil, some minced garlic, and a pinch of sea salt all followed in rapid succession. Since the bread wasn't toasted and the brotherhood wouldn't be eating right away, I added a tiny bit of my balsamic and stirred everything together. It wasn't exactly the presentation I'd choose, but it was more important for the food to taste good and not let the bread get soggy.

"How was your trip?" I asked. "I heard you had to quell rumors of shape-shifters."

"Ah yes, the heretics who came here from the Friuli district after the Inquisition are telling some interesting tales. Mighty warriors—whose spirits leave their bodies in animal form—to protect crops from malevolent forces have indeed returned." He snorted. "At least that's the story we were told in the village I was assigned to. They're convinced there's a spirit assembly where a goddess is teaching them ways to protect themselves from evil. It's hard breaking old beliefs." He met my gaze and a world of trouble brewed in his eyes. "Your nonna isn't the only one who thinks demons have arrived."

"I—"

A voice sounded in the corridor, too low to make out words clearly. Antonio held a finger to his lips. Whoever it was spoke again, a little louder. I still couldn't understand what they'd said, but they did not sound friendly. I fumbled for a knife. A hooded figure stepped into the chamber from the shadows, and slowly extended its arms toward us. "Heathen*s-s-s*."

Goose bumps rose like an army of the undead across my body. Nonna's cries of demons were replaced by my true fear of witch hunters. They'd found me. And there was no way I could use magic in front of them, or Antonio, without giving myself away.

I jumped back so quickly, I tripped over my skirts and crashed into the basket of supplies. Silverware clattered to the ground. The bottle of my special balsamic shattered.

Antonio clutched a wooden rosary that had been hidden under his robes, and stepped forward, placing himself between me and the intruder. "In the name of Jesus Christ, I command you to be gone, demon."

Suddenly, the figure doubled over and…giggled. Terror stopped coursing through me, and was swiftly replaced with anger. I pushed myself away from the wall and glared. "Vittoria."

My twin stopped laughing and tossed her hood back. "Don't mind me. I'm picturing the expression on your face again, and it's even more hilarious the second time."

Antonio slowly moved away, frowning down at the mess of glass and vinegar. I took a deep breath and silently counted to ten. "That wasn't funny. And you made me break my balsamic."

Vittoria winced at the bits of glass scattered across the floor. "Oh, Emilia. I'm really sorry." She crossed the small room and crushed me against her in a giant hug. "When we get home you can break my favorite white sage and lavender perfume as retribution."

I blew out a long breath. I knew she sincerely meant it; she'd happily hand over her bottle and watch me smash it to bits, but I would never choose revenge. "I'll settle for a glass of the limoncello wine concoction you make instead."

"I'll make an entire pitcher." She kissed each of my cheeks loudly, then nodded to Antonio. "You're very intimidating with the whole lord's command, brother Antonio. If I were a demon, I'm sure I would've definitely been banished back to Hell."

"Next time I'll brandish holy water. Burn the devil right out of you."

"Hmm. You might need to bring a jug for that to work, especially if I summon him here."

He shook his head, then turned to me. "I should be going; the brotherhood needs my help preparing for tomorrow. Don't worry about the spilled vinegar—I'll come back later to clean it up. Thank you again for the food, Emilia. After the festival, I'll be traveling for a little while to dispel more superstitious rumors, but I hope to see you when I return."

Not two breaths after he left the chamber, my stupid sister started dancing around the room, pretending to passionately kiss what I could only assume was Antonio. "Oh, Emilia. I hope to see you when I return. Preferably naked, in my bed, screaming the lord's name."

"Stop that!" I swatted at her, mortified. "He can probably still hear you!"

"Good." She wiggled her hips suggestively. "Maybe it'll give him some ideas. It's not too late for him to leave the brotherhood. There's no law or decree that says once he's accepted orders he needs to stay forever. There are *plenty* more interesting ways for a man to find religion. Maybe you can bathe in holy water and show him."

"You're impossibly blasphemous."

"And *you* are cherry red. Why not tell him how you feel? Or maybe you should just kiss him. Judging by the way he looks at you, I doubt he'd mind. Plus, the worst that can happen is he'll wax poetic on his religious orders, and you'll have to strangle him with his rosary."

"Come on, Venus. You've had enough matchmaking for one day."

I grabbed her hand and hurried out of the room, relieved to find the corridor empty.

No Antonio. Or any other member of the holy brotherhood. Thank the goddess. We rushed down the shadowy halls, and didn't stop running until the monastery was a speck in the night.

From the comfort of our home kitchen, Vittoria gathered blood oranges, limoncello, red wine, and a bottle of prosecco. I watched from the island as she methodically added everything to a pitcher. A cup of this, a splash of that, a few sugared peels—potions and perfumes were where her magic shined brightest, and it often translated to drinks. It was one of the few times she was entirely serious, and I loved watching her get lost in pure happiness.

My mouth watered as she sliced oranges. This was my favorite drink by far—Vittoria was inspired by sangria, which in recent years had also become quite popular in France and England. Some English families who'd moved to Palermo brought their recipes with them, adding to our already eclectic history. Nonna said the Spanish had actually been influenced by an Ancient Roman spiced wine called hippocras. No matter where it originated, I simply loved the taste of orange juice mixed with the wine and the fizzy bubbles created from the prosecco.

Vittoria dipped a spoon into the mixture, stirred vigorously, then tasted it before pouring a generous glass for me. She swiped the bottle of limoncello and motioned us up the stairs.

"Hurry, Emilia, before anyone wakes up."

"Where were you earlier?" I quietly shut the bedroom door behind us. "Nonna was one step away from using all of our olive oil to see if evil entered Sea & Vine, and probably the rest of the island if she could."

Vittoria collapsed onto her mattress, bottle of limoncello in hand, and grinned. "I was summoning the devil. An ancient book whispered its secrets to me, and I've decided to take him as my husband. I'd invite you to the wedding, but I'm pretty sure the ceremony takes place in Hell."

I gave her a sharp look. If she didn't want to tell me the truth, fine. She could keep her secret romance with Domenico to herself for however long she liked. "You need to stop drawing so much attention to yourself."

"Or else what? The Malvagi will come and steal my soul? Maybe I'll just sell it to them."

"Or else things will end badly for our family. Two girls were murdered last week. Both were witches. Antonio said people in the last town he visited were talking about shape-shifters. Now isn't the time to be joking about the devil. You know how humans get. First it's shape-shifters, then demons, and then it's only a matter of time before witches are targeted."

"I know." Vittoria swallowed hard and looked away. I opened my mouth to ask what she'd been doing at the monastery, but when she turned back around, her gaze sparkled with mischief. "So. Have you had any special wine or spirits lately?"

I let my interrogation go. "Special wine or spirits" was her code for "supernatural witch sense." She often used code to discuss topics we wanted to hide from humans, or nosy grandmothers. I nestled against my pillow and drew my knees up. Before I told my story, I whispered a spell of silence to cover the sound of our voices. "Well, the other night I dreamed about a ghost..."

"Wait!" Vittoria set her limoncello down and grabbed her

diary, pen in hand and ink pot at the ready. "Tell me everything. Every last detail. What did the ghost look like? Did you see any shimmering outline or shadow, or was it more like a thing you sensed? Did it speak to you? When did this happen, right as you fell asleep, or later in the night?"

"It was closer to the morning. I thought I was awake at first."

I sipped my drink and told her about the strange dream—the disembodied voice whispering too low to hear anything other than what sounded like the nonsensical language of dreams—believing it had only been my overactive imagination at work, and not the first signs of the horror to come.

THREE

I quickly broke down fish carcasses for stock, ignoring the muffled crunch of bones. We were already deep into prepping for dinner service when I realized I'd forgotten my basket at the monastery. Since it was a holy day and crowds were already out en masse, I had to wait until Sea & Vine closed to retrieve my things.

Maybe it was a blessing from the goddess. Since the brotherhood would be out celebrating La Santuzza—the Little Saint—I wouldn't have to worry about seeing Antonio. I *really* didn't want to run into him after Vittoria's mortifying charades last night. She could get away with being bold and brazen, and people adored her for it. Unfortunately, it was a skill I hadn't mastered.

I looked over at my sister who'd been unusually quiet all morning. Something was troubling her. After I told her about my dream last night, she seemed on the verge of confiding in me.

Instead of talking, she'd set her diary aside, turned over on her mattress, and went to sleep. I wondered if she'd gotten into a fight with her secret boyfriend. Maybe she was supposed to meet him in the monastery and he didn't show.

"I know we're going to be busy tonight," Vittoria said

suddenly, breaking into my thoughts, "but I need to leave a little early."

Nonna scooted past my mother—who was making espresso to serve with the dessert—and hoisted a wicker basket full of tiny snails up onto the island, and nodded to my twin. "Here. Boil these for the *babbaluci*." She swatted at my twin's hand. "Not for too long. We don't want them turning to rubber."

I raised my brows, waiting for Nonna to forbid my twin from leaving. She said nothing. While Vittoria quickly boiled a few handfuls of snails at a time, Nonna minced garlic and set a pan of olive oil on the fire. Soon we were all in a rhythm, and I pushed whatever was bothering my sister aside in favor of mastering my fish stock. I'd make her tell me everything later.

Vittoria scooped snails out, Nonna added them to the oil and garlic, lightly fried them and finished them off with salt, pepper, and fresh parsley. She whispered a blessing over the plates, thanking the food for its nourishment and the snails for their sacrifice. It was a small thing, and not necessarily magical, but I swore it made the food taste better.

"Nicoletta?" Nonna called. My mother set her last tray of dessert aside and tossed a cloth over her shoulder. "Bring your brother this bowl of *babbaluci*, and tell him to go outside and give a bite to anyone who looks hungry. It will help with the line."

And it would draw more people into our trattoria. Nonna might not use magic *directly* on customers, but she was skilled in the art of luring humans in by using their own senses. One whiff of the fried garlic would have plenty of hungry patrons gracing our tables.

Once my mother was gone, Nonna pointed her carved wooden spoon at us. "Did you see the sky this morning? It was as red as the devil's blood. Tonight is not a night to be out. Stay in and work on your grimoires—sew dried yarrow inside your skirts. There's plenty to do at home. Are you wearing your amulets?" I pulled mine from under my bodice. Vittoria sighed and did the same. "Good. You haven't taken them off, have you?"

"No, Nonna." I ignored the heaviness of my sister's gaze as it landed on me. I wasn't technically lying. *She'd* taken her amulet off when we were eight—I'd kept mine on. As far as I knew, neither one of us had ever removed them again.

Nonna took a deep breath, seeming pacified. "Thank the goddess for that. You know what would happen otherwise."

"Our world will turn to nightmares and ash." Vittoria held her arms straight out like she was a slow-moving demon and staggered forward. "The devil will roam free. We will be bathed in the blood of innocents, our souls cursed to Hell for eternity."

"You shouldn't irk the goddesses who've sent signs, Vittoria. Those amulets could set the demon princes free. Unless you'd like to be responsible for the Malvagi entering this realm after La Prima locked them away, I'd heed the warnings."

Any bits of lingering humor left my sister's face. She turned back to the next batch of snails, and gripped her *cornicello* tightly. I swallowed hard, recalling the hellhound we'd heard that night so long ago. Nonna had to be wrong—her warning was more superstition. The devil and his entire demon realm was imprisoned. Plus, Nonna always said our amulets couldn't be brought *together.* I hadn't let them touch—I'd just held my sister's while still wearing mine. The princes of Hell were where they belonged. No demons were roaming Earth. All was well.

Still, when our grandmother's back was turned, Vittoria and I shared a long, silent look.

FOUR

I stared at the dark monastery, unable to shake the feeling that it was staring back, its fangs bared in a vicious sneer. Which was a sign Nonna's superstitions had managed to unnerve me after all. Unless a powerful witch had cast an unheard-of spell to animate limestone and glass, it was only an empty building.

"*Grazie*, Nonna," I said under my breath, not really feeling thankful at all.

I headed for a wooden door set deep within shadows. Thick iron hinges groaned in protest as I slipped inside. Somewhere in the rafters above, a bird took flight—its wings beating in time with my heart.

The Capuchin Monastery was less than a mile from our restaurant and was one of the most beloved buildings in Palermo. Not due to its architecture, but because of the catacombs located within its holy walls. I liked it well enough during daylight, but couldn't shake the chill clinging to me in the dark. Now that it was completely empty, an eerie premonition crawled over my senses. Even the air felt strained—like it was holding its breath from some wicked discovery.

Nonna's cries of demons continued to haunt me as I crept deeper inside the silent monastery, and steeled myself against a growing sense of dread. I *really* didn't want to think about red-eyed, soul-stealing monsters invading our city, especially while I was alone.

I hugged my arms to my chest and walked briskly down a darkened corridor lined with mummies. They'd been posed in standing positions, dressed in garments of their choosing, their clothing dating back hundreds of years.

I tried not to notice their empty, lifeless stares as I hurried along. It was the quickest way to the room where I'd left my basket, and I cursed the brotherhood for the creepy layout.

Though it never bothered my sister. When we were younger, Vittoria wanted to wash and prepare the bodies of the deceased. Nonna didn't approve of her fascination with the dead, and thought it might lead to an obsession with *le arti oscure*. I was torn on the subject, but it didn't matter in the end; the brotherhood chose our friend Claudia for that task.

On rare afternoons when we all weren't working and could walk along the beach, picking shells for Moon Blessings, Claudia shared stories of how the mummies came to be. I'd squirm my toes in the warm sand, trying to banish goose bumps, but Vittoria would lean forward, a hungry gleam in her eyes, ravenous for every morsel of information Claudia served us.

I did my best to forget those morbid stories now.

A window was cracked open high above, allowing a gusty breeze to barrel through the corridor. It smelled of turned earth and salt—like a storm was blowing in. *Fantastico*. The last thing I needed was to get stuck running home in the rain.

I moved swiftly through the darkness. One torch was lit at

each end of the long corridor, leaving much of my path in shadow. Out of the corner of my eye, I noticed movement and froze. *I'd* stopped walking, but the sound of cloth brushing against stone continued a good breath or so before falling silent, too. Someone or some*thing* was here.

My entire body buzzed with nerves. I shook my head. I was already scared about the Malvagi and my mind was playing tricks on me. It was probably Vittoria again. I gathered what little bravado I could muster and forced myself to turn around, scanning the corridor of silent, watchful mummies for my sister.

"Vittoria?" I stared into the shadows, and almost screamed when one formed a denser silhouette that rose from behind the bodies. "Who's there?"

Whatever it was, it didn't answer. I thought about the rumors Antonio mentioned yesterday, and couldn't stop picturing a shape-shifter hiding in the dark. Little hairs on my arms stood on end. I *swore* I felt eyes on me. Tiny bells of warning sounded in my head. Danger lurked nearby. Nonna was right—tonight was no night to be out. I was contemplating how quickly I could dash back outside when wings flapped in the rafters. I blew out a breath. There was no apparition, or mythological shape-shifter, or demon stalking me. Just a lost little bird. I probably frightened it more than it scared me.

I slowly backed down the corridor and made my way to the next chamber, ignoring the jitters claiming my bones. I hurried into the room where I'd forgotten my basket and snatched it up, shoving my supplies back in, hands shaking the whole time.

"Stupid bird."

The faster I gathered my things, the faster I could get Vittoria from the festival and go home. Then we'd *borrow* a bottle of wine and crawl into bed, drinking and laughing together over Nonna's dire proclamations about the devil, warm and snug in the safety of our room.

A scraping of a boot against stone had me frozen in place. There was no mistaking that sound for the wings of a bird. I stood there, barely breathing, listening to an all-consuming silence. I reached for my *cornicello* in comfort.

Then, something quietly began calling me. Slow and insistent; a silent buzzing I couldn't push aside. Goddess knows I was trying. It wasn't a strictly physical sound, more like a peculiar feeling in the pit of my stomach. Each time I considered running away, it grew more demanding.

I gripped the knife from my basket in my other hand and tiptoed down the corridor, pausing to listen at each chamber. My heart pounded with each step. I was half-convinced it might stop working altogether if I didn't calm down.

I took another step, followed by another. Each one more difficult than the last. I strained against the drumming of my pulse, but no other sounds emerged from the darkness. It was as if I'd conjured the earlier noise from fear. But that *feeling*...

I followed it farther into the monastery.

At the very end of the next corridor I halted outside a room with its door ajar. Whatever had been calling me led inside; I felt it. A slight tug in my center, a summoning I had no hope of fighting. I didn't know what sort of magic was at play, but clearly sensed it.

I dropped my amulet and held my breath as I slipped in unseen, wary of what drew me. Nonna always scolded my ability to sneak around undetected, but, at present, it felt more like a blessing than a curse.

Inside, traces of thyme mixed with something metallic and

some burnt paraffin wafted around. It took a moment for my vision to adjust, but once it did, I bit down on a gasp, wondering how I'd missed him. Perhaps his preternatural stillness was to blame.

Now that I was aware of his presence, I couldn't drag my gaze away. It was too dark to make out his features clearly, but his hair was a shade close to onyx, almost iridescent like the wings of a raven catching sunlight. He was tall and powerfully built, like a statue of a Roman warrior, though his clothes were that of a fine gentleman.

There was something about him that made me cling to the shadows, though, uneasy about detection.

He loomed over a shrouded body. My mind churned with a dozen stories. Perhaps the love of his life died tragically before they could live out their dreams together, and he was angry with the world. Maybe she passed away peacefully in her sleep. Or maybe she was the murdered witch Nonna mentioned yesterday.

The one whose body was discovered in our city.

That thought was like a pail of ice water being poured over me. I stopped playing out mental fantasies and focused harder on the chamber. A strange assortment of half-blown-out candles were carefully placed in a circle around the stone altar where the body lay. Fragrant wisps of thyme wafted over to me again.

Odd for a human man to set up candles and burn herbs. I recalled the scent of thyme last night, and wondered if he'd been here while Antonio and I were cooking a few chambers down.

I stared at him, pulse thrumming, trying to determine if he was the source of magic that originally caught my attention. I didn't think so. There was no pull to him, only this chamber. Without warning, the air pressure suddenly felt wrong—like there was some distortion occurring in the space around us. Even the shadows seemed to bow in acquiescence.

Right. It was a ludicrous thought. First, invisible ghost demons were following me through the corridors, and now this. There was nothing menacing about a young man saying good-bye to the girl he loved. Placing candles around a body wasn't so strange, either. Plenty of people lit them while praying to their god. Once again, my—

He suddenly bent toward the body, his hands skimming the area above her heart, and I waited for him to tug the shroud away and kiss his beloved good-bye one final time. When he removed his hand from beneath the cloth, his fingers were coated in blood. Slowly, as if in some devil's trance, he brought those fingers to his mouth and *licked* them. For a moment, I stared, unable to process what I'd seen.

Everything inside me buzzed and went immobile. Fear and rage swirled together in a cacophony as I finally understood my earlier innate sense of wrongness.

Warnings rang through me, screeching about bloodthirsty demons, but I was incensed beyond reason. This wasn't a midnight creature, born of darkness and moonlight like Nonna claimed. This all too human monster had broken into the catacombs and committed the vilest of acts; he tasted the blood of the dead. Before I could heed the warnings my grandmother had beaten into our thick skulls from birth, I was out of my hiding spot, screaming like *I* was a feral creature of the night.

"Stop!"

Either from the raw command in my voice, or more likely the ear-splitting shrillness of it, the stranger jumped back a few feet, his movement almost too fast to detect. There was something else odd... something... I grabbed my *cornicello* and concentrated on his aura; his *luccicare* wasn't lavender, but a shimmering, multi-toned black with specks of gold. It reminded me of Nonna's titanium quartz. I'd never seen anything like it before.

He glanced from the kitchen knife I held to the body lying on the table, probably debating his next move. For the first time, I noticed the dagger in his hand. A gold snake with lavender eyes twined around its hilt, fangs bared. It was beautiful. Wicked. Deadly.

For a moment, I thought he'd aim it straight at my heart.

"Stay away from her," I warned, taking a small step in his direction, "or I'll scream loud enough to summon every *fratello* in this building."

It was a lie. The whole brotherhood was out doing their duties for Santa Rosalia. As far as I knew, he and I were the only ones in the entire monastery. Deep as we were within the catacombs, no one would hear my screams if he lunged for me. But I wasn't defenseless.

My hand dropped from my amulet and moved toward the moon-blessed chalk Nonna insisted we carry in our secret skirt pockets, ready to fall to my knees and draw a protection circle. It would work against a human just as well as it would protect against any supernatural threat. I hesitated just in case he was a witch hunter and using magic gave my secret away.

He opened his mouth about to say—whatever it was a person said after they were caught licking blood from the dead—when his gaze landed on the area near my chest. The heat of his focus almost singed my dress off. He'd tasted blood then had the nerve to stare at me like I was another delicacy put on this earth for his pleasure alone. Or was that...

"Liar." His voice was deep, rough, and elegant at once. A serrated blade wrapped in silk. All the hair on my arms rose.

Before I unleashed a torrent of curses, he did the last thing I expected; he turned on his heel and fled. In his haste to leave, his serpent dagger clattered to the floor. He either didn't notice or didn't care. I waited, kitchen knife pointed in front of me, breathing hard. I didn't hear retreating footsteps, only a slight crackle like fire. There and gone too quickly to be sure.

If he charged from the shadows, I'd defend myself through any means necessary. No matter if the thought made me queasy. Another moment passed. Then another. I strained against the loud roaring of my pulse, listening for any signs of footsteps.

There was no sound aside from my frantic heartbeat.

He didn't return. I contemplated chasing him, but found neither my breath nor my shaking legs were cooperating. I glanced down, wondering what had made him appear so uneasy, and saw my *cornicello* glinting in the darkness. How—

The silent calling was back in force, urging me to listen closely. I shoved the whispers into the deepest recesses of my mind. I didn't need any more distractions. It took a few moments of slowing my pulse to realize the body on the table wasn't where the brotherhood brought new corpses to be washed and prepared for mummification.

In fact, this room didn't appear to be used for anything. My attention drifted around the chamber, noticing a thick layer of dust. Aside from the stone altar set in the middle, it was a small room carved from limestone. There were no shelves or crates or storage. It smelled of mold and stale air, as if it had been sealed off for hundreds of years and had only recently been opened. The must was a much stronger scent than the earlier faint aroma of thyme.

An uncomfortable prickle began at the top of my spine and worked its way to my toes. Now that the stranger was gone, there was no doubt the body was calling me. Which was never a positive sign. I hadn't had the pleasure of speaking with the dead before and didn't really find the thought all too appealing now. I wanted to run away and definitely *not* peer under the shroud, but couldn't.

I gripped my knife and forced myself to walk over to the corpse, obeying that silent, insistent tug, cursing my conscience the whole way. Before I looked at the body, I snatched the stranger's dagger from the ground, replacing my flimsy kitchen knife with it. Its heft was a small comfort. If the blood-drinking deviant returned, I had a much better weapon to threaten him with.

Feeling as comforted as I could, I turned to the covered body, finally giving in to its summoning. I permitted no fear to enter my heart as I wrenched the shroud back from its face.

I was silent for an entire breath before my scream shattered the tranquility of the monastery.

FIVE

Magic is a living, breathing entity; it thrives on the energy you give it. Like all forces of nature, it is neither good nor bad—it simply becomes based on the user's intent. Feed it love and it blossoms and grows. Nourish it with hate and it will deliver hate back to you tenfold.

—*Notes from the di Carlo grimoire*

The face I stared into was a mirror of my own. Brown eyes, dark brown hair, olive skin bronzed by both the sun and our shared ancestry. I reached over, tentatively brushing a strand of hair off Vittoria's brow, and yanked my hand back at the warmth that still lingered.

"Vittoria? Can you move?"

Her eyes were fixed and empty. I waited for her to blink, then wheeze with laughter. She never suppressed her giggles for long.

Vittoria didn't move. I didn't inhale or exhale, either. I stood there, looking down at her, caught somewhere between denial and terror. I could not make myself understand the sight before me. I tugged at my hair. I'd seen her just an hour or two earlier.

This had to be another one of her stupid pranks.

"Vittoria?" I whispered, hoping for a response. Seconds stretched into minutes. She stared, unblinking. Maybe she was unconscious. I reached over and shook her a little. "Please. Move."

Even with her eyes open, she looked so peaceful, laying with a shroud tucked up under her chin. Like she was in a deep enchanted trance and a prince would soon come and kiss her awake. Something twisted deep inside me. This was no fairy tale. No one coming to break the spell of death. But *I* should have been here to rescue my sister.

If I'd only left the restaurant sooner, maybe I could've done something to save her. Maybe that murdering beast would've taken me instead. Or maybe I should've insisted that she listen to Nonna and stay in. I could have told our grandmother about the amulets. There were a hundred different choices laid out before me, and I'd done nothing. Maybe if... I closed my eyes against the rush of darkness surging through me.

Which was worse.

This had to be another horribly vivid fantasy I created—there was no way this was real. And yet, when I opened my eyes again, there was no denying that Vittoria was dead.

A steady drip broke into my thoughts. It seemed so strange, so mundane a noise. And yet I focused on it intently. It helped to drown out the insistent buzzing and whispering I could still hear.

Maybe madness was creeping in.

The drip slowed. It meant something—the absence of it. I couldn't think of it now. The strange whispering finally grew too quiet to hear. Like whatever had caused it had moved far away.

A sob broke the growing silence. It took a moment to realize it came from me.

The chamber spun until I nearly collapsed. My twin. My best friend. *Gone.* We'd never drink or laugh or plan our future. She'd never mock Nonna's superstitions or jump out from the shadows again. We'd never fight or make up. She'd never push me to be bolder, or tell me to grab my dreams by the throat. I didn't know who to be without her. How to go on.

"No." I shook my head, refusing to accept it. There was magic and trickery at play. Vittoria couldn't be dead. She was young and vibrant and so full of *life.* Vittoria danced the hardest at festivals, praised the moon and the goddess of night and stars the loudest, and always made everyone feel like her very best friend. I didn't know who this still, silent person was.

Through my tears I pulled the shroud completely off. The dress she wore was white, like an offering. It was finely made silk accented by lace. I'd never seen it. We weren't poor, but we certainly couldn't purchase something like that. Not unless she'd been saving for the last few summers.

The delicate bodice, destroyed, her *cornicello* missing, her—

I screamed. Her heart had been ripped from her chest. The hole jagged and angry. It was a gaping black and crimson chasm in her body, so unnatural I knew if I lived a thousand years, I'd never erase the sight of it from my memory. I stared at the blood, finally understanding the source of the incessant dripping. It pooled under her body and splattered down the altar.

There was so much blood. It looked—I fell to my knees, heaving up everything in my stomach. I retched again and again until there was nothing left.

I closed my eyes and the image there was even more terrible.

I dragged in breath after breath, but it didn't help the dizziness.

Now that I'd seen the blood, all I could smell was the metallic scent of death. It was everywhere, permeating everything. I went hot and cold in flashes.

I slipped forward and splayed across the stone. I tried pushing myself up and fell again. I was covered in my twin's blood. I curled onto my side and trembled. This was a nightmare. I'd wake soon. I'd wake soon, I had to. Nightmares didn't last forever. I just had to make it through the night.

Then everything would be okay.

I'm not sure how long I stayed there, shaking and sobbing on the floor, but at least an hour or two had passed. Maybe more. I needed to get help.

Not that anyone could save Vittoria now.

With weak arms, I finally pushed myself back up and stared at my sister, unable to reconcile the truth before me.

Murdered.

The word clanged through me like a death knell. Fear cleaved through my despair. My sister had been murdered. I needed to get help. I needed to find safety. I needed to—I dragged the stranger's blade across my palm and held my bleeding hand over my sister's body.

"I swear on my life, I will make whoever did this pay, Vittoria."

I looked at her one last time, then ran like the devil was coming for my cursed soul next.

SIX

Revelers jostled into me, splashing cups of wine down their tunics and dresses, laughing and trying to swing me into a dance. To indulge in their merriment. To celebrate the victory of life over death their blessed saint brought them all those years ago.

In a daze, I walked past our darkened restaurant, long since closed for the night, and found my way into our neighborhood. The hem of my skirts were soaked from goddess knew what. The material clung to my ankles and itched like mad. I kept moving, ignoring any discomfort. I had no right to feel anything when my sister would never feel again.

"Little witch all alone."

It was no louder than a hiss, but the voice sent a violent shudder down my spine. I spun on my heel, and stared into an empty street. "Who's there?"

"Memories, like hearts, can be stolen."

The voice was behind me now. I jerked around, heart racing, and saw . . . nothing.

"This isn't real," I whispered. My mind was just taunting me with horrific things after finding my sister's mutilated body. It seemed my invisible ghost demon had found a voice—a thought so ridiculous I couldn't even entertain it as truth. "Go away."

"He wishes to remember, but only forgets. He's coming here soon."

"Who is? The man who did this to Vittoria?"

I pivoted, skirts twisting around me. Not a single living thing was in the street. In fact, it seemed eerily still—like someone had snuffed out all life. No lights were on inside homes. No movement or noise. I couldn't hear the bustle and excitement of the festival, either.

Thick unnatural fog crept along the ground and curled around my feet, bringing with it the scent of sulfur and ash. Nonna would claim it was a sign demons were near. I wondered if some murdering human was hiding in the shadows, waiting with a knife.

"Who's coming?" I demanded, feeling more and more like I was trapped in some terrible nightmare. I closed my eyes and forced myself to snap into reality. I couldn't fall apart now. "When I open my eyes again, everything will be normal."

And it was. There was no sulfuric fog, sounds of families sitting down together floated through open windows, and jeers of drunken festivalgoers echoed all around.

I rubbed my arms and hurried toward my house. Ghostly demons. Disembodied voices. Devilish fog. I knew exactly what was going on—I was suffering from hysterics. And now was *not* the time. Vittoria's body needed to come home for death rites. I could hide my own despair and delusions away long enough to do that much for her.

After a few more minutes of mindlessly pushing forward down familiar streets, I stood outside our stone house and paused under the trellis covered with plumeria, unable to formulate the words I needed to say. I had no idea how to deliver the news to my family.

In moments they'd all feel like they'd been beaten and broken, too.

From here on out, our lives would never be the same again. I imagined my mother's scream. My father's tears. The horror in Nonna's face, knowing all her preparations to save us from evil had been pointless.

Vittoria was dead.

I must have cried out or made some small noise. A swath of golden light cut through the darkness before fading as quickly. Nonna was at the window, waiting. She'd likely been there since she came home. Worrying and fretting. Her warnings about the devil stirring the seas, and the sky being the color of his blood didn't seem like silly old superstition now.

The door swung open before I finished climbing the steps carved into the front of our home and reached the knob.

Nonna started shaking her head, her eyes watering, as she grabbed her *cornicello.* I didn't have to say anything. The blood staining my hands said enough. "No." Her bottom lip quivered. I'd never seen such despair and undulated fear in Nonna's face before. "No. It can't be."

The hollowness inside me spread. All her lessons, all of our charms... for nothing.

"Vittoria is..." I swallowed hard, the action nearly choking me. "She's..."

I stared down at the serpent dagger I still held, but had no memory of taking. I wondered if it was the weapon that had taken my sister's life. My grip on it tightened.

Nonna took one look at the dagger and wrapped me in her arms, holding me fiercely against her. "What happened, bambina?"

I buried my face in her shoulder, breathing in the familiar

scent of spices and herbs. Hugging Nonna made everything real. The whole goddessless nightmare.

"Your worst fears."

Flashes of my twin and her missing heart crossed my mind, and whatever thread of strength I'd been clutching to snapped, plunging me into darkness.

The day after we laid my sister to rest, I sat alone in our room, an unopened book in my lap. It was so quiet. I used to cherish peaceful days like this, when my twin was out being adventurous and I was adventuring with a favorite character. A good book was its own brand of magic, one I could safely indulge in without fear of getting caught by those who hunted us. I loved escaping from reality, especially during times of trouble. Stories made everything possible.

My attention moved to the door the same way it had all morning, searching for a sign Vittoria was about to charge through it, her face flushed and her grin wide. All remained still.

Downstairs a spoon clinked against the cast iron cauldron. A moment later herbal scents wafted up. Nonna had been making spell candles nonstop. She lit them for the *polizia,* helping to guide them in their search. Or so she claimed. I'd seen the juniper berry and belladonna candle she'd made with a dash of salt and a pinch of pepper. It was her own recipe and it wasn't used for clarity.

I set my book aside and went downstairs, hovering near the edge of the kitchen. Not quite hungry, but feeling empty, hollow. I hadn't felt like cooking or creating, and couldn't imagine ever feeling that light and free again. Living in a world without my sister felt dark and wrong.

Nonna glanced up. "Come sit, Emilia. I'll make you something to eat."

"That's all right, Nonna. I can fix something."

I went to the ice box and almost burst into tears when I saw the pitcher of limoncello wine Vittoria had made for me. No one had touched it.

I quickly shut the door, and perched on the edge of the closest stool.

"Here." Nonna set a bowl of sweetened ricotta in front of me, her expression kind. "Desserts always go down easy."

I pushed the creamy concoction around. "Do you think someone found out . . . what we are? Maybe Vittoria joked about the devil or demons to the wrong human."

"No, bambina. I don't believe it was a human who attacked her at all. Not with the signs we've been receiving. Or the blood debt."

I'd forgotten all about the mysterious blood debt. It seemed an entire lifetime had passed since Nonna first mentioned it. "You believe the blood debt is responsible for Vittoria's murder?"

"Mmh. It was part of an ancient bargain struck between La Prima and the devil. Some believe La Prima cursed the Wicked, others believe the devil cursed witches. A warning came one day: 'When witch blood spills across Sicily, take your daughters and hide. The Malvagi have arrived.' Now there's been three witch murders."

"It doesn't mean the Wicked killed them. What about witch hunters? Don't you think that sounds more logical than demon royalty breaking out of Hell? You know as well as I do how much humans fear witches, and how willing they are to commit the very sins they accuse us of. In fact, Antonio said a village not far from here is convinced shape-shifters have been cavorting with a goddess. Maybe someone like that saw Vittoria whisper a charm and killed her."

"The devil stirred the seas and made the sky bleed. What more will convince you that danger is knocking at our door that has nothing to do with mortals? What use do humans have with witch hearts?"

I took a deep breath, trying to calm the anger building inside me. This wasn't the time to believe stories passed down from generations ago. Now was the time to consider the facts that made the most sense. Starting with the first victim in Sciacca—more than a week before Emilia's murder—not a single witch family had come forward with information about the Wicked's arrival. Until new evidence or proof was uncovered about the demon princes, I'd stick with my theory of a human being responsible.

"Are we going to speak with the police, Nonna?"

"If they investigate too closely and discover what we are, do you think your fate will be any different than your sister's?"

I shook my head. I didn't want to fight with my grandma. I also couldn't quite figure out a way to tell the police witch hunters might be to blame without casting suspicion on us.

I was so frustrated, I could scream. My twin had been murdered. No one who knew my sister would ever wish her harm. Which meant it *had* to be a stranger, or someone who'd figured out what she was. According to Nonna, the other two victims were also witches. That wasn't a mere coincidence—it was a connection. A woman with a little power was terrifying to some.

I curled my hands into fists, focusing on the pain of my nails sinking into my skin. Someone chose to hurt Vittoria. And I wanted to know who. *Why.*

What had Vittoria been doing in the hours leading up to the attack? She didn't usually visit the monastery, but I'd seen her there twice in as many days.

It was possible she was meeting that strange dark-haired man there. For what purpose, I wasn't sure. She could have been secretly involved with him. Or maybe the murderer dragged her there against her will. Maybe she didn't know him at all and he'd intercepted her while she'd been on her way elsewhere.

I couldn't recall exactly what time she'd left Sea & Vine. That day had started off like any other—we'd gotten up, dressed, shared a morning meal, and went to work with our family to prep for the busy festival day.

I hadn't even asked where she was going. I didn't know she wouldn't ever return.

Tears threatened, but I held them in. If I could go back in time, I'd do so many things differently. I shoved the heels of my hands into my eyes, and commanded myself to keep it together.

"It's not easy for any of us, Emilia," Nonna said. "Let this go. Let the goddesses take their vengeance in their own way. The First Witch won't allow things to continue like this—trust that she has a plan for the Malvagi, and work on your protection charms. Your family needs you."

"I can't sit here while the person who killed her walks free. Please don't ask me to trust in a witch I've never met, or in goddesses I'm not sure really exist. Vittoria deserves justice."

Nonna cupped my face, her eyes watering. "You must put this to rest for your family. Nothing good will come from knocking on doors best left closed. Find forgiveness and acceptance in your heart, or darkness will seep in and destroy you."

I excused myself and went back upstairs. I needed to be alone with my thoughts. I dropped onto my bed, haunted with memories of that cursed chamber where I'd found Vittoria.

I'd gone over it again and again in excruciating detail, trying to figure out what brought my sister there. I was missing something vital. Something that might help find Vittoria's killer.

I closed my eyes and concentrated as hard as I could, pretending I was standing in that room again with her body. I kept thinking about how she was dressed. I had no idea where she'd gotten the white gown. She wasn't wearing it the last time I saw her. Which begged the question of what she'd been doing that afternoon. Was she secretly about to marry Domenico? Or had she planned something else?

Then there was the mystery of her missing *cornicello*. Nonna told us to never take off our amulets and apart from that one time when we were eight, we never did. Or at least I never did again. Maybe my sister had, but I couldn't fathom why. We didn't have to see or even fully believe in the Wicked to fear them. Nonna's stories were terrifying enough. Vittoria joked about Nonna's superstitions, but she was out digging up grave dirt, swiping vials of holy water, and blessing our amulets by the light of a full moon each month right along with me.

I rolled onto my side, contemplating the most troubling questions of all; if she hadn't taken her protection amulet off, who did and where was it now?

If a witch hunter discovered who she was, it was possible he took it as a prize. Maybe he suspected it was an actual magical object, unlike other human-made amulets. My thoughts turned to that dark-haired stranger again. Dressed in such fine clothes, he certainly wasn't a member of the holy brotherhood. And he didn't look like the sort to turn his life over to God. He seemed too defiant for religion. I hadn't met a witch hunter before, so I couldn't rule that out. Maybe he was a thief—he'd certainly moved around the shadows with ease.

I cursed myself for not chasing after him when I had the chance. When he fled, he took all of my answers with him. Except things weren't entirely hopeless. I sat up, heart racing, and yanked open the drawer on my nightstand. Metal glinted in the light. He'd made one giant mistake; he'd dropped his dagger. Surely someone, somewhere would recognize such a unique blade.

My thoughts settled. That was it, then. I had something to focus on aside from falling apart and reliving that night over and over.

I took a few deeps breaths, steeling myself against the next wave of tears and vowed—one way or another—to find the mysterious stranger and discover exactly who he was, what he was doing, and how he knew my sister.

And if he was the person who'd stolen her from me, I'd make him pay with his own life.

SEVEN

No matter how hard I dug my heels in and tried to halt time, three weeks passed since we'd buried my sister. Three weeks of laying in her bed in our shared room, crying into the sheets that were slowly fading with her lavender and white sage scent.

On good days I came downstairs and sat before the fire in our kitchen, staring into the flames. I imagined myself burning. Not like our ancestors at the stake. An ember of anger was slowly igniting within me, reducing the person I used to be to ash.

At times my simmering rage was the only indication I was still alive.

After dinner service tonight, Nonna kept casting wary glances my way, muttering charms of good health and well-being while scouring our family grimoire. She didn't understand the hatred I was being consumed with. Didn't see how I longed for revenge.

Vengeance was now a part of me, as real and necessary as my heart or my lungs. During the day I was a dutiful daughter, but once night fell, I scoured the streets, spurred on by a singular need to set right a terrible wrong. I hadn't found anyone who knew the mysterious stranger or recognized his deadly blade, and

I wondered if they just didn't *want* to admit anything for fear of retribution. Each day that passed fueled my growing wrath.

That dark-haired man had answers I needed. And I was losing what little patience I had. I'd started praying to the goddess of death and fury, making all sorts of promises if she'd help me find him.

So far, the goddess couldn't be bothered.

"*Buonasera,* Nonna." I set my satchel of knives on the kitchen counter in our home and dropped onto a stool. My parents insisted I spend a few hours in the restaurant each day. We could only afford to close Sea & Vine for a week to mourn Vittoria. Then, whether any of us liked it or not, life resumed. My mother still cried as often as I did and my father wasn't doing much better. But they pretended to be strong for me. If they could try, the least I could do was trudge into the restaurant and slice some vegetables before collapsing back into my grief.

"Emilia, hand me the beeswax and dried petals."

I found a few squares of wax and a tiny bundle of dried flowers on the sideboard. Nonna was making spell candles, and judging from the colors—white, gold, and pale purple—she was working a few different charms. Some for clairvoyance, some for luck, and some for peace.

None of us had had much peace this month. The *polizia* tied my sister's murder to the two other girls. Apparently they also had their hearts ripped out, but there were no suspects or leads. They swore it wasn't for a lack of effort on their part. But after the initial meetings, they stopped coming by our home and restaurant. They stopped asking questions. Young women died. Life resumed. Such was the way of the world, at least according to men.

No one cared that Vittoria had been slaughtered like an

animal. Some more-vicious gossips even hinted that she must have deserved it. She'd somehow asked for it by being too bold, or confident, or ungodly. If she'd only been a little quieter, or more subservient, she might have been spared. As if anyone deserved to be murdered.

My family almost seemed relieved when talk shifted to new scandals. They wanted to mourn and fade into the shadows again, hoping to escape scrutiny from neighbors and police.

Nosy vendors from the marketplace came to our restaurant, ate at our tables, hoping for news, but my family was too practiced with secret-keeping to give anything away.

"Claudia stopped by," Nonna said, breaking into my endless worries. "Again."

I sighed. I imagined my friend was desperate if she braved speaking with Nonna. Because Claudia's family practiced the dark arts, and because we were not supposed to associate with other witches for safety reasons, our lifelong friendship was a source of tension for each of our families. It was a rotten thing to do, but I'd been avoiding her, not ready to share our tears and grief just yet. "I'll visit her soon."

"Mmh."

I watched the cauldron Nonna hung over the fire in our kitchen, breathing in the herbal mixture. I used to love when she infused her own oils. Now I could hardly sit through the process without thinking of my sister, and the times she'd beg Nonna to make special soap or cream.

Vittoria loved crafting perfume as much as I adored blending ingredients into sauces. She used to sit where I was, head bent over secret potions, tinkering until she got the scent right. A bit of floral notes, a touch of citrus, and she always included an undertone of something spicy to balance it out. She'd whoop with delight and make us all wear her latest creation until we were sick of it. One fall, she made everything out of blood orange, cinnamon, and pomegranate and I swore I'd never so much as *look* at any of them again. The memories were too much...

I pushed away from the island and kissed my grandmother. "Good night."

Nonna inhaled deeply, like she wanted to impart some wisdom or comfort, but gave me a sad smile instead. "*Buona notte*, bambina. Sleep well."

I climbed the stairs, dreading the silent empty room that was once filled with so much joy and laughter. For a second, I considered torturing myself with watching Nonna make spell candles again, but grief weighted my eyelids and tugged at my heart.

I slipped out of my muslin dress and into a thin nightgown, trying not to remember that Vittoria had the same one. Except where my ribbons were ice blue, hers were pale pink. The air was thick with summer heat, promising another restless night of tossing and turning.

I padded barefoot across the floor and pushed the window up.

I stared out across the rooftops, wondering if Vittoria's murderer was out there now, stalking another girl. Nearby, I swore a wolf howled. A singular, mournful note hung in the air, sending a shudder down my spine.

In my haste to get into bed, I knocked over a glass of water. Liquid ran over a spot I'd forgotten about. It was a place in the floorboards where Vittoria hid things. Little trinkets like dried flowers, notes from the latest boy who loved her, her diary, and perfume she'd made.

I rushed across the room, dropped to my knees, and almost

broke my fingernails as I pried the board up. Inside were all the objects I remembered.

Plus a gambling chip with a crowned frog on one side, and two thick sheets of black parchment tied with matching string. I blotted them on my nightgown, hoping I hadn't ruined this precious piece of my twin. My hands trembled as I unrolled them. Gold roots edged the border, the ink shiny against the darkness of the oversized page. They were spells torn from a grimoire I'd never seen. I scanned the script, but couldn't quite identify what it was used for. It listed herbs and specific colored candles and instructions in Latin. I pushed the sheets aside and pulled her diary into my lap.

I was willing to bet my own soul that this was the key to unlocking what she'd been doing—and who she'd mistakenly trusted—in the days and weeks leading up to her death.

I ran my fingers across the scarred leather. Holding her diary made me ache with memories. At night she'd write in it constantly, recording everything from each of my strange dreams, to Claudia's scrying sessions, notes about her perfumes, spells and charms, and recipes for new drinks. I had no doubt she also told this diary each secret she'd been keeping from me.

All I had to do was crack the spine, and I'd discover everything I needed to know.

I hesitated. These were her private thoughts, and I didn't want to commit one more violation when she'd already suffered so much. I sat quietly, considering what she would urge me to do. I easily heard her voice in my head, telling me to stop thinking about the fall and to just jump. Vittoria took risks. She made hard choices, especially if it meant helping her family.

In order to find out who killed her, I needed to follow in her footsteps, even if it made me uncomfortable. I inhaled deeply, and opened the diary.

Or I would have, if the pages weren't stuck together.

I pulled a little harder, not wanting to destroy it, but worried the water had somehow damaged it. The book didn't budge. I yanked it with all of my strength. It didn't even bend. I scooted over to the wall, placed my feet on the lip of the back cover and my fingers along the front and tried prying it, and... nothing. A dark suspicion took shape.

I whispered a spell of unveiling, and tossed a pinch of salt over my shoulder for luck with deciphering the enchantment. Faint spiderwebbing in a violet-blue hue rose around the diary like a tangle of thorny vines. My sister had spelled it shut using magic I'd never seen before.

Which meant she'd known *exactly* how dangerous her secrets had been.

EIGHT

Vittoria had done more than dabble in the dark arts. I couldn't open the diary using force, so I tried a spell of un-making, burned herbs that helped with clarity, lit candles and prayed to every goddess I could think of, but the stubborn diary gave none of its secrets away.

I tossed the book on the floor and cursed. Vittoria had used a spell I'd never encountered. Which meant she'd probably figured out I'd snooped in her diary a few weeks ago. She *really* didn't want me to know her secret. And that made me even more determined to find out why.

I paced around our little room, watching the sun slowly rise. I needed a plan. Now. Aside from a forbidden truth spell here and there, I knew little of dark magic and how it actually worked. Nonna said the dark arts demanded payment since they took from something instead of using what already was. I'd happily sacrifice whatever I needed to in order to get what I wanted. I had one large clue and no way to access it. Except . . . I smiled as an idea struck. I couldn't break the spell, but I knew someone who might be able to: Carolina Grimaldi.

Carolina was Claudia's aunt and had taken Claudia in when her parents left for America a year or two apart. She was well versed in the dark arts, and was slowly teaching Claudia everything she knew. I didn't want to involve my friend, so I decided to go directly to the source of her knowledge. Carolina had a stall in the busy marketplace and, if I hurried, I might catch her before she opened her booth.

I grabbed a satchel and stuffed the grimoire sheets and diary inside, then ran for the door.

Nonna stepped into my path, frowning. "Is the devil chasing you?"

I hoped not, but that was up for debate. "Not that I know of."

"Good. Then you can sit a minute and tell me where you're running off to at this hour."

"I—" I almost confessed everything, but thought about my sister. Vittoria kept her secrets close, and was willing to die with them. There had to be a good reason why. "I wanted to stop by the marketplace for some spices before we start prepping for dinner service. I have an idea for a new sauce."

Nonna stared at me hard, trying to see through my lies. Her expression was a cross between disappointment and suspicion. I hadn't shown much interest in food or creativity since Vittoria's death. Just when I convinced myself she'd send me back upstairs with a list of charmwork, she stepped aside. "Don't be late. There's much to do."

"Signora Grimaldi!" I hiked up my skirts and charged through the streets. Luck was finally on my side. I caught Carolina right before she crossed the road into the marketplace.

Carolina shielded her face from the rising sun, and stepped into the shadows of a nearby alley when she spotted me. "Emilia. I'm sorry for—"

"I don't have much time, signora. I need your help with something...delicate." I pulled the diary out and glanced around, ensuring we were alone. "There's some enchantment on here I've never seen. I was hoping you might tell me what it is and how to break it."

She took a small step away, staring at the diary like it was an abomination. "Nothing of this realm will do what you seek. Put it back where you found it, child. Its very presence calls them."

"Them?"

"The Wicked. This magic stinks of their world—it wants to be found."

I stared at Carolina, wondering if Nonna had somehow figured out my plan and had gotten to the dark witch first. "This is my sister's diary, not some demon book."

Carolina nodded to my satchel. "Show me what you've got in there." I did another subtle sweep of our surroundings before pulling out the grimoire sheets. I handed them to her, watching her face swiftly drain of color. "This is a summoning spell."

"I—I don't understand. Why would my sister need a summoning spell?"

"Maybe she was trying to control a demon."

I studied the black sheets. "That's impossible. All demons are trapped in Hell. Just like they've been for nearly a hundred years."

Carolina snorted. "Is that what your nonna's been telling you? Go home and try summoning one yourself, see what happens. Unless you have an object that belongs to a prince of Hell, these spells should only call forth a lower-level demon. They're easy to control and often trade information for little favors or trinkets.

And I promise you, they aren't *all* trapped in the underworld. Almost every witch—whether they pray to the goddesses of light or dark magic—knows that."

I stared at the dark witch, heart thudding. "Are you suggesting my sister was summoning demons and asking them for favors before she died?"

"There's no way to know for sure what she was doing, but I guarantee those spells are strictly for summoning. I doubt a demon aided her without some sort of bargain. They don't believe in doing charitable work. There's always some gain in it for them." She looked me over, her expression softening. "Forget what I said, child. Don't dabble in the demon realm. Whatever your sister was doing, I promise you'll want no part in it."

She sounded just like Nonna.

I thanked her and said good-bye, then quickly made my way to Sea & Vine. Instead of answers, I had more questions. If Carolina was right about the spell on Vittoria's diary not being of this realm, then opening it was impossible. Unless... An idea slowly formed, one that made my pulse race. If my sister *had* summoned a demon, maybe she'd had it use its brand of magic to seal her diary. I couldn't imagine any other reason my twin would summon a demon aside from that.

Despite the stories Nonna told us growing up, Vittoria knew I didn't really believe in the demon princes. I wasn't as skeptical about lesser demons, but I thought they were trapped in their realm with no means of escape. It would have been the perfect way for her to ensure I'd never unlock the secret she was so desperate to keep. And Vittoria was almost right, except for one detail.

She never could have predicted the way her death would change me. There was nothing in this world or the next that would keep me from solving her murder. And I *would* solve it.

I mulled over different theories during dinner service, barely concentrating at Sea & Vine. I kept trying to think like my twin. Some thoughts were wildly outlandish, others more plausible. But one idea stuck out from the others. This was the one I carefully considered as the day dragged on.

Maybe because it seemed so impossible. Or maybe because Vittoria didn't believe in the word. Whatever the reason, the idea stayed with me as I chopped vegetables, and cleaned my knives.

I thought about it on the walk home.

Then while I changed into my nightgown, and brushed out my hair.

It haunted me and I welcomed it.

Later, once I was tucked into my bed, I pulled out the grimoire sheets again. I scanned the unfamiliar script and grinned. It was my first true smile in weeks, and it was as dark and vicious as my thoughts had been lately.

Vittoria had at least tried to summon a demon. The longer I sat with the thought, the more I accepted its truth. Tomorrow night, I'd try and summon one myself. Then, if it worked, I'd make a bargain of my own. In exchange for a small favor, I'd ask it to break the spell on her diary. I had nothing to lose—the summoning would either be successful, or it wouldn't. I'd never know what happened to my sister if I didn't set aside my doubts and try. With that, my decision was made.

All I needed now were some bones.

The next day at the restaurant passed by tortuously, but I managed to make good use of my time in the kitchen. I gathered everything the grimoire page listed, and no one suspected a thing. Except maybe Nonna. My grandmother stared at me across the island, silently chanting, as if she could read my mind and conjure a spell to pluck out the next thought before it took root.

Little did she know I'd been cultivating this idea since last night. I'd taken the bud of a plan and tended to it, urging it to blossom. Now it was full grown. I knew what I had to do.

I just needed the supplies and opportunity.

Nonna told us to hide from the Malvagi, to say our charms and bless our amulets with silvery shafts of moonlight and holy water, to never speak of the Wicked when the moon was full, and to do all the things a good witch did. Otherwise they'd steal our souls.

In the end, the monster we feared didn't come from Hell. He came from privilege.

That man standing over my twin—with his fine clothes and expensive knife—deserved punishment like anyone else. He couldn't just take what he wanted without facing the consequences. I was almost certain that the people I'd shown it to must have recognized his blade, but refused to speak out against him, fearing the repercussions. He might be powerful and wealthy, but justice would find him.

I'd make certain of it.

I still wasn't sure if he acted alone, or if he was a member of the mysterious *strega* hunters, and it didn't matter. He was the only one there that night. I would hunt him down first and find out more information later. If there were more people like him, I'd deal with it then.

I also had a plan to keep my family safe while tracking down Vittoria's killer. Instead of one simple bargain, I'd make two. First,

I'd have the demon I summoned break the enchantment on Vittoria's diary, and then I'd have it locate the mysterious dark-haired man. Thankfully, having a possession like the snake knife would allow for this.

A demon I could control was the answer to a prayer.

It seemed I'd been wrong earlier; the goddess of death and fury hadn't ignored my pleas. She'd simply been biding her time, waiting for me to turn my despair into something she could use. A twig was just a bit of broken wood until it had been sharpened into a spear. Grief carved me in half. And fury honed the pieces into a weapon.

Now it was time to unleash it.

NINE

Bone magic when used improperly can be part of the forbidden arts. Using the bones of animals—claws, nails, fangs, shells, and feathers—allows a witch to connect with the underworld. They must be gathered ethically, not sacrificed, as is popularly thought by humans. To harness their power, create a bone circle and include herbs and objects of intent.

—*Notes from the di Carlo grimoire*

I stood inside the lip of the cave, listening as the sea smashed into the rocks below, angry and insistent.

Salty spray raged up over the cliff, prickling the exposed skin on my arms and neck. Maybe the water was mirroring my mood. Or maybe it sensed the darkness of the rolled parchment tucked beneath my arm. I certainly could.

Witches were connected to the earth and channeled its powers into their own. I wouldn't be surprised if the sea was wary of what was coming—the dark power I was about to unleash upon our realm. The sea might be worried, but I was not. I had to wait hours for Nonna to finally fall asleep in her rocking chair before I collected my supplies and snuck out. Any lingering sense of worry was eclipsed by cold determination to carry out my plan.

I had no idea how Vittoria came across these grimoire pages—it was another mystery to add to an expanding list—but I'd use them to my advantage. A strong gust of wind forced me deeper into the cavern. I'd not been entirely sure where I was going when I left the house, but felt drawn here. Vittoria used to find reasons for us to venture up to this cave as often as she could when we were children. It was almost as if she were here, guiding me now.

The night air was balmy, but chills trailed sharp claws along my flesh.

I held up my lantern, trying not to cringe away from the shadows dancing around the light. Summoning a demon—in a dank cave where my screams couldn't be heard if something went wrong—wasn't exactly how I would've envisioned my life three weeks ago.

Back then I would've happily spent my nights creating new recipes for Sea & Vine. I would have read a steamy romance, and wished a certain *fratello* would forsake his oath to God for one night and worship me instead. That was before I found my sister's desecrated body.

My current wishes centered on two things: finding out who murdered my twin, and why.

Well, three wishes if you counted my dream of gutting the bastard who killed Vittoria. That was more than a wish, though. That was a promise.

Satisfied there wasn't anything lurking in the cave with me—like rats or snakes and other unpleasant surprises—I set my lantern on a flat rock and my basket of supplies on the packed dirt. I'd studied the summoning spell until my eyes crossed, but shivered a little anyway as I pulled out the items I needed.

Black candles, fresh fern leaves, animal bones, a tiny jar of animal blood, and a bit of gold. I didn't have much of the latter lying around, so I brought the gold serpent dagger with me. It seemed only fitting that the mysterious stranger's blade would be used to hunt him down.

If everything went smoothly, a lesser demon would be contained within the circle. I knew it wouldn't be able to leave the designated area, but I was still less than excited to be in a darkened place alone with a monster from Hell. Even one easily controlled and magically bound.

I glanced over the sheet of carefully written notes again, stalling. For the summoning to be successful, I needed to follow the rules of the ritual *precisely*. Any deviations could unleash the demon in this realm. First, I needed to set up the circle, alternating the candles, ferns, and bones. Next, I'd set the tiny jar of blood inside the circle's boundary. Then I had to formally invite a demon to join me, using Latin, their native tongue.

I hesitated on that point. Latin wasn't my favorite subject Nonna tried teaching us. There were so many words that were similar but whose definitions were vastly different. One slight shift in meaning could bring disaster. It would've been less worrisome if I had more than a base understanding of the dark arts. Or if Vittoria's summoning spell also included a trusted ancient phrase to use instead of simply indicating one was needed based on the witch's intent.

My true intention was to find out what my sister had been doing before her death, then track down the person who murdered her and kill him. Violence and blood vengeance wouldn't be the politest way to open a summoning, though. And I worried about the repercussions it could have. Luckily, I'd given great thought about what I wanted from the demon. I didn't want to offer it any opportunity to escape the circle, and I certainly didn't want it to harm me, so I decided on *aevitas ligati in aeternus protego.* Which roughly translated to "Bound forever in eternal protection."

Forever seemed like a wise idea when it came to making sure a demon couldn't leave the circle. And if it was forced to protect me, it couldn't very well attack me. For the final portion of the spell, I needed to prepare an exit. Apparently, demons were creatures of strict rules and had to adhere to them, so if I invited one to join me, I had to formally uninvite it and send it back to its realm. Good manners were advised, but I wasn't sure how well I could carry out *that* part.

I took a deep breath. "All right, Emilia. You can do this."

I slowly set objects down in a circle. Bone. Fern. Candle. With varying lengths, they looked like rays of an occult sun. I lit the candles and walked around the perimeter, clutching a bird's skull to my chest, the final piece I needed to make it complete. I hesitated.

If I placed this last bone in the formation, the circle would be set.

I inhaled, then slowly exhaled. I had no idea what kind of demon would answer my call. Some looked human and others were walking nightmares, according to Nonna. She never gave us specifics, which I wasn't sure was a blessing now. My mind was exceptional at picturing fang-toothed, claw-tipped, wicked creatures that crab-walked backward on multiple legs.

Clouds floated across the moon, creating a distorted effect on the cavern walls. Chills caressed my spine again. The goddess of storm and sea wasn't pleased.

I stared down at the skull I held, wondering if this was really the path I should take. Maybe I *should* blow out the candles and take myself back home and go to bed, forget about demons, witch hunters, and the devil. Nonna said once darkness was invited in, trouble shortly followed.

A flash of my twin's face—dark eyes sparkling with mischief, and her lips quirked up on one side—crossed my mind. Before I lost my nerve, I bent down and quickly fit the last bone into place. Silence swept around the chamber, sealing off the pleas of the sea. I crept over to the edge of the circle, the tiny jar of blood in hand, when a powerful blast of wind tore through the cave.

Bats screeched and flew at me. Hundreds of them. I screamed, tossing up my hands to protect myself as they raged around me like a living storm. Distantly, I heard glass break. I dropped to my knees, covering my head as little wings and claws tore at my hair and neck. Then, as quickly as it had happened, the bats were gone and the cave went still.

I took a few deep, shuddering breaths and slowly pushed a tangle of hair from my face. During the brief attack, it came undone from its simple braid. Long loose curls tickled my back like spiders, bringing on more goose bumps. Flower petals littered the ground like soldiers who'd fallen in a skirmish they hadn't seen coming. I'd forgotten there was a closed-off tunnel near the very back of the cave.

I pressed my lips into a thin line, furious with myself. If I could summon a demon, I could get over a bunch of bats.

In theory.

I stood on shaking legs and brushed myself down, shifting my attention to the summoning circle, and cringing at the broken glass winking in the moonlight. Blood splattered the ground around the perimeter, which was no good for me. It needed to be *within* its border to entice the demon.

"Stupid bats from Hell." I didn't have another jar of blood, and walking all the way back to the restaurant would take forever. The spell needed to be cast at night, and daybreak was only a couple of hours away. I'd never make it there and back in time.

I glanced around the cave, desperate enough to kill something if I needed to. Of course, now that I could *use* a bat or snake or another creature, it was truly empty. Kicking at rocks and muttering the sort of foul language that would make both my mother and Nonna's heads spin, I finally looked over Vittoria's mysterious grimoire sheet again.

Technically it didn't specify that *animal* blood was needed. It only advised using it.

I relit the candles and picked up the serpent dagger, reasoning that I needed it to complete the spell anyway. The time for hesitation and interruptions was over. Whether I liked it or not, if I wanted to break the spell on Vittoria's diary, this was my best option.

If I had to offer a little of my own blood, it was a small price to pay.

I ignored the pain as I dragged the blade over the top of my forearm; I needed my hands for cooking later and couldn't afford to cut my palm. The metal glowed as if pleased with my offering. Not wanting to think too hard about a blade that gloried in a blood sacrifice, I held my arm over the summoning circle and began chanting as soon as the first drops hit the ground.

"By earth, blood, and bone. I invite thee. Come, enter this realm of man. Join me. Bound in this circle, until I send thee home. *Aevitas ligati in aeternus protego.*"

I held completely still, waiting. For the earth to crack, the gates of Hell to snap open, hordes of witch hunters to rush me, or my heart to stop. Nothing happened. I was about to start chanting again when it began. Smoke swirled around the circle's edge like it had been trapped in a jar, never crossing into the rest of the cave. It pulsed with energy; almost lovingly caressed my hand. I dropped the dagger and yanked my arm back, hugging it to me until the sensation ceased.

I couldn't believe what was happening. A stronger wave of darkness shifted around the circle, obliterating the inside of it completely from view. Black, glittering light emerged from the center. I could hardly breathe. A sound like a crackling fire in winter preceded the demon's arrival. I'd done it. I'd actually summoned a creature from Hell! If I didn't pass out from the shock, it would be a true success. I waited, heart hammering, for the smoke to clear.

As if answering my unspoken wish, a phantom breeze carried it away, revealing a tall, dark-haired man. His muscular back was to me and he wore only low-slung black pants. He wasn't at all what I expected from a lesser demon. Golden skin glistened in the candlelight, the smooth perfection broken only by an assortment of shimmering ink. His beauty was an affront to what evil ought to look like. I supposed I should be thankful he didn't have a serpent tail or wicked horns.

The demon rotated in place like he was getting acclimated to his new location. His chest and torso were chiseled in a way that indicated he was well-acquainted with weapons. My attention dropped to a metallic gold tattoo that started on top of his right hand, and coiled up and around his arm and shoulder. A fearsome snake. I didn't have time to catalogue its details because he was now fully facing me. I sucked in a sharp breath as I finally met his gaze. Dark gold irises with flecks of black stared back at me.

Beautiful. Rare. And lethal. Even though Nonna claimed their eyes were tinged red, I knew in the very marrow of my bones what he was.

"Impossible," I whispered.

He raised a brow. His expression was so human, I forgot, for a second, how he'd arrived in this cave. He shouldn't exist. Yet there he was defying all of my expectations. Tall, dark, and quietly seething. I couldn't drag my attention from him, worried he was either a figment of my imagination, or proof of madness. I'd used the dark arts. Maybe this temporary delusion was my price.

It was much easier to think that was true, rather than accept I'd done the impossible—I'd bound one of the Wicked to this realm. Which was very, *very* bad.

He was human looking enough, but was the physical embodiment of a nightmare.

Blood drinking, soul stealing, immortal creature of the night. I fought the urge to jump away from the circle and held his gaze instead. A storm raged within those eyes. It was like standing on the edge of a darkened shore, watching lightning dance closer across the sea. A lick of fear trailed down my spine as he defiantly stared back. I had never been more grateful that I'd also bound him to protect. Instinctually I reached up and held my *cornicello* for comfort.

He looked ready to—*sweet goddess of fury*. His *luccicare* was black and gold. I'd only ever seen that once before. Recognition slammed into me, and I immediately dropped my *cornicello* and snatched my dagger from the floor. *His* dagger.

The hilt was as cool as the icy rage now rushing through my veins.

"I'm going to kill you," I snarled, then lunged for him.

TEN

Bones scattered as I attacked. The blade arced down, slicing a long, thin line across his hard chest. It should have pierced his heart. And it would have, if he hadn't maneuvered back so swiftly. A strange, searing pain erupted under my skin. I didn't want to consider what it meant—that maybe the mixture of our blood on the strange blade created a charm of its own. Or maybe the protection incantation also prevented me from striking him with a killing blow.

He yanked the dagger away with ease and tossed it on the ground.

I balled my hand into a fist and aimed for his center. It was like hitting a rock wall.

The demon stood there, allowing my assault to continue. While I exhausted myself with kicks and punches, he calmly looked around the chamber, enraging me more with his nonchalance. The demon didn't seem too worried, and I wondered how many times he'd been summoned and subsequently attacked. He studied the circle and his attention jerked down toward me, immediately narrowing in on the fresh cut on my arm. A slow frown formed before he hid it.

"Why. Won't. You. Bleed? Monster!" I was feral as I kicked and punched. My hatred and wrath so strong I almost got drunk on the intensity of it.

I glanced up in time to see him close his eyes, like he was enjoying those dark feelings, too. Nonna said demons pulled emotions to them, allowing them to wriggle and writhe around theirs. From the expression on his face, I was beginning to think that was true.

Disgusted, I stopped punching him and took a moment to catch my breath and regroup. Blood slipped down my arm and dripped to the ground. It wasn't his, though. It was from the cut I'd made to summon him. I didn't care if I bled myself dry if I took him to Hell with me.

"Bit of advice, witch. Yelling, 'I'm going to kill you' takes the surprise out of the attack." He grunted as I landed a swift blow to his stomach. My punches were slowing and he didn't look any worse for the wear. "You won't succeed in killing me, but it would be a vast improvement in skill."

"Maybe I can't kill you, but I'll find other ways to make you suffer."

"Trust me, your very presence is accomplishing that." Blood drops hissed within the circle. That strange searing under my skin was growing unbearable, but I was too mad to pay attention. "What spell did you use, witch?"

I stopped, breathing hard. *"Vaffanculo a chi t'è morto."*

I wasn't sure if he knew exactly what the curse meant, but he must have deduced it had something to do with fornicating with dead family members. He looked ready to drag *me* back to

Hell now. He suddenly staggered away, cursing. *"What spell did you use?"*

"Well, considering you're standing here, angry and unable to attack, I'd guess summoning spell, demon." I crossed my arms over my chest. "And one for protection."

Out of nowhere, gold light flashed over my arm before disintegrating into pale lavender. A tattoo in the same shade of purple—twin crescent moons laying sideways within a ring of stars—appeared on my outer forearm, burning almost as violently as my wrath.

I stood there, panting, until the searing in my arm finally ceased. I watched as he looked down at his own arm and gritted his teeth. Apparently he was also experiencing that awful pain.

Good.

"You demon-blooded witch. You *marked* me."

A pale tattoo had appeared on his formerly bare left forearm. Double crescent moons laying in a circle of stars. For a moment, he looked like he could hardly comprehend that I'd managed something so impossible. Honestly, I wasn't sure why he and I now had matching tattoos, either, but would rather die than admit that to him.

It must be the cost of the dark magic I'd used to summon him. I almost laughed. When Carolina told me the spells would summon a lesser demon, I'd had a hard enough time believing her. I wondered if I was having a nightmare—there was no way I'd *actually* summoned a prince of Hell. It would take more magic than I possessed to control a creature like him for any good length of time.

"This is impossible."

"On that much we can agree." He thrust his arm at me. "Tell me the exact phrasing of this spell. We need to reverse it before it's too late. There's only precious minutes left."

"No."

"You have no idea what you've done. I need to know the *exact* phrasing. Now, witch."

I was pretty sure what I did, aside from royally annoy him, was ensure neither of us ended up dead by the other's hand. The tattoos likely acted as a magical bond of sorts. Unbinding us so he could rip out my heart like he'd done to my sister was the last thing I'd do.

"Unbelievable," I scoffed. "Demanding things when you're not the one with the power here." His expression was one of pure disgust. I hoped it mirrored my own. "*I* need to know who you are and why you killed my sister. Since you can't go back to your Hell dimension without me allowing it, I suggest playing by my rules."

I couldn't be sure, but there was a shift in the atmosphere around us, and I had the strangest impression his power slithered out, circled me, then slunk away. His nostrils flared. He was raging against the magical leash I'd put on him, straining to snap free. I watched, a small spiteful smile curving my lips. If he didn't hate me before, I'd accomplished that tenfold now. Perfect. It seemed we finally understood each other.

"One day I'm going to be free of this bond. Think very carefully about that."

I stepped close to him, angling my face up. "One day, I'm going to find a way to kill you. Think very carefully about *that*. Now, tell me who you are and why you wanted Vittoria dead."

He offered me a smile that probably made men piss themselves; I refused to give in to fear. "Very well. Since you only have minimal time to hold me here, and have already wasted precious minutes with your poor excuse of an assassination attempt, I'll play your game. I am the Prince of Wrath, general of war, and one of the feared Seven."

Before I could blink, he trailed a finger down my throat, pausing at the vein that throbbed beneath my skin. Undiluted dread shot through me. I shoved his hand away, and stepped out of the summoning circle. I noticed the scattered bones and scrambled to put them back in place.

His grin turned into something sharp and wicked.

"Congratulations, witch. You've succeeded in getting my full attention. I hope you're prepared for the consequences."

Arrogance dripped off him. Only a fool wouldn't be terrified of the beast I sensed lurking beneath his skin. He radiated power—vast and ancient. I had little doubt he could end my life with nary a thought.

All the same, the corner of my lips twitched.

Then, without warning, I bent over and began laughing. The sound bounced off the walls of the cave, magnifying until I wanted to plug my ears. I clutched my stomach, practically heaving from my outburst. Perhaps I *was* going insane. This night had gone from bad to worse faster than I could have ever imagined. I couldn't believe I'd summoned a prince of Hell. I couldn't believe royal demons existed. The world was downside up and upside down.

"I'm glad imminent death is so amusing," he snapped. "It'll make it all the more satisfying to slaughter you. And I promise your death will not be quick. I will glory in the kill."

I waved him off like he was no more fearsome than a housefly. I could practically *feel* anger vibrating off him and winding its way into me. Even still, I had a feeling he was holding himself back. A lot. It was unsettling.

"Why, pray tell, are you laughing so hard?"

I straightened and wiped the corners of my eyes. "What, exactly, should I call you? Your highness? Oh, Feared and Mighty Seven? General Commander of Hell? Or Prince Wrath?"

A muscle in his jaw strained as he held my gaze.

"One day you'll call me Death. For now, Wrath will do."

ELEVEN

A prince of Hell will never give their true name to their enemies. They can only be summoned through an object that belongs to them along with a powerful emotion. Their powers are tied to the sins they represent. Beware, for they are selfish beings who wish to use you for their gain.

—*Notes from the di Carlo grimoire*

"Wrath?" I didn't bother hiding my incredulous tone. Setting aside the extremely melodramatic "you'll call me Death" line, the whole obscene night ceased being funny in the this-can't-be-happening-cruel-fate kind of way. First, I'd been convinced he was a witch hunter and had murdered Vittoria because of what she was, only to discover he was one of the creatures we'd been hiding from our whole lives. Then, to have the demon who killed my sister within my grasp and not be able to harm him...

I must have *really* annoyed some goddess to be punished this horribly. His stupid name and all of his titles were the least of my concerns, but the anger pouring off him as I laughed made me inclined to torment him over it.

"That's ridiculous. I'm not calling you by an emotion. What's your true name?"

He pinned me with a cold stare as I retrieved his dagger. "My true name doesn't concern you. Address me by my House title. Unless you'd like to call me His Royal Highness of Undeniable Desire. That's always an acceptable option. If you want to bow, I wouldn't mind that, either. A little groveling goes a long way. I may grant you a boon and make your death swift."

My lip involuntarily curled. "Are you sure you're of House Wrath? If I didn't know better, I'd say you were general to a vacuous, shirtless battalion belonging to House Narcissism."

His expression was anything but friendly. "You flatter me. If you're so repulsed by my company, why not set me free?"

"Never."

"Dangerous word. I'd avoid speaking in absolutes if I were you. They have a tendency to *never* stick."

I forced myself to breathe. What I had wanted before I recognized him were answers. Now I wanted to carve him into a thousand bloody pieces and serve them to sharks. "Why did you murder my sister?"

He slowly paced around the summoning circle, likely testing its strength. "Is that what you think? That I ripped out your sister's heart?"

"You were standing over her body, *licking her blood from your fingers,* you revolting beast." I drew in a furious breath, watching him closely, though it was an effort in futility. His expression was inhumanly blank. Not one emotion betrayed his thoughts. Without thinking, I reached up and clutched my *cornicello* again. "*Why* did you murder my sister?"

"I didn't."

"Why should I believe you?"

"Her death was most inconvenient."

"Inconvenient?" I gripped the hilt of his dagger, debating how fast I might shove it into his heart before he hit me back. Not that he had. In fact, he didn't so much as lay a hand on me while I'd kicked and punched him. Odd for a demon of war. I shook my head. My protection charm was at work, not his conscience. "Yes, I imagine it must've been terribly inconvenient for *you* to find my sister murdered. Why were you in the monastery, then?"

A faint shimmering gold light flared up and fell back to the earth like a waterfall. It took a second to realize he was only answering me because of the summoning circle. And apparently he was fighting it. Feeling bold, I stepped near the line of bones and asked again, "Why were you there that night?"

Hatred burned in his eyes. "For your sister."

"What did you want her for?"

He smiled again, but it was more a promise of payback than amusement. "She made a bargain with my brother. I came to collect on it."

I turned away quickly, hoping to hide my surprise. I'd suspected that Vittoria had made a bargain with a demon to spell her diary, but I didn't think she'd summoned one of the Wicked. My focus slid to the basket I'd brought. My twin's diary was hidden a few feet away. Carolina said it called to the Malvagi, and I wondered if Wrath felt it now. I didn't want him getting his demon hands on whatever was in there, and decided against asking him to break the spell. I faced him again. "What were the exact terms of the bargain?"

"Not sure."

I narrowed my eyes. He was obviously lying, but I had no way to force the truth from him. Unless I used one of the Forbidden spells. And that seemed like too much dark magic for one night. I was only willing to tempt Fate so much. "What did you do with her heart?"

"Nothing." He gritted his teeth. "She was dead when I got there."

I winced. Even though there wasn't anything particularly cruel about what he said, the cold assessment of my sister's death still hurt. "Why are you so concerned with the exact phrasing of the spell?"

This time his answer was much slower in coming, as if he was choosing his words very carefully. He finally said, "In order to adhere to its rules, I need to fully understand the protection spell, as you called it. Knowing the phrasing will also help me make sure others adhere to it. We have strict rules we're governed by in the Seven Circles, and severe penalties if they're broken."

"By 'others' do you mean me?" He shook his head. "Who, then?"

"My brothers."

I knew there were seven demon princes, but I didn't think they were related. Imagining demons having families was disturbing. "Do all demons have to obey these rules, or just princes of Hell?"

"If we're exchanging secrets now, I'd like to know how many witches live on this island, and the name of the coven elder from each city. Then you can tell me where the First Witch's grimoire is and I'll consider us even." He smirked at my look of repulsion. "I didn't think so. But I would like to know the Latin portion of the spell you used tonight."

I weighed the benefits against the disadvantages of telling him the protection spell. He couldn't harm me, that much was clear. And it wasn't like he could reverse it, only I could do that.

"Aevitas ligati in aeternus protego."

For a second, he didn't appear to be breathing. He stared at me, his expression close to horror. A deep sense of satisfaction filled me. It wasn't every day a witch caused that much fear in a demon prince, especially the mighty demon of war.

"No snide remark?" I asked, not bothering to hide my smug tone. "It's all right. I know it's an impressive one."

"What's impressive is how wrong you are." He crossed his arms, his countenance once again carefully blank. "Regardless of your pedestrian attempt at dark magic, I'll offer you a bargain in return. The length is negotiable, how we bind it is not."

My face heated. Nonna said the Malvagi's bargains almost always involved kissing—that once they'd locked lips with someone, that person lost their senses entirely. Always craving more, going so far as offering up their soul for another taste of the wicked sin they'd gotten addicted to. I didn't know if all that was true, but I refused to find out.

"I'd rather die than subject myself to kissing you, demon."

His expression held little humor as he took my measure. It was a slow, deliberate sweep of my body, my stance, the way I aimed his own dagger at his heart. If he looked at the bleached bones that surrounded us, he didn't give them more than a cursory glance. When he dragged his attention back to my face, something dark lurked in his gaze, forged deep in the pits of Hell.

Chills ran down my spine, tingling in warning. This was not the kind of prince written about in fairy tales. There was no golden crown sitting atop his dark head, or promises of safety waiting in his sculpted, tattooed arms. He was death and rage and fire and anyone stupid enough to forget that would be consumed by his inferno.

"One day you might beg me to kiss you." He stepped close enough for me to stab him. Heat radiated off him. Around me. A bead of sweat rolled between my shoulders, slipped down my spine. I shivered. He smelled of mint and warm summer days—so at odds with the darkness of his *luccicare*. "You might hate it. Or love it. But temptation will surge through those magical veins of yours, obliterating all common sense. You'll want me to save you from the endless torment by giving you everything you love to loathe. And when I do, you'll thirst for more."

An image of him pressing me against the wall, the stone sharp as talons in my back, his lips soft but demanding as he tasted me, crossed my mind. My mouth went as dry as the bones in my summoning circle. I would sooner sell my soul than be with him.

"Don't worry," he whispered, his lips brushing the delicate skin on my neck. I froze. He'd moved so swiftly, I hadn't even seen him take a step. "You'd need to be the last creature in all the realms combined for me to want you, witch. Even then it might not be enough to tempt me. What I'm offering is a blood trade."

TWELVE

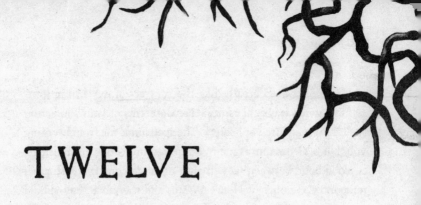

Never enter into a bargain with a demon, but most especially a prince of Hell. The Malvagis' lies are like sugar—sweet, but deadly when too much is ingested over time. Beware: Very few antidotes can be crafted for such a wicked poison.

—*Notes from the di Carlo grimoire*

My heart thrashed from his proximity, the sound almost as loud as the waves attacking the cliffs below. He lingered a moment before stepping away, like he not only heard it, too, but relished the rhythmic, primal beat. I wondered if it reminded him of war drums, and if he suddenly craved battle. I certainly did. Too many emotions were swirling inside me, making my decision especially hard. My sister's possible bargain with his brother. Wrath's blood trade. This whole strange, impossible night. I was barely able to wrap my mind around the fact that the Wicked were not only real, but that one was standing before me, offering a bargain.

"Well?" he asked. "Do you willingly accept my blood trade?"

"You haven't bothered to explain *why* you're offering it, so no."

He took a deep breath, like the very act of explaining himself to a witch was exhausting. "Per the terms of your *protection* spell, I must ensure your safety. The spell binds me from harming you, but it also requires me to grant you protection from others. A blood bond between us will alert other demons that you are a temporary member of House Wrath, and therefore they should not kill or maim you too terribly. There. Will you agree to the blood bond now?"

Not maiming me *too terribly* wasn't the same as not maiming me at all. I stared, lips pursed. After a minute, I slowly shook my head. "No, I don't think I will. You're bound until I release you, and I don't plan on summoning any other demon. Therefore, I don't need your *protection*."

"First, I'm bound to this circle for three days. Not until you release me. Your... protection charm is different—that is, unfortunately, for eternity now." He rolled his shoulders, though it didn't appear to undo the tension in them. "Second, the blood trade will allow me to sense when you're in danger. Without it, I can't guarantee your safety. Which puts me in violation of the rules that *you* made when you crafted that spell."

"Is that so." My tone accused him of being the worst liar I'd ever met. "None of that matters. When our time's up, I'm releasing you back to Hell, not the shopping district."

"Blood of a half-dead demon. This was your first summoning spell, wasn't it?" He watched me carefully. I glared, but said nothing to deny it. He sighed. "Of course I'm bound to an incompetent fledgling until the end of time. Do us both a favor and don't accept my offer. I'd prefer to not be your lapdog anyway."

I cocked my head to the side. "You'd have to come whenever I called for you?"

"Not exactly, but like I said before, I would know when you needed me."

"Why do you care about protecting me?"

"I don't. But thanks to your spell I'm forced to, or I'll risk having my powers diminished. Therefore, I am adhering to the terms. *Some* of us graciously accept our duty."

Sure. When we were magically required to. "How *exactly* does the protection work?"

"Demons will sense the bond and reconsider harming you. It might not persuade all of them not to kill you, but it would give them pause. They'd know they'd incur my wrath as punishment for interfering in House matters."

Much as I was loath to admit it, having the demon of war as a guardian angel wasn't the worst luck. I didn't have to trust or even like him—I only needed to have faith in my own instincts. Right now they were telling me he wasn't responsible for murdering my sister. I was fairly certain this bargain was more beneficial to him, but I'd eventually find a way to bend it in my favor. And even if I couldn't, it didn't matter. Wrath didn't seem to want me dead, and I needed to be very much alive to discover what happened to Vittoria.

"Fine. I accept your offer of a blood trade."

"Willingly?" he asked. I nodded. "Hand me my dagger."

I hesitated for only a second, recalling the protection charm I'd cast on him. For the first time since he appeared in the cave, he looked elated as I slid the blade into his waiting grasp. Before I changed my mind, he cut his finger and enticed a few blood drops to bead up. The wound sealed almost immediately after.

"I won't have to... drink it, will I?"

He cast a quick glance my way. "What sort of stories have you been told about us?"

I mumbled "wicked blood-drinking deviants," and he must have heard me because he didn't bother asking for clarification.

"Unless you enjoy drinking blood, mixing mine with yours will do."

Challenge rose in my steady gaze as I lifted my still-bleeding arm and he pressed his finger to my wound. He seemed just as repulsed by it as I was. I gritted my teeth, trading blood with a demon wasn't my ideal evening, either, but here we were.

"Repeat after me, I... whatever your full name is, willingly accept this blood trade with House Wrath for the term of six months."

"Six *months*?" I yanked free of his grasp and bunched my hands into fists. "That's absurd! What if I don't want your protection for that long?"

He rubbed his temples. "What is it that you want, witch? Why did you summon me?"

"To find out who murdered my sister."

"And?"

I hesitated. I originally wanted to summon a demon to break the spell on my sister's diary. I definitely didn't want Wrath knowing about it now. At least not until I knew why Carolina said they'd come looking for it. "That's it."

"You're lying."

"And you haven't?"

He shook his head. "Being bound to you prevents me from lying. It would be... discourteous to do so."

"Of course. One must always have good manners while ripping the hearts from their enemies." I looked him over, appraising. I wasn't simply going to accept his word without proof. "If your magic wasn't tethered by the protection spell, would you harm me?"

"If I had to, yes."

And he didn't sound all too put off by the idea. At least I knew he was telling the truth about being unable to lie. Instead of responding, like he seemed primed for, I waited. Nonna said a lot could be gained from reading the silence. He was a demon of war, but I understood strategy, too. It didn't take long for him to fill the quietness.

"Believe what you will, but we're aligned in the common goal of finding your sister's murderer."

He and I weren't aligned in anything and never would be. Fury whipped around the cave, faster and mightier than the wind now howling outside. He gave me a bored look that made me seethe more. "Why do you care about finding justice for my sister?"

"I don't," he said. "Do not confuse me with a human with noble intentions."

"If you want me to trust you enough for a blood bargain, or whatever it's called, I need to know *why* you want to solve her murder."

He was quiet a minute, seeming to consider what information to share. "I want to stop the murderer before he strikes again. Aligning myself with you isn't ideal, but it's the hand I've been dealt and I'm playing it to my advantage. Not only are you a witch, like each victim before your sister, you're also connected to the most recent victim. At some point, I believe you may prove valuable in drawing out the killer; therefore, I'd like to sense when you're in danger so I can remove the threat."

I opened my mouth, but he held up a hand to stall me.

"I will not give you any more details unless you agree to the blood bond."

Wrath wasn't lying—he wouldn't tell me anything else unless I agreed. I might be *willingly* choosing his offer, but it didn't really seem like I had any other options. I thought about my sister—I knew exactly what she would do. I inhaled deeply. "You'll tell me more about my sister's involvement with your brother?"

"I'll exchange all necessary information."

Tricky demon. All "necessary" information didn't equal *all* information. I stared at him, trying to work out the uneasy feeling growing inside me. He claimed the blood bond was part of the protection spell I used, but I wasn't sure that was all. I thought about him having a link to me. He said he could tell when I was in danger, but I didn't like the idea of him knowing where I was. Demons might have rules and etiquette, but I knew nothing of them.

Maybe he considered dragging someone to Hell to reign there for eternity a high honor.

"Answer one more question for me," I said. "Aside from not being able to lie, what else are demons forbidden from doing?"

He waited a beat before responding.

"We also cannot enter a human home without an invitation. We're permitted to use our powers, but not to cause direct physical harm. And, once summoned, we are forced to remain in this realm until our invitation is withdrawn."

"If I withdrew your invitation now, would you have to leave right away?"

"Yes. Do we have a bargain?" He looked relaxed, casual. But his eyes were focused, sharp. He very much wanted me to agree to his offer. I thought about the stories Nonna told us as children, about how the Wicked could never be trusted. Wrath had been specifically named.

I wanted very much to be more like my twin. But I couldn't help being me.

"No, Prince Wrath. I do not accept your blood trade."

THIRTEEN

A witch must never enter into a blood trade with a prince of Hell. By doing so, it allows the one conjured to have a direct link to the witch. It is unclear how long the bond lasts or if it can be broken. Never forget: forging a bond made from love is as dangerous as those made through hate.

—*Notes from the di Carlo grimoire*

Nonna glanced at the dagger strapped to my hip, then pounded chicken like she was envisioning someone's skull instead. I'd commandeered the weapon again before I'd left the cave, and Wrath had looked very much like Nonna now. If she was that put off by the demon prince's blade, I couldn't imagine how upset she'd be if she knew about the magical tattoo we shared.

I'd chosen a blouse with long fluttering sleeves to hide it. Before I went to bed, I inspected the two crescent moons within the circle of stars. The ink shimmered like moonlight. Despite the fact it bound me to Wrath, I didn't mind it all that much. It was delicate and pretty.

Thwack. Thwack. Nonna beat the poor chicken with singular focus. At least today's house special would be mouthwateringly tender for our customers. It was good some people still had an appetite. I'd certainly lost mine.

I ignored the way my stomach churned each time I thought about the events of last night. If Nonna knew I'd not only summoned one of the Malvagi, but almost willingly entered into a blood trade with one... I closed my eyes and fought the urge to lay down.

Nonna might stop pounding the chicken and walk herself off the nearest cliff instead.

My focus slid to the little clock above the stove. I wanted to finish dinner service and get back to the cave where Wrath was trapped before dark. Tonight I'd demand answers. Aside from his royal standing in Hell, I didn't know anything about him. For all I knew he *was* the devil and had his own evil agenda.

Regardless of all the unknowns surrounding Wrath, I was certain of at least two facts. The first being he wanted to locate my sister's murderer and probably kill whoever it was. And the second was his desire to form a blood bond with me. I had no intention of going through with the creepy bond, but it gave me excellent leverage to use when I interrogated him. His brother seemed to be interested in bargaining with witches, and I wanted to know why.

If his demon brethren weren't responsible for murdering my twin, that made it all the more likely *strega* hunters were responsible. Having Wrath around to guard me while some witch-hating zealot was ripping out hearts might be wise. I'd let the demon prince fight him and run for safety. And if they destroyed each other in the process? Good riddance.

I sliced mushrooms for the sauce, adding it to the pan of garlic and shallots already simmering in butter. My work was mechanical today, the kitchen held little magic like it once did. It didn't help that my focus kept straying to the clock. I was worried about leaving a demon by himself all afternoon. Whether he was a prince of Hell or something worse, he was still undeniably wicked.

Before I'd left the cavern at daybreak, I'd cast an extra spell of containment that didn't go over very well with him. He couldn't harm me because of the protection charm, and I was fairly confident he wasn't lying about being trapped for three days, but I enjoyed taking extra precautions.

Especially when they made him spitting mad. Nonna told us the Malvagi couldn't stand sunlight, so I planned to be back before nightfall just in case my spell hadn't worked, or he'd somehow broken it.

Nonna set her rolling pin aside and handed the platter of flattened chicken to my mother to drench in flour. She watched me slice more mushrooms as she uncorked a bottle of marsala and splashed it into a hot pan, and I pretended not to notice.

"Distractions in the kitchen lead to accidents, Emilia." She wiped her hands and tossed the towel over her shoulder. "Do you need to sit down?"

I glanced up, pausing my assault on the mushrooms. "I'm fine, Nonna. Just tired."

And more than a little anxious about the last twenty-four hours. It was hard to grasp the fact that the monsters from my childhood stories were real. They didn't have red eyes, or claw-tipped fingers, or horns. The creatures from Hell were elegant, regal, well mannered. It upended my idea of how evil was supposed to present itself to the world. Wrath was supposed to be fang-toothed and drooling, not a shirtless wonder any artist would dream of painting.

"Nicoletta, do you have some advice for your daughter?"

Nonna turned to my mother for help, but Mamma was lost in her own sadness today. She placed a piece of chicken in a bowl of flour seasoned with salt and pepper, shook it free, then dropped it into a waiting skillet. Butter crackled and spit, pleased with the offering.

My mother took another piece of chicken and repeated the motion. All body memory, no conscious thought. I quickly looked away.

Nonna grabbed my chin, forcing me to meet her unflinching gaze. "Whatever trouble you've been seeking ends tonight, Emilia. The moon is almost full and it's no time to be playing with forces you have no hope of controlling. *Capisce?*"

"I haven't been searching for trouble, Nonna." I'd only summoned it to me. "Everything is fine. *I'm* fine, I promise."

Nonna released my face and walked away, shaking her head. "Nothing is fine, child. Hasn't been for a month and I imagine it won't be for many more to come. Vittoria is gone. Nothing will ever bring her back. It's harsh, but it's true. You need to accept it and grieve. Let go of your vengeance, or it will curse us all."

"You want *how* much for this shirt?" I scowled at Salvatore, the thief parading as a vendor. I shook the offending garment at him. "We are both speaking about this one, right? The one that's practically threadbare in the elbows?"

"It's a fair price." He held up his hands and slowly backed behind his table of goods. "Carolina is selling hers for a good bit more. See?"

Sal nodded to the stall across the alley. He had a point, but everyone around here knew—and admired—Claudia's aunt Carolina as "the schemer." Only wealthy people who enjoyed a stroll through the crowded marketplace paid her inflated prices, though.

I imagined it had more to do with the fact she'd spelled the items to be irresistible to certain clientele. I fought the urge to look toward her booth, just in case she called me over to ask how my demon summoning went.

Even practitioners of the dark arts feared the Wicked.

I handed Sal the coins and shoved the shirt into my sack, grumbling the entire time. As much as I'd love to stay and haggle over the poor excuse for clothing, the sun would slip past the horizon soon, and I needed to make sure the demon was still trapped in the circle.

I hurried through the rush of the early evening crowd, ignoring people calling out for me to sample cheese, try their street food, or buy a lovely set of earrings. Unless they could sell me a demon spell to unlock my sister's diary, I wasn't interested.

"Emilia?"

I halted at the end of the street that eventually turned into the steep, winding path of the abandoned cavern. Maybe I'd imagined her voice. I closed my eyes, praying I had. I wasn't ready for this meeting and even if I was, I was running out of daylight. Wicked creatures came out in the dark, and I knew at least one who wanted to slip his leash.

"Emilia! It *is* you, thank the stars. I've been hoping to see you here."

I took a deep breath and pivoted to face my friend. "Hi, Claudia. How—"

She crushed me in a hug, her sudden tears soaking my collar. "It's been a whole month and I still can't believe it. Even after seeing her laid to rest." Claudia stepped back and shook her dark curls. Her hair was shorter than the last time I'd seen her. It looked good. "I've had the strangest . . . dreams lately. My aunt thinks they're urgent messages."

We both scanned the street, but no one was near enough to overhear us. By "dreams" my friend meant "visions." Claudia's magic worked best with scrying. Sometimes her visions were more than visions. And other times they weren't. The trouble was, we could never tell which was a gift from the goddess of sight and premonitions and which was purely her imagination.

I hated that I'd left her alone to worry over potential meanings. Vittoria used to jot notes and ask a hundred different questions. I desperately wished she were by my side now.

"What did you see?"

Claudia glanced around. "It's more a warning than a true vision, I think."

And whatever it was, it clearly terrified her. My friend looked ready to jump out of her skin. I reached over and gripped her hand in mine. "What is it?"

"I don't know . . . I saw black wings and an empty pitcher being filled and emptied. It was all very strange. I think some terrible darkness is coming," she said. "Or it's already here."

Goose bumps rose across my body in waves. I swallowed my shame. I had no doubt Claudia had seen me summoning Wrath. Dragging a prince of Hell from the underworld was a huge feat—I couldn't imagine the kind of magical tremors it must have set off. I'd disrupted the natural order of this world. I brought forth that which didn't belong. It was the darkest sort of magic, and I wasn't surprised a dark witch sensed it.

"Maybe it's just the way your mind is explaining away Vittoria's . . ."

"You're probably right," she agreed quickly. "Domenico is a mess, too. He visits the monastery at least twice a week to pray."

I was happy we'd steered the conversation away from the Great Big Evil I'd invited into our world, though thinking of my sister laying in the monastery brought on its own awful feelings. I tried not to focus on Claudia's tear-stained face. The last thing I wanted was to start crying and show up red-eyed and splotchy when I confronted Wrath. I wanted to project fearlessness and ferocity, not a sobbing, snotty mess.

It was the only thought that kept me from breaking down. Well, that and hearing my sister's secret lover had been praying so often. With my grief and then the desire to unlock her diary, I'd forgotten all about him. "I didn't know they were publicly..."

I wasn't sure what to call it. Not a courtship, because Domenico hadn't spoken to my father and Vittoria certainly hadn't mentioned him. If I hadn't seen his name scrawled in her diary, we wouldn't know she liked him at all. That thought ached, so I shoved it deep down where it couldn't hurt me, with the other unpleasant feelings I'd been storing lately.

"What else has Domenico said?"

"I'm not sure. He hasn't talked to me about anything. He mostly locks himself in one of the empty chambers, and lights prayer candles until after midnight. I think he's there now, actually. He always looks so sad."

I wanted to speak with him and knew I should, but didn't feel ready to just yet. I reasoned it might be cruel to show up, looking like the mirror image of his murdered lover. The truth was, I wasn't ready to confront one of my sister's secrets without my heart breaking the rest of the way.

Claudia looped her arm through mine and guided us off the main road. "Fratello Antonio is worried about you. Since you were the one who…" She swallowed hard. "Now that he's back from his travels putting rumors of shape-shifters to rest, it might be good to speak with him. Just to help find solace."

Solace was the furthest thing from vengeance and I wanted nothing to do with it. The brotherhood would advise me to say prayers and light candles like Domenico. Neither of which would help avenge my sister, or break the spell on her diary. Even if I confessed the darkest desires in my heart, there wasn't anything Antonio could do to help me. He was just a human.

I mustered up a smile, knowing Claudia was coming from a place of love. And she had enough to worry about with her own unsettling visions. "I will talk to him. Soon. I promise."

Claudia studied my face. "Make sure you visit me while you're there, too. I miss you. I can't imagine what you're going through, but you're only alone if you choose to be, Emilia. Please don't forget that you're still living and are loved. And, if you let me, I can help."

I pictured confirming her fears about her dream, telling her all about what I did last night; about the demon I'd plucked from the underworld and stashed away in ours. And not just any demon, but if he was to be believed, a prince of war. A demon so vicious and mighty he was the living embodiment of wrath.

If Claudia knew what I was planning next, I wondered if she'd still be willing to help.

I took one look at the determination in her eyes and decided she might.

"I…" I inhaled deeply. I didn't trust Wrath with this secret, and Carolina couldn't help, but maybe Claudia could. I pulled my sister's diary from my satchel. "There's a spell on this I can't break. Your aunt said the magic wasn't from this realm. It's possibly demonic in origin."

Claudia's eyes widened as she brushed her fingers over the cover. "It's . . . ancient."

"Do you think you could find out what sort of magic was used?"

She nodded vigorously. "I can certainly try."

"It's dangerous," I warned. "You can't tell anyone you have it, or show it to anyone."

"I won't. Promise."

I let the diary go. As I turned to leave, a shadow loomed above my friend and hissed, *"He's here."*

"What?" I half-screamed and stumbled back. It was the same disembodied voice I'd heard the night my sister had been killed. I'd never forget the sound. "Who is?"

"Who is what?" Claudia glanced around and then reached over to steady me. "Are you all right, Emilia? You look as if you've seen the devil."

"I—"

"Did you hear that?" I dragged a hand through my hair and tugged at the roots. Nothing was there. No menacing shadow or dire warnings from beyond. Maybe I needed the church after all. I could certainly use all the prayers I could get. "It's nothing. I thought you said something else."

Claudia seemed unconvinced, but after a strained moment hugged me good-bye with a promise to learn everything she could about the mysterious spell.

I heard Nonna's voice in my head as I hurried out of the city, constantly tossing looks over my shoulder to see if anything followed. She'd been right—*nothing* was fine.

And I was starting to think it might never be again.

FOURTEEN

"Put this on. No one should be subjected to *that* all night, demon."

Wrath snatched the shirt a second before it hit his face and actually cringed. Honestly, I couldn't blame him. Wrinkled tawny suede, elbows worn thin, and crisscrossing drawstrings at the chest. He stared like I'd dragged in a decaying carcass and told him to skin it and sew it into a jacket.

He set his jaw. "No."

"No?" I tilted my head like I hadn't heard him correctly.

"It looks like you balled it up and left it in the bottom of a drawer for months, and it smells like you wiped out pig innards with it." He tossed it back at me. "Fetch me something more suitable, or deal with me as is."

"Excuse me?" I marched up to the line of bones and crossed them without hesitation. I stood toe-to-toe with him, fuming. A wild gleam in my eyes dared him to tell me no again. "Put. The. Shirt. On. *Now.*"

"Does the sight of my bare skin get under yours? Did you have sinful thoughts about me last night?" He gave me a lazy grin. "That's usually my brother's specialty, but fear not, we've all got bedroom talents."

"Pig."

"Care to roll around the dirt with me?"

Anger poured off me. "You wish."

"I don't." I swore the temperature dropped to match the iciness of his tone. "You call *us* wicked, but you witches are vengeful creatures without soul or conscience." He nodded to his dagger I'd strapped to my hip. It looked ridiculously out of place against my dark flowing skirt and matching blouse with fluttering sleeves. But I didn't care. He wasn't getting it back. "Stab me if you must, but I'm not putting that monstrosity on."

"You can't possibly be serious. It's a shirt." I stared up at him and I couldn't begin to understand the new look in his eyes. "Need I remind you that you aren't in any position to make demands or deny me?"

His annoyance joined mine in unholy matrimony.

"Here's a little lesson since you seem to be woefully uneducated, witch. Summoning does not equal *owning*. Containment isn't forever."

He moved near enough that I either had to remain and feel the heat of his body, or shift away to hold his gaze. It took a moment for me to yield a step, but I finally did.

I couldn't believe he wanted to argue over clothing while I was reeling over my personal ghost from Hell. *If* it was even real and not some sinister creation my mind conjured to haunt me.

"I can and will deny you whenever I choose," he said, his voice now dangerously low. "Do not *ever* make the mistake of thinking you wield any power over me other than the spell that contains me here. And even that won't last."

He took a deep breath, like he was enjoying the anger emanating from me. I thought about punching him again, but refrained. "You can't break the spell without me, demon."

"Maybe not. But containment spells—like summoning spells—last three days. After that, I'm free to leave this circle and do as I please." He finally stepped back and leaned against the cavern wall, watching me digest the information. "Have you come to verbally spar all night, or have you changed your mind about the blood bond?"

"Neither. I've come to interrogate you about witch hunters." His sudden laughter startled me. I recovered quickly and crossed my arms. "Why is that funny?"

"Information is currency where I'm from. No one expects to get something for free. If you walked into any of the royal houses and demanded information, they'd skin you alive."

I hoped he couldn't hear the pounding of my heart as I let that visual take shape.

"Agreeing to a blood trade doesn't count as payment?" I asked. He straightened up and immediately lost the grin. That got his princely attention. "I believe in making informed decisions. Therefore, I request an exchange of some basic information. Surely that won't be too much for you to agree to."

He inspected me the way someone might look at a cat if it suddenly started ordering the servants around. "Very well. I will indulge you by answering *some* questions. Choose wisely."

"Have you heard of any humans who have banded together to hunt witches?"

He shook his head. "Not at this time. Though history has shown them to be active, so I'm sure they exist."

"Which of your brothers bargained with my sister?"

"Pride."

I closed my mouth. In human religion the devil was often associated with that particular sin. Last night Wrath only told me my sister had made a deal with his brother; he hadn't mentioned the actual devil. Which meant...

A memory sprang to the forefront of my mind. The night before Vittoria was murdered, I'd demanded to know what she'd been doing at the monastery.

"I was summoning the devil. An ancient book whispered its secrets to me, and I've decided to take him as my husband. I'd invite you to the wedding, but I'm pretty sure the ceremony takes place in Hell."

Blood and bones. Vittoria hadn't been teasing. Questions swarmed around my head like angry bees.

"Was that all you wanted to know, witch?" Wrath stepped into view, breaking into my thoughts. My sister had told me the truth, and I'd let her down. I didn't ask questions, or take her seriously. I should have known better—she always said outlandish things to humans, and delighted in them thinking she was lying. If I wasn't so annoyed with her for embarrassing me in front of Antonio, I would have paid closer attention. I *should* have paid closer attention.

I took a steadying breath. I'd start noticing every detail now.

"Why did Pride want to marry her?" I asked. Wrath's expression became impossible to read. My patience frayed. "I know my sister agreed to marry him. She told me so herself."

He didn't move, but I pictured his mind whirling as he probably formulated a thousand different scenarios, and tallied benefits against costs to information sharing. I honestly didn't think he'd respond. He didn't look pleased when he finally did. "Pride needs to marry in order to break a curse that was placed on him."

"Why are you helping?"

He flashed his teeth. "I was bored. It seemed like fun."

If he really couldn't lie to me, that had to at least be partially true. "So, what… your mission is to find someone who's willing to marry Pride?"

"Yes. He's in need of a witch bride, specifically. Part of my task involves ensuring his betrothed makes it to our realm safely, should she accept his bargain."

"Why does he need to marry a witch?"

"He requires someone with magical abilities to break the curse."

"What if she refuses?"

"Then she's made aware of opposing… forces… that wish her harm."

It was a very polite way of saying if she declined the offer, she'd risk death.

"The other two victims were also witches. Which means they were offered the same bargain as Vittoria," I said mostly to myself, thinking over the new information aloud. Wrath nodded politely anyway. "Were they killed before or after you spoke with them?"

"After."

"You allow them time to consider the deal?"

"Of course. They're given a full day to think it over."

I was surprised by this. If I needed someone to accept a bargain to break a curse, time would be the last thing I'd want to give them. Too much could go wrong.

"How do you choose the witch?" Wrath gave me a look that said question time was drawing to an end. "At least answer this, demon. How many others from your world know who you're offering the bargain to?"

"Only Pride and I."

I mulled that over. That actually made the list of suspects greater. Instead of worrying about a spy in Wrath's kingdom, it opened up the possibility of the victims telling people about the devil's bargain in this world, too. Then those people who'd been told could have said something, or were overheard by others. A full day was a long time for the gossips to get to work.

Except... there was one major issue with that theory. *Streghe* didn't spill their secrets. I thought about witch hunters again. Wrath didn't sound like he thought they were a threat, but I hadn't found any evidence to completely rule them out. It still made the most sense that they were responsible. Perhaps they'd somehow uncovered who the true witches across the island were, and the devil's bargain timing was a coincidence.

"Will you tell me who the next witch is?"

"No."

I considered my options. I could send notes to the twelve other families in Palermo, but there was a chance they could be intercepted. Showing up at their homes or businesses was also risky in case we were being watched, so that wasn't an option. In these strange times, I had to be very cautious about each of my moves. My good intentions might end up costing someone their life. Hopefully the others were taking precautions after the recent murders.

Wrath stepped to the edge of the bone circle, looking like trouble. "Well? Are you ready to become a member of House Wrath?"

"No. Until you decide to work with me as an equal, I decline your offer of *protection*."

His smile was filled with venom. "You weren't ever planning on accepting the blood trade, were you?" I ignored him and plucked my satchel up from the ground and headed for the cave entrance. Wrath called out, "Where are you going?"

"To the monastery."

"These are dangerous times; you shouldn't go alone. Set me free and I'll come with you."

As if I'd let that happen. "Next time."

"*Benediximus.*" Good luck. "It's your funeral."

His dark chuckle followed me all the way back to the city.

FIFTEEN

Two streets away from the monastery, I felt the unmistakable sensation of being watched. I pretended not to notice for a solid block before casually making my way down an empty street. If I had to resort to magic, I didn't need any witnesses reporting my so-called devilry to the church. When we were much younger, a *fratello* named Carmine used to search for anyone with evil in their soul. I'd heard the church had sent him to northern Italy, but I thought of him every now and again. Especially when outside the monastery, primed to use magic.

I gripped my *cornicello* and squinted into the alley beside me, searching for purply *luccicare* that indicated a human was near. At first, I didn't see a thing. And then...

A low, smooth voice spoke from the shadows. "Well, this is *quite* a surprise."

Hair on the back of my neck stood on end as a man emerged from the darkness. His hair was black silk, and his eyes were an animal-like green. No human had eyes that color, and the strange, glittering *luccicare* surrounding him indicated what I already suspected: Malvagi. I wasn't sure why, but I let go of my amulet and subtly tucked it inside my bodice.

"You're..." Another demon prince. One I *hadn't* summoned to this realm. Which meant there were other ways for them to get here. Something I should have realized sooner since Wrath had been the one standing over my sister last month. Impossible was becoming quite the joke.

I stepped back, and silently prayed to the goddess of battle and victory. The new demon smiled as if he'd read my thoughts. I wanted to look away, but couldn't. It was as if that odd, pulsating energy of his held me captive no matter how much I wanted to scream.

Instead of panicking, I catalogued details. He was almost as tall as Wrath, and was arresting as opposed to classically handsome, but drew greater attention because of it. He had well-trimmed facial hair that accentuated the hard angles of his face. Staring at him, I almost felt a twinge of—

"Envy." The demon managed to make a singular word sound both threatening and inviting. "And you are... intriguing."

I didn't want to be intriguing. I didn't want to be alone with him. I wanted to escape. I didn't manage to accomplish any of those things. I stood there, frozen with bone-deep terror. The Wicked hadn't been seen in this realm for almost one hundred years. Now at least two of them were here.

I couldn't quite grasp why, but I felt this prince was different from Wrath. There was something about him that came across as lethally angelic. But if he ever had a halo, it was broken now. I wanted to drop to my knees in supplication and also scream for mercy.

Envy lurked at the edge of the alley. Just as Wrath had been the first evening I'd encountered him, his brother was dressed in fine clothes. His suit was solid black, but his shirt and vest were several shades of swirling green shot through with silver threads. He also had a dagger strapped to his side, but this one had a giant green gemstone lodged into its hilt.

All my senses tingled with warning. And fear. This midnight creature wasn't bound to protect me, and I was acutely aware of my vulnerability.

This skirt had no secret pocket, so I'd left my moon-blessed chalk at home. Which meant I had no way to draw a protection circle, no herbs to offer the earth, and I had a feeling running would only amuse him. I almost choked on terror. I was at the mercy of this devil.

My panic abruptly shifted into something else. A fierce, overwhelming dark feeling fluttered around me like expansive leathery wings. It was cold and ancient—with no beginning and no ending. Like all magic, it just *was*.

And I longed for all of it to be *mine*. Every last drop.

I was suddenly jealous of the immense power these demons wielded. Why did the Hell creatures deserve it all? Why was I less worthy of possessing some power of my own?

I was goddess blessed, not demon cursed!

If I had even a *fraction* of that magic, I could force others to tell me what happened to my twin. I could stop another witch from losing her life in a demonic bargain. And I could bring the underworld to its knees. I wanted what they had so badly that I burned with hatred. It was an ice-cold hate so potent that I was frozen down to my very core.

It was too much. Wanting that which would never be mine...

Envy leaned forward, a hungry gleam in his strange eyes. I had the oddest impression that he suffered from those same feelings. That he envied his brothers in a way that almost drove him mad. I could never imagine feeling that way about my twin. It must be so lonely, so isolating.

I held the dagger I'd taken from Wrath, pressed it into my chest, and almost groaned with pleasure as blood beaded up. It pierced my skin with such terrible ecstasy. I was ready to carve out my own heart just to stop the consuming pain of knowing I'd never possess that power—

A little electric current pulsed from my tattoo, sending sparks of energy across my skin, and the spell shattered. I blinked as if coming out of a vivid dream. I glanced from the blade in my shaking hand, to the green-eyed demon whose attention shifted to my arm.

Envy must have been either feeding me his emotions, or turning mine against me.

"Exceptional," the demon prince said. "Did you feel as I did?"

If he felt like an endless abyss of nothingness, hatred, and ice, then yes. "What did you do to me?"

"Allowed your inner desires to surface. Some call them sins."

I shivered, feeling violated in a way I'd never known and hoped to never experience again. I'd almost shoved a blade through my heart. If my tattoo hadn't stopped me, I'd be dead. I couldn't help but wonder if I'd been wrong about witch hunters; maybe Nonna had been right all along and humans weren't to blame.

It definitely felt like this demon was responsible for the bodies with missing hearts.

Envy had affected me even with my *cornicello*. My little charm had been no match for a prince of Hell. I wasn't even sure if he'd used all of his power, or a small part of it.

If he'd done that while I was in the kitchen with my family . . .

I closed my eyes, not wanting to even *think* about what he could have forced me to do to them. And how powerless I'd be to resist him. I wondered if any of our precautions and spells or charms truly worked, or if they'd only succeeded in giving us a false sense of security.

With creatures like Envy roaming the earth, I didn't believe we'd ever truly be safe. I had the sudden urge to cry. No wonder Nonna told us those stories and tried to hide us.

These demons were worse than nightmares. And now they were here.

"Strange." Envy set his animal-like gaze on me, curious. I glanced down at my tattoo, startled to see snakes now twined around the crescent moons, forming a larger circle around them. I'd been so distracted by fear, I hadn't felt the burning in my forearm. Envy's attention cut to the dagger now safely tethered to my hip again and a slow, cunning smile touched his lips. "How very interesting indeed. Such tangled, tangled webs. Summoned through hate, bound by blood."

"What do you mean?"

He shoved gloved hands into his pockets. "You have something I want."

"If it's my still-beating heart, I'm afraid I must decline."

"No, but I imagine you'll end up giving that to my brother one day."

His tone was flat. I wondered if Wrath knew how jealous he was, but said nothing.

"Perhaps we can strike a bargain. If you agree to sell your soul to House Envy, I will help you find what you seek." His expression was inhuman and ice cold as he waited. The hair on the nape of my neck stood at attention. "I covet unique things. You would make an interesting gift to my court. Do you sing?"

"I'm not unique." Nor was I a "thing" or a "gift" to be passed around like a curiosity at a party.

"Aren't you, though?" He smiled. "It's been a great long while since I last saw a shadow witch. I should like very much for you to join my House."

I didn't know what he meant by shadow witch, and it was the least of my worries. An image of humans and witches frozen solid as morbid displays on a grand checkerboard crossed my mind. Envy seemed like the kind of demon who'd proudly show off his trophies, hoping others would be struck with jealousy over his *coveted* possessions.

I swallowed my growing panic, unsure if it was an image he'd fed to me. I didn't want to ever find out if that fear held any kernel of truth.

"Well?" Envy asked, an edge creeping into his tone. "Are you willing to join my House? I can offer protection from my realm and my brothers. You'll certainly need it, especially with all of the unfortunate murders here of late."

My heart drummed madly. There was an old proverb Nonna always muttered that claimed "better the devil you know than the devil you don't" and I'd never felt the truth in something more. If given a choice between bargaining with Wrath or Envy, I'd choose Wrath.

I had little doubt that Envy would love nothing more than to take his deadly blade to my skin and slowly peel away the layers, discovering what *exactly* made me a shadow witch.

Whatever that was.

Knowing a little of their rigid, well-mannered ways, I didn't want to anger him by declining too soon. After what felt like an entire millennium had passed of me pretending to consider his offer, I finally said, "Not at this time, thank you."

He seemed on the verge of arguing his point, but suddenly inclined his head as if in deference. His gaze tracked back to the tattoo on my arm.

"Very well. Even we princes of Hell don't know what the future may hold. You may change your mind, or alter your views yet. I will still accept you when and if you choose my House over my brother's." The demon turned and headed for the opposite end of the street, pausing at the crossroad to glance back. "Be warned; the others grow weary. If they haven't already started hunting, they *will* come for you soon. Let this serve as your warning, and as a boon from House Envy. Pick a House to align yourself with, or the decision will be made for you."

SIXTEEN

Nearby, fire crackled. Smoke followed soon after, slithering through the air like a fleeing serpent. When I first saw the Prince of Wrath in the monastery, I'd heard a similar sound. Maybe fire and smoke had something to do with how demons traveled between realms.

Now that Envy was gone, my breaths were coming hard and fast, almost matching the frantic pounding of my heart. Eighteen years of hiding from the Malvagi, and I'd just been trapped with one who'd used his powers on me. And I survived. I wanted to either laugh or vomit. Before I managed either, I needed to convince my knees to stop quaking.

Holy goddess, that was the most harrowing experience I'd ever had. If my sister had gotten involved with the Wicked, unraveling her secrets while remaining safe just got harder. I wasn't sure I'd be so lucky the next time I met a prince of Hell alone. They altered the very space around them. And it didn't look like it had taken much energy—if any at all—for Envy to do that. I glanced down the street. It was still blessedly empty. Before Envy showed up, I'd been on my way to the monastery. Claudia mentioned Domenico was there, and I thought it might be time to ask him if he knew what—

Fear gripped me until I could hardly breathe. Envy said I had something he wanted. Besides my *cornicello,* which I'd tucked inside my bodice where he couldn't see it, and Wrath's dagger, I didn't have anything on me. But Claudia had my sister's diary, and if the Malvagi could truly sense it, then Envy might already be hunting her down this very moment.

If anything happened to her...

I took off toward her home, running so fast I almost lost my sandals as my feet pounded uneven stones. I ran harder, focusing solely on getting to Claudia's house before the demon did. I jumped over baskets laid out, past chamber pots and chickens that ran through the side streets. I dodged laundry lines and managed to only bump into one unpleasant fisherman as I skidded to a halt outside Claudia's door.

I grabbed the iron knocker and pounded until a candle flared to life upstairs. Claudia poked her head out from the window on the second story.

"Emilia? Blood and bones. You scared me! Hang on."

I whipped around, scanning the dark street. There was no sign I'd been followed. I also didn't feel any sort of presence watching, and I hoped that meant Envy was somewhere far away.

A moment later, the bolt slid loudly and the door swung open. Claudia motioned for me to come inside. I rushed in and slammed the door behind me, breathing hard.

"What the devil is wrong, Emilia?"

"Is your aunt home?"

"Not yet. She stayed a little later at the booth tonight. What happened?" She held up her candle, searching my face. "You look terrible."

I blew out a shaky breath. "Did you find anything out about the spell on the diary?"

"Not really. The magic is old, definitely not of this realm. But there's something else that's strange about it. I need more time to really—"

"No!" I reached over and gently squeezed her shoulder to soften the blow of my words. "I want you to forget all about the spell and the diary. Please. It's too dangerous."

Claudia narrowed her eyes. "Does whatever happened have to do with the vision I had?"

"Maybe." I rubbed my temples. A giant headache was starting. "Listen, I—I'm not sure what happened tonight, but the Wicked are here. And I think their arrival has something to do with Vittoria's diary. Whatever the reason, I don't want to draw any attention to the book. Or you."

"Did you speak with one of them?"

I nodded. "The Prince of Envy and I just had a lovely conversation. It started with me almost carving out my heart."

I expected a sharp intake of breath, or some indication that my friend was completely terrified that the Wicked were indeed roaming around Sicily. Maybe she thought I'd hit my head. She calmly went to the cupboard and pulled out a bottle of herbal spirits she'd made. She poured us each a mouthful and set my glass in front of me.

"Sit." She pointed to one of the wooden chairs. "Drink this. It'll calm your nerves."

I plopped into the seat and brought the glass to my nose. It was mint and something citrusy. Maybe lime. I tossed it back, relishing the sharp flavor. *"Grazie."*

Claudia drank hers down, and put the bottle away.

"You don't seem surprised," I said. "Did you know they were here?"

"I suspected." She pressed her hip against the table and sighed. "When the murders started and the hearts were stolen, I immediately thought of the curse."

"You mean the blood debt between the First Witch and the devil?"

"No," she said slowly, "I mean the curse."

I drew my brows together. Wrath said the devil wanted to break a curse. "Was the curse placed on witches, or someone else?"

"That's just the thing." Claudia moved around the table and dropped her voice. "No one knows for sure. Dark witches believe it was the price La Prima paid for the vengeance spell she cast on the devil."

That was plausible. Dark magic demanded payment. But casting a spell on the devil... I shuddered despite the sweltering summer heat. I vaguely recalled Nonna mentioning it, but she didn't seem convinced of its validity. "Why did she curse the devil?"

"Old stories claim he stole her firstborn's soul. From that day forward the devil was trapped in Hell for eternity. His brothers could travel between realms within reason, typically the days before and after a full moon, but he would never set foot outside the underworld. And that wasn't all. Supposedly he'd only retain his full powers if a witch sat on the throne beside him, wearing the Horn of Hades to keep the balance between realms."

"The Horn of Hades? Is that a crown?"

"There's no written documentation on what it is, or how it

works exactly. My aunt thinks part of the curse included removing or blocking our memories. She also believes that's what really happened to old Sofia Santorini; that her scrying session unveiled something about the curse it wanted forgotten."

"By 'it' you mean the curse? Like it's its own entity?"

Claudia nodded. "It's strange that no one recalls certain details. Everyone has a slightly different myth or legend, but no one knows the truth."

"Nonna never mentioned any of this."

"Not surprising. My aunt said witches of the light don't believe La Prima would cast such a dangerous spell. It goes against their image of what it means to be goddess blessed. Who knows?" Claudia lifted a shoulder. "Stories twist each time they're told. Maybe it's all fiction now. The only way anyone might know the truth is if they had the first book of spells created by La Prima. And I've heard tales that the Wicked are searching for it. There may be a spell in it that will allow the devil to break the curse and travel between realms again without needing a witch queen."

Unease crept through me as I thought about the strange grimoire sheets Vittoria had hidden away under the floorboards. There was no way my sister had found La Prima's missing spell book.

And yet…there was the ancient magic binding her diary that wasn't of this realm. Was the secret location of the first book of spells written within those pages? I'd think it was impossible, but I'd been learning that impossible was another figment of the imagination.

So if it *was* true, then how in the world did my twin find it?

I scooted my chair back from the table and stood. Until I

figured out the answers to all of my questions, I didn't want anyone else near Vittoria's diary. If it had a spell the devil was after that could release him from Hell, it was more dangerous than I'd originally feared.

"Will you get the diary for me?"

SEVENTEEN

That night I found the first clue hidden beneath the floorboards in my room. As with most seemingly insignificant details, I'd overlooked the gambling chip when I'd first seen it. I'd been too preoccupied with the diary and strange grimoire sheets to pay much attention to another trinket my sister had collected. Especially something as small and unimportant as a gambling chip.

I carefully flipped the trinket over and read the Latin etched lightly on the back: AVARITIA. Greed. I set the chip down, and stared at the crowned frog stamped onto the front. A month ago I wouldn't have thought much of the crown or the Latin. Now I'd had the misfortune of meeting two of the seven deadly princes of Hell, and I couldn't escape the nagging suspicion that the owner of this gambling chip was another terrifying creature I'd like to avoid.

If he was anything like Envy, I couldn't fathom seeking him out. There was no telling what kind of horror he might try inflicting on me. But... Vittoria must have encountered him if she held on to this chip. Whatever the connection between them, it was important if she left a small piece of him for someone to find. So far, while I hadn't entirely ruled out the possibility of witch hunters being responsible for the murders, I also hadn't come across any solid evidence pointing to them.

For now, I needed to concentrate on this clue and set my other suspicions aside.

I glanced toward my window at the stars winking in and out of the darkness as clouds swept past them. I wished my twin had trusted me with her secrets. But wishes wouldn't get either of us anywhere now—action would. I pulled a piece of parchment out from our shared nightstand and sat with a pen and pot of ink. Writing out things to research more might help reveal another thread for me to pull. The Wicked were a promising lead, but I had a nagging feeling I was missing something.

There had to be a connection tying everything together.

Spelled diary—what magic did Vittoria really use to seal it? how did she find it?

Deal with the devil—why did she agree to become his bride? does it have to do with the curse Claudia mentioned? or did she think she could break it and remain here?

First book of spells—if it belongs to La Prima, how can the Wicked sense it?

Horn of Hades—what is it? a crown? how powerful is it?

Witch hunters—are they involved? if so, are they watching the Wicked, or is there a connection between them and the devil's bargain?

I scanned the notes, nothing stood out. Except...I thought back to when Vittoria first started acting strangely. It had been roughly three weeks before she died. Right around the time of our eighteenth birthday. I'd assumed it had to do with her secret affair with Domenico, but it seemed more likely now that that was when she'd started summoning demons.

One week later, the first murder occurred in Sciacca. Then the first witch in Palermo died a few days after that. Within a week from the second murder, my twin was killed. I didn't know if Wrath would share any detailed information with me about the bargains, but there was a strong possibility that my sister's first summoning correlated to the devil's sudden desire to break the curse.

Maybe her use of demon magic awakened something in the underworld that had long been slumbering. If she'd managed to summon a prince of Hell, anything was possible. Or maybe none of that was true. If she didn't summon a demon or find the first book of spells, maybe she found the Horn of Hades and its discovery set everything into motion.

I pushed those thoughts aside and focused on the theory I'd started with. Witch hunters. They were human, but humans used folk magic as part of their religion throughout the Kingdom of Italy. Perhaps they had some way of being alerted to that kind of dark magic.

I sighed. The witch hunter theory still didn't quite fit, no matter how hard I tried making sense of it. It did, however, look more probable that there was a link between the demons being summoned, the devil's bargain, and the murders that followed. I'd summoned a prince of Hell, so it was likely Vittoria had accomplished the impossible, too. Which still begged the question of where she'd gotten the summoning spells to begin with. I scribbled another note.

Grimoire sheets—was Vittoria summoning a demon to control, or did one of them give her these summoning spells? if so, who and why?

I stopped writing and carefully considered the last point. What if Vittoria didn't summon a demon first...maybe one was already here, like Wrath. If that demon prince gave my sister the grimoire sheets, did that mean he'd convinced her to help in some wicked scheme? What could a demon prince possibly gain by angering the devil, and slaying his brides? Was it a bid for the dark throne? No matter what secrets my sister kept, I knew with utter certainty that she'd never help someone if they murdered witches.

I picked up the gambling chip, wondering if it wasn't something Vittoria had taken, but something that was gifted to her. Maybe it was a token of good faith, or...I needed to stop speculating and start hunting. I had a new plan for the morning, and it made my stomach twist.

"Have you seen this before?" I flashed the gambling chip at Salvatore. He may have been a mediocre clothing vendor, but he was an extraordinary source of knowledge. I'd gotten up with the sun and rushed out of the house before Nonna interrogated me about the devil again. He might not be chasing me yet, but I was certainly trying to find him and his wretched brothers.

A bead of sweat rolled down my neck after my brisk jog to the market, and I probably looked a little wild with my loose, damp curls. Hopefully Sal wouldn't scrutinize me too closely when there was something much more interesting to pay attention to. Out of anyone in the city, Salvatore was the most reliable gossip.

And the most likely to share every detail he knew with anyone who asked.

"Is that . . ." He leaned across a pile of folded shirts, squinting. "That's it! That's the club everyone's talking about these days. It's real mysterious. No name, just the crowned frog stamped onto the door. I hear it changes locations and you need one of those chips to get in." He rummaged through a pile of clothes, and held up a pretty crimson dress. It was one of the finer garments in his stall. I immediately became suspicious. "Trade? I'll give you this for that. It's a real bargain."

"*Grazie*. But I'm going to hang on to it for a while." I stuck the gambling chip down the front of my bodice. "Do you know the last location of the gambling den?"

"Somewhere near the cathedral, but that was days ago. It's probably long gone by now. If you don't have any luck there, ask old man Giovanni, who sells granita near the front entrance. He likes to gamble."

I decided to try my luck with the cathedral first. I spent a good thirty minutes walking down each alley and side street. I stumbled across a man urinating near a palm tree, but the mysterious gambling den remained hidden. I searched for a few more minutes before seeking out old man Giovanni. A sign on his granita stand was flipped to CLOSED.

Of course. He was probably at the gambling den.

I was about to give up and try my luck elsewhere when I felt the sudden urge to clutch my amulet. Maybe the goddess of death and fury was still guiding my path, or maybe, buried some place deep down where I didn't want to examine too closely, I sensed the slight lure of demon magic.

I could have sworn I heard a faint humming, guiding my path. I didn't know if I was losing myself to phantoms, or if it was a latent skill that was emerging each time I held my *cornicello* and concentrated. I didn't care what the reason was, I only needed to let my instincts guide me.

After a few minutes of wandering down side roads that spiderwebbed away from the cathedral, I stopped in front of a door with a crowned frog burned onto it. I'd done it!

And now I felt a little queasy. I dropped my amulet, and considered my next move. I could turn back, go to Sea & Vine, and forget this nightmare. Leave princes of Hell to someone better equipped with dealing with them. Or I could try to be a little more like Vittoria.

I pulled the gambling chip out from my bodice and held it against the door, praying I wasn't following a little *too* closely in my sister's footsteps.

EIGHTEEN

For spells of courage, anoint a red candle with the following items during a waxing moon and burn until flame extinguishes: one part cayenne pepper, one part clove, twice-blessed oil, and a heaping tablespoon of crushed charcoal.

—*Notes from the di Carlo grimoire*

The door swung open, and I traveled down a creaking set of stairs before entering a subterranean lair. Based on the grimy dead-end entrance, I thought the inside of Greed's den of sin would be dark and derelict. Which was only partly the case. The overcrowded room was indeed dark—brick walls, a gleaming ebony bar that spanned the length of the room, and several velvet-topped tables in deep burgundy dotted the tiled floor.

Each table featured different card games. One colorful round of scopa drew the most attention. Men and women gathered, their gazes fixed on what they hoped was their winning hand. I had a feeling the only true winner was the demon prince in residence.

The gambling den oozed with the promise of riches. Desire for wealth and power was so potent, it almost took physical form.

I pictured it reaching for my throat, squeezing until I drew breath in greedy drabs. My attention darted from one sinful tableau to the next.

Greed in its many forms made an appearance. There was greed for power, wealth, attention—excess was the poison of choice here, and patrons couldn't seem to get their fill. I wondered if they knew what time it was, that the sun had just risen and beckoned to them to step outside, to live. Some were haggard, tired, as if they'd been up for days, addicted to whatever their chosen form of greed was. There was also an edge of violence lurking in the atmosphere, like a simple want or desire could twist into something deadly at any moment. It wasn't hard to imagine someone knifing their competition, and taking what they wanted by force.

Sharp gazes cut around the room and I followed the stares. In one corner a man held court with dozens of expensive liquor bottles, doling out drinks to those who luxuriated in his presence. On the opposite end of the room, men and women slowly removed layers of clothing, swaying their near-naked bodies in hopes of capturing the greedy gazes of those content with watching. Attention was their vice, and, even though it felt wrong to participate in something that was surely enhancing Greed's power, I couldn't stop from indulging in their sultry show.

I shook myself from the trance, and looked for the demon I suspected was around.

A door along the far wall was flanked by scowling guards in fine clothes. I'd wager anything I'd find Greed there. *If* I could make it through the crowded room. There were so many patrons that I had to tread carefully. I tried weaving around groups of people standing behind card players, but barely squeezed through immoveable bodies. Servers carried silver trays overflowing with food and drink, making the progression more difficult than it already was. I managed to shoot between a line of people topping off prosecco glasses before a fight broke out behind me.

Cheers and jeers erupted at the nearest table. I stood on tiptoes and peered past a crowd of people who'd moved in to see what had drawn such a reaction. The door was still impossibly far.

I debated hopping up onto the tables, and running across them when I heard her name—it was a blade to my heart.

"Vittoria!"

I spun slowly, searching for whoever'd called out for my sister. My attention landed on a man around my father's age, half sitting in his chair, half falling to the floor. Gambling chips and empty glasses were stacked in haphazard piles around him. He lifted his gaze, and I drew in a sharp breath. Domenico Nucci Senior.

"Signore Nucci. Do you—"

"Vittoria, be a good girl and see about my drink, will you?" His focus slid to the next card someone slapped down. "Maybe get some of those fried calamari with extra arrabbiata to dip them in, too. It's gonna be another long game. These cheaters are making me feel wolfish."

He smiled like we were sharing some big secret.

"I'm not—I'm Emilia, my sister is..." Signore Nucci was obviously intoxicated and probably thought he was at Sea & Vine, ordering dinner. The spicy marinara and fried octopus were one of our most popular dishes to share. It also explained his confusion over calling me Vittoria—she used to help our father and uncle in the dining room sometimes. "I'll make sure someone brings your food soon."

I turned and smacked into a hard chest. One of the nicely

dressed men who'd been guarding the door glared down at me. "The boss would like a word with you. Come this way."

Whatever pain I'd felt about being mistaken for my sister was immediately replaced with fear. I followed the muscular man as he cleared a path to the door. Power seeped from whatever lay beyond it, and I knew it meant a prince of Hell was in residence. I steeled my buzzing nerves.

The man wasted little time with entertaining my trepidation, and shoved the door open. He barreled into the room without a second glance, and, with little choice, I followed.

"She's here, signore."

I don't know what I expected to find—maybe a fire-breathing dragon guarding a mountain of gold and jewels, or a really large poisonous frog lashing out with a whiplike tongue covered in spikes—but a lavish room fitted with layered Persian rugs, an oversized desk, plush leather chairs, and a dazzling crystal chandelier wasn't it. Everything was elegant and warm. So very at odds with the shivers running down my back.

The Prince of Greed sat behind the mammoth desk, fingers steepled beneath his chin, a bored look on his finely carved face. He was, in a word, bronzed. From his dark auburn hair to the deep russet of his eyes, he reminded me of copper coins melted and recast in a humanoid form. If he had a dagger like Envy and Wrath, he'd hidden it well. Which made me trust him even less.

"I wasn't anticipating this meeting, but I am pleased nonetheless." He smiled. There was something off about it. Something not quite natural. "Please, sit."

He motioned to one of the chairs in front of him, but I lingered near the door. Either his powers were greatly diminished despite the greed pouring from his gambling den, or he'd tamped them down for this meeting. A demon game—feigning weakness to lure in prey, though, in this room he didn't really seem to hide who he was or where he was from.

Two demon guards stood behind him with their arms crossed, growling deep in their throats. One had pale green reptile skin and matching eyes. And the other was covered in short fur—similar to a deer, and had liquid ebony eyes. Two antlers curled up and away from the top of the fur-covered demon's head. It was disconcerting, seeing something that almost looked human with the skin and eyes of an animal. I tried to convince myself to cross the room, but couldn't force my body to carry me anywhere near those demons. "I..."

Greed's attention slowly shifted from me to what had caught my eye. He snapped his fingers and the room cleared. When he looked at me again, there was a hunger in his gaze—one that spoke of possession. He didn't want to seduce me, he wanted to *own* me. I wouldn't be a trophy to him like Envy, I'd be a tool for power.

"Emilia. Please," he nodded to the unoccupied chair, "no one will harm you while you're here. You have my word."

Said the wolf to the little hen. His use of my name unnerved me, but I managed my best impression of a confident stride and sat down. "Did my sister tell you my name?"

"No. You did. Pardon my rudeness, but I have informants stationed throughout the club. They heard your exchange with one of my regular customers." His smile was almost convincing this time. I wondered if he sensed my fear and adjusted his responses accordingly. That thought brought on a new rush of nerves I didn't need. Being alone with Greed was a terribly rash idea, but I really couldn't think of a better way to get information from him. "Vittoria didn't mention you at all, actually. This is quite a surprise."

He poured two glasses of water from a pitcher I hadn't noticed and slid one to me. Crowned frogs were etched onto the glasses. I accepted the water, but didn't drink. "Why a frog?"

"They're greedy creatures. Content with neither land nor water, they desire both."

Made sense. In a demon logic sort of way. "Did Vittoria summon you?"

"You're full of questions." He studied me closely. "It's strange . . . how identical you are."

His tone didn't hold any clues to his emotions. It was a statement of fact. Nothing more. He didn't seem to mind one way or the other that my sister was dead.

"I know my sister came here before she was murdered. I want to know why. What did she want from you?"

"Hmmm. Right for the jugular. A bold move, little mouse." He leaned back, his gaze sharp, calculating. I did my best not to squirm under his scrutiny. "It seems I have valuable information that you'd like. And you, Signorina di Carlo, also have something of great value to me. I will answer your questions to the best of my ability, only in exchange for your amulet."

My hand automatically moved to my *cornicello*. "Why do you want it?"

"Do you know what it is?"

"A folk charm to ward off the evil eye." Unlike Malocchio charms humans wore, it would also bring the world into eternal twilight if I brought it together with my sister's amulet, according to Nonna. I decided to keep that to myself, in case he started drooling on his finely trimmed suit.

"Mmh." Greed removed a velvet pouch from the desk drawer, and dropped a necklace into his palm—a gold chain with a ruby the size of a quail egg that twinkled in the light. A strange essence came off it, almost like a high-keening wail in the distance, setting my teeth on edge.

I wanted him to put it back where he'd found it. Immediately. "What is that?"

"It's called the Eye of Darkness, and it grants whoever wears it true protection from creatures of malevolent intent. Give me your amulet, and it's yours."

A gift like that didn't come without a price. "What else do you want?"

"For you to join yourself to House Greed."

I stared at Greed and I swore my skin physically tried to crawl away from my body in protest as he gazed back. He was classically handsome, but there was something off about him. His eyes were void of human emotion. He looked alien and wrong. I couldn't imagine my sister falling in love or even lust with him. Which meant her reason for coming here was not a result of seduction. He had information she wanted. And I wanted to know what it was.

"Why do you want me to align myself with you?"

"Because I believe you'll be very useful to me in the future. If you become queen, you'll owe me a favor. A powerful one, too, if this charm ends up saving your life."

Greed didn't strike me as a betting kind of creature, which made me even more hesitant to accept this little present. I had no plans of becoming Queen of the Wicked, and would be damned if I gave him a reason to help put me on that dark throne.

"Did you offer the Eye of Darkness to my sister?"

"Accept my bargain and find out."

"If you won't answer simple questions, I'm afraid we're through." I stood, ready to be as far away from this prince and place as possible, when his chair scraped across the floor.

"Wait." He sat back down and put the ruby necklace in its pouch again. Some of the unease in my shoulders loosened. "In a show of good faith, I will answer *one* of your questions."

"In exchange for..."

"Nothing. You have my word. Remember, the offer is for one question, anything else will cost you."

I reclaimed my seat, calculating my next move. There were so many questions I needed answers to, but none of them would be worth the cost of handing over my *cornicello*. I thought carefully about the list I'd written out last night, and focused on one detail that bothered me the most. It meant something. I wanted to know what. I chose my words with exacting precision.

"Tell me about the Horn of Hades."

If he was surprised by my choice, it didn't show. "It's a key that locks the gates of Hell."

"I heard it was part of a curse. That if a witch wears it she'll have power over the devil."

"Witch legends are fascinating in their falsehoods. The Horn of Hades was a gift. Your sister knew the true story."

I desperately wanted to ask him what it was, but there was something more important I needed to know. "How do you break a demon spell that was cast on an object?"

Greed's answering smile was toxic. "I told you about the Horn of Hades. The rest will cost you. I don't believe in giving without gain."

Now my smile turned sharp. "Per your rules, that was my first actual question."

He rolled his shoulders back, his nostrils flaring a bit. I was half convinced he was about to spring across the desk and wrap his hands around my neck. A long moment passed before he spoke.

"Clever girl." He reached for his glass and drank deeply, his knuckles turning white while he probably thought over my phrasing. "Sacrifice a bit of yourself."

"That's not an honest answer."

"Oh, but it is."

Greed took another sip of water. "Would you like to ask another question?"

I would like to ask another dozen questions, but dragging useful information from a prince of Hell was harder than I thought. I pressed my lips together.

He kicked his boots up onto the desk, and steepled his fingers again. "Allow me to be blunt, Signorina di Carlo. Your sister gave me her amulet, knowing the importance of it. I need both hers and yours to work a spell. Give me your amulet, and I vow to protect your world."

Sure he would. Right after he pillaged and destroyed it. Suspicion coiled around me. There was absolutely no way my sister had willingly given him her *cornicello*. If he did have it, then he'd taken it. I knew for a fact Vittoria had been wearing it the day she died. I swallowed hard. It was looking more and more possible that I was sitting across from my twin's murderer. I mentally crossed witch hunters off my list of suspects. Thus far, all of my clues kept pointing to demons.

I wondered if Greed told my sister a similar story and she refused him. I was more than a little afraid of what he might do if I also tried walking away. He could probably sense fear, so I shoved it as far down inside me as I could, and bluffed. "If Vittoria gave you her amulet, show it to me."

"Ah." He blew out a long breath. "That isn't possible."

"Not possible, or you won't do it?"

"Both. A Viperidae was summoned to this realm. Its nest is below the cathedral and, well, they're very protective about their space. The amulet will stay there until it decides to give it up."

I didn't bother asking what a Viperidae was, or who'd summoned it. I doubted he'd tell me anything else after I'd tricked information from him.

"And you put the amulet there..." I didn't expect an answer and he didn't offer one. It was highly unlikely that he would put something he wanted so badly in a place he couldn't gain access to it. But I had a feeling my sister would. I knew, beyond a shadow of a doubt, Vittoria would never willingly give anyone—let alone one of the Malvagi—her amulet.

Greed's story didn't add up. I wanted to hope against all odds he was being semi-truthful, but it was a gamble I couldn't risk taking. He did give me another short-term goal to focus on—I'd get my sister's *cornicello* back, and ask Nonna why a demon would be so interested in them.

"Well?" he asked. "Do we have a deal, Signorina di Carlo?"

"*Grazie*," I said, standing, "but my answer is still no."

NINETEEN

A prince of Hell is the most dangerous of the demons. He appears angelic, but will claw out your heart. To combat his power, wear or draw a cimaruta charm—a branch of a rue with five stalks sprouting designs that correlate to your needs. Choose five images needed to banish a demon prince back to his realm. Example: a key, dagger, owl, snake, and moon will send him straight to Hell.

—Notes from the di Carlo grimoire

Blood was the key to unlocking demon magic.

I'd been thinking about Greed's seemingly innocuous answer all afternoon, and puzzle pieces slowly clicked into place. I tallied up a few instances where blood had been integral with demon magic. In order to summon a demon, I needed to offer blood in sacrifice.

Then there was Wrath and his blood trade. The supposed blood debt Nonna mentioned.

I tried and failed to hide my repulsion. Would it be too much for demons to accept a bit of wine instead? I sighed and pricked my finger with a pin, letting a single drop splatter onto Vittoria's diary. Breath held, I stared at it intently, waiting for some sign the spell held or disintegrated.

There was no cataclysmic event or flash of lightning. One minute I couldn't open it, and the next I could. I hesitated with the spine half cracked. I'd been trying to get into this diary for so long, and now I was a little afraid of what I was going to find. This might reveal my sister's murderer. The more I learned, the more I doubted witch hunters. Demon princes were taking the lead as the most likely to commit murder. But if the devil needed a witch, it didn't quite make sense for them to thwart his efforts. Which meant someone in our circle might have been responsible. I shivered in place. It was easy to think she'd been killed by a demon, but the thought of it being someone she knew...

I took a deep breath and began reading Vittoria's most private thoughts.

The first several pages were dedicated to the perfumes she'd crafted. A few random spells, or charms for Moon Blessings and luck. A sketch or two of a *cimaruta* and a few other symbols I didn't recognize. I paused on a page where she'd written down one of Claudia's scrying sessions in great detail. I was about to scan the opposite page when something caught my eye. A tiny, almost insignificant note she'd left for herself.

Am I hearing magical objects, or the souls attached to them over time? Sometimes the whispers are louder, clear. Other times they're frantic and hard to understand. Similar to Claudia's scrying, or different?

Hearing magical objects? I stared at the line, unblinking. I had to be misunderstanding somehow. Vittoria never mentioned this ability before. We told each other everything. I was her twin, her other half—but then again, I'd never told her about the *luccicare*, either.

I turned over the events of the night when we were eight. It was highly probable that she'd developed some latent ability, too. I had. Though I had believed I was an anomaly because I'd been the one holding both of our amulets. I hadn't confided in my sister because I didn't want her to worry about the repercussions, or blame herself since it had been her idea.

I quickly turned to the next page, but there was nothing out of the ordinary. No clue to her magic. I flipped to another, and another. I'd gotten to the middle of her journal before finding another passage about the strange, secret magic.

I was out near the sea collecting shells and sea salt when I heard it. It started as a whisper, frantic, too low to hear clearly. I set my basket down and clutched my cornicello, which seemed to help me focus on the voice. Voices. There were many. And they were speaking all at once. They begged me to come help. They said the time was upon us. I followed the whispers until they turned to chatter, indistinct and out of sequence—like they were speaking in tongues. It reminded me of old Sofia Santorini. Of the time her mind got trapped between realms. I wanted to walk away, to run back and get Emilia, but something warned me not to. I followed the hum of voices into a cave, high above the sea. I don't know why, but I dropped to my knees and started digging. I found it there, buried deep within the earth. I managed to understand one line before it descended into chaos.

Unfortunately, my twin didn't write down the line she'd heard. I exhaled loudly, hands shaking as I flipped through the rest of the diary. There wasn't any other passage about the mysterious "it" she'd found buried beneath the earth. I scanned doodles of flowers and hearts, Claudia's dreams, and all of the questions Vittoria had recorded the answers to.

I couldn't bring myself to read the part about what ended up being our last night in the world together. So far there were no names, no people she'd mistrusted, or demons she'd struck bargains with. How she'd ended up agreeing to marry—my attention fastened on to something that made my palms dampen.

I didn't plan on listening to it again. I'd already decided to hide it, far from where they could ever find it. Then it whispered something that sounded a lot like nonsense, but my blood prickled. The Horn of Hades is a key to locking the gates of Hell, but, according to it, what it really is, is two somethings. They are the devil's horns, cut off by his own hand. I held my cornicello, feeling the truth in the hum and whispers. The root of my power. Emilia and I, for reasons I am unsure of, have been wearing the devil's horns our whole lives.

So if that's true, how did they find their way to us?

I slowly closed the diary and exhaled. Holy goddess. The devil's horns. It was hard to believe and yet...I knew it was true. We'd been wearing the Horn of Hades our whole lives. No wonder Greed was so interested in our amulets—I couldn't even begin to imagine the damage that he could cause if he managed to get his hands on them both. I shoved that destruction from my mind and read over the last line my sister wrote again. It was an excellent question. One I fully intended to get the answer to immediately.

"It's about time you tore yourself away from dark pursuits, bambina. Your mother and father are sick with worry." Nonna eyed me from the rocking chair she'd dragged across from the simmering cauldron. Spell candles for peace and restful slumber burned all around her. "All day, petrified you were laying somewhere with your heart ripped out, alone. Like your sister. Do you have any idea what you put us through?"

I did. And I hated it, but I wasn't the only di Carlo who had explaining to do. I moved fully into the kitchen and laid Wrath's dagger and then my *cornicello* on the island. "Is this one of the devil's horns?" Nonna's face paled. "Have we been wearing the Horn of Hades?"

"Don't be silly. Who filled your head with these stories?" Nonna got up and walked over to the cauldron, added a sprinkle of herbs and stirred them into her newest essence. It smelled of spruce and mint. I wondered where she got the evergreen, but didn't ask. "We don't believe in such things, bambina."

"A Viperidae was summoned, and is guarding Vittoria's amulet."

She stopped stirring the mixture. "It's true, then. The Malvagi have returned."

I waited for her to start muttering protection charms, or rush around the house, checking all the windows and doors for herbs and garlands of garlic she'd hung to keep wicked things out. She didn't ask me to grab olive oil and a bowl of water to make sure evil wasn't in our home this very moment. This calm, collected version of my grandmother was completely foreign to me. For as long as I could remember, she'd worried about the devil and his soul-stealing demons.

Human children had nursery rhymes, but we'd been taught about the seven demon princes and the four—in particular—di Carlos should fear the most. I hadn't forgotten that Wrath had been named. Nor had I figured out if he was the one who'd crave my blood, capture my heart, steal my soul, or take my life. Honestly, I could picture him fulfilling any of them.

My grandma moved the wooden spoon around the boiling mixture, her attention stubbornly fixed on its ornately carved handle, and said nothing. Of course now that all of the nightmarish stories were coming to life, she stayed silent.

"Nonna, you have to tell me about the Horn of Hades. Vittoria knew about it, and she was killed. *Please.* If you don't want that to be my fate, too, you need to tell me what it is and why we're wearing it. I deserve to know."

She stared into the cauldron and sighed.

"Dark days are upon us. It's time to be a warrior of the light." Nonna left her essences and removed a pitcher of wine from our sideboard. She poured herself a glass of chianti, then sat in her rocker. "I never wanted it to come to this, child. But the hands of Fate work their own magic. Who are we but puppets on their cosmic strings?"

Cryptic as usual. I decided to start with the smaller details, and work my way up to the harder questions. "Is it really a key for locking the gates of Hell?"

"Yes and no. It has the ability to open and close the gates, but that's not all it does."

"Are they the devil's horns?"

"Yes."

"And you've known the whole time?"

Nonna nodded. I stared at her, trying to process the fact that my grandmother—who'd been making us bless our charms to protect ourselves from the demon princes our entire lives—had placed such things around our necks. "La Prima cast a spell that turned them into two smaller amulets, hoping to hide them from all who'd seek them."

"Because they belong to the devil?"

"Because if brought together, they not only have the ability to lock the gates, they can also summon him. They grant the summoner a certain bit of power over him."

I stared at the amulet I'd worn for as long as I could remember, wondering why my sister hadn't come to Nonna when she'd found this out. I still had so many questions about her bargain. If we had a means of controlling the devil, why didn't she just ask me for my *cornicello*?

It made sense why Greed was after it; his sin was closely tied to power. But if all princes of Hell craved power why, then, didn't Wrath try to snatch my *cornicello*?

Something Envy said resurfaced amidst my confusion. "What's a shadow witch?"

Nonna made a disgusted sound. "Shadow witches are what demons call us. We are known as *Stelle Streghe*."

Star witches. "*We* are known? Since when are we known as Star Witches?"

Nonna gave me a sardonic look. "Since the dawn of our bloodline. We hail from an ancient line of witches who had ties to the Wicked prior to the curse. We were guardians in a sense, ensuring creatures of the underworld remained there, never interfering with the human world. For a time we worked beside the Malvagi. That was before—"

Nonna's wine glass flew across the room and shattered against the wall. Chianti dripped like blood. I screamed, but not because of the glass. A floating blade hovered against my grandmother's throat. My ghost demon was back, and it didn't seem like just a figment of my imagination now. It had been quiet the last few days, and I'd forgotten it. Now it was hard to ignore Wrath's serpent dagger as it glinted in the light.

"Little tricksy witch."

The demon's blade pressed into Nonna's skin. I shook my head and stepped forward. "Please. If this is about what I did to Greed, she has nothing to do with it. Leave her alone, she's innocent."

"Innocent?" It accentuated the "c" until it sounded like a hiss. "She is no such thing."

Before I could dash across the room and knock Nonna away, her head jerked back and the invisible hand dragged Wrath's blade across her throat. Blood gushed from her wound. She gurgled, the sound one of the most horrendous things I'd ever heard. The weapon clattered to the ground. I watched everything happen as if it occurred in slow increments.

A window burst open, and I imagined the invisible demon fled through it.

Then reality crashed into me and I was in motion. I was across the room a breath later.

"No!" I snatched a cloth from the counter and held it to her neck, stanching the blood. Then I screamed until my voice broke, rousing the whole house from the spelled slumber Nonna had enchanted them with. There were spells to help slow the flow of blood, but I couldn't think of any through the panic screeching at me. It was as if my mind shut down and all I could focus on was one basic need: hold the wound.

My mother rushed into the kitchen first, her attention immediately falling on Nonna. And the growing lake of blood. Tears streamed down my face, blurring my vision.

I would not let my grandmother die. Not like this.

My father appeared a minute later, his eyes widening at the sight. "I'll get bandages."

I stopped paying attention to anything other than keeping the cloth pressed firmly against my grandmother's wound. Time ticked by. Blood saturated the cotton, my mother prayed over a thick herbal paste she'd made. I held firmly. I wanted to be the kind of person who didn't panic and could act calmly. But logic didn't penetrate my terror. Mamma tried yanking my hands away, but I refused to budge. I had to keep applying pressure. Nonna needed me.

"It's all right, baby. Let me get this on her. It'll seal the wound."

"I can't."

"You can. It's all right."

It took another bit of coaxing, but I finally relinquished my grip. Nonna slid to the ground, her breathing labored. I'd seen this in injured animals before and it wasn't a good sign.

My mother slathered the thick paste across the injury, then wrapped one of the clean bandages around it. My father had brought them in before he went to work checking for any more intruders and securing our window. My mother finished tying it off with a prayer to the goddess of good health and well-being to heal Nonna quickly. I offered up a prayer of my own, hoping she listened to us both.

"Help me get her into bed, Emilia."

I swiped at my tears and did as I was asked. Once we'd laid her across the mattress, my mother pulled up a chair to watch. I sat against the wall and stayed there until the sun set, turning the room bruised shades of purple and black. Nonna's breathing finally evened out, and she fell into a deep, restorative sleep. She'd made it, no thanks to me. Praise the goddess.

"You should go get some rest, baby. Your grandmother will be fine. The worst is over."

I nodded, but couldn't sleep now. I wasn't sure I could ever rest again without seeing the gory scene replay in my mind. And the worst part was, Nonna was almost killed because of me. Then, when she needed me the most, I'd failed her again. I'd lost all memories of spells or healing charms. I'd shut down and let fear take control. If I hadn't started investigating my sister's murder, or tricked Greed, none of this would have happened.

I crept into the kitchen, wanting to clean up the blood before my parents saw it again. I scrubbed until the floor shined and my fingers ached. Then I repeated the routine. Pouring water, scrubbing. I needed to remove the stains from the grout. It took most of the night, but I finally managed to erase all physical signs of the attack. But the memory would never leave me.

I rinsed out the rag and leaned against the island, sipping a glass of water. It took a while for me to notice at first, but eventually I realized the invisible demon came here with a mission. I absently reached up, thinking of Nonna's injury, and went to hold my amulet. My hand dropped away, empty. I forgot I'd taken it off. I went to pluck it off the counter and froze.

My *cornicello* was gone.

TWENTY

"You look like hell, witch."

I glared at the demon of war by way of greeting. In a few short hours he'd be free, and I wasn't sure he'd answer any questions once the containment spell dissipated. After the brutal attack on Nonna, I left the house and wandered around Palermo, deciding what to do next. I'd made a terrible mistake and it almost cost my grandmother her life. I shouldn't have ever gone back to my house after confronting Greed. Of course he'd send spies after me to steal my amulet. It was reckless to think a prince of Hell would simply let me walk away unscathed after besting him.

Now that I knew my sister and I had been wearing the devil's horns, and how powerful and dangerous they were, I had to get them back. I might not know where mine was at the moment, but thanks to Greed, I knew exactly where Vittoria's was. I just needed some information from Wrath about the Viperidae first, and then I'd set out to retrieve it.

"You'd know better than most what that's like." I smiled sweetly. "I met two of your brothers, by the way. They're absolute gems."

Wrath looked neither surprised nor interested in the news. He sat with his back against the wall, legs straight out, surveying the circle of bones that contained him. Of course he wasn't wearing the shirt I'd bought for him; it was lying in a discarded heap on the ground.

"I have six brothers. You'll have to be more specific."

"Don't you know who's here?"

His attention subtly dropped to my hip before he jerked his gaze back up. "Have you come crawling back to beg for help? I'm not feeling very charitable today. Captivity doesn't suit me."

Demons invading my city, attacking my grandmother, stealing my *cornicello,* and murdering my sister didn't suit me, either. Instead of arguing, I pulled a cannoli from the brown paper bag I'd tucked into my satchel. Nonna said you could catch more flies with honey than vinegar. I figured a cannoli would help me catch a prince of Hell just fine.

He looked startled when I handed it to him. "What is that?"

"Food. Unless you've been catching vermin, I doubt you've eaten."

"I neither need human food, nor do I wish to taint my body with the foulness of it."

I stared at him, horrified. After all the terrible things that had happened, this was putting me over the edge. "You really are a monster, aren't you?"

"That doesn't even look edible." He took the cannoli between his two fingers and held it closer to inspect it. "What do you expect me to do with it?"

"Engage your enemies."

He poked at the ricotta filling. "Is it poisoned?"

I sighed. "Just eat it, oh, mighty warrior. It's for pleasure, not pain. I made them myself. I swear they're not poisoned. This time."

He looked skeptical, but took a bite. His attention flicked to mine as he chewed. I couldn't help but grin as he took a larger mouthful, then grabbed a second cannoli from the bag. He was halfway through it when he noticed me still watching and scowled. "What?"

"I do not wish to taint my body with the foulness of human food," I mocked. "But desserts are acceptable."

He didn't deign to respond. Instead he rummaged in the bag, frowning at the emptiness. He set it aside and looked me over again. "I imagine these delicacies were part of a larger scheme to infiltrate my defenses. You smell like blood that isn't your own, your hair is tangled like some wild creature built a nest in it and invited its kin. My blade is missing from your hip. And you look ready to curse the world. What is it you desire to know, witch? What scared you?"

My hand moved to the place I'd been strapping his dagger. After the damage it had inflicted on my grandmother, I couldn't stand the thought of holding it. Now I felt its absence almost as much as I missed my *cornicello*. "How would someone summon a Viperidae?"

"Someone with a sense of survival wouldn't."

"Maybe someone immortal and arrogant already did."

"Doubtful." Wrath wasn't amused with my assessment of demon royalty. "Viperidae are unique creatures. If they choose to guard something, or bring it into their nest, no denizen of the underworld may interfere. They must choose to give it up on their own."

I made a mental notation to bring him dessert anytime I wanted information. He was downright pleasant and chatty. "What does it look like?"

"Its namesake. Like a viper, it's got long, hinged fangs. It also happens to be larger than I am and is twice as deadly. Very few antidotes exist if someone is bitten. And the ones that do exist aren't to be taken lightly. There's a cost for using them, like all magic. Make your own choice, but know you may not survive to see another sunrise if you disturb one."

I rubbed at my arm, not because his warning frightened me, but because there was an annoying sensation burrowing beneath my skin. Like someone was scratching back and forth over the same section with a pin. Wrath tracked the movement and then glanced at his own arm.

It seemed our tattoos were transforming once again. Winding around the serpents—which I noted Wrath now sported around his twin crescent moons, too—were wildflowers.

Before my eyes, my snakes were given shimmering, even scales. I didn't want to think it was beautiful, but it was. Undeniably so. Wrath curled his hand into a fist. I couldn't tell if it was because of the pain, or because of our strange, ever-changing ink. I decided not to press the issue; I had one more question for the demon before I left on my mission.

"If someone was to attack a Viperidae, what sort of spell might they use?"

He dragged his attention from the magical ink on his arm, his look a study of resignation. "No one should be attacking a Viperidae. But, if someone was a foolish witch with a death wish, then that witch might try casting a sleeping spell. It might be the only way to sneak around it."

"I . . ." I stopped myself from thanking him. If it wasn't for him and his cruel brothers, my entire family wouldn't be in this mess. I inhaled deeply, thinking about the sleep spell. It was simple. I liked simple plans. It meant there was less that could potentially go wrong.

"One final word of caution." Wrath pushed himself up from the ground and moved to where I stood near the edge of the bone circle. I ignored the expanse of toned, golden skin in my face. "Freedom will be mine soon. If you are foolish enough to attack such a creature, I will not come for you."

I stared up at him. "Good."

Last month if someone told me I'd *choose* to wander through forgotten tunnels beneath the cathedral alone, tracking down an ancient snake demon guarding one half of a sacred key that not only locked the gates of Hell but were actually the horns of the devil, I'd think they needed medical attention.

Emilia Maria di Carlo didn't do danger. My sister was the adventurous one—I was satisfied with safe, clean fun. Give me a steamy romance novel with forbidden love and impossible odds.

That was the kind of adventure I could get behind.

A little more than a month ago I would've laughed with my sister over the possibility that something like a giant, netherworldly snake even *existed*, thinking Nonna's superstitions were hard at work again. Even with magic running through my veins, I never fully believed in the stories she told us; they were too fantastical. Immortal, blood-drinking creatures like the Wicked couldn't be real.

Now I knew better. Every tall tale was rooted in truth.

I followed a strange, foul egg odor and bits of snakeskin that had been shed, wishing I'd gotten over my aversion to Wrath's dagger and had taken it with me. Light from grates above dappled the ground every once in a while, but I traveled mostly in darkness.

I paid attention to the slightest shift in the atmosphere, allowing my senses to guide me. I had a suspicion the demon wouldn't want to draw attention to itself or its precious treasure.

Plus, I already had a good idea where its nest was—Greed said it was under the cathedral, and I was quickly approaching the turnoff for it. I paused at the corner and collected myself.

I'd been mentally running through my plan, and now that I was almost facing my enemy, it seemed like it was much too simple to actually work. Maybe Wrath had decided to send me to my death armed with an impossible scheme. Diabolical demon.

I drew in a deep breath. I could do this. But I needed to move quickly. The longer I stood around, debating, the more my fear grew. I imagined what my sister would do if she were here instead. She'd charge in to save the day—like she tried doing when she'd agreed to the devil's bargain. Granted, that didn't turn out to be the wisest decision, but at least she was brave enough to *try*. Compared to what she'd done, casting a simple sleep spell and retrieving a necklace was easy.

I exhaled slowly and peered around the corner. Amber-colored light spilled into the chamber from above, illuminating the snake-shaped demon. Wrath hadn't exaggerated—the Viperidae was bigger than he was. Oil-slick midnight scales covered a body coiled in the center of the tunnel. Even curled up, the demon took up most of the space; its prone form was taller than me by a good head or more. When it was alert and upright...I didn't want to think about facing something like that.

I pulled a handful of dried chamomile leaves from my skirt

pocket, offered them to the goddess of night and slumber, and whispered, *"Somnum."*

Steady breathing indicated the beast was now in a deep slumber, a gift from the goddess. I exhaled. Now I just had to find the amulet and sneak back out the way I'd come. The Viperidae faced the opposite direction, and its head was easily twice the size of our biggest oven. I didn't have to see its fangs to know they'd skewer me with one bite.

I scanned the nest and almost whooped with victory when I spotted a familiar horn-shaped object. My sister's amulet glinted on the ground next to the beast. As luck would have it, the *cornicello* was on my side of the tunnels. It seemed like it should be fairly easy to sneak over, grab it, and retreat without waking the demon. I looked around, cataloguing every exit I could make out in the dim light. Two more tunnels formed offshoots in a *Y* layout. Easy.

And it would have been, if it wasn't for all the pebbles and debris littered on the ground. One small misstep and, regardless of the sleep spell, the Viperidae would be on me in an instant. I gave one last prayer to a goddess I hoped was listening, and took the first step into the tunnel.

I didn't so much as breathe too deeply, fearful of making the slightest sound. Unnatural silence blanketed the chamber like freshly fallen snow. Once, when we were little, Nonna brought us to a cabin in northern Italy where we met one of her friends. I was too young to remember what the exact circumstances were, but I never forgot the smothering quiet of snow.

I was more than halfway to the amulet when I noticed the beast had stopped breathing evenly. I paused, foot midair, and waited for death. The trouble with sleep spells was, there was no way to prevent someone or something from waking normally.

When the Viperidae didn't move, I decided to finish what I'd started. If it was lingering somewhere between sleeping and wakefulness, it wouldn't remain that way forever. My attention split between it and the ground, careful to not make any noise. I didn't so much as allow one pebble to skitter out of place.

Finally, after what felt like a thousand cursed years, I reached the amulet and slowly, painstakingly, bent to retrieve it. I kept my eyes on the demon, which turned out to be a terrible mistake. The instant my fingers clasped the *cornicello*, the chain swished across the ground.

The Viperidae struck.

Its tail whipped out, knocking me off my feet in one quick blow. I gripped Vittoria's amulet with one hand, and a handful of dirt and pebbles in the other. I waited until the demon was almost on me before tossing the debris in its eyes. The Viperidae released a multilayered scream that sent chills racing down my spine.

Holy goddess above...I'd *really* pissed it off. The snake-like demon coiled in and around itself, screeching and thrashing. Chunks of stone fell from the walls in an avalanche of chaos. Dust clouds filled the air, choking me. One tunnel was now completely sealed off. I had to get out of there immediately, but couldn't.

I huddled as far away from the demon as possible, trying to crawl along the wall. It was moving too quickly, and I couldn't chance getting hit with its tail.

It wouldn't be long before it worked the grit from its eyes. The Viperidae's powerful body crashed into the tunnel on the right, and I didn't waste my only opportunity for escape. I shot past it, heart hammering, praying it didn't swing back around and clip me. I took my first step into the tunnel I'd used to get here when it happened.

A fang the size of a sword pierced the fleshy part on my lower back. The bite was lightning fast—over and done with before I could scream. I stopped moving, my whole body prickled and went ice cold. I knew enough of herbal folk medicine to know the signs of shock. Major trauma sometimes took a few seconds to catch up to nerve receptors in the brain. Just as I'd thought it, the pain hit me a beat later. Hot, searing, all-consuming.

I dropped to the ground and turned in time to see the Viperidae closing in for the kill. I rolled a second before it tore out my throat. The sudden movement made my wound split wider and throb. Blood splattered around me, and I did my best to not focus on the possibility that the demon had already struck a death blow. It came for me again, and this time, I let it get close enough to see my reflection in its slitted eyes. I shoved the screaming pain aside, heart pounding. I waited...waited...it lowered its head, ready to sink its fangs—

I struck hard and fast, shoving Vittoria's amulet into one of its eyes. Warm liquid gushed over my hands, as the Viperidae shrieked one last time. I shoved harder, until I was almost certain I'd pierced its brain.

I didn't wait to see if it was dead or badly injured—I turned and fled.

For a little while, anyway. The venom had other plans for me.

TWENTY-ONE

Everything spun wildly—like the few times I'd mistakenly had too much wine with Claudia and Vittoria. I staggered back down the tunnel and collapsed under the grate I'd snuck in through. Escape was so close, yet impossibly far. I needed to gather my strength and drag myself up; and vowed to do just that…

…once my head stopped spinning and the nausea passed.

A soft thud landed near me, followed by a series of exquisitely foul curses. If I wasn't convinced opening my mouth would bring on the vomit I was barely suppressing, I'd have laughed over the colorful litany. I couldn't exactly remember his name at the moment, but I recalled he wasn't normally prone to such outbursts. For some reason, the situation struck me as funny when it was anything but.

My head suddenly ached—the pain sharp and vicious. It felt like a thousand needles were pricking my brain simultaneously. I groaned, which only made it worse.

"Where are you hurt?" His voice was too loud. I batted him away, but he was an annoyingly persistent devil. "Focus! Did it bite you, witch?"

"Stop."

Fingers probed my skull, my throat, then hesitated at my neckline. Somehow I'd managed to loop the *cornicello* over my head. He rolled me onto my side, and I nearly passed out from the next wave of agony. He clearly didn't care about my pain and suffering. Maybe he enjoyed it. I vaguely recalled hating him. Now I knew why.

He paused for less than a heartbeat, then the sound of fabric tearing was followed by a blast of ice down my back. Air battered against my ripped flesh, the pain absolutely blinding in its fury. I think I might have screamed.

"Shit."

Two solid arms hoisted me up, caging me against a body that had to be made of steel, not muscle and bone. We started moving swiftly, his steps fluid and graceful. Which was a good thing—if he bounced while running, I'd throw up all over him. I didn't think he'd like that.

Wind whipped at my hair—we were traveling at an impossible speed through city streets. I made the mistake of looking at buildings flashing by once, and instantly regretted it. I nestled against his warm chest and squeezed my eyes shut. Pain was all I knew.

"We're almost there."

My teeth chattered uncontrollably. I had no idea where *there* was, but hoped it had blankets and a fire. A coldness was spreading through me, all-consuming and terrible. I had the worst feeling I'd never know the comfort of warmth again. Which was strange, since I thought the day had been especially hot. Icy numbness slowly spread up my legs. A door clattered open, then slammed shut. It felt like we ran up a set of stairs and then I was laid onto a soft mattress.

Shouts rang out around me. Muffled voices were hard to distinguish. Water splashing into a basin overtook my senses, followed by the unmistakable scent of smoke. I thrashed. Somewhere, deep in my memory, I knew what the smoke meant. Danger.

"Don't worry." Another voice. Male. Unfamiliar. "He knows what to do and will be back soon." Blankets tucked me in so tightly, I could barely breathe. I must have gasped; warm hands were on my forehead. "Shhh. Don't struggle. It makes the venom spread faster."

Time narrowed into the smallest fraction of itself. I knew nothing but random seconds, and unrelenting agony. My heartbeat was so loud, it made my head pound. Moments passed. Pain persisted. Then a crackling fire, the scent of smoke, and he was back, prying my eyes open.

"I'll fix this. But you have to grant me permission. Do you?"

I tried to nod, but could barely move. He crouched beside me, placed his hands on either side of my head, and repeated the question. He must have felt the nearly imperceptible movement this time—before the next wave of pain struck, he was a blur of action.

"Watch the perimeter and do not interrupt us, no matter what," he barked at someone I couldn't see. Panic set in again. Perimeter? Was I in Hell? He scooped me up, a door shut behind us, and his voice turned noticeably gentler. "I need to get us both into the water, all right?"

I tried to say yes, but the numbness spread to my throat. I think he saw the answer in my face anyway. It sounded like he whispered, "Live long enough to hate me for this."

The next thing I felt was warmth—like I was floating on a cloud near the sun. Words in a language I didn't understand were spoken at my ear. Lips brushed against my skin, one of the last pleasant sensations I experienced before darkness closed in.

"Drink."

I wanted to, more than anything, but couldn't. He tilted my head back, parted my lips and poured nectar down my throat. I tried thrashing against the cloying taste of it, so sweet and thick that I almost choked, but I'd long since lost the ability to move on my own.

A tear slipped down my cheek and strong fingers brushed it away. Water splashed. A different kind of warmth encompassed me. Soft, gentle lips met mine. It was a whisper, a promise, an unbreakable vow. It shattered the pain and felt like home. I think I wanted more, but was denied. He quietly chanted, his words foreign.

Brilliant light flashed and then my true hell began.

A soft sound roused me from the worst dream I'd ever had. I cracked an eye and kept my breathing deep and even. I was soaking in a tub. For a second, I had no idea how I'd gotten here.

Then flashes came to me. I couldn't tell if they were dreams or memories.

A metallic snake inked onto an arm banded around my body—not in possession, but solidarity. Like Wrath had followed me into my nightmare, battled Death, and dragged me out.

At some point, I thought his tongue flicked over my jugular, tracing an invisible *S* along my skin. I remembered the feeling of every nerve ending, every molecule sizzling, instantly attuned to where I wanted those lips to move next. I swore I still felt heat lingering from the brief contact. I was surprised that I didn't hate it.

I squeezed my eyes shut as more images resurfaced. A giant serpent. A deadly fight. Fangs. Blood. My grandmother's neck, slashed. Drinking something thicker than honey and so saccharine, I had to gag it down. Strange words spoken fervently. A kiss followed by a blinding spark.

Then the nightmares began.

Demons screeching, claws scraping, an unfamiliar woman with midnight eyes and fire in her soul, cursing me. A city of fire and ice. An obsidian throne room. A crown forged of flames and smoke. Enormous gates crafted from bone and leathery wings, bursting open. Betrayal.

I shoved the dream from my mind and focused on my surroundings, then promptly wished I hadn't. I vaguely recalled the sensation of warm, wet-slicked skin against mine. Muscular legs. The feeling of complete safety. I didn't know if that was real or imagined, either.

I closed my eyes again and silently counted until my pulse slowed. It took a second, but I realized my wound was completely healed.

Wrath had worked an enormously powerful spell. I felt recharged, almost buzzing with excess energy. I'd been an empty vessel before being poured beyond capacity with life. I wanted to jump up and dance, or fight, or make love. Maybe all at once.

To avoid thinking about forbidden kisses while I was naked, I concentrated on the room. I was in a bathing chamber that was ornate yet shabby. The chipped marble tub was beautiful, white with veins of gold. Mosaic tiles covered the walls, depicting winged creatures and fields of flowers.

A slight rustle from the corner to my left caught my attention. Wrath stood with his back to me, as if offering a bit of privacy. Rivulets dripped off the planes of his tanned upper body. His very toned and naked upper body. Goddess above, he needed to put a shirt on. Immediately.

Until he did, I stole a peek at the ink I'd seen in the cave the first night I'd summoned him. Shimmering gold and charcoal tattoos crossed from shoulder to shoulder. They appeared to be lines of Latin, but I was too far away to be sure. I swallowed hard and averted my focus. It looked like he'd gotten out of the tub moments before I'd awakened. Those foggy bits from last night were definitely memories then, not dreams. My face heated. He probably already figured out I was awake and was waiting for me to say something. This was... painfully awkward.

Not wanting to delay the inevitable, I cleared my throat. He rotated until we were face-to-face. Tousled damp hair made him appear almost human, but the energy radiating around him shattered the illusion. It was like soaking in a tub while lightning struck perilously close by. He was alert and looked like he had been for quite some time. It was strange, seeing him outside of the summoning circle. Stranger still that he'd saved me. I wasn't sure what that meant, if anything. I settled against the side of the tub and took a deep breath.

Despite his proclamation about not coming for me, he didn't let me die.

I don't know what powers he'd invoked to bring me back from the edge of death, but he'd given all he had. And I didn't think my protection charm was the only reason he'd helped me. I'd felt something last night, more intimate than if we'd shared a bed. For one strangely long second, I swore we'd been inside each other's minds. What I saw there, deep where he couldn't hide it, wasn't simple hatred he felt toward me. It was much more complex.

Light filtered in from an arched window with no coverings, accentuating the chiseled angles of his face. If I didn't know exactly what he was, I might mistake him for an angel. Which, in a way, I supposed he was. I wondered what he'd done that was evil enough to be cast out of heaven. I didn't ask. I doubted he'd confess his sins.

His focus roved over my features, his expression unreadable. I fought a chill.

"I had these...dreams," I said slowly. "Or memories. Maybe both. You used powerful magic last night." I watched him carefully. He didn't move or break eye contact. For a horrible second, I wondered if he'd gone catatonic. Then he cocked his head, waiting. "Before I went after the Viperidae, you said there was a great cost for an antidote."

I glanced down at the water. I remembered the way we'd been sitting—his legs and arms and body flush against mine...I'd seen illustrations before. Only a few ancient rituals required bare skin contact—in essence, they were a rebirth of sorts. Like he'd transferred some of his power to me, using water as a conductor between our flesh. None of the rituals were to be taken lightly. I wasn't sure if his magic was the same as a witch's, but figured it was close.

I flicked my attention back to his. "What was your price for saving me?"

The temperature seemed to plummet. He held my gaze as he slowly crossed the room. Unyielding anger shone in those golden eyes. "You should be more concerned with the price you had to pay. I hope it was worth it."

He turned to leave. Before he could, I hopped up from the water and blocked his retreat. "You can't say that and just go. What was the price?"

"Would you really like to have this conversation in the bath?"

"Why not? Suddenly feeling shy?"

He exuded the opposite of shyness. Honestly, with a body like that and all of that power, I wasn't surprised by his confidence. He crossed his arms over his broad chest. Up close, the gold snake tattooed on his arm was breathtaking. "You want to talk, witch. I'll start. You made a choice last night that had catastrophic consequences. If I hadn't been there, you'd be dead."

It was annoyingly true. "Getting my sister's amulet back was worth whatever it cost me. And if I had to do it all over again, I would without hesitation."

"Which proves you're either reckless, or foolish, or both."

"If I'm so foolish and reckless, why save me?" I held up a hand. "Spare me from the protection charm excuse. You and I both know that's not the whole truth." He opened his mouth and I cut him off again. "I don't know the exact spell you used, but I know enough of certain rituals and their requirements that I have a pretty good guess. Tell me why you saved me. Now."

He arched a brow. "Do you have any more demands, your highness? Or may I go?"

"As a matter of fact, I do. Did you use a rebirth spell on me?" He shook his head. "Then why weren't we wearing clothes?"

A smile slowly tugged at the corners of his mouth. His expression resembled that of an immensely pleased yet smug male. "Because you ripped mine off like a hell beast in heat." I shot him a dirty look. He blew out a breath that almost sounded like a laugh. Since he couldn't lie to me, it had to be true enough for him to say it. I rolled my eyes. I'd been clearly out of my mind, and I told him as much. "Also, because the Viperidae inject venom that acts like ice, we needed to reverse the effects quickly. Body heat and hot water were the most efficient and quick ways to prevent hypothermia from killing you."

It was true. But I also heard him whispering in that strange language. Wrath wasn't lying, but he was keeping secrets. "You kissed me."

He abruptly looked away. "Fever dreams have peculiar side effects."

I grinned. I might not know the full spell, but I knew the chaste kiss was part of whatever magic he'd summoned. He probably neither wanted to, nor had much of a choice in the matter.

But I'm glad he suffered through it, or else I'd be dead.

When I'd found myself inside his head last night, his expression wasn't one of love, but fear. That, despite his best efforts, I was a splinter slowly burrowing under his immortal skin, and one day I might travel deeply enough to pierce his stone heart. He wouldn't be wrong.

No matter if he sacrificed some small portion of his power to save me, I'd never forget who he really was. He was a self-centered demon with a mission to protect his own world using any means necessary. He didn't really care about this realm, or the witches who'd been murdered. His focus was on what it all meant for *him*. The fear I saw in his heart had nothing to do with me, personally, but what emotional entanglements represented in general. Death.

As in death of all he was and chose to be.

Princes of Hell were loyal to none but themselves. Wrath would take an enemy to his bed in an instant if it meant garnering information or power. And I doubted he'd loathe it.

I moved until we were nearly touching. He didn't back away, but he didn't reach for me, either. His behavior had nothing to do with goodness, or blossoming friendship, or even lust, and everything to do with gain. I just didn't yet understand how or why he needed me alive.

But I would do everything I could to find out what his true goals were.

His attention slipped to my mouth. There wasn't anything kind or sweet in his gaze. In fact, there was hardly anything soft in it at all. Sometimes when he looked at me, I swore I sensed a beast hiding beneath the mask of skin he wore. It was restless, feral. I had a feeling he kept the monster locked away, but it was never far. I fought a shudder. I didn't ever want to be around when he decided to let his inner animal out of its cage.

A taunting smile curved his lips. "Is this the part where you thank me with a kiss?"

"Hardly. I'm not like you, demon. I don't kiss people I hate. And I never will."

"Never? Are you certain you'd like to make such a declaration?"

I wasn't certain of anything at the moment. I was confused and buzzing with magic that wasn't entirely my own. I'd lived through twenty-four hours from hell—with Nonna's attack, my own brush with death, and being saved by my enemy. His power thrummed through me, filled me. For a second, I wanted him to reach over and drag his hands down my body. Which made no sense.

I couldn't think with him standing so near. I desperately needed a moment to myself. To collect my thoughts and decide how to proceed. And I couldn't accomplish any of those things with the half-naked demon crowding my space. Power surged through my veins.

Before Wrath dazzled me with more charm, I whispered a containment spell that must have been fueled with his demon magic because it did *not* go as planned. One second he was standing there, and the next he was gone. Winked out of existence. It happened so quickly, but I'd managed to catch a glimpse of his face before he'd disappeared. He'd looked so... betrayed.

A mix of emotion haunted me for several minutes. He was my enemy. Even if he'd saved me. That one act of goodness didn't erase that fact. And yet I wasn't sure if I hoped I'd sent him back to the underworld, or if I hoped he was imprisoned in the cave again. It shouldn't matter where he was.

Even if I felt slightly guilty for using his own magic against him, I refused to let it color my judgment. He had his mission and I had mine. That was it. I rummaged around on the floor, but couldn't find my clothes. Damned demon. Of all the ways he could take his vengeance, I didn't predict walking through city streets naked to be one of them.

I glanced up, ready to curse Wrath to Hell again, and noticed a new dress folded in a neat pile in the corner where he'd been standing. I lifted it up, surprised by its beauty. Dark skirts had tastefully placed gold glitter sprinkled across them—not unlike his shimmering *luccicare*. Black sheer sleeves fell gracefully from an off-the-shoulder top. And a gold corset with thorns and wings stiched across the back finished it off. I forgot my clothing had been torn during the Viperidae attack. Some feeling I'd rather not dwell on took shape as I held the gown. I shoved it away.

The demon prince's magic crackled under my skin, infected my soul. I didn't want to like how alive it made me feel.

I quickly dressed, needing a mundane task to focus on while my feelings darted from one extreme to the next. With Wrath gone, it was only marginally easier to think. Mostly because my thoughts kept returning to him—to the expression on his face. I'd hurt his feelings. And it... bothered me. What a ludicrous turn of events. His family sent invisible ghost demons to attack my grandmother and steal my *cornicello,* and *I* was feeling bad about potentially banishing a demon to Hell. Where he lived and ruled. Probably happily. In the height of demonic luxury. With fire and brimstone and an orchestra of the screaming souls of the damned.

Still, it might have been a rash decision. Unpleasantness aside, Wrath could be useful to my quest for justice. I was almost positive he had ulterior motives for aligning himself with me, but when I really needed him, he'd been there. That act, above everything else, told me enough.

My soul was safe with him.

Which meant we could set our differences aside and work together to solve Vittoria's murder. Neither one of us would love the idea, but at least I could trust that he wouldn't kill me. As of now, the evidence was pointing to a prince of Hell being responsible for the murders, not witch hunters. After what happened with Greed and the attack on Nonna, I needed Wrath on my side.

I blew out a long breath, hoping it was a sound decision.

Goddess curse me, now I had to find out where I'd sent the Prince of Wrath.

I grabbed his shirt, and stole into the city to track down my missing prince of Hell.

TWENTY-TWO

"If you want me to speak with you now, ask nicely."

I wouldn't call it relief, but a knot in my chest loosened when I found Wrath stuck in the summoning circle again. He wasn't angry like I'd expected, only a touch bemused. I supposed he didn't expect to be banished right after saving my life. Which was fair. To be honest, I hadn't expected to repay him that way, either. "Are all demons mad, or is it just you?"

He blew out a breath. "You're not the most pleasant viper in the pit, are you? Thanking someone who saved your life by imprisoning them isn't how things are done in my realm. There's no denying you could stand to work on your manners."

All thoughts of striking a tentative alliance left me. A demon lecturing about manners was the most ridiculous thing I'd ever heard. The very *nerve* of him. I fired off a dozen different suggestions—that included farm animals—for what he could do with his remaining time on earth.

"Charming. I wonder where your creativity comes from, perhaps personal experience?" Bickering wasn't getting us anywhere, and I had more important things to do. Apparently, Wrath felt the same way. He narrowed his eyes, scrutinizing me. "What's got your skirts all twisted, witch?"

"Nothing."

"If it's about the spell I used, or the dress..."

"It's not." For some reason, now that I was near him again, I wasn't quite ready to ask for his help solving my sister's murder. I needed some other assurance that this was the best course of action. And there was one thing he might be able to answer that would help me make up my mind. If he didn't laugh himself to death first. I closed my eyes and counted to ten. "An invisible demon attacked my grandmother yesterday. And before that, I think... I think it was stalking me."

I expected him to mock me, or ask if I'd recently indulged in too many spirits. Instead he studied me very carefully. "Did it speak to you?"

I nodded. "It said, 'he's coming.'"

Wrath paced around the bone circle. "Sounds like an Umbra demon. But for it to be here and speak to you... did it say anything else?"

"I—I don't remember exactly. The first time it said something about memories and hearts being stolen."

"The *first* time?" He swung around to stare at me. Wrath wasn't very good at showing a wide range of emotions, probably because he was an immortal being spawned in Hell and not a human, but was clearly surprised at this news. "Exactly how many times have you encountered it?"

"Maybe three? I thought I was being followed in the monastery... that night... then I found my sister and didn't think about it again." I started walking around the outer edge of the circle. "What's an Umbra demon?"

"Mercenary spies, mostly. They sell their services to any royal House that has use for them. There are a few who are only loyal to Pride. They're mostly incorporeal and are very hard to kill. Magic doesn't always work on them the way you'd imagine it to."

Very hard to kill wasn't *impossible to kill.* A silver lining if ever there was one. "If it's supposed to be spying, why reveal itself?"

"That's the question, isn't it, witch? They typically don't speak at all."

"Do you think Greed hired it?"

"Why would I think that?"

I looked him over for signs of deception. Surely he knew his brother was here. "Because I spoke with him in his gambling den right before my grandmother was attacked. And I may have tricked him into giving me more information than he'd originally agreed to. It's not his sin, but I'm sure his royal pride was injured."

"Funny." Wrath gave me a dry look. "It is nearly impossible to fool a prince of Hell."

"Well, unless he was lying about who he was, tricking him wasn't that hard." I couldn't tell if Wrath believed me, and I didn't care. "You said that some Umbra demons are loyal to Pride... do you think he sent them?"

Given the fact that it stole one of his horns, it seemed likely. But Wrath didn't know that's what I'd been after when I'd invaded the Viperidae nest. I was interested in his response.

"It's possible, but not probable. Not when I'm here. An Umbra demon can't *transvenio* to the underworld. They can only slip between realms if a prince sends them, or if they're summoned. And even then that sort of power can only be used during specific periods."

"How does traveling between realms work?"

"It's like plucking threads of time, and weaving them in different places."

Vague. "If someone was trying to summon the devil...would you be able to tell?"

Wrath cut a sharp glance my way. "He can't be summoned."

"What if someone had the Horn of Hades? Could Pride be summoned then?"

The demon prince went very still. His surprise only lasted a second before a slow smile spread across his face. "You've been busy."

I had been, and I'd done a decent job so far of tracing my sister's steps, but now I needed help. Wrath might be my enemy, but he'd saved my life. I hoped it meant I could trust him.

I thought carefully about what I wanted to do next. His responses about the Umbra demon reminded me of my twin and the way she'd take notes in her diary, and it put me at ease. It was like Vittoria was giving her blessing for this most unusual of unions. I reminded myself that Wrath could have easily tried taking my soul or bargaining for my life as I lay dying. And he didn't do either of those things. Instead, he sacrificed his own power without expecting payment.

"Will you help me figure out if...that happened?"

"If someone summoned Pride?" he asked. I nodded. He looked highly skeptical. "We'd need to know the place where the summoning was attempted. And nothing is guaranteed. Was the Horn of Hades combined, or was just one horn used?"

"Just one." I inhaled. "And I know where to start. So you'll help?"

"You need to be more specific when asking to break the containment charm. And don't forget to use my title. It *is* polite to do so." I glanced down at his dagger I'd retrieved from home, then flicked my attention back to his. He grinned again; this time it was filled with genuine amusement. "Not my rules."

"Will you please leave the bone circle and assist me in finding out if someone summoned Pride, Prince Wrath?"

It was the first time I'd ever broken a containment spell, and it was strange. I didn't have to whisper an incantation, simply requesting him to leave the summoning circle did the trick.

An electric charge in the atmosphere filled the cave, expanding slowly until it pushed the containment circle's border away. There was a slight crackle and then the outside world returned in full.

Wrath suddenly towered over me. "If you value our new alliance, do not ever use that containment spell on me again, witch. Trust goes both ways. My patience grows weary."

"Fine. If you want my trust, stop helping Pride find a wife."

"I can't."

"Then don't be surprised when I defend myself using any means necessary."

He paced away, running a hand through his hair. I watched impassively as he strode back over to me. Determination flashed in his gold eyes. "Hand me my dagger." I shot him an incredulous look. "I only need it for a moment. And no, I won't stab you with it."

Though he probably wanted to. Badly.

I unstrapped the serpent dagger from the holster at my hip, and handed it over.

Wrath dropped to one knee.

"Emilia Maria di Carlo, you have my word that I will not physically harm a witch, nor force her into a marriage with Pride."

He dragged the blade across his palm, and pressed his bleeding hand against his heart. "On honor of my crown and my blood, I vow that my current mission is to save souls, not take them."

He stood and handed his dagger back to me, hilt first. Another show of trust. I replaced the blade and looked him over. His wound was already sealed. "Aren't you going to ask me to accept your blood trade from earlier?"

"I would prefer if you accepted it, but I will not force you to. Are you satisfied by my vow?"

"For the time being."

"Good enough."

He brushed past me, stopping near the edge of the cave. Resisting the urge to shove him into the sea below, I silently followed, taking in the silver-backed waves, undulating like a mammoth ebony creature beneath the full moon as he stretched. *Blood and bones.* Of course. A full moon meant more trouble. And my hands were already full of around six foot two of it.

"Here." I slapped the shirt I'd bought him against his chest. "I don't care if you hate it, if it smells, or if you're too princely for peasant clothes, but you will wear this while we're walking through the city. The last thing we need is to draw any more attention to you."

Wrath and I settled against the building adjacent to the monastery, watching lights snuff out one by one. Soon the brotherhood would be asleep in their bedchambers. "What possessed you to swear a blood vow to me?"

"I wanted to offer a twig of trust."

"You mean an olive branch."

"Same concept, witch." He tipped his face up at the moon. "Also, I might have wanted more of those . . . things you brought. If you died then I'd have to hunt them down. It would have been inconvenient."

"The cannoli?" I asked, feigning incredulity at his attempt at humor. "You saved me in part for some sweetened ricotta?" Thank the goddess he didn't seem to grasp how popular they were, or how widely they could be found in the city. "Do you think the Umbra demon is watching us?"

Tucked snugly between the shadows, it was too dark to see his features clearly, but I pictured his look of resignation anyway. "Are you scared?"

A perfect nonanswer to my question. I knew he was referencing the Umbra demon, but the truth was Wrath scared me, too. Anyone who wasn't a little afraid to enter a chamber with the demon last seen with their murdered loved one would be an idiot.

A couple streets over, voices rumbled like distant thunder. Laughter followed, bold and boisterous. Palermo was a city that worshipped the night as much as it basked in the glory of the day. Festivals, feasts—there always seemed to be some occasion worth celebrating, especially with food and drink. I hoped to stop the monster bent on destroying that before it struck again.

Several minutes of quiet later, the last golden light inside went dark.

"All right. It's time," Wrath said, straightening. "If you'd prefer to stay here, then stay. I don't coddle."

I ignored him and slipped into the shadows, letting him talk to himself. He seemed to enjoy the sound of his own voice well enough. It felt rude to interrupt.

"I won't comfort. Or tend to your wounds. Emotional or otherwise. I despise—"

When the door across the alley creaked open, his mouth snapped shut. I flashed him a scathing look as I pushed it wider in invitation. He stood there, scowling. I'd wager anything he hadn't heard me move. I wondered how many people ever surprised him. Probably not many, given the way his annoyance seemed to build at the thought of being bested by a witch.

"Are you coming, or not, demon?"

TWENTY-THREE

Thankfully, there were no supernatural whispers waiting for me in the chamber where Vittoria died. No insistent summoning tug, or magical request from the Great Beyond. Only silence and the slight scrape of Wrath's boots as he moved around in the dark. At his quiet but gruff request, I handed him my satchel of supplies, grateful for a few moments to collect myself while he searched inside of it for candles.

According to Wrath, we'd only have a few minutes for him to sense traces of any summoning magic. He warned me there might not be any hints since more than a month had passed. I hadn't been back in this room since I first found my sister's mutilated body. If I had a choice, I'd never set foot in this cursed monastery again. I knew Vittoria wasn't here, but the ghost of that night haunted me all the same. I closed my eyes against the memory of her torn flesh. The utter stillness of death. And the blood.

I rubbed my hands over my arms, though the air was pleasantly warm. It was odd how unexpected life could be. A month ago, I never would've pictured returning with the very creature I'd first found licking my sister's blood, yet here we were. Working together.

Suddenly, I was no longer lost in grief. With everything that had happened, I'd forgotten all about that morbid, blood-licking detail. I spun around, relishing the weight of the demon's dagger as it bounced at my side. "Just to be clear; I permitted you to leave the containment circle tonight for *my* benefit alone. It doesn't mean I like you."

"And here I thought binding me for all eternity meant we were good friends."

"You haven't explained why you were licking my sister's blood."

He finished digging through my bag and struck a match. Light flared up, gilding the edges of his face. Shadows darkened his gaze, but didn't hide the shimmering gold of his irises. His attention slid to the dagger and lingered. He stared at it often enough during our walk here, that I couldn't help but think he was plotting creative ways of getting it back.

I fought a chill as the familiar feeling of danger returned. Sometimes, especially since he agreed to help me, it was easy to forget he was one of the Wicked. "You didn't ask me to."

"I most certainly did."

"What you said was 'You were standing over her body, *licking her blood from your fingers,* you revolting beast.' " Obviously, it made a lasting impression. He lit the candles and handed me one. I avoided his fingers and he replied in kind. "Don't touch anything, witch. We don't want to disturb any lingering scent."

"Do I even want to know what you mean by 'lingering scent,' or is that some Hell creature fact best left to the imagination?"

"Tempting though it may be, it's best not to imagine me at all."

I rolled my eyes. If he didn't want to elaborate, that was perfectly fine. I didn't give a rat's tail about his precious demon senses, but I *did* care about Vittoria.

"Fine. Why were you licking her blood?"

He held up his candle and pivoted in place, scanning the chamber. "I was testing it."

I drew in a deep breath and prayed to the goddess of strength and reasoning to keep me from butchering him right here and now.

"Listen, this little alliance will work much better if you elaborate without constant prompting. Pretend I know nothing about your wicked ways. Testing her blood for *what*?"

"Forgive me, your highness." A small smile played across his face. "I was testing it for any hints of a demon House she might have aligned herself with."

"Like the blood trade you offered me?"

He nodded.

"What did you discover when you tested Vittoria's blood?"

"She hadn't yet aligned herself with anyone. But that doesn't mean she hadn't interacted with a prince of Hell."

"So even though I summoned you here, no one would know you and I are... working together... without a blood trade, right?"

"Correct."

Blood and bones. That meant Vittoria could have summoned Greed or even Envy, and, if she hadn't agreed to a blood trade, there was no way to track that.

"Do you think Greed or Envy would want to stop Pride from marrying?"

He considered that. "Greed enjoys ruling his House, so no. And Envy wouldn't attempt anything that would bring war to his House. He's more likely to brood about all the things he doesn't have and wants, but lacks the ambition to take it."

Conversation over, Wrath shifted back around with his candle, and something caught my attention. I bent down, scraping a bit of wax with my nail. The wax was pale rose. I suddenly remembered the candles that had been here that horrible night. I moved my light in a slow arc to see the floor better. Another smaller wax splotch was gray. I rotated, spying the same alternating pink and gray wax impressions.

This was definitely the place where Vittoria had created a summoning circle. "Envy said the others will come looking for me, did he mean your brothers?"

"I imagine so."

"Could he mean the Umbra demons, too?"

"Perhaps."

I stared daggers at the demon prince. After he went out of his way to save my life, I wanted to scream over his short responses. I thought again about his inability to directly lie to me and narrowed my eyes. "What did he mean about not knowing the future?"

"I wasn't there. I'm not sure exactly what he was referencing." Wrath avoided my gaze. "He could just be using it as a fear tactic to get inside your head."

"What's a shadow witch?"

He flicked his attention to me, and gave me a look that said if I didn't know, he wasn't going to be the one to tell me. I shot him a glare that promised a long, violent death if he didn't start talking. He relented. "You've got a bit more demon blood in you than other witches."

"That can't be true. You're—" I shut my mouth. He couldn't lie, but there was no way what he said was true. Our family was goddess blessed, not daughters of darkness. "How would that even be possible?"

He arched a brow. "You do know how children are made, don't you?"

"Of course I do."

"Good. Saves me from explaining how one of your ancestors had a fine romp with a demon, and produced an heir. Probably not so distantly if Envy could tell by . . . looking."

"My grandmother said we were guardians between realms. And that 'shadow witch' was the nasty name the Wicked gave us."

His attention was fully on me now, and I suddenly didn't want him knowing anything regarding my family's secret history. I nodded at the candle wax, changing the subject. "I remember thinking the air smelled like thyme. And paraffin. Is that proof she tried summoning Pride?"

"No. Pale rose and gray candles are used by House Greed." He walked around the chamber. "Thyme and copper are also required when summoning a demon who belongs to that court."

"Demons can only be summoned using the right color candles?"

"Among other things, yes. Demon courts are broken down into seven royal Houses. Each have their own rituals and requirements. Candle colors, plants, time of day, objects of intent, and metals all vary."

I pointed to the objects around us. "None of this can be used to summon Pride? Or does having the Horn of Hades negate that part of the summoning spell requirement?"

"Even if your sister had possession of both horns, it still wouldn't work without the correct candles, metals, and plants." He held his candle up. "Whatever happened in this chamber that night, I know your sister didn't summon Pride. And it doesn't look like she was trying to, either."

"She told me she was."

Wrath watched me closely. "It's impossible to know what her

intentions were. She very well might have wanted to summon him, but changed her mind along the way. Or, if she did attempt to summon him, she didn't do that here."

I collected my growing frustration. If she didn't summon Pride, that meant Greed was to blame. He had to be. I thought about the attack on Nonna, and his desire to have the Horn of Hades. It made sense that Greed wouldn't be content being a prince of Hell when he could become the king of demons. Part of his sin included never being satisfied, always wanting more. Not caring who or what was destroyed in the pursuit of his goals.

Unexpected fury rose in me, and coiled around every inch of the room. It was so powerful, my knees almost buckled from it.

"I vow on my blood that I'll destroy the demon who did this to Vittoria, and take pleasure in doing it." Wrath glanced at me sharply and, judging from his flash of surprise, I imagined my gaze went nearly black. My emotions were getting stronger, darker. I blamed proximity to the warrior prince. If Envy inspired feelings of jealousy in me, it made sense that Wrath—intentionally or not—stoked my anger. "You will help me interrogate Greed again. And if I can't kill him, you will."

My sister's amulet glowed an unearthly purple. Wrath's focus drifted to it, then back to my face. I'd put it on after I'd stolen it from the Viperidae. So far, the gates of Hell hadn't sprung open, and Wrath hadn't tried cutting it off my neck.

"Impressive as your rousing speech and temper is, I won't be bringing war to anyone. And neither will you. At least not without irrefutable proof. The likelihood of it being Greed is very slim."

"Then how did he get here? Someone summoned him." I tossed an arm around the chamber. "From the looks of it, he was summoned in this room."

"Not necessarily. Aside from Pride, princes of Hell can travel here on their own. Plus, there is no trace of Greed's power in this chamber. Unless your sister had a personal object belonging to him, it's far more likely she—or whoever else may have set up this particular circle—summoned one of his subjects. And there are *thousands* of them."

"But there's only *one* demon prince from that House who's currently in Palermo. I don't see thousands of other demons running around here, do you?"

"Are you asking rhetorically or do you expect an answer?"

I opened my mouth and shut it. I had so many more questions about the demon realm, but could almost see Wrath begging me to ask them. I decided today wasn't so lucky for him.

"What kind of object would she need to summon Greed? A dagger, like yours?" I couldn't remember seeing the blade on him when I paid his gambling den a visit. More evidence that he was summoned. "Maybe it's still in our bedroom."

"Afraid not." He shook his head. "It would have been here the night she was murdered. Whoever killed her must have taken it when they left. There's no scent in here that can be traced, though. If it's a demon, I'll have to track it a different way."

"Unless you were right earlier and she didn't actually summon a demon," I mused aloud. "Maybe she stumbled upon someone else trying to summon Greed and they killed her. Or maybe they'd summoned a lesser demon and it attacked."

Because the manner in which her heart had been ripped out... only some terrible creature could have done that. I wouldn't let myself forget that I knew of only one demon who was in this chamber with my murdered twin, mere moments after she'd lost her life.

"It's possible, but I don't believe it was a demon." He stared at the altar where my twin's body had been discarded. "A lesser demon would typically go for the throat, the viscera—it wouldn't target one organ and leave. Especially something large and fierce enough to inflict that sort of damage on a body."

No Pride. No Greed. No clues. This excursion wasn't going as planned.

I thought about the grimoire sheets I'd found. Wrath said certain color candles and objects were required when summoning a particular demon House. Trouble was, neither of the two sheets Vittoria had contained a spell that included pink and gray candles. Anger built inside me again, needing a release. Or a target.

"It's funny." The air was warm, but the blade I pressed into Wrath's back felt like ice in my hands. He stopped breathing. "You can't lie, and I believe that's true enough, but why can't I find evidence to support your claims of innocence?"

"Are you asking me to comment on your own perceived incompetence?"

"Did you place the candles here as evidence that night to shift blame to Greed? You must have realized my sister had summoning spells for your House, and it would implicate you."

"I was unaware you summoned me using any spell other than your own. I've never had contact with your sister, aside from the night I discovered her body. You do recall that I need to find out who's killing the witches, too, correct? Maybe more than you do."

"Why? Because of the curse?"

"If we're to simplify, yes."

"Tell me everything about it. I want to know who cursed the devil, why, and why it matters to me or this world." He tossed a look over his shoulder that said that line of questioning wouldn't be answered, regardless of the dagger. I considered stabbing him anyway, but it would probably only end with him refusing to answer any other questions. "Have you been pretending my protection charm works?"

"If I was pretending, why wouldn't I have snapped your neck or used my influence by now? It's certainly not because I enjoy your spellbinding company."

"Give me one reason I shouldn't shove this blade through your heart. That *is* how you can die, isn't it? By your own weapon. And only in that one spot."

"Hardly."

"Are you sure?" I angled the tip of the blade against his spine. "I think you're omitting the truth. Know why?"

"Enlighten me."

"I feel your gaze on me when you think I'm not paying attention. You track the dagger every time I move. You need to know where it is. That's why Envy was surprised I had it. You're almost immortal, except for that one little weakness. So, oh, mighty Prince Wrath, if you don't want to die tonight, tell me why Pride really sent you here."

TWENTY-FOUR

Wrath spun around and leaned forward, pressing the tip of his dagger into his chest before I could even blink. A drop of blood slipped down the metal, briefly illuminating it. I stared mutely as the demon's wound healed before my eyes.

He angled his head down. If either of us moved, our lips would touch. I didn't so much as breathe too deeply. "A dagger to the heart hurts, witch, but it'll take much more than that to destroy a prince of Hell. If you still think I'm lying, go ahead and stab me."

A wild part of me wished to test the theory, if only to determine if he was being honest. Another, quieter part still reeling with grief wanted to hand him the blade and see if my protection charm really worked. I decided now wasn't the time for foolish risks and sheathed his weapon.

I stepped away from him, trying not to think of it as retreating. He made no move to stop or pursue me, only watched as I put a few feet of space between us.

"Will you at least tell me about the curse? I think we could—"

Wrath set his candle on the stone altar and was before me a breath later. And he was entirely too close—his back brushed against my chest. I lifted my hands, ready to shove him, when I heard the faint sound of footsteps heading our way.

"Did you tell anyone we were coming here?" Wrath asked. I shook my head, terrified Greed or Envy had tracked us. Wrath's body was coiled, ready to strike. I did my best to calm my breaths.

"Hello?" A familiar, deep voice called out from the corridor.

"Blood and bones." I threw my head back and groaned. "Not now."

Wrath shot me a look over his shoulder. "Someone you know?"

I nodded and the demon relaxed his fighting stance. Light from a lantern preceded our visitor into the room, and I internally cursed the interruption. Wrath stepped aside and appeared downright jovial at my annoyance. I ignored him as Antonio walked in and promptly halted.

"Emilia." Antonio's gaze warmed when it landed on me, only to narrow when he saw I wasn't alone. He glanced between me and my minacious companion, clearly at a loss for words. "I heard voices..." His focus drifted back to Wrath, took in the serpent tattoo that started from the top of the demon's hand, coiled around his wrist, and disappeared up his sleeve. Then his gaze shifted between the matching ink on both of our forearms. His look was unreadable. Antonio stood straighter. "Is everything all right?"

Wrath inspected Antonio in a way that sent goose bumps skittering over my body.

I quickly put myself between them and offered my old friend a sheepish smile. "I'm sorry if we were too loud. I asked..." I hesitated. I couldn't very well call him "Wrath." The demon prince shifted into view. He gave me a slight shake of his head. It was hard to tell if it was a warning to not give his name, or if he was simply getting a better look at my discomfort. "My friend Samael is visiting and we wanted to light a candle for Vittoria."

Antonio didn't seem convinced and I couldn't blame him. I wasn't a very good actress. I really hoped he didn't keep asking questions. If I had to guess, lying to a holy man in a place of worship in the presence of a demon who was on a secret mission for the devil was probably bad luck. "Unusual name," he finally said. "Where did you say he was visiting from?"

"She didn't. Would you like to fetch us some sacramental wine and delve into my lineage?" Wrath flashed a look that bordered on predatory. "I wouldn't mind getting to know you better, either. Especially if you're such a good *friend* of my Emilia's."

Wrath said the word "friend" like he thought Antonio was anything but. My mouth hung open for an entirely different reason, though. I couldn't begin to understand why Wrath had said "my Emilia's." Honestly, I wasn't sure if the demon even remembered my name since he only ever tossed around "witch."

Antonio seemed just as stunned. "Your—"

"Apologies, Antonio." I recovered quickly and shot Wrath a warning look as I slipped my arm through the *fratello*'s, swiftly angling him toward the door. I'd wager anything the Prince of Wrath was only trying to make my friend angry so he could siphon those emotions, just like Envy had done to me. "You'll have to forgive his rudeness; his journey was long and it's not under the most pleasant circumstances."

Antonio's arm had a surprising bit of muscle hidden beneath his robes, but he didn't try and stop me as I guided him into the corridor.

"Is it all right if we stay for a few more minutes to say our prayers?"

Antonio looked down into my eyes, and his expression softened. "Of course. I'll be in the next corridor near the *colatoio* if you need me."

"Thank you."

I exhaled as he slowly made his way down the hall toward the preparation room, waiting until his lantern could no longer be seen before I reentered the chamber. Wrath leaned against the altar and stared at me, one brow arched. It was one of the most human expressions I'd ever seen him wear. "Samael, really? *That* was the best name you could come up with?"

"He was a prince of Rome and an angel of death. I'd say that sounds pretty fitting. You're more than welcome to tell me your real name. Then you won't have to get your undergarments twisted about ones I make up."

He strode over to me, stopping at an almost decent space. "Do not *ever* call me that again. I am no angel, witch. Never make that mistake."

"You don't say. And here I was under the impression most humans considered Samael the devil." I brushed past him and went back to the traces of wax left from Vittoria's summoning circle. "Do you—"

"Have you and that human ever shared a bed?"

I spun around, completely taken off guard by his question. I expected to see a smirk or sneer and wasn't prepared for the genuine curiosity I found. I wasn't sure which was more disturbing. "First, that's none of your business. And second, why would you ask such an asinine thing? In case you didn't notice, he's a man of God."

"He hasn't always been."

I clamped my mouth shut. He'd only recently become a member of the brotherhood, and it hadn't stopped me from pining over him. Truth was, I often dreamed of him trailing kisses down my throat, knotting his fist in my hair, and choosing me instead of his holy brotherhood.

Right before he took that oath, I swore he seemed interested in pursing a romance with me. He'd stop by Sea & Vine, offer to walk me home and linger outside my door. A few times I was convinced he was working up the nerve to steal a kiss. He'd chatter nervously about his favorite books. Vittoria would waggle her brows and slip inside, leaving me alone with him, but he never closed the distance between us.

And none of that mattered now. For multiple reasons.

"Are you able to find anything useful here to help us with Vittoria's murder?"

"Your pulse is pounding." Wrath made to reach for the vein in my neck, but stopped shy of making contact with my skin. "Just like your human's when I claimed you. Odd for such a pious man to get so jealous."

His attention moved across my face, and he took his time shifting it to my eyes, my lips, tracing each curve and whirl of the tattoo my fluttering sleeves couldn't hide. Wildflowers continued to bloom across each of our arms along with vibrant frangipani blossoms. It must have happened after the spell he'd used to save me. He studied me carefully, as if he was imagining what Antonio saw, and slid his focus down inch by inch until he'd taken in everything from my face to my sandals then dragged it back up just as slowly. I had little doubt that he'd catalogued minute details and stored them away for future analysis. Perhaps he was memorizing my size for a coffin.

I commanded my heart to steady itself. "Is there a point to any of this, or are you simply trying to evoke my wrath again?"

"There's a point to everything, witch. We just have to figure out how it all connects. Don't discount your *friend* simply because he's mortal. Emotions are powerful forces. People kill for much less than greed or jealousy."

I tried to imagine Antonio sneaking around at night, murdering young women. I'd say Wrath was wrong, but I knew enough of man to believe that anyone was capable of anything at any time. While I wasn't convinced Antonio had any *motivation* for killing, I'd keep all options open just in case. For all I knew, he really was running around summoning demons and ripping out hearts between prayer sessions.

"If we can't find proof Vittoria summoned Pride," I said, "what should we do next?"

He stared at me a moment too long before looking away. "I'll send a message to the next potential bride. Hopefully she'll meet us tomorrow and we can be done with this."

The world stopped spinning. I stared at him a beat, processing the fact that another witch had made a bargain, and he'd been aware of it. "You promised to stop helping Pride. And you knew about another witch?" He nodded. "Why is this the first you're telling me?"

"First, I agreed to not harm a witch or force her into a bargain. Second, I was going to share the information after the Viperidae attack, but you banished me to the summoning circle before I got the chance to."

How convenient for him. "Did you return to your realm to get this information?"

"No. Once summoned, I cannot leave this world until you send me back. Or unless my connection is severed with a demon blade."

"What about the transve-whatever?"

"*Transvenio.* My ties to you prevent me from freely traveling between realms. But they also allow me to stay here longer than I normally could. Put simply: our bond anchors me here."

"So how did you get the information about the new bargain?"

"Pride sent a messenger."

It was too simple for comfort. I didn't like that the devil could send messages between realms. It made me think of the Umbra demon again, and how it had taken the blade to my grandmother with ease. Maybe the devil was tired of witches wearing his horns.

"If you can only leave this realm when I send you back, how are you planning on delivering her to Hell?"

A spark of admiration lit his gaze. "I'm only speaking with her tomorrow. I said nothing of taking her to Hell." He gave me a once-over and I wondered if he found me to be a formidable opponent. "I'm going to secure a building tonight. Once I find a location, I'll send a note telling you where I'll be. If you don't hear from me by dusk, meet me back at the cavern."

TWENTY-FIVE

I pulled the mortar and pestle from the shelf, face strained in concentration as I gathered up the olive oil, garlic, almonds, basil, pecorino, and cherry tomatoes for the pesto alla Trapanese. On days such as this, when the sun was sweltering before noon and even the thinnest dress clung like a second skin, I enjoyed adding fresh mint to the tomato pesto. Unfortunately, we were out of it at the moment.

I set my supplies down and pulled up my wavy hair, allowing a few shorter strands to frame my face. There were no flowers in my locks today—they'd go limp and wither in moments. The back of my neck was already sticky and the day had only just begun. I was seriously reconsidering my choice to wear white as I tied an apron over my sleeveless dress. I would have prefered to keep my magical tattoo hidden, but there was no way I'd survive the heat, even with sheer sleeves. Hopefully, no one in my family would notice the pale ink, especially if I angled my arm away.

I was deep in thoughts of picturing Wrath trying the tomato pesto when my mother joined me in our little kitchen and grabbed sardines from the ice box.

"You didn't come home." My mother wasn't asking, and her tone was almost as sharp as the knife she was using to debone the fish. "Would you care to explain where you were all night?"

I would sooner sell my soul.

I kept my attention on the pesto, crushing the almonds just right. There was no way I was admitting to working with a blood-drinking demon to solve Vittoria's murder. And not only had I temporarily aligned myself with one of the Malvagi, but I had also spoken with two others.

Oh, and, by the way, an invisible mercenary demon was following me around, sputtering cryptic warnings, attacked Nonna, and might assassinate me if ordered to. Then, I'd almost died in a Viperidae attack, and a prince of Hell saved me using ancient, dark magic that required both of us to be naked in a tub. My mother's head would spin. But at least the tattoo wouldn't seem half as bad.

"I was at the monastery."

"I know."

I jerked my gaze to hers, startled. "How?"

"Fratello Antonio stopped by this morning, concerned." She went at the next sardine with gusto. Slipping the knife under the skin, dragging it down the spine. "He said you were with a young man. A friend of our family's. Said his name was an odd one."

"I—"

"Save your lies, child." Mamma's grip on her knife tightened. "They're the gateway to Hell."

I snapped my mouth shut. My mother must know. She must have seen through my ruse, and had somehow pieced together that I'd used the dark arts. And Fratello Antonio Bernardo had confirmed her fears. I swallowed hard, debating how honest I should be with her.

"Well, you see—"

"Tumbling around dark places with handsome young men might distract from the pain for a little while, but it won't ever take it away. You need to find your own inner strength for that."

"I—*what*?"

Mamma shook her knife in my direction. "Don't go pretending you have no idea what I'm saying. You're lucky your grandmother was sleeping and didn't overhear him. She has enough to worry about while she's healing. She doesn't need to stress over devilish men. Fratello Antonio told me all about that young man. From the sound of it, you've bewitched him, too. Antonio said he called you his Emilia. You're no one's but your own, girl. Don't ever forget it."

Sweet goddess above. This was *so* much worse than Nonna finding out I'd summoned a demon. Heat blossomed across my face and crept down my neck that had nothing to do with the soaring temperatures. My mother thought Wrath and I had been...

I might die of mortification.

Even *picturing* him naked, tugging me to his solid, tattooed body, radiating his infuriating heat as he put his stupid mouth on mine and I gripped him back like he was both my eternal damnation and salvation as we...

I needed to stop that train of thought immediately. I wasn't as disgusted by the image as I'd thought I'd be.

I knew Wrath's juvenile taunt would come back to sink its nasty fangs into me one day. I just hadn't quite pictured it occurring like this.

Mamma set her knife down, her expression softening. She completely misread the reason behind my reddening face. "Love or enjoy whoever's company you want. But you need to be more careful. If your father had answered the door…" she trailed off, not having to finish the sentence to drive the point home.

Pummeling the person who was "tumbling" his daughter would be the perfect way to work out some of his own grief. Defending a daughter's honor was an age-old male pastime. Antiquated human behavior aside, I couldn't believe Antonio had come to our home.

My attention sought out the little clock for the thousandth time. The afternoon was dragging by. There were hours left until I had to meet Wrath. To give my hands something to do besides fantasize about wrapping themselves around Antonio's neck, I removed the damp cloth from the mound of dough and began rolling the pasta for the *busiate*.

I couldn't believe I ever wanted to kiss that nosy fool.

"Oh, and Emilia?" I paused my assault of the dough and looked at my mother. "Make extra *busiate*. I promised Antonio you'd bring some over today with your apologies."

I smiled. I'd happily make extra pasta and dump it all over the troublesome *fratello*'s head.

"Buon appetito." I slammed two baskets onto the long wooden table in the dining hall, not bothering to remove the covered trays of food within them. The small gathering of men waiting for their meal went silent. Antonio paused his conversation with another member around his age, concern crinkling his brow.

I gave him a look that I hoped promised a slow, torturous death and it must have worked. He shot to his feet and hastily escorted me into the corridor. I tolerated his hand on my bare arm until we were out of sight, then shrugged him off.

Sleeveless bodice or not, I didn't appreciate the liberty he'd taken with touching my skin.

"Is something wrong, Emilia?"

"I cannot believe you told my mother I was here with someone last night," I hissed. "What I do, and who I spend my time with, doesn't concern you."

Antonio's jaw tightened. "Your sister was murdered here and a month later, I find you in the same chamber with someone I've never seen and whose name you refuse to give. Forgive me if I wanted to check to make sure you were all right."

"If you were that worried, you could have easily waited in the monastery and walked me home. You didn't have to show up at my house before dawn."

He closed his eyes, leaving me to wonder what exactly was going on in his head. He had to know how much trouble he could have caused. No one was *that* naïve. Finally, when he looked at me again, the fight seemed to leave him.

His voice was quiet when he said, "Another girl was murdered after we spoke last night. And…and I couldn't stop worrying it was you. After what happened with Vittoria, I had to be sure it wasn't. I apologize for any trouble—I wasn't thinking clearly."

I sucked in a sharp breath. We were too late. Someone must have discovered the identity of the witch Wrath had planned to meet later. But how?

My mind spun. Wrath said he was the only prince who knew about the potential brides, but that didn't mean other princes didn't have ways of figuring that out. Spies were utilized in human royal courts—the same likely held true in the demon world. I thought about the invisible Umbra demons who worked for Greed. If he'd sent one after me and it attacked Nonna, it was probable one of them was also passing the names of potential brides along to him.

I still hadn't quite figured out *why* he wanted the witches dead, though. Maybe it was just to ensure the devil didn't break the curse and never left Hell.

Antonio reached over and tucked a loose wave behind my ear, his fingers lingering a moment too long. A few weeks ago my heart would have fluttered madly in my chest. Now I couldn't help but remember how easily one could be torn from a person.

"Do you know who it was?" I asked. Antonio stepped back, looking a bit dazed as he dropped his hand. When he still didn't answer, I clarified, "The girl from last night?"

He shook his head. "Rumors, but nothing that's been confirmed. The consensus so far is she had dark hair and eyes like the others. Which isn't much since nearly everyone on this island fits the description."

"Where was her body found?"

"That, I don't know. If anyone from the brotherhood was called there to bless the body, I haven't heard about it. But I'm sure the market will be abuzz with information tonight. It always is."

Antonio was right; the vendors knew everything and everyone. Customers from all over the city were in and out of their stalls all day, trading information and gossip while they shopped.

Of course stories were often embellished, but the truth usually remained tucked somewhere inside the exaggerations. Luckily I had another, more reliable source who knew the name of our victim. It was almost dusk, so Wrath should be in the cave by the time I got there. I'd grab the demon, ask him everything he knew about the witch, then go to the market and find out the location of the murder.

Hopefully, Wrath could test the scene like he'd done before, only this time we'd be successful with finding out which demon prince was responsible.

Then goddess be with him. I had little doubt the demon of war would take almost as much pleasure in destroying the murderer as I would.

TWENTY-SIX

Throngs of people elbowed their way through the busy marketplace, but still managed to give Wrath a wide berth. I wondered if they sensed his otherness and just didn't know what to make of it. There was a quiet assurance about him—a confidence in himself and the space he occupied. Men and women paused in their gossiping, their gazes tracking him as we passed by. Some appreciatively, some with open distrust and scorn. Though that might be because murder was the topic of the evening, and Wrath looked like trouble.

I imagined wandering through the crowded, twisting streets with a leashed panther would give off the same aura of primal danger. If someone was temporarily out of their senses, I admit there *could* be a certain level of excitement, being close to something so lethal.

My senses were *mostly* intact, though. I knew there was no taming the wild beast, only the illusions of domesticity it cast when it felt like toying with its next meal. The fine clothes and impeccable manners were all part of a well-crafted trap to lure prey, likely honed eons before man walked the earth. Wrath was a predator through and through. I had a feeling if I let myself forget that even for a second, he'd happily sink his teeth into my throat and rip it out.

He caught me staring and raised a brow. "Enjoying what you see, witch?"

"Only if I had a death wish."

"Do you?"

"Not even a little one."

His eyes glittered with dark amusement. Of course the topic of death would appeal to him. "Which vendor do you believe knows about the murder location?"

I nodded toward the center of the marketplace where the apparel section began. Booths with fabrics and silks rustled in the slight breeze, beckoning us over.

"Salvatore is one of the best gossips in the city. If anyone has reliable information about Giulia, it's him." I glanced down at Wrath's shirt. "He's also the vendor who sold me that."

"I see. You brought me here to commit murder while we investigate one."

The good humor promptly left Wrath's face. I hid my grin as his nostrils flared. For a vengeful prince of Hell, he certainly was touchy about clothing. And I was pretty sure he was only teasing about killing the vendor. I hoped.

In fact, I was surprised he was joking at all. After I left the monastery, I went straight to him and delivered the news. I'd been convinced he'd lay waste to the whole city. Instead, he calmly reported everything he knew about the potential bride. Her name was Giulia Santorini, and he hadn't been able to get a message to her last night. I'd taken a second to digest this latest revelation.

I thought over everything again now. I knew her family. They sold spices in the Kalsa District, and Vittoria used to volunteer to stop by their shop to pick up orders for Sea & Vine when Uncle Nino or my father couldn't. Giulia's grandmother Sofia was the witch whose mind had gotten trapped between realms, shifting between realities so swiftly she no longer knew what was real and what was a vision.

As far as I knew, after what happened to Sofia, the Santorinis never dabbled in the dark arts again. Maybe I was wrong. Maybe Giulia decided to invoke the dark arts like her grandma. And maybe she was the one who'd given my sister those mysterious grimoire pages.

That thought stopped me cold.

If Giulia had somehow given my sister a spell to summon a demon, it made sense that she'd taken it from her grandmother's grimoire since Sofia was known to use the dark arts. Maybe the grimoire was the missing link... I thought again about the first book of spells. About the magic binding my sister's diary. Was *that* the connection between the murders? Maybe not the dark arts, but the source material?

"What's wrong?" Wrath asked, breaking into my thoughts. "You look strange."

"Are you *sure* you didn't tell Giulia to meet you last night?" I asked. Wrath shot me a look that silently communicated he might strangle me if we went over this again. To be fair, I might have already asked him half a dozen times on our walk into the city. And half a dozen more once we were here. "Maybe you're double-crossing Pride and killed her."

He let out a long sigh. "I assure you that is still not the case. I have no reason to kill anyone. As I said before, my message never made it to her."

I knew he wasn't double-crossing anyone, but liked hearing him get flustered. "Do you think one of your brothers killed her?"

"No."

"And we're back to one-word answers."

"Careful, witch, or I might think you're interested in having a civil conversation." The barest hint of a smile ghosted across his lips as I rolled my eyes. "Simple answers don't require padding."

"Why don't you think one of your brothers did it?"

"What reason would they have?"

"Let me count the ways, oh, wicked one." I ticked off motivations on my fingers. "Greed might be interested in taking the throne. Maybe Envy is jealous and wants more power. If Pride doesn't marry, then he remains cursed and can't leave Hell. Which is a pretty decent motivation if one of your brothers wants to rule this realm. Shall I go on?"

Wrath glared at me, but didn't respond. Apparently he didn't like my accusations, but couldn't find a way to discredit them as foolish theories. We turned the corner, stepped around a pile of precariously towering wooden crates, and narrowly avoided getting speared by a swordfish head. Wrath took in all the sights and colors silently. I wondered if he had anything like it where he was from, but didn't ask.

A sea of people standing in line for gelato parted for us as we crossed the road and entered the clothing section. Salvatore was in the middle of arguing with someone over another threadbare tunic when Wrath stopped at his table, emanating that quiet menace he was so good at. Conversations ceased. The other patron took one look at the expression on the demon's face and bolted into the crowd, the clothing in question discarded and forgotten.

"You and I have business, vendor."

"I don't believe we..." Sal's attention shifted to the shirt Wrath wore, then shot to me. I gave him a little finger wave. I'd tried warning him about the condition and cost. Now he could deal with an angry demon. I felt the not-so-subtle rattling of Wrath's namesake emotion as it slithered toward Sal and wound around him.

The vendor's hand trembled as he pushed it through his dark hair. "Signore, h-how nice. The shirt is—"

"Being exchanged for that one."

Wrath jerked his chin toward the row of clothing hanging behind the stall; the most expensive pieces judging from the drape of them. Sal opened his mouth, took in the set of Wrath's shoulders, then closed it and plastered on a big false smile. Smart man.

"A bargain indeed!" Sal cringed as he removed the black shirt from a hanger and handed it over. Well, he tried to hand it over. He clutched it before Wrath finally snatched it away. "This is a fine, fine garment, signore. It's a perfect match for your trousers. May you wear it well."

I rolled my eyes skyward. Sal cracked under pressure from the demon faster than an egg hitting the ground. Next time I wanted a good deal, I'd have to try scowling and summoning some quiet menace, too.

Wrath was out of the tawny monstrosity a breath later and tossed the offending garment back at the vendor. If the demon prince hadn't already caused a disturbance before, his bare, sculpted chest certainly did now. He slipped the new shirt on, seemingly unaware of the effect he had on the people nearest us. Muscles, supple and sinuous, moved with practiced ease. His serpent tattoo also caused quite a stir. Someone nearby commented on how large it was, how lifelike. Another person whispered about its possible meaning.

A line of people that had been meandering through the clothing stalls halted to watch.

I begged the goddess of serenity to send me some in buckets, then turned to Salvatore to get what we actually came here for. "Do you have any information about Giulia?"

"I sure do. Reliable sources, too. I heard from Bibby down at the docks, who spoke to Angelo who makes ricotta near the palace, that her heart was ripped clean from her chest." Despite the graphic nature of his gossip, Sal looked immensely pleased with himself. "Her nonna was the one who went a bit..."

He lifted his pointer finger to his temple and made circles, an offensive gesture indicating madness. I went to admonish him when a member of the brotherhood walked by the stall and touched his forehead, heart, and each shoulder in the sign of the cross.

"Anyway...whatever got her was vicious. Angelo said blood sprayed all over the building. Looked like animals ripped her apart. He had a devil of a time cleaning it up. Chunks of..."

"I'm sorry, but where was her body found?" I asked, cutting him off mid-description. I had my own nightmares about how that looked firsthand, and didn't need any more details. "You mentioned someone who works near the palace?"

"That's right. Angelo with the ricotta said it was near his stall out front. Prime location." Sal jerked his chin to the right. "The police are still there, so you won't miss the crowd. If you hurry, you might still see the body."

It was impossible to get within sight of the murder scene. Sal's information was indeed reliable. And it looked like he'd told a few hundred of his closest confidants the same thing he'd shared with us. Wrath was about to barrel his way through, but I reached out to stop him.

"How close do you need to be to..." I glanced around. There were too many humans around for me to start talking about demons. "To do your special investigation?"

Wrath was well versed in the art of deception. He didn't miss a beat. "I'd like to get a better visual, but I can tell from here that none of my brothers have recently been in the area."

I scrunched my nose. His heightened sense of smell was unsettling. I rolled up onto my toes, trying to see over the heads of everyone. Wrath startled me by briefly placing a hand on my back so I wouldn't wobble. I couldn't see the body, thank the goddess, but I saw a priest tossing holy water around and assumed he was doing some sacramental blessing for her soul. It would be a long while before the crowd dispersed, so there was no point in waiting here until then. We might as well return tomorrow night when all was quiet.

"Follow me," I said, turning toward an alley. Wrath didn't protest and kept close as we maneuvered out of the thickest part of the crowd. A little food stand that had already closed up for the night caught my attention. There was a painting on its side—a pawprint clutching a stalk of wheat, and something about it made me think of Greed. I waited until we were far enough away to speak openly. "You're sure you didn't find any traces of Greed?"

"Unless he's come up with a way to mask his magic, no. He wasn't here. Why are you so convinced he's to blame? What evidence do you have?"

"I'm not convinced of anything. I'm just trying to tug on threads that seem likely." I bumped into a few people still on their way to the murder scene, muttered apologies, and turned down another street. "As for evidence? Based on my conversation with him, his desire to possess the Horn of Hades, and the attack on my grandmother immediately following my meeting with him, Greed makes the most sense right now."

I felt Wrath's attention on me as we moved into a narrower street, a constant prickle of energy between my shoulder blades, but he didn't ask how my grandmother was or offer apologies.

And to be perfectly honest, he was the last creature in the world I wanted comfort from.

I stopped at the turnoff to my neighborhood. "Who is the next witch on your list?"

"I don't know yet."

"That needs to be our next priority," I said, glancing past him. The street was quiet in this quarter. "Once you find out who she is, we'll have to hide her somewhere safe."

Wrath pressed his lips together, but finally nodded in agreement. "I'll send word to my realm tonight. I should have an answer by morning."

It wasn't cold, but I rubbed my hands over my arms anyway. My dress was creamy white and sleeveless. Perfect for warm summer nights, but terrible for fighting chills brought on by fear. Wrath tracked the movement, his attention focused on my forearm. Wildflowers twisted and tangled all the way up to my elbow now. I didn't have to see his arm to know his tattoo was the same. I looked down my street, relieved to see a few children out playing. I didn't want to be scared of Greed or Envy lurking in the shadows, but I was.

"All right," I said. "I'll see you tomorrow then. Where should we meet?"

"Don't worry." Wrath flashed a wolfish grin. "I'll find you."

"You know that's deeply unsettling, right?"

"Iucundissima somnia." Sweetest dreams. And then he was gone.

TWENTY-SEVEN

"I was thinking of making cassata for tomorrow's dessert."

Mamma turned to me, her expression worn, but hopeful. Somehow I managed to hide the swift emotional punch from registering on my face. The sponge cake with sweet ricotta layers was a favorite of both mine and Vittoria's. We used to request it each year for our birthday and Mamma never disappointed us. She'd roll out a thin layer of marzipan, covering the whole cake in the sweet paste before decorating it with brightly colored candied fruit. I loved how that slightly chewier upper layer contrasted against the soft deliciousness of the wet cake hidden inside.

I wasn't sure I could ever eat it again without feeling crushed by a wave of sadness, but refused to dampen my mother's spirits. When I smiled, it was genuine.

"That sounds delicious."

My mother shuffled over to the dry goods cabinet, seemingly exhausted again from her brief spurt of conversation, and pulled out a bowl, filling it with sugar and all the supplies she needed for the cake. Today was a bad day for her. I watched her, then went back to removing the *sarde a beccafico* from the oven. I inhaled the fragrant scent of stuffed sardines.

Nonna's recipe called for golden raisins, pine nuts, and breadcrumbs in the stuffing, then she'd drizzle melted sage butter and thyme over it before finishing it off with large bay leaves to separate the fish while it baked. The result was a symphony of flavors that melted in your mouth and stuck to your ribs.

I'd no sooner set the fish on a platter when my father stepped into the kitchen, waving around a folded note. He expertly swiped a piece of stuffing that had fallen out, and I shook my head, but smiled all the same. My father was always *very* helpful in the kitchen, sampling each new recipe for quality purposes. Or so he kept claiming.

"Salvatore dropped this off for you, Emilia," he said around a mouthful of food. "Said your friend asked him to deliver it right away."

Mamma wore a rosary like other humans, and I imagined she'd be kissing it later, uttering novenas if she ever found out who my "friend" really was. I hastily snatched the note before she could. "*Grazie,* Papà."

My father pulled a stool over and started loading a plate, drawing my mother's attention. I used the distraction to hurry into the corridor and read the short message.

Piazza Zisa and Via degli Emiri.
Eight in the evening.

I didn't recognize the careful, neat penmanship but it dripped regal arrogance and made my stomach twist. The address he'd given was Castello della Zisa. La Zisa was a sprawling Moorish palace that mostly sat in ruin now. The king who'd had it built was called Il Malo—"the bad one"—so it was more than fitting the demon prince had taken up temporary residence there.

I refolded the note, shoved it down my bodice, then made my way back into the kitchen. I'd have just enough time to finish dinner service and hurry over to the palace before dark.

I crept into the abandoned castle from the rear garden, and roamed around several desolate yet ornate rooms before finally circling around to the main entrance and finding another note tacked to the front door—the last place I'd expect a secret meeting location to be posted. I stared out across the lawn at the reflecting pool, and shook my head.

Subtlety was an artform lost on the demon, apparently. Though I supposed when he was the biggest, baddest predator around, he had little to fear.

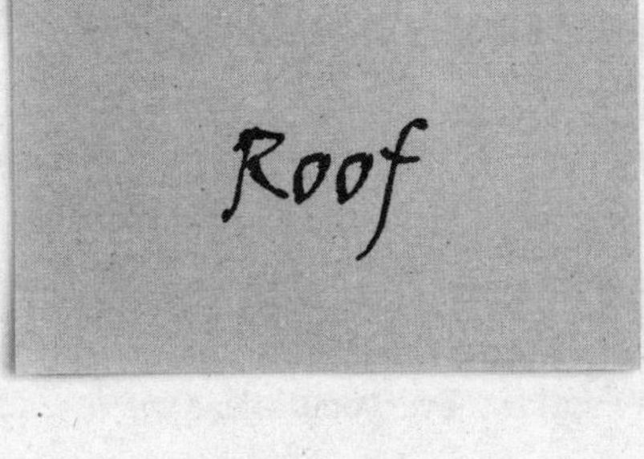

I inwardly sighed. This palace had been built in such a way that cool air filtered through it like an ice box, but of course a creature from Hell would be happiest in the scorching heat. I was dripping with sweat, and spitting mad by the time my foot hit the last stair.

I marched across the roof, determined to flay the demon alive, and halted.

Wrath lay stretched out on his back, hands laced behind his head, soaking in the last rays of the sun as it hovered above the horizon in the distance. Light gilded his profile and he turned his face toward it, smiling at the warmth. He hadn't noticed me yet, and part of me was relieved.

His expression was serene, a look I hadn't seen from him. Though his body was relaxed, an undercurrent of alertness remained that made me believe he could spring up and attack in less than a breath. He was like a serpent, laying in a patch of sun.

Lethal, beautiful. Wholly untouchable.

I wanted to kick him for being so dangerously breathtaking. His head snapped in my direction, his gaze capturing mine. For a minute, I forgot how to breathe.

He slowly took me in. "Did something happen on the way here?"

"No."

"Then why do you look confused?"

"I thought you couldn't bear daylight."

"Why is that?"

I rolled my eyes. As if he didn't know. "Because the Malvagi turn to ash in the sun. That's why we always meet at dusk."

He looked at me oddly. "What else, exactly, have you heard of the Wicked?"

I lifted a shoulder. Everyone knew the legends. Since they

concerned him, I doubted he was that clueless. "You're bloodthirsty demons. You've got red flecks in your eyes, your skin is like ice, you're beautiful, and your kisses are addictive enough to make someone sell their soul for another."

A bemused smile touched his lips. "It's nice to know you find me so attractive, but I'm not one of *those* demons. My eyes aren't red. And if you'd like to find out if my skin is warmer than ice, that can easily be arranged."

To further his point, he undid a few buttons on his shirt, exposing a patch of bronzed skin. A light sheen of sweat glistened, as if beckoning. My face heated, having nothing to do with the sun. "I work in a kitchen and can break down a chicken carcass in under three minutes, I imagine doing the same to you wouldn't be that different."

"I assure you, there's no truth to these stories." His eyes sparked with mischief. "Though I can't promise my kisses wouldn't be sinfully good."

"I thought we were supposed to meet later tonight. Did something happen to change that?"

Wrath stared at me a moment longer and for some reason, I held my breath. He looked like he wanted to say something else, but an inner battle was being waged. Finally, he laid back down, face tipped up at the sun, and closed his eyes. I exhaled.

"No. Nothing of note."

"Do you know who the next witch is?"

"Not yet."

I stood there, waiting for him to elaborate. When he didn't bother, I walked over and glared at him until he looked up grudgingly, shielding his face with a strong hand. "If you don't have information on the next witch, why did you ask me to come here?"

"I…" He squinted at me. "I've secured the building with my magic so, unless you invite something in, it'll be safe from humans, my brothers, and most supernatural creatures. I wasn't sure what you'd had planned for the evening, and thought you might like to see where we'd be staying. I'll be out for a little while, so please look around, make yourself comfortable, and grab your things."

I stared at him, ignoring the whole "moving in together" scenario. "Where are you going?"

"To meet one of Pride's messengers."

"Is he the one who gave you Giulia's name?"

Wrath nodded. "My associate has been watching him since late last night, and witnessed him passing information this morning to someone wearing a hood. I believe whoever he spoke to is our murderer."

"Why didn't your associate follow the hooded figure?"

"He tried. When he closed in, the person crossed into a crowd and disappeared."

I blew out a breath. Of course. "What's the plan?"

"I'm supposed to meet Pride's messenger to retrieve the next name soon. Instead, I'll interrogate him, and will hopefully discover the identity of the robed figure that way."

"Or I could just use a truth spell."

"Too dangerous. Plus, you'll be grabbing your things. I won't be gone for long."

"I see." Something in my tone made him sit up again, a wary expression on his face. So, he could be a smart demon. "You know I won't stay when there's a chance we can find out who killed my sister," I said. "Either take me with you, or I'll follow you."

He studied me for a long minute then sighed. "*I* will not be pleasant. I can have the meeting, and tell you about it. I promise to not hunt down the murderer without you."

"Wait... are you suggesting you've *been* pleasant?" I snorted. "I pity your enemies."

His grin was anything but friendly when he said, "That might be the wisest observation you've made yet, witch."

A clock in the city square chimed the hour. He stood, then ran his golden gaze over my clothes, appraising. "We leave in forty minutes. Try to wear something less... pedestrian. Better yet, I'll have something more appropriate sent to your home."

I glanced at my dress, frowning. It was a modest cotton gown I'd dyed a deep lavender last summer. It didn't have a corset, which I was very pleased with, but it still had a pretty shape. I liked how it was fitted through the bust and waist and then dreamily flowed down to my ankles. It was hardly *pedestrian,* and yet... "What if I don't want to wear your fancy clothing again?"

He didn't bother responding.

I looked up, ready to snap about his rudeness, but he was gone. I cursed him the entire way home, wondering why I'd gotten stuck with such a clothes-obsessed snob of a demon.

Perhaps Nonna was right about the cost of *le arti oscure;* being subjected to Wrath certainly felt like a punishment for using the dark arts.

I was so annoyed, it took far too long for me to focus on the most important detail of all that he'd let slip—Wrath knew where I lived.

TWENTY-EIGHT

I looked down at my new, finely made dress and frowned at the dark layers. "Why do villains always wear black?"

"Better to hide the blood with, witch."

I eyed the demon standing in the alley next to me, thinking his response explained a lot about his personal style. Then I wondered how much blood he planned to spill tonight if he'd dressed us both like living, breathing shadows.

I was *almost* disturbed the thought didn't terrify me more.

"Who are we meeting? Human? Demon? Werewolf?"

"Werewolves are like puppies. It's hellhounds you need to watch out for." Wrath chuckled at my look of horror. "We're meeting a mortal who sold his soul. Speaking of, I need my House dagger back before he arrives."

I gave him a flat stare. Arming a demon didn't seem very beneficial to me. Then again, he needed me to be his precious anchor. He'd mentioned it before, but had shared a few more details on the walk here. I handed the blade over.

"Say I were to die... how long would it take for your powers to start diminishing?"

"Depends on how much magic I expend. If I don't use much, I could retain them for a small amount of time."

A small amount of time for an immortal was probably a decade for me. "Can someone else act as an anchor?"

He blew out a breath. "Technically, yes. Any human or denizen of this world can strike a bargain, and agree to anchor a demon. It is rare and not worth the time it would take to find someone, and agree to terms both parties accepted."

Several moments of silence passed. I tapped my fingers against cool stone. We were hiding in a little alcove off the cathedral square, and it felt like we'd been waiting years for the mysterious messenger to show up. Five minutes in, I quickly discovered standing still wasn't something I enjoyed very much. When I wasn't moving, all I could do was think about my sister.

"Why do demons steal souls? Do you need them for something specific?"

I felt the weight of Wrath's attention as it settled on me. I shifted to see him, surprised to note the level of incredulity he wasn't bothering to hide. *Right.* Like he'd have a nice long chat about soul collecting with the enemy. I lifted my hands in placation, and looked away. Inexplicably, I turned back to him a breath later.

"Why do you think hearts are being taken?"

"Are you asking so many questions in hopes of frightening off the messenger before I can scare information from him?"

"I want to know what you think."

There was such a long pause, I didn't think he'd answer. "We don't have enough information to speculate. And it's unwise to make assumptions without fact."

"Do you believe anything would want to…"

"Eat them? Yes. Plenty of creatures find freshly beating hearts to be the most supreme delicacies, witch. Then there's the ritualistic significance. Sacrifice. Sport. Summoning. And plain old depravity. That level of sadism isn't limited to one species, so we're back where we started."

I felt sick. "A simple yes would have sufficed," I said quietly.

"What you want is for me to say something comforting." His voice was like steel when he faced me. "Lying and saying your sister felt no pain serves no purpose to *you*. I imagine, no matter the reason, whoever or whatever took her heart, did so while she was very much alive and very conscious. I promise you, there is *no* strategic value in getting lost in emotional entanglements. Hone your anger and sorrow into weapons of use, or go back home and cry until the monsters come for you. Because come for you they will."

"I'm not afraid of monsters."

"You may think so now, but my brothers delight in bending creatures like you to their will. They'll feed you their emotions and siphon yours until you don't know where you end and they begin. There are many forms of Hell. Pray to your goddesses you never have to experience them firsthand. You need to be sharp and focused, or you'll end up just as dead as the others."

Tears pricked my eyes. Not from sadness, but pent-up rage. "I am focused, you steaming sack of horse manure. All I dream about is avenging my sister. Don't you *dare* accuse me of being too emotional. I will destroy *anything* that gets in the way of achieving my ends. Even you. And I'm not scared, or else I never would've summoned you to begin with!"

"You should be terrified." His gaze practically pinned me in place. "Vengeance is a potent emotion. It makes you easy prey to both humans and demons alike. *Never* let someone know what your true motivations are. If they know what you want more than anything, they'll craft all sorts of sweet lies and half-truths to manipulate you. They'll know *exactly* how far they can push, what to offer, and what you would never refuse, giving them the upper hand. Your first goal should be to remain alive. Figure out everything else as you go."

"You know my true goals."

"Yes. I do. And it was an extremely foolish mistake on your part to tell me. Make no bones about it. All it takes is a bit of prodding, a tiny push to annoy you and you immediately fall into the trap of lashing out in fury. And in that burning rage you told me *everything* I need to know about what you want." He shook his head. "What will you promise me, Emilia, in exchange for your deepest desire? What *wouldn't* you do to achieve justice for the sister you love? Now I know there's no price too high to demand. I can ask anything, and you'd give it."

We were standing very close now, each of us breathing very hard. I hated that he was right. He didn't even manipulate my emotions like Envy had; he didn't have to. He'd simply goaded me into telling him my deepest desires out of anger. And he only had to push a little bit to get me to snap. Furious with myself for being outmaneuvered by a demon, I did the best thing I knew how—I lied like the devil.

I stuck my finger in Wrath's chest and poked him hard. "If you think that's everything that motivates me, you're sadly mistaken, demon. And why do you care anyway?"

He slowly wrapped his fingers around mine, halting my assault on him. He didn't let go and I wondered if he realized I'd stopped poking him the second his blazing skin touched mine. Now he was just holding my hand against his chest, his heart hammering beneath my touch.

And I was allowing it.

I regained my senses and stepped away.

"That's the fourth time you've lied to me, witch."

It *really* stoked his anger, too. I smiled demurely. "Maybe you should tell me more about the curse. I'd like to know more about that part."

"Fine. You want to know the bloody details? The curse—"

"Signore, is . . . should I return in a little while?" A man somewhere between thirty and forty stood a few feet away, wringing a letter in his hands. "Your brother said—"

From one breath to the next Wrath had the messenger up against the wall, his forearm pressed hard against the man's windpipe. Blood dripped from the messenger's nose onto his tunic and the demon closed his eyes as if in utter rapture.

"Hello, Francesco. Pardon my rudeness, but I hear you've been selling my secrets. If we were in the Walled City, you'd already be dead. Consider this a favor."

I stood there, frozen. Half in shock, half in horror. Wrath had exploded in violence faster than it took me to suck in a startled breath.

"Did I ever tell you the scent of blood drives me into a near frenzy, witch? Your kind believes we crave the taste of it, but princes of Hell don't usually drink blood. It's power we're intoxicated by. The more I allow someone to bleed, the more power I hold over their life."

I blinked. I could barely form a coherent thought. I forgot, through our bantering, who Wrath really was. I imagined I was seeing only a small fraction of what he could do.

He leaned harder into the human whose face was now a deep purple. If Wrath pushed any harder, the man was going to die. I made to step forward, then stopped.

"I crave power more than money, or blood, or lust. And there's no greater power than choice. I'd lie for it. Steal, cheat, maim, and murder. If I could, I'd sell my soul again for it, witch."

"Sell your..." I shook my head. Demons were soulless creatures.

Wrath opened his eyes and turned to me, his irises glowed bright gold in the dark. There wasn't anything human in them, and I realized he'd been keeping this part of himself under lock and key. Some claimed the Wicked were angels before they committed unforgivable sins, and were cast out of heaven. Now I understood how those stories started—Wrath's gaze blazed with heavenly fire. He was wrathful justice: pure, swift, and completely unforgiving.

Ignoring my growing fear, I turned over his admission, and understood what he was really saying; he was offering me a choice. I had the power to walk away from what he was about to do. Or I could choose to stay and take part in it.

I thought of my sister's ravaged body, and the other witches who'd died just as brutally because this man shared information about the messages he carried. Wrath said he was going to scare the messenger to find out who he'd been selling secrets to. His sudden burst of violence shouldn't have surprised me. I nodded, almost imperceptibly, but the demon understood.

Wrath faced the messenger again. "Who paid you to open my letter, Francesco?"

The man's attention shot to me, searching for assistance. Wrath looked me over slowly again, waiting. Francesco made his choice. Now it was time to make mine.

"The prince asked you a simple question, Francesco. I'll repeat it once for your benefit and then I'll let him ask *his* way. And I'm sure you already know that won't be pleasant." I injected a ruthless charm into my tone like Wrath's, and the man flinched. "Who paid you to open his letter?"

Wrath kept staring at me. And even though his expression hadn't shifted in the slightest, I swore I almost sensed... approval. My stomach tightened and I fought the urge to be sick. If I'd done the right thing, I didn't think I'd feel so ill.

Francesco gurgled and scratched at the arm still pressed against his windpipe, his nails snagging on the demon's cuff. I hoped Wrath wouldn't strangle him to death before we got our answers.

The demon prince must have suddenly eased up on the pressure because Francesco gulped air like a fish yanked from the water. "Would you feel more comfortable talking with my blade at your throat?"

Francesco's golden skin blanched, but I noticed his hands fisting at his sides. Wrath was using his powers, and the messenger was getting mad. His chest rapidly rose and fell. "Do what you want, but I won't tell you a thing, demon pig."

"Really?" Wrath smiled, a flash of teeth that seemed to put Francesco on the verge of pissing himself despite his newfound rage. "Let's test that out, mortal. Who do you work for?"

"God." The man spit in the demon's face, and the glob slowly dripped to the ground. Wrath's blade was under the man's chin in an instant, the tip pressed hard enough for blood to slide along the metal. It looked like it took all of his willpower to not shove the dagger through the human and into the stone he leaned against, severing his spinal cord. Shadows seemed to pulse from Wrath. For a second, I wasn't sure if the demon of war would end him right there.

"Apologies, Francesco. But my patience is growing thin. Your actions sent four women to their deaths. Do not think I will not send you to yours just as brutally."

"Go ahead and kill me. I won't tell you anything." Francesco's head cracked against the wall when Wrath slammed him back. Blood dribbled from the human's mouth as he laughed, delighting in the violence. He smiled, teeth stained red with blood. "I hope you all rot in Hell."

I felt Wrath's rage turn from a simmer into a full boil. Soon, whether he meant to or not, he'd kill Francesco. And we'd lose our biggest chance at discovering who murdered my twin. I heard both Nonna's and Wrath's warnings singing through my head, but it didn't matter.

We were out of options and the anger raging around us was growing intense enough to burn. Wrath was about to snap. I pulled his emotions to me, using them as fuel for my truth spell as I clutched my sister's amulet.

"Did you open the letter?" I asked, my voice laced with magical command. Wrath's attention snapped to me and if I didn't know any better, I'd think fear entered his features.

Francesco nodded before answering. "Y-yes."

"Did anyone pay you to do it?"

"Yes."

"Who paid you, Francesco? Greed?"

"No."

"Tell me who paid you then."

"I do not know his name."

"Is he human?"

He lifted a shoulder. "He wore a hood. I didn't see his face."

"Did you tell him where Giulia would be the night she was murdered?"

He swallowed hard. "Yes."

"Did you meet with him today?"

"Yes."

My anger flared up. "What information did you give him?"

"A-a-another address. And a time to meet. I didn't have a name this time, I swear!"

"What time and address did you give him, Francesco?"

"Th-th-th-the Piazza Vigliena. M-m-midnight."

I looked at Wrath for further instruction, but he shook his head. The truth spell was nearly up. Blood spilled from the human's nose, and his eyes had turned glassy. If I pushed any more, he'd die. I glanced down, noticing my whole body trembled. Wrath stepped close to him.

"If you ever share my secrets again, I'll cut out your tongue. Then I'll carve out your heart. Have I made myself clear?" He gave Wrath the barest hint of a nod, careful to not slice his own throat. Sweat dampened his hairline. He really didn't look well. "Next time you're tasked with carrying a message for me, don't let curiosity or greed get the better of you. Those conditions often prove deadly."

I couldn't help but notice the trickle of urine streaming down the man's leg as the demon let his weapon drop. He stared from Wrath to me, a deep crease forming in his brow. He blinked slowly as if awakening from a dream. Or a nightmare.

"Who... who are you? Why am I here? P-please... don't hurt me. If you're looking for money, I don't have any." He turned out his pockets. There was nothing but lint. "See?"

My nausea from earlier was back and almost had me doubling over. I'd invaded his mind, and must have destroyed his recent memories. Dark magic demanded a price. And it didn't always come in the form someone expected. Guilt swirled through me. Just because I had power, didn't mean I should abuse it. "You're—"

Wrath flashed me a warning look. "You're Francesco Parelli Senior, and you're on your way home. You had too much to drink. You better hurry before Angelica gets mad again. Do you remember the way?"

Francesco swiped at a tear and shook his head. He seemed so fragile now, so lost. And *I'd* done that to him. Not some demon, or horrible creature from Hell. Me. I'd broken the most important rule of this world. I'd taken his free will, and I'd bent it to mine.

Wrath turned Francesco toward the cathedral, handed him a coin purse, and whispered in his ear.

I stared at the demon's back, heart racing. Wrath could've easily left the man alone in his new hell, but didn't. Just like he could have easily demanded I trade my soul in exchange for justice for my twin. He knew what I wanted and what I'd be willing to give up for it, and had asked for nothing. I didn't think there was mercy in Hell. But maybe I was wrong.

Wrath gritted his teeth. "What?"

"You could have killed him."

"Don't. I beat him and you stole his freedom of choice. His memories will eventually return, but that piece of your soul will not. I would have gotten our information without magic. There's an old saying about fools rushing in where angels fear to tread. From now on, I suggest you heed the warning. Come on." He walked deeper into the shadows. "We need to get to Quattro Canti."

If he didn't want to discuss the forbidden magic I used to get our information, that was fine with me. I already felt like my skin was crawling with grave worms. "Why?"

"The real messenger is waiting for us there."

TWENTY-NINE

Before we waltzed into the middle of the baroque square, Wrath situated us in another crammed alley. He claimed it was to get a better idea of the layout, and any traps other demons—like Greed or Envy—might have set. He politely asked me to wait while he strode over to a young man with a scar carving a path through his right cheek. Since he asked nicely, I decided to agree... temporarily. Letting him go ahead afforded me an opportunity to observe him, and the new messenger, on my own.

The human was intriguing. His stunning combination of dark features and upswept eyes hinted at North African and Asian ancestry. He hadn't noticed me peering from the shadows nearby, but I saw him clearly enough.

He leaned against a building, digging imaginary dirt from shorn nails with a deadly looking blade. He projected a sense of boredom, but his gaze tracked the movements of everything around him with a predator's focus. Even the demon prince.

Wrath marched over without hesitation, and I was unfortunately a *little* too far away to make out their conversation. Judging from the amount of eye-rolling the human was doing, I imagined Wrath was lecturing about something. I quietly drifted closer.

"...suspects the truth, Anir. I'm sure the others will in time, too."

"Too late for regrets now," the human, Anir, said. His voice was familiar, I just couldn't place it. "With everything going on... it might be a good thing. I mean, you chose to do the ritual. Right? Is it really *that* bad?"

"She's a demon-blooded damned *witch*. What do you think?"

Were they talking about *me*? I curled my hands into fists, my nails creating little crescent moons in my palms. *He* was a high-handed, arrogant, no-good demon from Hell. But I wasn't harping on his less-than-appealing qualities, was I? No. *I* was mature enough to set them aside to work together to stop a murderer from slaughtering any more witches.

"Sounds like a lovely girl. Will you be properly introducing us? You've only got—"

Wrath yanked Anir up by his collar, his feet swinging a good inch or two off the ground. I sucked in a quiet breath. It didn't look like lifting a grown man caused any strain for the demon prince at all. "Finish that sentence, and I'll give the other side of your face a scar, too."

"Apologies. Did I strike a nerve?" Anir held up his hands in mock surrender, not bothering to hide his grin. It held no fear and little humor. I decided if I wasn't so aggravated, I might like him. He was either very brave or very foolish to taunt the demon of war. "Don't get pissy. Right now it's only temporary. And she's—"

"Behind us." Wrath dropped the human and he gracefully caught himself from stumbling. "Emilia, this is Anir, my most trusted associate. He knows who agreed to marry Pride next."

I slipped out from the shadows and inspected the young man. "You were there the night I was attacked by the Viperidae."

"Yes." Anir seemed unsure of what else he could or couldn't share.

I turned to Wrath. "He's human."

"You're very astute."

I took a deep breath and counted until the urge to send him back to the bone circle passed. "What I meant is, if you have a human as your associate, why can't he be your anchor? If something were to happen to me, you'd be all right."

Wrath opened his mouth, then shut it. I raised a brow, waiting.

"Anir no longer claims the human world as his, therefore, he cannot provide the same . . . benefits you can."

Anir snorted, and quickly tried to choke the rest of his laughter down when Wrath turned his blazing glare on him. "That's certainly one way of looking at it."

"What's he talking about?" I asked, staring hard at the demon. "What aren't you telling me?"

Wrath gave me a look that said "a good many things," but didn't bother answering aloud. Instead he said, "Anir was just leaving. He was waiting to see if the robed figure arrived, but they never showed up. Now he's got House business to tend to back home."

"Who's the poor girl?"

"Valentina Rossi."

My whole body went numb as I let that information sink in. Valentina was Claudia's cousin. If anyone would want to readily agree to become the Queen of Hell, Valentina would take up that shadowy mantle with pride. She wasn't bad; she just seemed regal and meant for a role larger than a weaver on our little island. I wasn't surprised she'd be intrigued by a deal with the devil.

I started for her neighborhood. We had to warn her before it was too late.

Wrath stepped into my path, halting my steps. "What?"

"I know her."

"And?" he pressed.

"I'm wondering why he's choosing witches with ties to dark magic."

"Well," Anir said, "that's because the—"

Wrath cut him off. "Time to go."

As he glanced between the demon prince and me, Anir's smile was that of a wolf who'd found a squiggling snack it wanted to shove down its throat. "Actually, I'd rather stay here for a while. Demon weddings are not for the faint of heart. Plus, you'll need some extra eyes and ears when you speak to the girl. Maybe the robed figure will follow us."

He winked at me like we were the oldest of friends sharing a secret. Wrath caught the look and stared until his "associate" shrugged and started walking across the square. I waited until he was out of earshot before turning to Wrath.

"Are you going to try and convince Valentina to go to the underworld with you?"

"I swore I wouldn't do anything but offer the bargain. And I will keep my word. However, once we get her to safety, I'd like to see if she'd be willing to help us draw out the murderer."

"You'd like to use her as bait."

"Yes. Someone is doing their best to ensure Pride doesn't break the curse. I intend to discover who and why before anyone else dies. Then I'll offer a bit of retribution of my own."

I shivered. It wasn't exactly what I was expecting him to say, but I appreciated his honesty. "I know Valentina's family very well. I'm going to tell her to decline Pride's bargain," I admitted. "I hope you understand."

Wrath's gaze clashed with mine. "Do what you must. The final decision will be up to her."

While we hurried to Valentina's home, Anir told me about his life prior to leaving this world for what he called the Kingdom of the Wicked. He was the only child of a Tunisian father and Chinese mother—and had been playing in a nearby olive tree during the brutal slaying of his parents. His father had witnessed a crime and was going to tell authorities what he saw. Before he could do that, they were killed.

Anir said the scar came later, once he'd grown into the sort of young man others feared. Wrath found him traveling through South America, fighting in underground rings, bruised and bloodied. Some battles were a fight to the death and paid handsomely. Anir was a reigning champion for more than a year when he'd been offered employment in House Wrath.

I stopped listening to them bicker over how many years passed—apparently time moved differently in the demon realms—as we turned down the next street and slipped into a darker, narrower alleyway. A strange tug I'd felt before took control of my senses, drawing me down a second side street.

I glanced around, recognizing the neighborhood, and a terrible feeling settled in. I took a few more steps and stopped, unsurprised by the body. I'd grown suspicious before we'd rounded the corner, and the slumped silhouette was all the confirmation I'd needed.

I scanned the area.

Laundry hung from one crammed building to the other over our heads, and snapped in the breeze like teeth. It might've stricken fear into my heart before, but now it seemed like the perfect cover for a crime. There was no evidence. Nothing to waste time sorting through. It was a targeted job—the killer had gotten in and out, leaving nothing but the body behind.

Wrath abruptly stopped walking.

Anir noticed the victim a moment before tripping over her. He shot the demon an irritated look, and sidestepped a growing lake of blood. "Next time, a little warning would be nice."

"A little less insubordination might make me more amenable to common courtesy in the future."

Anir narrowed his dark eyes. The movement made the scar on his cheek stand out more. Wrath went to step around the body when his associate yanked him to a halt. I watched it all happen as if the scene was playing out on a stage, far from where I actually stood. I couldn't believe another body lay brutalized at our feet. Bile slowly rose. Wrath seemed entirely unaffected, as if coming across maimed bodies was part of his daily life.

The demon turned on his heel, gaze locked onto the human's hand. "What?"

Anir jabbed a finger toward the cooling body. "Aren't we going to send for help?"

"What do you propose we do? Call for human authorities?" Wrath didn't give Anir a chance to answer. "If you were them, would you take our word as good Samaritans and let us be on our way? Or would you look at your demon-forged blade, and my devilish demeanor, and toss us in some shit-filled cell and throw away the key?" Anir pursed his lips but didn't say anything. "Do you have any more noble suggestions, or can we leave?"

"Sometimes you really are a heartless bastard."

Wrath glanced down at me, his brows drawn together. "Are you all right?"

No, I was most certainly not all right. The body of another murder victim was lying at our feet. And I'd just gotten a look at her face. She was my best friend's cousin. I stared in horrified silence at her broken body. I still couldn't understand how this scene was real. My head spun with shock. Claudia wasn't close with her cousin, but would still feel her loss greatly. I shoved the heels of my hands into my eyes.

"Emilia?"

I shrugged away from Wrath's touch. "That is . . . was Valentina Rossi."

"I assumed as much."

I couldn't believe another witch had her heart ripped out. This brought the death toll up to five. I fought the bile searing its way up my throat again. Seeing something so horrific . . . I'd never get used to it.

Francesco, the treacherous human messenger, didn't know the name of the next bride, only the meeting location for Anir. And I doubted Anir would betray Wrath, which meant the information had gotten out some other way. I was nauseated for a new reason—I'd tortured a man for nothing.

"There must be a spy in the kingdom," Anir said, putting my thoughts into words.

I imagined he'd seen his share of horrible things, but he still looked shocked. He pulled his dark hair back, and tied it with a string of leather he ripped from his wrist.

Wrath paced around the alley, careful to avoid stepping in the blood. I averted my gaze from the gore. We needed to send word to the authorities. Valentina couldn't just lay there, cold and alone. The demon stopped close to where I stood, shielding my view of the body. "Which means one of my brothers *is* responsible. Somehow, some way."

My earlier encounter with his brothers sprang to mind. "Greed and Envy are both here."

Wrath shook his head. "Envy wouldn't chance a fight with me. Greed . . . I still can't see him jeopardizing his House. Not after he's built a formidable stronghold."

"Either way, the implications of a betrayal within the Seven . . . forget the curse, your highness," Anir said. "Personal feelings about witches aside, finish the marriage bond with Emilia and secure your own House before war comes. You'll need your powers at their fullest. Whoever is organizing this must have killed Pride's wife."

It felt like I'd been drenched in an ice bath. "What marriage bond?"

Anir missed the note of panic in my voice. "The one you started when you bound the prince to you."

Wrath stopped moving. Stopped breathing as I gaped in horror. Time seemed to freeze as I silently repeated what Anir said. I wanted to shout that it wasn't true, but Wrath's reaction said otherwise. The demon prince didn't break my stare. "How?"

"Leave us." Wrath barely spoke above a whisper, but Anir jumped to obey the command. Once he was gone, the demon nodded toward our matching tattoos. "Your protection charm wasn't a bond of protection like a guardian to their ward. The translation of *aevitas ligati* means 'bound forever' as in holy matrimony. It wasn't needed for the summoning to be successful."

"Are we . . . are you saying we're *betrothed*?" I waited, heart pounding, but Wrath said nothing. He didn't need to. The truth was there in his eyes. He'd known all along what I'd done. No wonder he'd looked so horrified that night. I'd basically ripped him from Hell, and forced him into a betrothal. Forever. "When were you going to tell me?"

His voice came out soft. "This doesn't change anything..."

"Everything's changed." A violent shudder tore through me as the demon continued to hold my unflinching gaze. This was all too much. The body of my best friend's cousin. My accidental engagement to Wrath. "What happens if I don't want to marry you? Will you force me to rule beside you in Hell?"

"Emilia..."

"Don't you *dare*." I shook my head. "Will I be forced to go there?"

"No."

Right. Demon laws were based on civility. Forcing someone into marriage probably broke all of their strangely rigid rules. But I bet he'd fashion a wicked bargain for me and make it so good, so tempting, I'd never say no. Especially if the marriage bond helped give him more power like Anir claimed it would. I locked my hand at my side.

"What did Anir mean by securing your House before there's war?"

A muscle in his jaw ticked. "I cannot share that information with you."

"Then we're through." I clutched my sister's amulet. "*Te libero.* I release you from whatever bond we have. When I marry, it will be for love. Not love of power or whatever other depraved thing you desire. And love is something you soulless, despicable creatures know *nothing* about!"

If he called out to me, or flinched, I wouldn't know. I turned and fled as far from the demon prince and the newest murder victim as I could. I wanted nothing more to do with the cursed creatures who'd brought this suffering on my family and my city.

From this point forward, I'd find out who murdered my sister on my own.

And Wrath could simply crawl back to Hell and rot with the rest of them.

THIRTY

I sat at a table facing the sea, sipping water with a slice of lemon. I'd left an anonymous note for the police with the location of Valentina's body, and still hadn't gotten over the horror of the night. I wanted to rush to Claudia's, but had to wait until the police told her cousin's family first. If they were already mourning when the authorities showed up, they'd start asking questions. Waiting invited all sorts of thoughts I didn't want to think about. Not now, or ever.

I couldn't believe I'd been so stupid as to accidentally betroth myself to Wrath, and he hadn't let the secret slip sooner. He must have absolutely loathed it. Especially with what Anir said about him hating witches. I fought the urge to bury my face in my hands. Knowing that he was fully aware of my error while I'd thought I was in control... it was humiliating. I didn't want to consider other missteps I'd taken that he'd been too polite to point out.

As soon as I'd tipped off the police, I'd realized I had nowhere to go. I couldn't go back home and put my family at risk. And while I *could* stay at the palace with Wrath, I needed time and space to sort out my thoughts and feelings. A lot happened in a short amount of time. Two more murders. A secret fiancé from Hell.

Nonna's attack. My stolen amulet. The Viperidae. It seemed the punches kept on getting thrown, and I was getting battered and bruised in the process.

The harder I clutched at normalcy, the more my world spun into chaos. Since I refused to see Wrath again for the moment, I decided to push everything out of my head and continue searching for answers in Vittoria's death by myself. If I could solve my sister's murder, I could prevent anyone else from dying. Every time I tried putting myself in Vittoria's shoes, I kept coming back to her diary. It didn't give up as many secrets as I'd hoped. And the ones it did reveal were still cryptic enough to keep me guessing.

I was going over a mental list of tasks to accomplish when the seat across from me was pulled out. Wrath dropped into it, eyeing me warily. I stared back at him for a few moments. Neither of us said anything. It seemed like my almost-husband was giving me time to collect myself. Or maybe he was waiting for me to banish him back to the bone circle again.

I took a few deep breaths.

"How did you know where I was?" He gave me a long, measured look, then glanced pointedly at the tattoo on my arm. I was definitely going to kill him. "You said you could only find me if I accepted the blood trade. You never mentioned the tattoo."

"If I told you the ink was part of a marriage bond, you would have immediately run. I needed you to have time to trust me."

I went to argue, but shut my mouth. It was true. If I'd known what the tattoo meant the first night I'd summoned him, I would have sent him straight back to his realm. "Trust is usually earned because both parties are honest."

"I have not lied to you."

I loosened a breath. "Not technically, no."

A waitress came out and cheerfully recited the menu. Wrath seemed skeptical, but let me do the ordering without complaint. Thirty minutes of strained silence later, she brought out our food. Wrath considered it as if it were a complicated equation he was sorting out.

One steaming plate of scampi, some arancini, a platter of antipasto—stacked with prosciutto, peperoncini, soppressata, provolone, marinated olives, and artichokes tossed with oil, vinegar, oregano, and basil—and a basket of grilled bread graced our little table.

I kept waiting for the demon to pull the waitress aside and ask for warmed blood or raw innards, but he seemed content with my choices and I certainly wasn't going to be the one to put the idea of uncooked offal in his head.

Wrath did surprise me by ordering a pitcher of red wine with orange slices, and poured a generous amount for each of us. I sipped my wine, enjoying the sweetness of it despite myself. I wanted to escape from my dark thoughts for a while, and the dinner and wine were helping. I hadn't slept all night and it felt good to just collect myself and regroup. Wrath piled a plate with food, and slid it in front of me before serving himself. It took all of my concentration to not topple out of my chair from the shock.

He caught my eye and scowled. "Good manners are hard to break, no matter how unpleasant the company I'm forced to keep. Plus, you served me the dessert. It's only fair to return the favor."

I smiled, which seemed to rankle him more, and tucked into my food.

After a few minutes of watching him poking around at the scampi, I skewered one with my fork and held it out to him. His suspicion deepened. "What are you doing?"

"This is langostino. It's like a baby lobster. I'm pretty sure you'll like it. Unless you're afraid..."

Wrath accepted the shellfish as if in challenge. He must have enjoyed it, because his focus shifted to his plate and he didn't look up again until he'd sampled a bit of everything.

While he experienced the wonder of human food, I ate my scampi, enjoying the fresh lemon they'd used to cut the richness of the butter. Theirs was a bit heavier with citrus than ours, and I decided to experiment one day soon.

Maybe if I sliced a lemon in half, and grilled it facedown—

I paused, fork to mouth. I'd been enjoying myself so much I almost forgot the reason I was sitting there, with one of the Malvagi, eating. A month. My twin had been gone for a little more than a month, and I was daydreaming about recipes for Sea & Vine while in the company of our worst enemy. The food turned to stone in my stomach.

I pushed my plate away, no longer hungry.

Wrath watched me in a way a human might study a fly buzzing over their dinner. "Experiencing a moral dilemma, witch?"

I couldn't muster an ounce of anger or annoyance. A hard blade of truth carved into me; I had no idea what I was doing. I was pretty sure my sister had summoned a demon, but didn't know which one. I knew about the Horn of Hades, but didn't know how we came to be the keepers of it.

Then there were the cryptic clues in Vittoria's diary about her ability to hear magical objects, and the possibility of the first book of spells being in this world. I knew my sister agreed to become the devil's bride, but still hadn't figured out *why* she'd made that awful choice, or why she didn't confide in me or our grandmother.

I had more questions than answers, and no one I could fully

trust. Nonna almost died because of my quest for justice, and I refused to put anyone else in my family in danger by going to them for anything related to the murder. While Wrath might have saved me, he was a prince of Hell, and even though he'd vowed to not force a witch into a bargain, I still didn't know how or why he was picked for this mission.

I leaned forward and dropped my voice. "I want to know everything about the curse."

I stared at him, and his gold eyes—speckled with black—gazed back. "Have you considered moving in with me until we find the murderer?"

A most unexpected deflection. "I have."

"Where are your belongings?"

"At home."

He swirled his wine around, and I wondered what, exactly, he was thinking. "Would you like me to escort you there while you retrieve them?"

"I haven't told you what I've decided." I eyed him. "And I want you to answer my question. If Pride is the one who's cursed, how does that affect you?"

"We should go back to the palace, and speak there."

"Not until you give me some answers."

Wrath looked like he was considering different ways to string me up using my innards. "I will. Later."

"Now." I refused to budge on this. He stared up at the sky and I wondered, if he was praying, why he hadn't glanced down instead.

"Fine. If I answer your questions, will you agree to stay in the palace?"

"No. But it will help me decide. How about that?"

He drew in a long breath and slowly released it. I waited. After fighting some inner battle, I saw the exact moment he decided to confide in me.

"In order for the curse to be fully broken, a consort needs to sit on the throne and help rule House Pride."

"Anir said the last consort was murdered. How?"

"Her heart was torn from her chest." He looked at me, but I had a feeling he wasn't really seeing me anymore. "Along with a few of her royal ladies."

"Did the First Witch really curse Pride?"

"Yes."

I allowed that information to settle in with all of the other tales I'd convinced myself were just stories. La Prima Strega was ancient—she'd begun the first line of witches. Or so the old stories went. Supposedly, she was the source of our power and belonged only to herself. No light magic, no dark magic. Just raw power slightly diluted from the goddess who'd birthed her. She predated human La Vecchia Religione—and the Old Religion was *old*.

At times La Prima was idolized, and at others, feared. Daughter of the sun goddess and a demon, she was created as the perfect balance between light and dark. We were told she was immortal, but I'd never seen her and didn't know anyone else who had, either. I always believed she was no more than a creation myth or legend.

"Why did she curse him?"

Wrath hesitated. "It was punishment for what she thought happened between her firstborn and him."

I sat up straighter. Claudia had mentioned this. "So, what, he stole her soul and La Prima took her vengeance?"

"Witches would believe that, wouldn't they?" Wrath scoffed.

"Pride didn't steal anything. He didn't have to. Her daughter willingly chose to wed him. They fell in love, despite who they were."

I thought about what Nonna had started telling me about *Stelle Streghe*, about how they were tasked with being guardians of the Wicked. "She was a star witch?"

Wrath nodded. "She was meant to be a guardian between realms—think of them as wardens of the prison of damnation. Her daughter should have known better, she was supposed to be a soldier first. La Prima, as you call her, commanded her daughter to give up her throne, and return to the coven, but she refused. The First Witch used the darkest kind of magic to remove her daughter's power and banished her from the coven. It had unforeseen effects for other witches, too. It's why some give birth to human daughters."

I mentally sorted out the story. "What you're saying is..."

True. I stared at him. Our whole lives we'd been told stories about the Wicked, and their lies. Yet Wrath couldn't directly lie to me because of the summoning magic. I'd tested it and knew it was a fact. What he was saying, no matter how impossible it sounded, had to be true.

Or at least he believed it was.

"Why are you helping him break the curse? If he's trapped in the underworld, I don't see why that concerns you or any other prince."

"Several human years ago, something fractured the gates of Hell. We'd been told it was part of a prophecy. Pride, being who he is, laughed it off. Then his beloved wife was murdered. His powers dampened. He was trapped in Hell, and lesser demons began testing us by trying to slip through cracks in the gates."

Aside from the curse, I couldn't believe Hell's second biggest problem was a rickety old door. I squinted at Wrath. I had a growing suspicion he hadn't revealed the worst part. "And?"

"Creatures that don't feel like facing trials in the Portals of a Thousand Fears have slipped through. The gates are continuing to weaken, despite our best efforts. It's only a matter of time before they completely break. We've tried keeping them away, but some things have already arrived in this world."

"Such as?"

"A few lesser demons."

"The Viperidae?"

"Not likely. They are summoned."

It wasn't exactly comforting. Demons were starting to invade our world. And I had a terrible feeling it would get much worse before it got better. "Anything we should be concerned about in particular then?"

"*You* should be concerned about the Aper demon, for one."

"The...what?"

"Aper demon. Head of a boar, tusks of an elephant. Huge reptilian bodies, cleft hooves. Dumb as an ox, but they've got a particular fondness for witch blood. A thousand tiny teeth in double rows make them very accomplished with swiftly draining a body."

Wrath's growing smile was positively wicked as he glanced over my shoulder. A wet snuff near the base of my neck had me breaking an instant sweat. One hoof clattered on the cobblestones, followed by another. The ground vibrated beneath whatever had taken those two mammoth steps. A shadow fell across the table. Sweet goddess above, I *so* did not want to turn around.

"Whatever you do, witch, don't run."

THIRTY-ONE

There is no greater threat to a witch than a demon who craves her blood. Once its thirst has been provoked, it will relentlessly pursue the cause of its addiction, stopping only when the source has run dry. To ward against this dark energy, pin a sachet of dried yarrow inside your clothing during each new moon.

—*Notes from the di Carlo grimoire*

Wrath's warning came a second too late. When I wasn't focused on running for my life, I'd later wonder if it was intentional on his part. I hiked up my skirts and plunged into the twilight-colored streets, the sound of pursuit ringing all around me.

I charged down one narrow alley into the next, jumping over baskets of dried goods. I didn't look back for fear of losing momentum. There was no way I'd end up drained of blood because curiosity got the better of me. As I dodged past closed doors and ducked under laundry lines, the clattering of cloven footsteps behind me never faltered or slowed.

I wasn't just terrified for myself, I worried about any unsuspecting human unfortunate enough to be in my path as I led a hungry demon through the cramped quarters. I almost stumbled as reality crashed into me. A demon was chasing me through the streets of my city. Somehow it had breached the gates of Hell. And, if this was only the beginning . . . I couldn't finish the thought.

I knocked into an empty barrel, and threw it in the beast's path. My netherworldly attacker halted for all of a second before wood shattered. Not good. My witch blood gave me a little more strength than a human, but the creature tore through the barrel like paper.

My foot caught in a cobblestone, and I couldn't stop morbid curiosity from taking over as I caught myself against a building and tossed a glance over my shoulder. I was ready to freeze from unrelenting horror as Death cornered me, its maw open wide, ready to devour me bones and all, but nothing was there. I warily glanced around. No demon lurked behind fluttering clothing. No wet-nosed snuffs broke the silence. The complete and utter *unnatural* silence.

Blood and bones.

Chills erupted out of nowhere. Like the first night I'd heard the disembodied voice of an Umbra demon, all sounds of life vanished around me. I wasn't alone—I just couldn't see any danger coming. But I sensed it closing in—a claw-tipped hand reaching out in the dark. Demons must have the ability to cloak themselves with some sort of glamour. Which was just *perfect.*

I turned and ran as fast as I could, and bounced off a body that was ice cold to the touch. I fell and crab-walked backward, slowly dragging my gaze up at my destruction. Apparently I'd been wrong about the glamour. It hadn't been hiding at all—it just moved too fast for me to see it. It wasn't moving now. The Aper demon was everything Wrath described and worse. Its enormous head resembled a wild boar almost perfectly, except for its bright red eyes. Slits of black carved down the middle of the irises, reminding me of a cat straight out of Hell.

I squeezed my eyes shut. Counted to ten, then opened them again. The demon was really there, and it was even worse than the first time I looked at it.

Holy goddess.

Thick globs of black drool dripped down its muzzle as its teeth clicked in anticipation. Its breath smelled like a fetid swamp on a hot summer day. I pushed up onto unsteady legs, and slowly inched away from those vicious, snapping instruments of death. The demon followed.

Every instinct I had shouted for me to flee, but I refused to break eye contact with it. I had a feeling if I turned my back, it'd pounce. No matter what I had to do to survive, I would live to see my family again. The demon moved swiftly when I went to turn left, so I moved in the opposite direction.

We maintained that same slow dance until we were trapped down a dead end. On my right there was a thick steel door with a pawprint holding a stalk of something painted onto the metal. The Aper demon stood before it, snuffing the air. Bloodlust gleamed in its strange red eyes.

Finally remembering the moon-blessed chalk in my pocket, I slowly reached down. One second I was standing, the next I was on the ground with teeth snapping at my neck. Pain shot through me, but was eclipsed by a more immeditate threat. Thousands of teeth were ready to slurp my blood. Hot breath touched my skin, and a low whine from the demon followed. Panic set in. I wouldn't die like this. I couldn't.

I fought wildly, but the demon was too strong. It drew back, ready to sink its teeth in and then . . . gray sludge exploded from the beast.

A blade shot through where the demon's heart used to be, and shadows writhed like snakes from the wound. I cringed away, watching the dagger pull the shadows in and seemingly absorb the demon's life force. The point stopped just shy of piercing my chest. I held my breath, waiting for Death to defy whoever had stolen its prize and claim me anyway.

I looked up, not into Death's face, but the demon of war's.

Wrath yanked the dead behemoth away and tossed its carcass aside. He sheathed his demon-slaying dagger, then knelt down. His expression was as hard as his tone. Which was helpful—I needed something to focus on besides the overwhelming terror coursing through me.

"Lesson number one: when fighting a demon, always have some weapon at the ready. Whether it's spell chalk or a defensive charm. If you don't have defensive magic, now's the time to acquaint yourself with that part of your lineage. Demons are apex predators. They're faster and stronger than you. Their sole purpose is to kill, and they're very good at it."

I leaned against the building, panting, waiting for the trembling to pass. If Wrath hadn't gotten to me when he did, my family would have buried another child. Well, if there'd been anything left of me *to* bury. Tears pricked my eyes. I'd been forced into a game I knew nothing about and I was losing. Badly.

"Can you stand?"

I could barely breathe. But that had nothing to do with terror anymore, now I was ready to strike out. And I had my sights set on the demon prince looming above me. I maneuvered into a sitting position, and swatted his proffered hand away.

"What, are you my teacher now?"

"An opportunity to turn this into a teachable exercise arose on its own. Lessons were never part of our bargain, so you're welcome."

I stared up at him, speechless at the flash of concern he was too slow to hide. He'd genuinely been worried about me. I was so startled, I forgot to jab him back.

I waited another minute before standing. Wrath's gaze traveled over me a second time.

I glanced down at gelatinous gray globs that I assumed used to be innards of the demon. Now *I* smelled like a fetid swamp. *Fantastico*. I never thought I'd long for the days when stinking of garlic and onion were my biggest worries.

"Do you recognize that symbol?" He nodded toward the door with the pawprint.

"I..." I tried wiping demon sludge from my dress. "I need a minute."

"For what it's worth, I wouldn't have let the demon kill you. Maybe a slight nip."

"Comforting as ever."

I stepped up to his side and stared at the door. I'd been terrified over the Aper demon attack, angry with Wrath about the impromptu lesson, and now fear took residence in my thoughts once more. I had no idea which of his brothers would use a pawprint, and wasn't eager to find out.

"Is this pawprint Envy's House symbol?" I asked. Wrath shook his head. "Do any of your brothers require a stalk of wheat for their summonings?"

"I believe that's actually a fennel stalk."

I shook my head. I didn't want to know how he'd gleaned that from the crude symbol on the door. But it did force puzzle pieces together in my mind. I'd recently seen that symbol before, but couldn't recall when or where. Possibly somewhere in the city while we'd been wandering the streets. Or maybe in Vittoria's diary? She'd had plenty of sketches and strange symbols in the margins. I had barely slept and the last few days had taken their toll on my memory. Once we left here, I'd go straight home and grab the diary.

Wrath shot me a sidelong glance. "Want to see what's inside?"

I most definitely did not. I couldn't escape a slow, creeping feeling of dread. Maybe it was simply a coincidence that we ended up here, or maybe it was part of a larger, more sinister design. Either way, I felt like we were about to enter a lion's den, and I was as excited as a fawn knowingly being led to slaughter. I swallowed hard. "Yes."

Wrath shook his head once before shouldering the door open for us.

"Liar."

THIRTY-TWO

We walked into a large room that was filled with crates and fishing traps. Ropes hung from rusted nails on the wall. Wooden floors creaked with each of our steps. I wasn't normally prone to feeling uneasy about buildings, but there was something unsettling about the space. A slight, strange humming set my nerves further on edge. Dust motes swirled in the moonlight.

I hoped we'd caused the disturbance and some demons weren't lying in wait. I really didn't want to face any more creatures like the dead demon outside. Wrath was annoyingly unaffected. He strode through the room with the ease of knowing he was the most lethal predator. He inspected the fishing gear, and kicked at a rusty anchor that had been discarded near a back exit.

"It looks like this location hasn't been used in some time," he said.

"Do you believe it was just a coincidence that the Aper demon led me here?"

He lifted a shoulder. "Anything look familiar?"

"I…"

I scanned the space. Fishing nets, ropes, various hooks in

strange shapes nailed to the far wall, and wire traps. Everything looked average. Except for that sensation I couldn't name. It felt familiar in a way. I slowly walked around the perimeter, pausing at each piece of fishing gear. There had to be some reason we ended up here. And I was so close to figuring it out...

I picked up a rusted hook and let it fall back against the wall. It was perfectly ordinary.

I blew out a breath. I didn't want to waste time, touching each old hook. Especially when I might possibly have a much better clue waiting for me at home in Vittoria's diary. Still...I couldn't quiet the insistent tug in my center. I did another sweep of the room, but nothing stood out. It seemed that the Aper demon attack and this empty building were unrelated.

"Well?" Wrath asked. "Do you recognize anything?"

Nothing aside from the symbol I was *almost* certain my sister had sketched in her diary. I shook my head, wanting to hurry to my house to retrieve it. "No."

"Very well. Let's go home."

I didn't point out that his stolen, ruined palace was not my home and never would be.

"I have to go collect my things," I said. "I'll meet you there soon. You should dispose of the demon outside."

Before he could argue, I slipped out the door and headed to my house.

I slumped against the doorframe in my bedroom and surveyed the carnage. Floorboards were ripped up and broken. Wooden splinters littered the little knotted rug Nonna made for me and

Vittoria when we were little. Feathers floated on the breeze blowing in from the shattered window. Someone had taken out *a lot* of aggression on my mattress.

Or something. Wrath said princes of Hell had to be invited into a mortal's home, but, as I'd recently discovered, that rule didn't hold true for *all* demons. Lower-caste creatures of Hell seemed to do as they pleased. The Umbra slipped beyond our protection charms, and no formal invitation had been sent to it. Wrath also mentioned magic didn't work on them the same way it did on corporeal beings, so it was likely more an issue with that than our protection charms.

Which still wasn't comforting.

Without even fully walking into the room I knew my sister's diary was long gone, taking her many secrets with it. An Umbra demon was the likely perpetrator of this theft. And that brought Greed back to the top of my suspect list. He was the only prince of Hell thus far that I knew used them to do his bidding.

I wondered about those nights I thought I'd felt someone watching as I drifted into sleep. It was unsettling and invasive, having private moments become a spectacle for prying eyes. All the times I'd gotten dressed, or collapsed in grief. Emotions raw and unchecked because I thought I'd been alone. I glanced out the window, wondering if someone was out there now, watching this latest horror unfold.

I rubbed my hands over my arms, trying to shake the sudden chills. If my bedroom wasn't on the second floor, and if I didn't travel through the rest of the house to get here, I'd think the entire place had been ransacked. Aside from my trashed bedroom, the rest of our home was untouched. And so were my family members. Somehow Nonna must not have heard anything unusual, because she was napping peacefully in her bedroom on the lower level. Everyone else was at Sea & Vine until they completed dinner service. Thank the goddess.

Just to put my mind at ease, I made my way across the debris, and peered into Vittoria's old hiding place. The grimoire pages I'd tucked back in there after I'd summoned Wrath were torn to shreds. Her perfumes smashed. The love notes were missing, along with her diary.

A tear hit the floor. Followed by another. I felt like I was falling, too. Slipping between cracks and losing myself to grief all over again. Seeing Vittoria's things smashed and broken... it was all too much.

I crossed the remnants of what used to be our safe haven, and collapsed onto what was left of my bed. It sank with my weight, sitting cockeyed and wrong. Like everything else in my world.

A sob tore loose. The harder I tried fighting it, the more uncontrollable my sobbing became. How foolish to think I had nothing left to lose. The demons went and proved me wrong. Even if I put our room back together, it would never be the same again.

My sister's belongings and everything she'd loved had been destroyed.

Vittoria had finally been erased from my world. And now I wasn't sure I knew how to go on. I laid on my side and tucked my knees up to my chin and cried. I didn't care if there was an incorporeal demon watching. I didn't care if there was a witch hunter, or prince of Hell, or sadistic human monster delighting in my pain. I lost something I'd never regain, and I mourned.

If the Aper demon was only a small taste of what was to come, my city would spend many nights crying over stolen loved ones. I felt so helpless. So lost and alone. How could I stop such powerful beings? The whole situation seemed impossibly hopeless. I'd been deluding myself into thinking I stood a chance at solving the murders, and saving other lives. I wanted to help, but it wasn't enough. I heaved and hiccupped until I had nothing left. I hated how altered this world had become.

It took a little more time, but I finally dried my tears. The demons stole my sister's life, and would keep taking and taking until they were stopped. So what if I didn't have all the answers? I would do everything I could to stop the gates of Hell from opening. I'd had enough.

I pushed myself up, clutched at my anger, and went to grab my pen and pot of ink. I wrote out a quick note to my family, telling them I loved them, and promised I'd be fine, but I couldn't stay here anymore. I vowed to keep them safe, no matter what.

No one else I loved would be taken from me.

I'd use the darkest of magic to be certain of it.

"How are you doing?" I asked Claudia. Her face was splotchy and her eyes were swollen.

"Please, come in." She opened the door to her home and I stepped inside. The curtains were all drawn tightly. Glittery black candles burned and flickered on almost every surface, giving off a peppery scent. An altar piled with animal bones and bunches of dried herbs adorned the top of a small chest in the sitting room. A mirror lay against the wall behind it, reflecting the macabre scene back at me. I'd almost forgotten poor Valentina had been murdered.

It felt like a year ago, not just a day.

"Are you all right?"

"I'm not sure. I feel a strange mixture of emotions." Claudia's voice was quiet. She motioned for us to sit on a threadbare sofa before the altar of mourning. "At first I felt like someone had ripped out my heart, too. Then I felt numb. And now..." she sniffled, shook her head. She wouldn't meet my gaze.

"Now you want vengeance."

She glanced up sharply, and swiped at her nose. "Is that wrong?"

"No. I used to think it was, but not anymore." I swiveled on the cushion and clutched her hands. "Do you have a spell to make a ward that's powerful enough to kill a demon if it tries crossing it?"

Claudia's grip on me tightened and she set her jaw. "I believe so."

"Even an invisible one?"

"Yes."

"Good," I said. "I want you to cast a ward around your home immediately, and mine if you can, too. Do you need blood for the spell?" She dropped her gaze again and nodded. I figured as much. Dark magic demanded payment. I let go of her hands and rolled back one of the sheer sleeves on my blouse. "I'll just need a knife, two vials, some lavender oil, and a bandage."

"Emilia, you can't—"

"I can," I said, firmly. "I want to help any way I can."

"All right." My friend pushed herself to her feet. Her sadness had been replaced by something sharper, angrier. Something I recognized in myself now, too. "I'll fetch the blade."

THIRTY-THREE

Wrath didn't utter one word when I barged into his stolen palace and marched up the stairs. I imagined he sensed my raging emotions and was courteous enough to give me a wide berth.

He watched in silence, one annoying brow raised, as I tugged at the bandage on my arm and disappeared from view. On the third floor, down the end of an elegant hallway, I found a room that was five times the size of the bedroom I'd shared with Vittoria.

I should have probably hated it for being so beautiful, but couldn't.

It had ice blue walls with a sunshine-colored tapestry and a four-poster bed—smack in the middle—that I could roll across at least three times and not topple off of. A tiled bathing chamber with a sunken tub and floor-length mirror was attached, and even with a few cracks and chips, I decided it would definitely do.

Though, given the newness of the bed and tapestry, maybe I hadn't been the first person to think I'd like this room. I wanted to be annoyed that Wrath guessed right, but was exhausted and didn't have the capacity to feel much of anything. It had been a long terrible day.

I unpacked my own blanket, flicked it across the mattress, and smoothed it down. I tossed the pillow on next, and even though it wasn't much, it felt a little more like home. Especially since home didn't feel like home after my room had been invaded and destroyed. Before I started crying again, I went into the bathing chamber and turned on the water.

After I scrubbed my face clean and brushed out my hair, I decided my next order of business was a nap. I walked into my room and halted. Wrath sprawled across my commandeered bed, one arm draped over his torso, the other bent behind his dark head.

His position was forced casual, but the sharpness of his gaze gave his tension away. He was dressed in black again, and looked like the kind of man who'd wear it from head to toe. I wondered who he planned on beating tonight, given his reasons for liking the color so much.

"Are you all right?"

I crossed my arms and gave him a flat look. "No."

He narrowed his eyes, his attention fixed on my bandage. "What happened?"

I lifted a shoulder. I wasn't in the mood to answer his questions. But I wanted him to answer some of mine. "Greed and Envy both want the Horn of Hades. You must want it, too. Why not take this half from me?"

Wrath didn't rise to the bait, but his expression hardened along with his tone. "Why don't you just ask the question you're really interested in knowing?"

"My sister's diary was stolen. Someone ripped our room apart and destroyed her things."

"And you believe I had something to do with it?" His eyes appraised me. "It's not just a diary, is it?"

"No." I blew out a frustrated breath. "She placed some locking spell on it, using demon magic. I managed to break it, but it didn't give me the answers I'd been looking for."

Wrath quietly considered the information I shared. It was a peace offering for snapping at him, and he looked like he understood that. "I would have helped you break the spell if you asked me to."

I crossed the room and flopped onto the bed next to him, ignoring the indignant glare he shot in my direction as he bounced in place. I was bone tired, and just wanted the day to be over. After the revelation about the gates of Hell weakening, my next priority was to find my amulet. If I had the whole Horn of Hades, I might be able to lock the gates before any other demons broke free. But I needed to get some sleep so I could think straight. "Do we have anything planned tonight?"

"Yes."

"Has someone else made a deal with Pride?"

He nodded. "Isabella Crisci."

"When do we leave?"

"Dusk."

I tugged the pillow out from behind him, stuffed it under my head, and closed my eyes. A solid thirty seconds of blessed silence passed before he poked me in the ribs. I cracked an eye. "Do that again, and I'll slap you with a containment spell."

"What are you doing?"

"Preparing for war. Now go away."

He muttered something under his breath I didn't catch. Nor did I care to. I hadn't been entirely sarcastic. I needed to be well rested and sharp to find my *cornicello*, and to prepare for whatever other hellish nightmare the evening would bring.

When I woke up several blissful hours later, Wrath was gone. Thank the stars. Sometimes, especially when I was exhausted, I had a tendency to roll around and talk in my sleep. Vittoria used to tease me endlessly, which was embarrassing enough, but it would have been painfully awkward if it happened in front of the demon prince.

I sat up and a blanket that had been carefully placed over me fell away. I glanced at it, frowning. I was almost positive I'd fallen asleep on top of it.

"Hello?"

I scanned the silent, empty room. Wrath wasn't lurking. Not that I expected him to be. It took a moment for me to realize why. It was almost dark outside, and he'd said we needed to leave at dusk. I hopped up from bed and raced down the stairs, yelling the demon's name.

All was as still as the catacombs.

"Blood and bones." The no-good prince left me to go speak to the witch on his own. I marched around the empty palace, seething. He should have woken me up. I had as much right to be there when he talked with Isabella as he did. Wrath obviously didn't want me to potentially dissuade her from accepting the devil's bargain. So much for being partners. I was so mad I could scream.

After the day I'd had, I needed to get my frustration out. I couldn't just sit around, waiting for someone else to make a move. Especially now that I felt invisible hands tick, tick, ticking away the time that remained before the gates of Hell broke entirely. I couldn't waste energy being angry. I had to go out and see if I could find my *cornicello.* I went back to my room and noticed a dress had been draped over a chair in the corner.

I picked it up. It was midnight black with gold roots sewn across the bodice, similar to the grimoire page I'd used to summon Wrath. Tiny serpents were also woven into the design. Exquisite didn't come close to describing it.

"Testa di cazzo." Only an asshole would think a pretty dress made up for a broken promise, though.

I slipped it on anyway. It suited my needs for tonight.

I whispered a prayer to the goddess of good fortune, and hoped she'd bless me with a little luck.

I didn't know where I was going, but I subtly held on to my sister's *cornicello* and followed a whisper of a feeling. It had worked when I'd needed to find Greed's gambling den, so I decided to think about my amulet and see what happened. I wasn't sure what I was sensing now, but I followed the feeling as it grew stronger.

I marched up steep streets clinging to cliffs and finally stopped to stare out at the sea. Multicolored fishing boats swayed just offshore.

It was peaceful, but I had no business stopping to admire the mundane world I no longer was a part of. Not that I'd ever really belonged. But before all of this, I could at least pretend.

I took a few steps past the cliff, and the whisper calling to me stopped. I retraced my path and it returned. I scanned the area, watching a bonfire as it started glowing below me. There was something here the magic wanted me to find. A shadowy group of people began gathering in a cove tucked into a space between two towering cliffs, mostly hidden from view. It was a nice night for a seaside party. I envied the people down there for their ignorance of all the creatures of the night.

I held Vittoria's *cornicello* in my fist and squeezed my eyes shut, silently commanding it to lead me to my own amulet. There was no time for parties or frivolity. I lifted my foot to start off again, but something wouldn't let me go.

I opened my eyes and glared down at the party. If my sister were alive, she'd be down there with them, dancing. I could almost picture her there now, swaying and laughing. Her arms thrown up to praise the full moon. I wanted her to be here so badly my eyes stung. I let go of her amulet and took a deep breath. Vittoria would have dragged me down there to dance and drink and live.

And now she was dead and I was standing up here, alone.

A powerful, glittering magic filled my veins. I was angrier than I'd been in a while. And maybe it was that fierce anger that made me decide to forget about finding my *cornicello.* There were twelve other witch families living secretly in Palermo. Any number of them could try and stop the demons from invading our world. And yet, no one had. Maybe I *would* be more like my twin. I'd dance and laugh and forget the world was a lonely, scary place for a few hours. There would still be nightmares to fight tomorrow and other battles to wage. Tonight I wanted to pretend things were normal.

Even if it was a lie. Everyone else seemed content to live in a fantasy world. They couldn't blame me for wanting to experience that for an hour, too. And who knows? Maybe if I found a way to release some stress I'd be able to think more clearly.

Decision made, I followed the steep, narrow path to the water and sounds of merriment. I ran my fingers over tall grass, taking careful steps down stairs carved into the cliffside.

In the distance, fishermen blew into seashell horns. The sea whispered, soft, fierce. Waves lapped the shore. Gulls cawed. Whispers followed me, taunted me, just out of earshot.

The goddess cried out in warning.

Caught up in my thoughts, I hadn't been listening to the signs. An overwhelming sense of fear crashed into me when my feet hit the sand, but by then it was too late.

I'd already reached the raging bonfire.

THIRTY-FOUR

Moon Daughter Rituals should be observed during each full moon. To release that which no longer serves you, you'll need a pale blue candle, bowl of water, pen, paper, and a handful of sage to burn.

—Notes from the di Carlo grimoire

It started innocently, like Pleasure took human form and dragged a cool finger down my spine, tracing little circles over my flushed skin. I lifted my arms and arched into the sensation. Happiness, pure, radiant, and all-consuming, filled me.

If I'd been angry a moment before, standing high up on the cliffs, it was a forgotten memory the second I walked across the sand. If I'd been worried about invading demons, I no longer could recall why. Now all I knew was bliss.

I was so preoccupied with happiness, I just wanted to dance; sway my hips and feel another body moving in time with mine. Rhythmic, joyful, unfettered. As if my desire summoned a dance partner, invisible hands roved across my bodice, down my sides, gripped my bottom.

I gasped. I didn't slap my bold partner. They'd given me what I wanted the second the thought entered my mind. And I *liked* it.

Music and laughter drummed all around. The beat was life. Enticing. It called to my most primal witch instincts. I moved without thought, giving myself over completely to nature and my senses. I spun away from my invisible dance partner, and my skirts and hair flew around.

The serpent and root dress I'd slipped on earlier reminded me of the wilderness—I tossed my head back and soaked up the dying rays of the sun. Maybe I'd left my body and was a cloud. It felt so good to just be free, to move and forget. Here, near the crackling fire and invisible dancing people, I didn't think about murders, or curses, or creatures of the underworld, and the devil's horns.

I didn't think about stolen amulets and diaries.

Dancing, down here on the beach, I only knew peace and joy and pleasure. I didn't need to worry about anything. I could stay here, drifting from one good sensation to the next, forever. He was coming for me. My king. My damnation. I don't know how I knew, but I did.

Balance. Light and dark. The sun and moon. Good and evil. A snake winding through a bed of wildflowers. Offering a taste of the most forbidden fruit. Scales of justice were tipped; a choice hanging there for me to decide. To right a wrong, or damn us all.

A tiny voice screamed in warning, this was all terribly *wrong,* but was silenced as music and movement swept around me, through me. Whispers grew louder, more frantic. I shoved them aside.

I must have kicked off my sandals, my soles slipped over warm sand, and I was overcome with the sensation of it. Everything felt so *good.* So intense. Like all my pleasure receptors had been spelled a hundred times their normal rate. I didn't know I was capable of so much *feeling*.

I wriggled my toes, laughing as grains of sand slipped between them, tickling and teasing. Someone handed me a glass of wine and I drank deeply. It tasted sweet, strong. Apples dipped in honey and blessed by the stars. It was one of the most delicious things I'd ever had. Vittoria would have loved it. I gulped more—maybe to forget, maybe because I wanted it.

Then my glass was gone and I was pulled into another dance.

I wanted to stay here for eternity, lost to these good feelings. And it felt like I had. Here I didn't have to feel grief. I didn't have to mourn. Here I could simply live.

Minutes passed, maybe hours or days; time had no meaning. I moved and swayed, closed my eyes and listened to the enchanting sounds of the water, the murmurs of voices that belonged to people I couldn't see. Those invisible hands from earlier became bold explorers, mapping the uncharted territory that was my body. They slid down, lower...

"Remember." A strange voice whispered to me. *"Inferus sicut superus."*

As above, so below. There was a memory buried there, skirting the outside of my mind.

Something piercing in my arm, cold and sharp, jolted me from my trance. My eyes flew open. Fear reached icy tendrils out to me again, but just as quickly as it happened, it was gone. Replaced with pleasure. Rapture. Complete and total freedom from all thought. I liked it there, deep in a cocoon of oblivion.

Then I saw him.

He cut through the crowded beach like a blade, his anger setting the peaceful joy ablaze. My invisible dance partner vanished, but I hardly noticed. There was a much more interesting creature stalking closer. The most terrifying and feral. Vaguely, I felt I should run in the other direction. That he was a carnivorous beast and I was a lamb, stumbling ever closer to danger. Amidst a group of shadowy figures, he burned brightly—the only form that wasn't hidden.

I thought about fire, about plumes of smoke and flames licking the air. Which made me think about dragging my tongue over *him*, seeing if he was as hot as the energy steaming off him. Drums beat. My heart pounded. I wanted to experience pleasure on all levels.

I wanted a spell to bottle this feeling and sip from it whenever I desired.

Magic was life and life was made by making love and feeling good and our bodies constantly tried to remind us to *live*. I'd spent the last several weeks consumed by death and destruction—I needed balance. I deserved it. As above, so below.

He stopped before me, his expression wary. "Time to go, witch."

Hardly. I twirled away, but he grabbed my hand, spinning me back until I crashed against his body. Heat poured off him, enveloped me. I had the strangest feeling I should hate it. "Hello, demon. Let's dance."

"You need to get out of here. Immediately."

"Why?"

"Because you're tearing your clothes off and looking at me like mine are next."

I glanced down and laughed in surprise. I was *trying* to undo the stays of my bodice, but he thwarted my efforts. His tattooed hand covered mine. I looked up at him, my brow crinkled. "Don't you want to see me naked?"

"I have."

"And?"

"If you still want to rip your clothes off when we get home, we can discuss it then."

A blast of ice on my arm doused flames of desire. Then they were back with a vengeance. I gave up trying to remove my dress and focused on him. I went for the button on his trousers, and he deftly moved back. He was a difficult creature. I placed my hands on his chest and dragged them down instead. Power thrummed beneath my touch. Responded to me. It was intoxicating.

"For the living embodiment of sin, you aren't very sinful."

I tugged him close. Drums beat. Passion stirred. He closed his eyes. I pressed closer, and he didn't stop me this time. The music grew sultry. I swayed automatically against him. I wanted him to swing me up into his arms, and dance us across the sky.

The stubborn demon didn't move.

"Why won't you touch me?" I ran my thumb across the seam of his lips and he gently bit down, holding my finger in place. If he meant it as a deterrent, it wasn't working. He opened his eyes and I was struck by the beauty of them. "Is it because I'm a witch?"

He trailed big hands down my arms. I leaned in, waiting for him to crush his lips against mine. In the far reaches of my mind, I recalled him saying one day I'd beg him to kiss me. That I'd love it or loathe it, but still crave it. He hadn't been wrong. I hated him... for denying me. The anticipation was building to a point that was almost painful. When he finally dragged his hands to my wrists, instead of pulling me closer, he gently pushed me back, holding me at arm's length.

"There are many reasons. One of which is because you're under my brother's influence." He glanced over my shoulder, his expression forbidding. "Lust."

Intrigued, I slowly turned. Desire scorched every last sentient thought I had. The Prince of Lust was golden skinned, dark haired, and had a body Michelangelo probably used as inspiration for his sculptures. I didn't just want him, I *needed* him. I craved his attention as much as I longed for his touch.

"Hello, Signorina di Carlo. You're absolutely delicious, aren't you?"

His voice was unearthly. Pleasure mixed with pain. I was enraptured and terrified. Ice prickled my arm. The same insistent feeling that kept haunting me. It dulled my emotions long enough for me to fully grasp the horror of what was happening. What he was doing.

Lust was using his influence on me. And it was worse than Envy by far. He made me feel so good, so happy, I forgot who I was. What I wanted. And what I hated above all. Or maybe I didn't entirely forget my hatred, but I certainly didn't care. Passionate flames razed my conscious thought, and I was once again gripped by pure animalistic need. I had a lust for life, for fun, for...

The demon prince circled me. He wore an unbuttoned, silver suit jacket—without a shirt—and matching trousers that hung so low on his hips, I could die. A circlet of flames sat on his head. His eyes were charcoal. Penetrating. In them I saw a bottomless pool of desire. I wanted to tear off my clothes and dive in.

I started moving toward him, but someone grabbed me around the waist. I stopped trying to escape, focusing instead on the warmth behind me. The solid frame. The power. I'd almost forgotten how much I wanted *him*.

Lust must have sensed my shifting emotions. He looked from me to his brother, his expression indescribable. He started speaking, but I was distracted by too many sensations. His voice, the warm breeze, the scent of Wrath, and the friction of his strong arms as he held me in place. Lust kept talking. My mind tried to focus on his words, not the shape of his lips.

He stepped close to where we stood. Wrath's arms were bands of steel around me. "Do you know what that means, witch?" I drew my brows together. His smile was crafted of beautiful nightmares. "Go, dance. Enjoy the party. This is a practice round before the Feast of the Wolf."

A familiar scent wafted toward me, beckoning. Lavender and white sage. Vittoria! She was here... if I left to go dancing I'd find—

Stop, the same voice whispered in the back of my head. It was a trick. Vittoria was dead.

"No."

I was as startled by my refusal as Lust was. His expression turned from desire to fury.

He snapped his fingers and his influence over me vanished. My knees buckled. If Wrath wasn't holding me, I would have fallen. All the happiness and bliss I'd felt were ripped away, leaving me hollow and trembling. Terror coursed through me. What he'd done... the things I'd felt. I wanted to claw my skin off. Or maybe I wanted to sink my nails into him, the creature who'd violated my emotions. Who made me forget and want things I should fear. The wine I'd had suddenly made a reappearance; I bent over, hurling everything up. Wrath didn't let go.

"Why are you here?" Wrath's voice was quiet, low. A chill slid down my spine.

"To deliver a message, dear brother. You're needed at home. Immediately." His gaze cut to me. "Don't worry. I'll watch over your little friend. I have much to tell her. Stories of demons and witches. Villains and heroes. Curses and a king's vengeance."

"No." My fingers dug into Wrath's forearm. "P-please."

I don't know if it was the way my voice broke, or if he'd been waiting for an opportunity for his own reasons, but one second Wrath had me in his arms, and the next I was behind him and his blade was buried deep in Lust's chest. Bones crunched. He twisted the dagger up, dark blood poured from the wound.

"Don't come back here again. I'll go home when I'm ready." He yanked the dagger out, wiped it across his pants. And waited. "See you in Hell, brother."

I wasn't sure what disturbed me more—the cold indifference on Wrath's face as he watched his brother die, or the brutal efficiency of the attack.

I knew he was dangerous, but seeing it…

Lust coughed, glanced down at his mortal wound. And was suddenly gone. As in, vanished completely from sight, like he'd never been here.

I collapsed on the beach, staring at the space the demonic prince once occupied. Tears streamed down my face. I heaved again and Wrath watched impassively. After I stopped retching, he knelt beside me. I couldn't bring myself to look him in the eye. "Is he dead?"

"No. Being struck with a House blade only severs ties to this realm. He's back in the kingdom, and won't be able to use his powers for a while."

A small blessing amidst the curse. "Good."

Wrath handed me a cloth to wipe my face. I don't know where he pulled it from, and I didn't care. "Lust takes the pleasant emotions you have and inflates them. You might experience a void now. Picture it like a well—his influence rapidly depletes the supply. Where you were once blissfully happy, you'll feel a sharp contrast. It is a hell in its own way. Giving someone ultimate pleasure, only to rip it from them before they fully grasp it. Done often enough, it drives mortals mad. You should be all right soon enough, though."

"He wouldn't have..." I fisted my hands at my side. "Made me..."

Wrath shook his head. "No."

"But I felt—there were invisible hands." I also didn't forget how hard I'd been trying to take my clothes off in front of Wrath. Or how much I'd wanted him to touch me.

"Manifestations of your desire. They were a part of you, not anyone or anything else."

There was little comfort in that. Lust might not have violated me physically, but the emotional manipulation was equally bad. He'd twisted goodness until it was cloaked in evil. Wrath was right. It did feel like I'd crashed—like I'd been soaring, and the wind abruptly stopped and I was plunged into the frigid sea depths below. A vast abyss of nothing swallowed me.

I wanted to curl up on the ground, and sleep for eternity. I didn't care about the curse. Or the nagging feeling I'd learned something important. I no longer worried about my sister's murder. Or vengeance. Nothing mattered anymore.

I must have said that last part out loud.

Wrath reached over and lightly brushed blood-smeared knuckles against the side of my neck. The exact place I thought he'd kissed me the night he'd saved me from the Viperidae. I shivered and he dropped his hand.

"Valeas." Be strong. "It will again soon."

THIRTY-FIVE

"Soon" turned into a week. I hardly noticed the passage of time. I stayed in bed, locked the sunlight out, and refused to bathe. I had little energy and less reason to care. I didn't visit my family, or the restaurant. I didn't look for my amulet, or think about the gates of Hell. I barely slept. When I did, I kept hearing a strange voice. When I awoke, the urgent message was forgotten.

I didn't care. It didn't matter.

The world felt like it was caving in around me, and sometimes I'd gasp for what felt like hours, unable to draw in enough breath. Life hurt. All pleasure was gone. Anything that once held meaning was long forgotten, buried deep in a void I couldn't break through. My sister was a faraway memory. Vengeance was rooted in passion, and therefore I had nothing left of it, either.

If Wrath was angry or annoyed by my inability to shake off the last vestiges of his brother's power, he didn't let it show. At least not in the ways I expected.

He wasn't always the most gracious or patient nursemaid. But he was never far, always prowling around near my borrowed room in the ruined palace. Sometimes, when I was in that foggy place between sleep and wakefulness, I saw him camped out in a chair beside my bed. His hair and clothing both rumpled. Once, I thought he held my hand. But when I roused myself from that near-impenetrable haziness, he was gone. He brought food three times a day and when I refused to eat, he'd sit there, glowering until I did. Fighting him took too much energy. So I ate.

Sometimes I'd stare at the careful lines of his tattoos. Up close, the metallic snake that started on his right hand and curled up and around to his shoulder was a masterpiece—each scale shimmered. It was more than gold, there were bits of silver and charcoal—shadows and light. I stared blankly at it while he brought my next meal. I wondered if our matching tattoos would evolve with intricate details over time. I stopped caring.

He held out more food.

Globes of plump red grapes. Hunks of hard cheese. Warmed milk sweetened with honey and spices. Cured meats and other things I stopped paying attention to. He was a mighty hunter bringing home spoils of war. I wondered when he'd give up and let me be.

"When you start doing it on your own."

I didn't think I'd asked aloud. I didn't care if he read my mind. I pushed his handful of grapes away, rolled onto my side. And let the world around me fade.

Somewhere, in the distance, I thought I heard Wrath speaking. He was telling me a story about a witch. One day her heart had been ripped from her, not physically, but emotionally. The void was only filled when she went out hunting for vengeance, and even then her grief was never far. Then, when she'd been close to discovering some long-forgotten secret, she met a terrible prince. He delighted in taking what little pleasure she'd clung to, leaving her empty and vulnerable.

I tuned out the sound of Wrath's voice. I didn't care for this story. I knew the ending.

Vittoria was gone. I'd been fighting grief over her loss with all I had, gripping my pursuit of justice like it was my only tether to the world.

Now that my will to cling to it was gone, there was nothing left.

Two weeks was where his patience ended, apparently. One morning, or evening—I'd stopped paying attention—I was scooped from bed and unceremoniously dumped into a waiting bath, clothes and all. I bobbed up from the water, pushed tangles of hair from my face, and glared at the demon. He glared right back and a tiny spark of anger finally ignited.

"Have you completely lost your damn—"

My scolding died when I took in the peculiar scene around us.

Candles set in a circle on the floor dripped waxy tears, their flames offering a soft glow against the twilight streaming in. I couldn't tell if it was dusk or dawn. The windows were thrown open, allowing fresh air to glide around the bathing room. At some point, during my convalescence, Wrath had hung window coverings. Beautiful gauze panels fluttered in the wind.

He hadn't stopped redecorating there.

A line of sand circled the tub along with dozens of fragrant orange blossoms and plumeria. My favorite flowers. My gaze shot to him in accusation. "What is this?"

"Representations of each element." He nodded to the items

in question. "Earth, air, fire, and water. I take it I don't need to explain further."

He didn't. I knew exactly what it meant. They were offerings for the goddesses to help guide a moon daughter back from darkness. I glanced around the chamber again, my pulse soothing. Adding orange blossoms and plumeria was a bit much—the sand would have done just fine for the earth portion of the ritual. I didn't point that out, though. I was . . . surprised the demon even knew this much of our ways. I relaxed against the lip of the tub and closed my eyes, letting the magic of the elements seep into my soul. A drowsy peace settled deep within me.

I heard retreating footsteps and waited until he was almost gone. "Thank you."

He must have heard me. I didn't whisper and—even with the windows open—there were no other noises drifting up from the streets. But the only reply he offered was the soft click of the door closing behind him. I inhaled the pleasing scent of orange blossoms and drifted off. Later, I'd pick some of them up and weave them into my hair. As I slipped deeper into the water, I finally understood why he'd brought the flowers. They weren't meant for the ritual. They were for me.

Their fragrance was the first bit of true pleasure I felt after mine had been stolen away.

THIRTY-SIX

"There are victors and victims. Decide who you want to be. Or the choice will be made for you, witch. And I doubt you'll like it."

I threw my head back and groaned. "It's a game of scopa, not a battle between life and death. Are you always this dramatic?"

Wrath scowled from behind his hand-painted cards. "Valuable lessons are often learned from games of strategy. Only fools discredit them."

"And only an ornery creature from Hell gets this serious over a simple card game."

I plucked another cannoli from the plate Wrath had set on my bed. When I'd come out of the bath wrapped in my new silky robe, he'd been waiting with the dessert and cards. He subtly watched as I devoured another one, seeming pleased he'd done an acceptable job at remembering the sort of human food I loved. I'd mistakenly assumed more relaxation was part of his master plan to restore me to optimum health and well-being.

I had no idea we'd be playing at war games. I suddenly longed for the bath again.

The elemental blessing worked wonders for my emotions. I was ready to get back out, and solve the mystery surrounding my sister's murder. And find my missing amulet. At least in theory. In reality, I was petrified of running into another prince of Hell. Each one I'd met thus far had been worse than the last.

"How long does it take for a demon prince to restore themselves after they're—"

"Gutted?"

"I thought you aimed for his heart, actually."

"I punctured a lung. Maybe broke a few ribs." His tone was filled with disappointment. "I imagine he's almost healed already." He looked me over. "He won't bother you again."

"Right. A prince of Hell who delights in tormenting others by removing all happiness and pleasure will suddenly grow a conscience, and never attempt *that* nasty trick again."

"Oh, he'll definitely try again. But you're going to stop him."

I gulped down the last bite of my third cannoli, suddenly feeling queasy. "Is there a spell or charm that mitigates demonic influence? Irish carve crosses from rowan wood and wear them to keep fae away. You must have objects that offer protection from you, too."

He was silent for an uncomfortably long beat. I glanced up, and fought the urge to flinch. It was becoming too easy to forget what he really was. Then, there were glimpses like this, which made me worry about when *he* might be the one to turn his influence loose on me.

"Me and mine make monsters wary, witch. I do not fear, I *am* fear. Twigs and berries and iron imprison the weak. Do you think I'm weak?" I shook my head and Wrath bared his teeth in a grin that was downright petrifying. "Are you scared?"

I swallowed hard. "No."

He stared at me for a minute, but didn't call me on the lie. "My world is broken down into one simple principle: *I believe I'm powerful, therefore I am.* If I am convinced of my abilities, others will pick up on my confidence. It will give them pause, if only for a second, while they reevaluate a potential threat. Any advantage you can give yourself will be helpful when dealing with my brothers. Their motto will always be 'know thy enemy.' Make that difficult. So to answer your question, no, you do not need a spell or charm or trinket of false protection. You need to trust in yourself and your power. Or they will torture and taunt you for eternity."

Once my heart stopped thrashing, I flashed him a skeptical look. "You think I can achieve all that by playing cards?"

"Yes."

"Fine, let's say you're right. How can a game of scopa prepare me for successfully battling a prince of Hell?"

"Life often deals you a hand you didn't choose." Wrath settled back, the tension in the room releasing with him. He studied his cards carefully, then placed one on the table. A sweep. I cursed. It was the third time in a row he'd done that. "It's how you end up playing it to your advantage that counts."

I scoffed. "That was luck, not strategy."

"Both are needed. But it can be argued that luck improves with a well-thought-out strategy." He glanced up. "You live by archaic notions of light and dark magic when power is neither good nor bad. It's intent that really matters. By not studying *all* power, you've closed off options. Not honing each weapon in your arsenal is a poor strategy on your part."

"Nonna would love that advice."

His gaze hardened. "If your grandmother is against you learning to defend yourself, I'd start asking questions." Wrath took a steadying breath, his tone turning more pleasant. "If you want to become a real player in this game of murder and deceit, start by studying your opponents. Know who they are, what they want, and watch them closely. Once you're well acquainted with their habits, you'll easily spot lies." One side of his mouth lifted as I lost another hand and cursed the devil. "Work on your emotions. You're ruled by fire—and are easily angered and excited. Qualities that are not bad in certain instances, but are detrimental when facing your enemy. Do not make it easy for them to read you. They will certainly be doing everything they can to thwart your efforts at uncovering their truth."

"Have you ever considered teaching classes in Hell? You certainly love to give lessons."

"Mock me all you like. It doesn't negate the fact I'm right."

"And oh so humble about it."

"The world and its inhabitants are constantly changing, therefore we princes of Hell continue to sharpen our minds and skills. It is the absence of arrogance that allows us to remain the most feared. We do not believe we know all, we believe in adaptation. Adopt those same principles or you'll end up extinct."

"I believe you love the sound of your own voice. Maybe you should let me teach you about experiencing a wider range of emotions."

"One day, maybe I will."

He set his cards aside and studied me. I couldn't tell if the dark gleam in his eyes was that of a predator circling its prey, or the sign of mild interest for other purposes. Or maybe...maybe he was admiring me in that way that someone did when they were noticing you for the first time in a different light. Stranger still, I wasn't sure which one I hoped for more.

A flash of my desires on the beach crossed my mind.

My pulse ticked faster as he slowly leaned forward, his gaze searing into mine. For one moment, I thought he was going to kiss me. He abruptly sat back. I released a breath.

"When you first stepped onto the beach, I imagine you sensed demonic influence. Being aware is the key to fighting it. Our power lies in sensing your emotions, inflating the ones we thrive on. Once you realize that, you have the power to shift your focus and feelings elsewhere. At any moment you could have walked away from Lust's gathering. You just needed to believe you could."

"Are you suggesting what he did was *my* fault?"

Wrath stood. I hadn't noticed how finely he was dressed, or the care he'd taken with styling his hair. He wore an inky black jacket with gold snakes embroidered on the lapels, black trousers, and boots that gleamed from a recent buffing. A few rings even glittered on his fingers. Onyx and gold, his favorite colors. He looked…good. He noticed where my attention had shifted and one side of his mouth edged up.

"I'm suggesting you have untapped power, Emilia. Twist my words, twist the meanings all you like. Such is the mortal way."

"I'm not twisting and I'm not human. Your brothers are sadistic."

"Princes of Hell are neither good nor evil. We just *are*."

"Yeah. They just *are* malicious monsters."

"And yet, you keep saying 'they' and don't include me in your assessment of my brothers." Wrath shook his head. "Why is that?"

"I…" I inhaled deeply. "Because so far, Greed, Envy, and Lust have all done terrible things. You haven't. But that's probably just because of the spell I used on you."

Wrath no longer looked amused. "Practice reading people, especially when their expressions seem cold or remote. Look for their mouth tightening, their eyes darting away. Any wince or minute sign of their true feelings when you're asking uncomfortable questions."

"Any other tips, adaptable one?"

"You live in a realm of free will—accept that and you've already defeated your foes. You *always* have the power of choice, even when those choices seem limited. Never forget that."

"Oh, really? *Always?*" My anger flamed. "Did my sister have a choice to live or die? Because I'm pretty sure someone else decided that for her."

"There are worse fates, witch."

"Such as?"

"Living in my world." He turned and headed for the door. "I'll be back in a little while. If you get bored, check the dresser by your bed." He paused in the corridor and glanced over his shoulder. "I don't suggest leaving the palace tonight."

"Why not?" I called after him.

He didn't bother answering, he was already gone. I wondered about his clothing, about the way he'd combed his hair. He looked like he wanted to make an impression.

I got up and paced around the room, peered out the window, then plopped back onto the bed. I absently twisted a lock of my hair, thinking about everything he'd said about victors and victims. Then I started thinking about free will and choices. And *then* I started to get annoyed that he was being a hypocrite by infringing on mine.

I sat for twenty minutes, contemplating why, if I had free will, I was listening to him. I had important things to do and had wasted enough time. I dressed in a simple dark gray sleeveless gown he must have recently acquired, and stole into the quickly falling night.

THIRTY-SEVEN

Candles of Darkness should only be used under the direst of circumstances. Light a navy or deep purple candle, sprinkle a handful of niter powder around its base, and call forth evil from the farthest reaches of the north and south.

—*Notes from the di Carlo grimoire*

Moonlight spilled like silver blood across the rooftops, and dribbled onto the streets. It was still early enough that quite a few people were out. Some carried packages from the market, others hurried along, looking tired and worn from a hard day's work.

Thanks to the recharging nature of the elemental bath I wasn't tired or drained anymore, but the last several weeks had taken their toll. When I'd stuck orange blossoms in my hair before leaving, I noticed the sharpness of my gaze, and the gleam of suspicion that hadn't been present before. I was still the same Emilia, just a bit more cautious and on edge. I thought back to my sister's final weeks and wondered how, if she'd encountered any of the princes of Hell, she'd hidden it from us.

Maybe she *had* been on edge, shaky. And maybe that was why Nonna had been pointing out all the signs from the goddesses. She knew the storm was coming. I'd been too focused on refuting fantastical claims to notice.

I hurried through the streets, grateful I wasn't alone. I didn't want to run into any demons, royal or otherwise. Remaining in the magically protected palace was undoubtedly wise, but I couldn't hide from my many enemies forever. Staying there also wouldn't help me hone my skills with watching people speak, and seeing if they lied. Each day that came and went could bring a new witch murder. When I'd finally shaken off the last of my demonically induced despair, I'd thought about something I'd missed before. Something that might not mean anything, or it could tie everything together. The monastery.

I couldn't stop wondering why my sister had been there two nights in a row. After Vittoria had been passed up for preparing the bodies of the dead, she hardly ever stepped foot in there. I thought about the summoning circle located in the chamber where my twin died. If she didn't set it up, that meant someone else did. Someone who might be responsible for summoning Greed and Envy. Maybe I could catch them in the act of making another circle. It wasn't much, but it was something.

Thanks to Lust's demonic influence, I'd lost the last two weeks and—

Claudia paced the small courtyard separating the dormitory from the monastery. Tears streamed down her face. She yanked at her hair, mumbling. Her skirts were dirty and torn, dark rusty splotches splattered her bodice. I rushed to her side; she didn't seem to notice me. She was an absolute mess—which wasn't surprising considering her cousin's murder a couple of weeks ago.

"Claudia?" I cautiously reached for her. She refused to look up. "Are you all right?"

"They said not to use them. To never use them."

"Use what?"

"Bones and black mirrors. Black mirrors and bones. Piles of bodies and ashes of the fallen. Bones of the dead, and the dead are dust because I've seen the raven's wings beating against the crescent moon. The moon is a fang, waiting to sink its teeth into us all. Devouring. Devouring blood and bone until we're dust."

She dropped to her knees, unsuccessfully trying to pry stones up from the street. Dried blood coated the beds of her nails. They were cracked and torn to the quick.

"I hear it. It whispers to me and sometimes it's so loud I can hardly think."

I stared down, horrified to note the ground was scarred with several long, thin lines as if she'd been clawing at it for quite some time.

"Claudia, please." I bent to place my hands over hers, but she craned around and hissed like a feral creature, her eyes void of recognition. I jerked away. "What happened?"

"Dust. Dust. We're mirrors in dust. We're skulls without flesh, bones without marrow. Death. Death would be welcome. None are welcome. And you"—her dark gaze shot to mine—"you'll burn and burn, and the moon will have her vengeance, and the sun will swallow us whole and there will be nothing left. Stars. The stars are out, and they're falling like feathers ripped from the mighty raven because he craves their meat and she wishes to feed him until he's gorged, but he will never be satisfied. He is sin and is glad of it."

Black mirrors were used for scrying, and some people also

used animal bones, though Nonna cautioned against using items touched by death. She argued the future should only be viewed by the living, that things rotting deep within the soil had broken down into something else, and moved on from this realm, and therefore were no longer worried about what was to come.

As far as I knew, Claudia only used a handful of gemstones or spell candles.

She rocked back and forth, whispering. Her words were rushed and laced with a frenzied panic. She wasn't speaking exclusively in Italian anymore, and I didn't understand half of what she said. I couldn't help but fear she was repeating messages from creatures I wouldn't want to meet in the flesh. I tried reaching for her again, not wanting to leave her alone in this nightmare.

She struggled to get away, but I wrapped my arms around her, smoothing damp hair from her brow. "Shh. Shh. The stars aren't falling. We're all safe."

"Safe. Safe in chains and locks and black mirrors with no keys." Claudia rocked in my arms. "I hear it, or them. It's hard to tell. They're all talking at once—the bones of the dead, and the dust of the stars, and the devouring moon with its vicious grin. The goddess who is and is not, is vengeance."

A terrible suspicion pooled in my belly. "Did you use human bones?"

"It said I would know. That they'd tell me. The dead shouldn't mind. The dead have no mind, no will. No memory. Our minds were made for forgetting. The locks don't fit the keys. I only used the bones because it said to. Lovely stars were supposed to light the way, lead me to them. I was supposed to help. They won't stop screaming…make them stop screaming!"

"Who's screaming?"

"The damned! They think they burn, but there are worse fates than fire and ash."

It was unnervingly similar to what Wrath had said earlier.

Claudia threw her head back and screamed, raising an army of goose bumps on my body. Lights went on in the monastery dorms. I held her tightly to me, trying to keep her from thrashing. She needed to be still before the brotherhood arrived.

"It's all right. Everything's all right. Breathe."

"Black mirrors. Burning eyes. Death comes bearing friendship. *Inferus sicut superus.* The book needs blood. It craves it. Blood breaks it." She shoved me away, and whipped around. "Hide your heart. Hide it before—" She tapped my chest, shaking her head. Tears streamed down her face. "Too late. They took the ticker, and tucked it away beneath rock and dirt. Death. Bones and dust and screams. Gone. Change is here."

"What change did you see?"

"*Angelus mortis.* He's coming and going, and is a cunning thief who stole the stars and drank them dry. He will take you. You're already gone. In the end, you choose. But he's also chosen. I'll mourn. I am mourning. Like leaves on the wind." Claudia plucked what I could only assume were imaginary leaves from the ground, and blew them from her palm. "The angel of death claimed you. Changed you. You are here, but not there, there is where you will be, your life is ended. Same but different. For eternity."

I knew enough of scrying to know her warnings were not simply rantings, or signs of madness. I imagined this was similar to what happened to old Sofia Santorini when her scrying went badly eighteen years ago. It sounded like my friend was trapped between realms and realities, hearing a hundred different messages at once. I couldn't imagine how terrified she must be, lost within the prison of her mind with no hope of escape. I hoped this wasn't a result of the spell I'd asked her to work. If it was...

I gently took Claudia's hand in mine. "Let's get you to Nonna."

"They're all talking at once. It's hard to understand. To listen. The same voice speaks above all others, cruel, smooth like silk and sweet like honey. Choose, it says. I wanted a taste. It was poison. I was not meant to know. He's coming. No, no, no. He's here, no longer there, but here. He walks among us, hidden in shadow. Like death."

"Nonna will know what to do to help. We must go to her at once."

She dug her nails into my arms hard enough to make me wince, and whispered, "Run."

THIRTY-EIGHT

"You mustn't linger; he's searching for you." For a moment, Claudia seemed perfectly lucid. Then her eyes went wide enough to show off the whites, and the screaming began again in earnest. It was awful; bloodcurdling and unrelenting. Like an animal caught in a trap as a predator closed in.

I fought the urge to plug my ears. Or burst into tears.

I took a few quick breaths, and pulled myself together—a spell of cleansing enchantment was what she needed, at least temporarily. But those required rose quartz, salt, water, and alkanet root. All of which were at home and didn't help us here.

A dormitory door flew open, and a few members of the brotherhood rushed outside. I tossed up a hand to stall them, and they reluctantly paused several feet away. I internally cringed when I saw Brother Carmine emerge from the back of the group. I hadn't seen him in years.

Long-buried memories from childhood resurfaced. When we were younger, a few years after old Sofia Santorini used dark magic, he would stand on a crate in the market, screaming about the devil. We needed to leave. Immediately. If he saw Claudia like this he'd believe she was possessed.

Fear made monsters of men.

Antonio broke away from the group, his expression filled with suppressed horror the closer he got to where we sat huddled together. He scanned Claudia's messy hair, torn dress, and the blood splotches. "Was she attacked? What happened?"

I couldn't very well tell him the truth—that she'd been playing with mystical forces in the holy corridors of the monastery, possibly used the bones of the dead in a scrying ritual for reasons I hadn't yet uncovered, and had paid a steep price. "I—I'm not sure."

It was close enough to the truth, at least.

Claudia made a high keening sound. Antonio knelt beside her. She lurched forward and grabbed the front of his nightshirt. "I shouldn't have looked. But she told me to. We needed to know. For Valentina. Rats scurry in and out, and there are many in our midst. They helped it. Strange little vermin, dropping secrets like excrement. Now it won't leave. He started it—his hatred and evil invited it in. She told me we needed to be sure. He is the chosen. He is death. He shouldn't be able to leave—those are the rules. But rules are made for breaking. Like bones. He loves to break bones. I think it's the marrow he's after."

"*Who?* Who told you to look?" I asked. Antonio raised his brows and looked me over. Clearly he thought I might be suffering from the same affliction if I entertained anything Claudia said as truth. I didn't care what he thought. I had a growing suspicion I already knew who she meant based on the mention of Valentina, but wanted more proof. "Was it your aunt Carolina?"

"She spun stories like sugar, and they were airy and sweet

until they burned, and now we'll all burn because he's here and mad, and the gates . . . the gates . . . she said to protect the gates. But he's not chained to them anymore, is he? The poison was sweet, I still taste it. Lingering. Stick, stick, sticking in my throat, choking. He has secrets. He wants to devour. Empty glasses poured full of him. No, no. Empty *glass*. How did he do it? A chalice or vase. Vessels empty until full. He has the book. The heart. He needs the body to steal the soul."

A flicker of movement caught my attention. I glanced up. Several more members of the brotherhood had joined us. They silently stood in a half circle, blocking us from the monastery. Some clutched long wooden rosaries in white-knuckled fists. Others looked primed for violence, their attention fastened on my friend. Claudia needed to get to safety before they tried exorcising a demon from her that didn't exist.

"What madness is this?" Brother Carmine asked, his expression hard. My heart thrummed wildly. "Is she possessed by evil?"

"No, no. She's all right." Antonio waved him off. "Just a little too much to drink."

I didn't think members of the holy order told lies, but I was glad he did. Antonio was still on our side, no matter what his brothers might think. "Will you take her to my house? I think she must have been exposed to . . . something. She needs rest and tea. Tell Nonna she should give her some of the alkanet root she has."

Antonio chewed on his bottom lip, looking doubtful about the likelihood of that folk remedy working, but didn't argue. He offered his hand to her. "Will you come with me, Claudia? We're going to go for a walk. It'll help clear your head. Fresh air always does."

She turned a troubled gaze on me, and I smiled. "He's right.

A walk will make you feel better. And so will some herbal tea and rest. Are you ready to go?"

"Yes. But Domenico isn't." Claudia slipped her hand into Antonio's, then cringed. "He said he's not ready, and he will not move. Time is slipping like water through his hands. But still he waits. He waits and waits. He wants her to choose. He knows she will. Soon. Then he will take her heart, too. And her soul. He wants to kill again. The ultimate prize."

"Domenico?" I asked, turning to Antonio when my friend retreated back into her own fractured world. "Was he here earlier?"

"I...I think so, but can't remember for certain. He's here most days. You don't think..." He slid his attention to Claudia, who'd begun mumbling in that strange tongue again. Concern filled his expression. "You don't think he hurt her, do you?"

"It's dark. Dark and musty, and death is lurking. It's gotten a taste and craves more." Claudia blinked rapidly, suddenly seeming more like herself. "Is he still here?"

"No," Antonio said, "Domenico's gone."

"But don't worry." I helped her to her feet. "I'll find him." I faced Antonio. "Do you know where he lives?" He shook his head. Of course things wouldn't be easy; they never were. "I'll check their arancini stand just in case they're working late."

"Alone?" Antonio's mouth pressed into a tight line of worry. Brown hair fell across his brow. He looked so young and inexperienced compared to Wrath. "If he did something...maybe we should go together."

I mustered up what I hoped was a reassuring smile. While I'd love to have him with me when I confronted Domenico, there were questions I needed to ask that he couldn't be privy to. And not just because he was human. I wouldn't be able to mention the dark arts, or toss around accusations of cavorting with demon princes in front of a member of the holy brotherhood.

"I'll be all right. I don't believe Domenico did anything sinister," I lied. "He might know if she ingested any strange food or drink. Who knows? Maybe there was some mold, or other toxin present for one of her desiccations. Or maybe she had a bad bottle of wine. Valentina's death is probably to blame if she drank too much. Murder isn't easy to accept."

That seemed to mollify Antonio. It was perfectly logical. And humans loved logic, especially when it explained away the unexplainable. "She did complain of the bay leaves being rotten earlier. I believe she burned them in the preparation room."

"See?" I smiled. "I'm sure that's all it is. She inhaled mold, or something equally bad. This will pass with some fresh air and sleep, you'll see."

With a polite nod good-bye, he escorted Claudia out of the courtyard. I waited until they were safely down the street and far away from the lingering brotherhood before I left, too. I tried not to think about the searing accusation burning in Brother Carmine's gaze as I hurried away.

Since I still didn't know where Domenico's family lived, and I was fairly confident their arancini stall had long since closed for the night, confronting him would have to wait until morning.

I knew where to find Claudia's aunt Carolina, though. And she and I were going to exchange some words. I understood how grief warped a person into doing things they'd normally never do—I'd prayed to the goddess of death and fury and had summoned a demon—but asking someone else to do that when she could have done it on her own... I hoped to reign my temper in before I saw Carolina.

I stomped off in the direction of her neighborhood, unable to wrap my mind around what she'd convinced her niece to do, and how dangerous it had been. I'd asked Claudia to use a powerful spell to ward our homes because I didn't know how, and because not much could go wrong. What Carolina did was much more dangerous.

I rounded the corner and felt a prickle of energy between my shoulder blades. I kept walking, picking up my pace. The sensation continued, which meant I was being followed. And whoever they were, they were furious. I could think of at least one demon I made that angry on occasion.

Wrath probably returned from his visit with whomever he'd been trying to impress earlier than expected, and wasn't happy I'd escaped my pretty cage. Good. Maybe his evening didn't go as planned, either. I turned and glared into the shadows. I really hated the stupid magical ink that connected us, letting him find me when I didn't wish to be found. I'd assumed when I broke the spell that bound us together, the tattoo would fade.

Apparently some gifts couldn't be returned.

"Stop lurking, it's beneath you. If you've got something to say, say it."

"Bold for a witch." The voice wasn't familiar, and his accent was hard to place—almost English but not. I peered down the street, pulse racing. A few paces away, a dark figure peeled away from the building. I instinctually stepped back. He followed, his movements smooth and quick. "Your blood smells like spiced wine. Give us a taste?"

"Who are you?" I fumbled for my moon-blessed chalk, forgetting this dress was a gift from Wrath and wasn't one from home with secret pockets. "What do you want?"

The man stepped into a shaft of moonlight. He wore a long duster that seemed to be cut from the thickest slice of night. Rings glittered on each of his knuckles. They made good weapons.

My gaze slowly traveled up. Ice-blond hair, eyes that looked like they'd been chipped from a glacier, a cruel slash of a mouth twisted up on one side. Human in appearance until he smiled wider, exposing a set of sharp fangs. *Vampiro*. I stopped moving. Stopped breathing. As a witch, I *really* needed to stop thinking some creatures were mere myths and legends.

"Y-you're…" I snapped my mouth shut, hating the stammer that gave away my emotions. So much for working on keeping them hidden from my enemies. Wrath would knock himself in the head with the dull end of his dagger if he saw me now.

"It's been so long since I drank deeply from one of your kind." His gaze traveled to my neck. He was before me in an instant. "Venom is pleasurable. At least if I choose to grant such a gift. Would you like a present, little witch? Untold ecstasy while I feed on you?"

I swallowed hard. "N-no, thank you."

He circled me, his long jacket blowing on a night breeze. My whole body tensed.

"Very well. Perhaps next time."

I sincerely hoped there would never be a "next time" I encountered a vampire alone in a darkened alleyway. One time was enough to give me nightmares for the remainder of my mortal life. His jacket brushed the back of my calf, and I sucked in a sharp breath. The corners of his lips edged up. He stepped closer. Fear seemed to delight him.

"Apologies. I can see my proposition of pleasure has frightened you."

He sketched a mock bow, but never took his attention from my throat. I thought quickly about the stories from childhood. In the legends Nonna shared with us, vampires weren't known for impulse control. I felt my vein throbbing and willed it to stop, which only made it pulse harder. I didn't want a slight temptation to turn into animalistic need.

"My name is Alexei. Prince Envy requests an audience with you. His highness has much to discuss. But first, let's go on a little stroll, you and I. That should give them enough time." He offered his arm like a perfect gentleman. I didn't move to take it.

"Give who enough time for what? Envy?" I asked, losing patience. "Stop talking in riddles."

The vampire's fangs gleamed in the moonlight. "*Mare e Vitigno.* Such a lovely name. Rolls right off the tongue."

Sea & Vine. I went very still. Blood roared in my ears. Envy knew about our restaurant. He would torture my parents and—I forced myself to calm down. There was no reason to panic anymore. Claudia had shielded our home against demons. It was late, and the restaurant was closed. Thank the goddess my family would be home by now and were protected. A dark smile touched the corners of my lips. I would very much like to have the demon test the deadly magic.

"Tell Prince Envy I decline his offer. And I dare him to try and enter my home."

"My prince said I ought to mention that spells, like witch bones, are easily broken. If one knows where to apply the correct pressure. Or in this case, who to target."

I went cold. "What are you talking about?"

"Did you think you could fool a prince of Hell, little witch? Do you truly believe Envy hasn't had spies watching your home?"

His smile was filled with malice. "Demon shields and wards are tricky, but can be broken. Especially by the witch who cast them."

"That's a lie." I stepped back, shaking my head. Claudia was safe. Antonio had taken her to my house—my stomach flipped. They could have been intercepted or attacked on the way. Fear clawed its way into my heart. "That can't be true. The wards . . ."

"Are down." He offered his arm again. "Your family should be with the prince by now; the more you struggle, the harder it will be on them. He does not like to be kept waiting. Boredom is a terrible affliction in the Kingdom of the Wicked."

"Envy is—he's at Sea & Vine with my family now?"

Alexei nodded.

I wasn't going to simply take a vampire's word for it. I offered him a hateful grin as I whispered a forbidden truth spell. Alexei wasn't mortal, so I ignored the glimmer of wrongness I felt by invoking a forbidden power.

"Did Envy have Claudia break the ward on my family's home?"

He gritted his teeth as the truth was wrenched from him. "Yes."

"Are they at my family's restaurant now?"

"Yes."

I dropped my sister's amulet as if burned. I recalled the way Envy had forced me to take Wrath's dagger to my heart, ready to gouge it out. Then I imagined him doing the same thing to my family and friends. In fact, he might have already started his games. Our kitchen had cleavers and knives and all sorts of tools that could be used as weapons, or torture devices hanging on the wall. I imagined that was why he'd chosen it as our meeting place.

Without wasting another moment, I ran.

I tripped over my skirts, and the taunting sound of the vampire's laughter followed me down darkened roads. I ignored him. He no longer mattered. Getting to Sea & Vine was my only focus. I charged down narrow alleys and uneven streets, jumped over buckets of waste and shoved through lovers holding hands and strolling under the light of the moon.

I covered the mile in what felt like moments, and burst through the front doors, panting. I quickly scanned the room, searching for blood and gore and signs of a struggle.

My focus landed on the demon prince.

"I do love punctuality." Envy shut a pocket watch with an audible snap. "You're right on schedule, pet. The show is about to begin."

THIRTY-NINE

"It's truly a shame about your grandma." The Prince of Envy sat at a corner table, his back to the wall, surveying the bounty of food set before him. The room was empty except for the two of us. I couldn't decide if that was comforting, or more terrifying. "All that power, gone."

Maybe I was too late, and my parents and Nonna and Claudia and Antonio were all lying dead in the kitchen. As quickly as the thought appeared, I banished it. He'd said the show was about to begin. I clutched onto the hope I could do something to stop whatever sinister thing he'd planned.

"Where are my family and friends?"

He acted as if I hadn't spoken at all. Envy picked up his wineglass and swirled the liquid, breathing in the scent before taking a careful sip. His suit tonight was a deep forest green. Ferns lined the lapels and cuffs. The hilt of his emerald-studded dagger glinted from a strap he wore over his jacket. "I hear your grandmother might not be able to speak again. Tough fate for a witch. I imagine it's hard to cast spells without a voice. Herbs and gemstones are fine, but those powerful incantations are nothing without words to set them ablaze. Isn't that right?"

So he'd been behind the attack on Nonna, not Greed. I thought about the human messenger and the mysterious hooded figure he'd sold secrets to. Envy was the traitor we'd been looking for. I'd wager all of my magic on it. Wrath had been so convinced Envy would never rise up against them, that he didn't even look into the threat. Which opened up an opportunity for the jealous demon. One Envy couldn't resist taking.

I wanted to scream and scream and scream. I considered it a gift from the goddess that I was able to maintain some semblance of dignity. I lifted my chin. "I *said,* where are my parents?"

"Locked in the kitchen."

"My grandmother?"

"I left her at your home. She's no use to me in her current state."

"And my friends?"

"Safe, for now."

"What do you want?"

"Sit." He motioned to the seat across from him. "Dine with me." When I didn't jump to obey his command, he leaned forward, his voice edged with menace. "I vow to personally torture your family, your friends, and anyone who ventures into this fine establishment if you reject my civilized offer, pet. Then I'll have Alexei hunt down those you love and drain them dry. Now be a good girl and take a seat."

"Or don't." Alexei appeared behind me, grinning as I flinched away from him. I hadn't heard his approach. "I'd like to feast before sunrise."

I glanced between the demon prince and vampire. I wasn't

sure which of them was the bigger threat. The prince poured a second glass of wine. He'd slicked his chin-length hair back tonight, placing attention on the unusual jewel tone of his eyes, the sharpness of his jaw. "Don't tell me you're choosing a bloodbath over a glass of wine and pleasant conversation."

I glared at him. I might be helpless, but I didn't have to appear so. "I'll sit as long as you promise to spare my friends and family, and leave here once we're finished. And by 'here' I mean this city."

"You're not in a position to be making demands. But I respect your effort. Now *sit*. Drink."

With little choice, I joined Envy at the table. He nodded toward the goblet of wine. I picked it up, and pretended to take a sip. I didn't trust him to not have tampered with it before I arrived. If he was planning to sneak me back to Hell, he'd have to take me by force.

"You're the one who's been working against Pride," I said.

He didn't deny it. He watched me in an unnervingly close way—like he was seeing through layers of skin and bone, and found the heart of who I was and all I aspired to be.

"I understand why Wrath is intrigued by you."

Intrigue was probably the last thing Wrath felt toward me. "Did you ask your vampire to deliver me here just to discuss your brother?"

"He loves a good challenge. It's the war in him; makes him want to conquer and win at any cost." He took another sip of wine, his attention straying to my neck. "It will be hard for him to give you up when the time comes. But he will. Do not delude yourself into thinking you matter to him. We princes of Hell are selfish creatures. We do not suffer the same range of sentiments as mortals, and those born to this peculiar realm. You are standing between him and something he's sought for a very long time. In the end, he will choose himself. As we all do."

I set my goblet down, the contents splashing onto the worn wooden table. "If this is what you came all the way from your wicked kingdom to say, that's unfortunate. You're not telling me anything I don't already know. Nor are you telling me anything I particularly care about."

I saw the exact moment I walked into the carefully laid trap he'd set for me. He cut into a stuffed sardine with impeccable manners. After he washed down the bite of food with more wine, he gave me a lazy smile, though his gaze was sharp enough to stab.

"If you've figured out my brother so well, why don't you tell me what he's really after? I'm sure a smart girl like you already knows, and doesn't need my humble assistance in that matter."

Envy wanted me to need him. To beg for knowledge out of mortal curiosity. Then he'd exchange it for something he wanted from me. And he must want something very badly if he'd go through this much trouble. I got a sick sense of satisfaction for being a disappointment to the demon. "What do you want, Envy? Why am I really here?"

"The first night we met, I suspected you were in possession of something I need. Do you know what that is?"

I thought back to that first encounter. I'd tucked my amulet inside my bodice right before he'd emerged from the shadows. Back then, I was worried he'd been after my sister's diary. Knowing what I do now, I bet he could sense the power of the amulet. "You want my *cornicello*."

"Close. I want both your amulet and your sister's. And you're going to give them to me."

"Why would I do that?"

"Because I have in my possession something you want."

I shivered in place. I knew what he meant; he had my parents. My friends. Nonna might be home now, but that didn't mean she was safe. I held very still, waiting for him to deliver the blow. He finished the last bite of food and exhaled, sounding immensely pleased. He pushed his plate back then snapped his fingers.

A demon that had the head of a ram—complete with rounded horns above its ears—and the body of a human dragged my parents out by their collars and tossed them down. Their eyes were cloudy, their movements sluggish. They didn't seem to be aware of what was going on.

I jumped up from my seat, but Envy shook his head.

"Sit, pet. We're not through. There's more."

With no other option available, I dropped back into my seat.

"Good. You're finally taking this seriously. I've waited long enough. Give me the Horn within the next twenty-four hours, and your loved ones will not be maimed. Tell anyone or fail to meet my demands, and they will be coming to stay with me in House Envy with the rest of my curiosities. And things will end much worse for you. This, I can promise, is no idle threat. Have I made myself perfectly clear?"

I glanced at my mother and father again. They hadn't moved from where the horned-demon unceremoniously dumped them, and stared blankly at nothing. In a way, it was a blessing from the goddess of mercy that they weren't entirely conscious for this.

My eyes burned with unshed tears. "What did you do to them?"

"You ought to be concerned with what will become of them yet if you don't give me what I'm asking for."

"I don't have the other amulet." I kept my focus on my parents, trying to think of a way out of this. "My half was stolen the night my grandmother was attacked."

"Then I suggest you start looking for it. One half won't do."

"If you attacked my grandmother, don't you already have my amulet?"

"Let me provide a bit of advice: accusations without evidence are worthless." Envy poured another glass of wine. "By this time tomorrow, I expect to be in possession of both amulets. I will move your family and friends to your home tonight. Meet me there once you have the other amulet and we will trade. Your family and friends for the Horn of Hades."

I went to remove my sister's *cornicello* from my neck, but he held up a hand to stall me. "Why not take this half tonight?"

"If I touch it now, it will...alert those I wish to keep in the dark. I don't want to draw any attention until I possess the entire Horn of Hades."

"Wrath didn't care about the Horn before. Why can't I ask for his help?"

Envy gave me an odd look. "Wrath will never be the hero in your story. He's carved from something other. In fact, he might be the biggest liar of us all." I scoffed, which only seemed to delight him. "If you don't believe me, then ask Wrath about the final soul he has to collect. The one that will grant him freedom from the underworld, regardless of the curse."

I stared at the smug demon prince. I'd say it was a lie, but deep down I suspected it wasn't. I knew Wrath had his own agenda, and this felt like the final piece I'd been missing. But a soul? I shook my head. He'd saved me when I'd been attacked by the Viperidae. If this was true, he could have bargained with me then. Or maybe . . . maybe he hadn't told me because he'd wanted to use it to his advantage when the time was right. I exhaled. I was getting paranoid.

"You're lying."

"Am I? I thought you knew better. Why do you think he, the mighty demon of war, cares about safely escorting a witch to the underworld?"

"Because he wants to break the devil's curse." As I said it, I heard the doubt creeping in.

"I have a secret, pet." Envy leaned across the table, his poisonous gaze alight with triumph. "Once he has collected his final soul, the curse won't matter to him. He will have full power, and the ability to walk this realm freely without an anchor. He can either choose to stay in the Seven Circles and rule his royal House, or he can roam the earth until the end of days. Choice is powerful. And we princes do love our power." He offered me a slow, vicious grin. "You didn't think that deep down he could be redeemed, did you?"

FORTY

A prince of Hell's greatest pleasure is causing discord. Before an attack, his irises turn darker than a starless night with flecks of red, a sign of his wicked bloodlust. Do not engage them in battle; you will never win.

—Notes from the di Carlo grimoire

The tall, arched door clicked shut behind me. It hardly made a sound, but Wrath emerged from the darkness of the abandoned palace, his face half-hidden in shadow. He'd discarded the serpent jacket, and his dark shirt was unbuttoned and rumpled. Much like his hair.

I thought about running my fingers through it, and my heartbeat quickened. I didn't want to believe Envy. Wrath had been there for me, even when he said he wouldn't be. And yet…

"Are you hurt? You look…" his voice trailed off as I slowly walked over to where he stood. He didn't move, hardly seemed to breathe as I backed him up against the wall, his shirt bunched in my grasp. His golden eyes latched on to mine, burning. I wondered if he sensed my emotions. If they somehow affected his, too. I held him captive there, caging his body with my own.

He could break from my grasp at any moment. But he didn't.

I eased my grip from his shirt, and slowly splayed my hands over his chest instead. He looked down into my face, his expression wary but intense. Having all of his attention directed at me was intoxicating.

"I want to trust you," I said quietly, holding his stare. His heart thudded solidly beneath my touch. "Why don't you tell me what you really want? Let me in."

His gaze fell to my mouth before he tore it away a breath later. I didn't think the flash of desire I saw was fake. I knew the emotion it stirred within me wasn't, either.

I'd always imagined he'd dutifully take an enemy to bed if it meant he'd gain something from it. Now I wasn't sure that's how he felt at all. There was a charge steadily building between us. And Wrath seemed poised to let it detonate. Because he wanted to. Maybe I did, too.

I moved a hand inside his shirt, keeping close contact with his skin. His pounding heart betrayed the response he was desperately trying to hide. My hand inched lower. The heat of him, the solidness . . . suddenly, I wanted this to be real.

One second I was standing there, and the next my mouth was on his, punishing, hard. It was damnation and salvation wrapped into one. I wanted to kiss him until I stopped being angry and terrified. Until I stopped thinking about my family being held against their will. Until the demonic world melted away, and all I had left was this one moment of pure oblivion.

Wrath was still for a beat before he met my lips with equal

hunger. His hands slid down to my hips, anchoring me in place. It wasn't nearly close enough. I pressed myself against him. He was gentle at first, then I swept my tongue into his mouth and he came undone.

He kissed me back hard, then his teeth were against my throat—in the exact spot he'd flicked his tongue over the night he'd used that spell to bring me back from the edge of death. I hadn't been sure it had actually happened, now I knew it had. For one startling moment, I imagined him ripping out my throat. The fear quickly passed and was replaced by pure desire.

I gasped from the unexpected sensation. I swore I felt the strange heat from that first encounter simmering beneath my skin now. I wanted him to devour me.

Or maybe I wished to devour him.

I hated how good he felt. How right. I'd kissed boys before—drunkenly and on dares. Chaste kisses and passionate kisses, but none that were like this. Powerful. Savage. Sweet.

A reckoning awoke in me. The more I gave, the more he returned. We traded kisses like blows. And if this were a fight, I wouldn't know who was winning. I understood why some thought kissing one of the Wicked was addictive. Each time his tongue touched mine, it felt as if the ground beneath me quaked. Like we were a cataclysmic event that shouldn't be.

It only made me kiss him harder, faster. I tugged at his shirt, wanting it off. I wanted nothing between us. Buttons hit the ground as I yanked at the material. I dragged my fingers down the ridges of his hard stomach. His hands on my body felt like magic. It was more intense, more seductive than any spell. Somehow, we were now up against a column. I don't remember moving. Maybe because all I could concentrate on was the way he was currently moving against me, hoisting me up. I wanted to rip off the rest of his clothes and see what else he could do. Discover what other feelings he could awaken in me. His hand slid down to my calf, then trailed up slowly, pulling my skirts with it. He didn't stop, and I didn't want him to.

I tipped my head back, giving him access to my throat again as he paused with his hand on my thigh. I leaned in to his touch, wanting him so badly I was almost driven to madness. Somehow I kept my hand on his chest, and pulled away from kissing him long enough to ask, "Was Envy lying when he said you need to deliver one more soul to gain your freedom?"

He startled away, but not before I got my answer in the form of a singular, thrashing beat of his heart. Understanding dawned before he shuttered his expression, and moved out from my reach. Anger filled the space around us, burning brighter and more furious than our passion.

"What is this, witch? Have you lowered yourself to kissing someone you hate after all?"

I stared at him, unblinking. It was true. I couldn't manage anything besides a slight shake of my head. My eyes stung with unshed tears. Envy hadn't lied—Wrath *was* after a soul. The realization hit me like a physical blow. I'd felt foolish when I discovered I'd accidentally betrothed us, but this?

I was going to be sick.

Wrath's anger seemed to dissipate when he noticed the look on my face. He stepped forward, hand outstretched, stopping only when I shook my head again. He let his arm drop. "Emilia, I—"

"Don't."

He seemed ready to argue, but listened. Long seconds passed. I concentrated on steadying my breaths, letting my feelings untangle themselves. I was angry with him, but I was furious with myself more. I realized I'd *wanted* to trust Wrath. More than I'd even admitted to myself.

Even though I knew better, I wanted him to be the shining prince of this nightmare. I'd fallen under his spell and while there were times I loathed him, I'd also started to enjoy his company.

He distracted me from the pain of losing my sister, gave me something to focus on. He was someone I could jab and who'd jab right back. And now...it was like Lust reemerged and wrenched every last drop of happiness from me again. Only this time, there was only me to blame. I'd let him in. And I should have known better.

"Emilia."

"I can't...."

Wrath curled his hand at his side.

"Envy whispers in your ear and every action I've taken is wiped off your imaginary tally. Tell me, Emilia, what has *he* done for you? Aside from trying to carve out your heart. What honorable thing did he do to deserve your trust? Spill the blood of those you love? Maybe you like threats. Maybe I should make some of my own."

The ground seemed to rumble with the force of his anger.

He'd wanted me to study my enemies closely, and I'd done just that.

"Tell me it's not true, then," I said, surprised when my voice came out hard, and not pleading. "That Envy was lying, that you don't need to collect one more soul to gain your freedom. Tell me part of the reason you accepted this mission wasn't to use a witch for your benefit. Better yet, tell me you haven't considered using *my* soul. Can you do that, or does our summoning bond make it impossible because it's a lie?"

For once, Wrath didn't seem to have an answer. He looked ready to lay waste to the rest of the crumbling palace. I was surprised when he didn't.

"Envy is many things," I said, my voice low. "Despicable. Selfish. Conniving. But he doesn't hide those things. He told me what you were really after. He told me what he wanted, and what he would do if I didn't listen. He's made terrible threats, acted on them, but he never deceived me or pretended to be anything other than what he is."

And there it was.

Despair crashed into me, hard. Wrath *had* lied. Maybe not outright, but he'd lied through omission. Which was still lying. I wanted to strike out at him, to make him hurt the same way I did. Instead, I turned and started walking away.

Nonna tried warning us about the Malvagis' lies. I should have listened.

He stepped into my path, moving almost faster than my senses could detect. "Have my actions not told you the truth? Forget the last several weeks. Saving your life from the Viperidae. The impenetrable palace. The elemental bath. Do you think I need to sleep in a place protected by magic? I, who cannot be killed?"

"I don't have time for this." I marched past him toward the stairs. "I'm going back home to stay with my family. Envy is holding them captive. Something else he said that turned out to be true."

He stormed up after me. "No."

"I don't recall asking for permission, demon."

"Envy will stick a dagger in your back the second he gets what he's after."

"Am I your prisoner now?"

"No, but I'd be happy to toss you in a dungeon, if that's what you'd like."

I ignored him and rummaged through new dresses that had magically appeared in a broken dresser sometime in the last few hours. Wrath had a serious obsession with providing clothing for me.

I found a simple charcoal dress that would be easy to run in and laid it across the bed. I couldn't believe I now had to choose my wardrobe based on if I could easily flee from a demon, vampire, or other nasty assailant.

Wrath crossed his arms and set his feet. If he thought I'd hesitate to change in front of him, he had much to learn of me. I stepped out of my current dress and the silky material pooled at my feet. Wrath watched impassively as I slipped into the new ensemble.

Now that I knew that Envy wanted the Horn of Hades, I *needed* to locate my amulet. Immediately. Before I handed it over, I'd strike a bargain with him. I'd make him vow to lock the gates of Hell before any more demons snuck through them, and then he could go to war with the entire underworld. As long as our world was protected, I didn't care what happened in their realm.

I tied my long hair up with a ribbon, fastened a small belt with a pouch around my waist, and added moon-blessed chalk and dried yarrow to it. It was the best I could do by way of protecting myself. I left the room and headed back down the stairs.

Wrath followed me through the corridor and paused near

the door to the gardens. I stuck an arm out and barred him from crossing the threshold.

"Do *not* come after me, I mean it."

"Emilia, please. Don't—"

"I swear on my blood, if you follow me, I will sever our summoning bond and send you straight to Hell."

Wrath pressed his lips together—the only outward indication he was less than pleased, but didn't argue, or make a move to come with me again. Feeling relieved, I slipped out the garden exit, pushed through a tangle of vines and overgrown shrubs, and darted into the night.

FORTY-ONE

Two doors away from my home, I became aware of the near silent footfall behind me. After the night I'd had—with my best friend's scrying from Hell, thirsty vampires, and devious demon kidnappers—I wasn't sure what to expect.

There were any number of nasties out for witch blood. Maybe the Umbra demon was back, or another Aper demon was in pursuit. For some reason, I thought about Envy and Greed teaming up to collect the Horn of Hades before divesting me of my skin, and shivered.

I wasn't at all prepared for Fratello Carmine. His dark robes swished across the stones, like little whispers of warnings to run and hide.

I quickly wedged myself between two buildings next door to my house, heart hammering as the sound of his pursuit grew closer. He kept a steady pace, head swiveling from side to side, as he passed me by. I wasn't sure who he was looking for. Maybe he was trying to find where Antonio had brought Claudia. I should have known he wouldn't let my friend leave without being sure the devil wasn't in her.

I waited a few beats before I peered around the side of the house. He'd stopped near the end of the street and was having a hushed conversation with another member of the brotherhood. Fragments drifted over to where I hid.

"Antonio . . . night . . ."

". . . unholy."

". . . missing."

"Found . . . signs?"

I leaned against the building and took a few deep breaths. Antonio was missing because a prince of Hell was holding him hostage. And it was all my fault for asking him to walk Claudia home. I needed to fix this before anyone else got hurt. Brother Carmine hardly needed a reason to start a witch hunt. The mere fact that he'd been called back from wherever the church had sent him was a sign they believed the devil was on the prowl.

I slipped out from the shadows and hurried into my house.

There were three demons crammed inside the kitchen with my family. One was the ram-headed demon that Envy still had guarding my parents. The other was nothing more than a dense shadow hovering above Nonna and a slumped and sedated Claudia—the Umbra demon. Antonio wasn't among the group, and my stomach twisted with worry. I wasn't sure how demons felt about humans who devoted themselves to God, but it didn't bode well for my childhood friend. I also didn't see the vampire anywhere. I hoped that didn't mean he was feasting on Antonio.

The final demon in the room was the traitor prince himself, Envy.

"Where's Alexei?" I asked, not wanting any other surprises.

"He's back in the kingdom, watching over House Envy until I return." Envy lounged on Nonna's rocking chair, his boots kicked up onto our island. Dirt splattered the stone top. The very place where my sister used to labor over potions and drinks. Something dark and vicious ignited inside me at the sight. Envy didn't appear concerned. "Unless you have the other amulet, pet, this visit is most unwelcome."

Maybe it was the simmering rage I'd tried smothering after my encounter with Wrath, or the sight of my loved ones huddled on the floor in our own home, or pure recklessness, but I'd had it. I marched over and smacked Envy's boots off our island. "Show a little respect, your highness. This might be how you treat things in your hellhole, but this is our home."

Envy's blade was at my throat before I had time to blink. "You asked Wrath about the soul, didn't you? I imagine you didn't like what he had to say." He pressed the dagger a little harder. I felt a slight prick as it pierced my skin. I held still, not daring to breathe. "Do not take your own wrath out on me, or I will turn this blade loose on your grandmother. There's nothing quite as satisfying as watching a witch bleed. Especially one who—"

"Silentium."

The spell rang through the room as if Envy's words had been cut off with the swish of a knife. Nonna rose up from the ground, a faint purple glow surrounding her. I couldn't believe it. She'd forced the demon prince into silence. She clutched her *cornicello* and began chanting a spell I'd never heard. I stared, unblinking, as her voice grew stronger. I didn't know she'd healed. The demons didn't seem to realize it, either, an error they were about to pay for. Nonna drew an image in the space before her, and a glowing, unearthly *cimaruta* charm appeared there.

I was so stunned by her show of power, I didn't notice the glittering black portal forming behind Envy. My mouth opened in shock. Holy goddess above...

The purple light surrounding Nonna ended in tips of silver now. Envy, for the first time, looked worried. He took a small step backward, eyes flashing toward his demons, but Nonna yanked a handful of dried fennel from her skirt pocket and whispered an enchantment that locked his feet in place.

A flick of her wrist and black thread spooled into the air before the prince of Hell, then slithered toward his feet like serpents. The other two demons moved toward Envy, only to be driven back by black shadows spun from the spell. I could barely hear over the pounding of my heart when I saw what my grandmother had done. She'd magically sewn his feet to the floor. Now he couldn't speak, or move. His eyes widened enough to show the whites.

Nonna returned to her spell. "A key to lock, a moon to guide."

My attention flew back to the magical image of a rue branch as each of the five stalks began shifting and stretching into different shapes. A key and a full moon formed at the end of two branches. I suddenly knew exactly what Nonna was doing. She caught my eye.

"Now, Emilia!"

I held on to Vittoria's *cornicello* and focused on the glowing *cimaruta*, feeding Nonna's spell with my own power. "A dagger to kill, a snake to die."

Two more images appeared on the glowing charm.

Nonna nodded in approval, and we said the final part of the

spell together, our voices ringing as a swirling vortex of wind howled inside the portal.

"Blessed owl go forth and fly."

The final image burst at the end of the *cimaruta*. Now all five charms pulsed with purple light. Nonna walked over to where Envy stood frozen, leaned in, and whispered something that made his eyes widen even more.

Then she planted both hands on his chest and sent him straight to Hell. The two remaining demons dove through the portal after him. Nonna dropped her amulet and slumped against the island. The *cimaruta* faded away. A breath later, the portal closed. Silence blanketed the room. I kind of felt like falling to my knees, or throwing up.

My attention shifted to my parents who were still in that foggy, near-unconscious state. Claudia was also slumped over, her eyes shut as if in sleep. Whatever magic Envy had used on them must need time to wear off. Nonna crossed the tiny kitchen and plopped into her rocking chair. "Grab the wine from the ice box and take a seat, bambina. We have much to discuss and not much time. That spell won't last for long. I have a feeling he'll be back."

I stared at my grandmother. She just drew a glowing *cimaruta* and banished a prince of Hell to the underworld. And instead of looking drained, her eyes were alight. In fact, if I looked closely, I swore little twinkling stars shined in her irises. "What kind of magic was that?"

"The kind that will demand payment. Now get me the wine." I poured two glasses and handed one to Nonna. She took a deep pull and exhaled. While she sipped from her glass again, I set mine down and pulled my hair back. The spell we used had made me break a sweat. Nonna's attention snapped to my neck, her color draining. "You've been Marked."

"By Envy's blade?" I rubbed at the place on my neck where he'd pressed his dagger. "I didn't think he'd cut me that deeply."

"No, bambina. You've been Marked by a prince of the underworld in a different way. It's supposedly a high honor among their ruling Houses. Very few are given them."

She had to be mistaken. Instead of arguing, I headed into our little bathing chamber. I moved my hair to the side, and leaned in. I didn't notice anything unusual, let alone a special mark.

"See?" Nonna appeared behind me and traced the area. She must have used some spell because suddenly a tiny, shimmering *S* gleamed back at me. I squinted. Or was that a snake?

I stood there, unmoving. It was the place Wrath's tongue moved across me the night I'd almost died in the Viperidae attack. He'd also traced it again earlier tonight. I tentatively reached up and brushed my fingers across it. Coolness bit into my skin. I frowned. "What does it do?"

Nonna didn't seem at all pleased. "It allows you to summon the demon who placed it there without the use of an object that belongs to him. As long as the prince of Hell draws breath, nothing will prevent him from answering the summoning."

"You mean . . . I can just summon him without his dagger?"

Nonna nodded slowly. She seemed on the verge of a lecture, so I quickly let my hair fall back down. "It's a dangerous thing, Emilia. Who placed that on you?"

There was no point in lying. "The Prince of Wrath."

"Are you certain?" she asked. I nodded. Wrath had been the only one who'd touched me. I tried not to think about his lips on my neck earlier tonight. Or how it had made me feel. Nonna just stared for another minute. "I suppose there's no denying it now."

"Denying what?"

"The prophecy. Back when I was a young woman, I was entrusted with being one of the keepers of the Horn of Hades."

I was at a loss for words. I replayed her confession and somehow managed to formulate a few decent questions. "Keepers?" I asked. "How many are there? And what prophecy?"

"Patience. I'll get to that, bambina."

My hand moved to my sister's amulet. "Did you ever wear them?"

"No, never. Each generation, dating back from when La Prima first handed them off, a witch was chosen to guard them. We were told of an ancient prophecy involving twin witches. When they were born, on the night of a terrible storm, only then could the amulets be worn."

I took a deep breath. It was a lot to absorb at once. "How do you know Vittoria and I are the subjects? Maybe there are other twins..."

"No other twin witches, both with magic, have been born into this line."

"Ever?" I asked. Nonna shook her head. "What exactly was the prophecy about?"

Nonna took another long pull on her wine, her expression sad. "The twins would signal the end of the devil's curse, and would be forced to make great sacrifices to keep the gates of Hell intact. If they choose to do nothing, Hell will reign on earth. The twins are meant to bring balance to both realms. As above, so below."

My heart thrummed. There was something about that phrase, something buried deep... I'd heard it before, twice. The first time when I was under Lust's influence. And then when I was recovering afterward with Wrath. "What does that part mean, exactly?"

"No one knows for certain," Nonna said, her attention shifting to where my parents were now stirring. "It has been a constant argument among the thirteen witch families of Palermo. Some believe it refers to the use of light and dark magic. Few think it means a prince will fall in love with a witch. Others believe it means one twin will rule in Hell to stop this world from being destroyed. And then there are others who think both twins are meant to sacrifice themselves to save both realms. One to heaven, and the other to Hell."

"How does being Marked fit in with—"

"If the prophecy holds true, there's not much time left. The gates are breaking." Nonna suddenly pushed me out of the small room and down the corridor. "You must run, Emilia. Leave us here and go. We'll wait a day or so and then go into hiding as well. We will find a way to meet again one day. For now, you must leave here and do not draw another prince of Hell's attention. Do you understand? Do not trust them, any of them. We will find a way to temporarily spell the gates. You concentrate on staying hidden."

"I can't—"

"You will. You will because you *must*. Leave here before that demon returns. We will find a way to stop the prophecy, we just need some time." Nonna cupped my face tenderly, her brown eyes watering. "Love is the most powerful magic. Above all else, remember that. It will always guide you where you need to go." She dropped her hands and stepped back. "Now go, bambina. Go be brave. Your heart will conquer darkness. Trust in that."

FORTY-TWO

I stumbled out of our house and into the street. Dawn painted streaks of red and gold across the sky. I stared up at it, trying to orient myself to my new reality. The world was the same as it had always been, but felt irrevocably changed. A prophecy foretelling disaster...I dragged in another breath. I couldn't believe no one told us about it before. Knowing my very existence might signal the end of Earth's days was kind of a big secret to keep, especially if there wasn't much time left before the gates of Hell crashed open.

I also could not believe Nonna had taken on a prince of Hell, and won. And being Marked by Wrath... Everything was happening much too quickly. I could barely process it all. I glanced over my shoulder at my home, hearing the slight murmur of voices. My parents were fully awake. Thank the goddess. I rushed back up the stairs and halted, hand hovering above the knob. I wanted more than anything to go in and hug my parents, to tell them I loved them, but couldn't. Tears stung my eyes as I hurried away. I didn't want to leave them, but if what Nonna said about the prophecy was true, everyone would be safer without me.

I quickly walked through the streets, trying to figure out a plan. I wondered if my sister had found out about the prophecy. If she had, it explained why she thought accepting the devil's bargain was necessary. Maybe she'd been trying to save me. Between the gates of Hell crumbling and the prophecy, the choices were dwindling on how to stop more chaos from arriving.

I walked past the marketplace, avoiding the stalls of vendors I knew, skirted the edge of the crowds, and ended up on a steep street that faced the sea.

I was thinking a lot about what Nonna said. About love being the most powerful magic. I wasn't sure if that was true in the literal sense, but love for my twin had made me stronger. In the months following Vittoria's murder, I'd left my comfort behind in favor of helping give her peace.

I'd summoned a demon and encountered four princes of Hell. I'd fought a giant snakelike demon, been chased and almost bitten by another, and had survived it all. I tricked information out of Greed, I learned cunning from Wrath. I didn't know I was a fighter before all this. Now I knew I could and would do anything for the people I loved.

I reached for Vittoria's amulet, wanting to feel connected to her. I wished she could have seen Nonna fighting off a demon prince. As my fingers clasped it, some tiny detail surfaced. I don't know how the connection was made, but suddenly there it was.

Fennel. Nonna had used dried fennel on Envy. And it wasn't the first time I saw fennel in connection with something related to fighting the Wicked. Wrath had pointed out that the image painted on the door to that old fisherman's storage building had a paw holding a stalk of fennel, not wheat like I'd originally thought.

Which meant... My pulse raced. I thought about more stories from our childhood. I knew that symbol—it wasn't in Vittoria's diary and it didn't belong to any demon prince, either. Quite the opposite. I hadn't thought about the legends since the night in the monastery when Antonio mentioned them, but it symbolized an ancient order of shape-shifters who were said to battle evil.

Almost everyone in the Kingdom of Italy had heard stories of the mighty shape-shifters growing up. Talk eventually turned them into myths, but that didn't mean they weren't real and still around. The villagers Antonio had spoken to seemed to think they were very much alive and well and gathering again. Excitement thrummed through me. If an ancient sect of warriors was living in Palermo, maybe it was time to see if they'd like to help rid the city of the demons invading it.

Regardless of anything, I'd felt something supernatural in that room with the fishing gear. And now I was going to find out exactly what I'd sensed.

Inside the abandoned building with the painted shape-shifter symbol, all was eerily still and quiet; like the room itself was waiting, breath held, for its secrets to be discovered. There was something in here I needed to find. I knew it. I *felt* it.

Now I scanned the miscellaneous items carefully, dragging my attention over each floorboard, each corner, and every last item I could see. Fishing nets and tackle still lay in the same heaps. This time, however, I decided to see if my *luccicare* would locate the magical object the way my sister was able to hear them quietly whispering to her.

I held on to Vittoria's *cornicello* and concentrated hard on my talent, trying to force the lavender aura to manifest. That didn't happen, but something strange did. The more I tried to focus on the *luccicare,* the more attuned I became to sounds. I closed my eyes, listening to a slight humming that called to me. There was something familiar about it I couldn't quite place.

I let go of rational thinking, and gave myself over to my senses completely.

I stepped to my right and the sound faded. I inhaled deeply, recentered my focus, and moved left. The humming came back. I inched toward it, pausing and refocusing each time it started to fade. The closer I got, the louder and steadier it became.

I took a final step forward, then stopped.

I opened my eyes. I'd been guided to the far wall where the fishing hooks were hung up in neat rows. I recalled scanning it the day Wrath and I had ventured inside. I'd been drawn to it then, but hadn't trusted my instincts. I ran my fingers over the hooks. Some were shiny, others dulled by use and rust. I came to the end of the wall and paused. One very ordinary-looking hook seemed to hum the closer I drew to it. I backed up and the sound disappeared.

I focused again and it returned. I blew out a breath, and let go of the questions I had no answers to. I wasn't sure what to do, but reached over to remove the old hook from the wall. As I tugged on it, a secret door behind it clicked open. Holy goddess above. I hadn't expected that.

I glanced sharply over my shoulder, worried there was an invisible spy lurking behind me, waiting to report back to whomever it worked for. I scanned the room slowly, but unless there were multiple Umbra demons in the city, the one hired by Envy was gone.

I shook the chills away and turned back to the secret door. I swore I heard the distant whispers of many voices coming from inside the hidden passage. I thought about Vittoria's diary, about the lines she'd tried to decipher that had been jumbled like Claudia's scrying session.

I followed the hum of voices into a cave, high above the sea...

...I found it there, buried deep within the earth. I managed to understand one line before it descended into chaos.

I thought about the "it" she mentioned. If we'd each been wearing part of the Horn of Hades our whole lives, then that couldn't be the mysterious "it" she'd been referring to. So what, then, had she heard whispering to her high above the sea? What had Vittoria dug up and decided to hide again, somewhere far from the Malvagi?

I peered at the secret door, wondering if I'd be brave enough to see where it led. Whispers called to me, a little louder, a little more insistent. My palms dampened.

Maybe wearing Vittoria's *cornicello* gave me access to her magic. Which meant, whatever had drawn my sister to that cave above the sea, was now calling to me.

If I truly wanted to find out what happened to Vittoria, I needed to see what was behind that door. With a quick prayer to the goddess, I held her *cornicello* tightly, and stepped into the secret passage.

FORTY-THREE

A crumbling old set of stairs greeted me. I hesitated at the top step, peering down into the darkness below. There were no torches or lights to guide me once I descended into the abyss. Only spiderwebs and the unmistakable urge to run in the opposite direction. The whispers were much louder and more excited in here, and covered up other noises. If someone or something followed me in, I wouldn't know it until they were almost on top of me.

I rubbed my thumb across the smoothness of the *cornicello.* I was a goddess-blessed witch wearing one of the devil's horns. Surely I could find a way to cast a little light. I concentrated hard on my sister's *cornicello,* imagining the times that strange purple light emerged, and the tiniest glow appeared. It wasn't much, but it would be enough to light my path. I exhaled, and began the long trek down.

I kept one hand around my amulet, and the other against the wall, making sure I didn't lose my balance and go tumbling to my death. It took a minute or two, but I finally reached the bottom. I swept my attention around, ensuring I wasn't about to be attacked.

I was in a tunnel that reminded me of the location of the Viperidae nest. I fought a shudder. I sincerely hoped I wouldn't run into it again. Keeping those fears from taking root, I forged ahead.

A few meters down, the tunnel forked off in two directions. The path on my left seemed to incline steadily, cutting off my view. The one on my right looked like it went on for a while before twisting to the right. Honestly, neither one seemed like a fun journey, but I wasn't here for a good time. I closed my eyes and listened to the magic leading me. The whispers were louder on the right. And the slight tug in my center pulled me that way. So that was the direction I chose.

I lost track of how much time had passed when I abruptly halted. My sister's amulet had gone from a slight purple glow to a strong pulsating light. I'd never seen either of our amulets act that way before, and immediately became suspicious. I glanced around, searching for the cause and saw a crude cross painted on the wall. I must be underneath a church. I went to look away, but something caught my attention.

There, buried a little by dirt, was a glint of silver. Whispers excitedly chittered.

Pulse racing, I inched close and bent to brush the dirt away. My missing amulet glowed in welcome. I snatched it up and went to loop it over my neck, then stopped. Nonna said they must never touch. I wasn't sure if that mattered anymore, but didn't want to chance another catastrophe. I took my sister's amulet off and stuck it into my secret skirt pocket. The moment my *cornicello* laid against my skin, my shoulders relaxed. I hadn't realized how much tension I'd been carrying. It might be one of the devil's horns, but it now belonged to me.

I stood up, and looked around. I'd been expecting to find a

secret meeting location of the shape-shifters, but there were no doors or offshoots. I was considering my options when I heard a sound that wasn't a result of magical objects whispering. Someone was down here. It might be whoever had painted that symbol on the door, or it might be something much worse.

I considered running, but that wouldn't be wise. Whatever big bad creature was out there would probably love to give chase. I glanced straight ahead, happy to see the turnoff a few short meters away. If I ran, I might be able to lose whatever was following me. I didn't waste another second considering it, I charged toward the next tunnel.

I rounded the corner and hurried into the shadows, drew a quick protection circle, then pressed myself into a damp recess, hidden from view.

A slight displacement of pebbles indicated my stalker hadn't given up. I held my breath, worried the slightest intake or exhalation would give me away. My pursuer paused close enough that I could just make out his features, and I bit back a string of curses.

"Are you completely—"

Wrath's hand shot out and covered my mouth before I finished my sentence. He'd crossed my protection circle without showing any indication it had affected him at all. Which should have been impossible because it was keyed with my power. I was too stunned to do something smart, like bite him.

"Now that you possess the Horn, there are three dozen Umbra demons closing in. Two dozen of which have been following you since you left your house." He removed his hand. "If they attack, I want you to run. Do not look back or linger. Understand?"

"What?" Nearly forty invisible assassins had been trailing me, but that wasn't even the most terrifying part. Imagining that

many demons invading this world, and the damage they could do...it was too much. "How did they get here?"

"I have two guesses. Either the gates are exponentially weakening. Or someone summoned them all." Wrath pressed us more firmly against the stone, his massive body swallowing up any bit of light from my amulet that might give us away. "If you agree to it, I can *transvenio* us back to the palace. Will you come with me?"

A slight tug of warning stayed my tongue. Which was odd considering I very much wanted him to magic us away from the danger. But it was also highly convenient that I only had *his* word about the invisible mercenaries. Envy had succeeded in one thing; he'd created doubt.

"How does that work, exactly?"

"Put simply, you travel through dimensions with me, and are deposited at a place of my choosing."

"You said I had to agree to it...does that happen each time?"

"Once you give permission, it is eternal."

Despite the danger closing in, there was still that nagging feeling I couldn't ignore. I'd rather take my chances with mercenaries than make an eternal bargain. "And what else?"

He hesitated now. Which worried me. "Essentially it feels like you're being incinerated while we shift time and space. It doesn't last more than a second or two."

I stared at him. Fire and witches mixed as well as demons and angels. It was settled. I'd try my luck with the assassins. "There has to be—"

"Run, Emilia!"

He whipped around, and landed a hard kick into what could only be an Umbra demon. I didn't see it go flying, but I heard a strange sound. If it was incorporeal, I wasn't sure how Wrath had made contact with it. He lashed out at another, and another. It was only when they collapsed that I understood the anomaly. Wrath's demon dagger severed their heads. Maybe holding the weapon allowed him to strike them, too.

As they died, they lost their invisibility. I wanted to run, but couldn't seem to move. I stared at the pale faces with deep black circles around their sunken eyes, and teeth carved to tiny points that pulled back from rotting black gums. They looked like corpses and smelled much the same.

I couldn't decide if not knowing their true faces was better or worse.

"Take the horns and leave!" Wrath dodged forward, struck, heads rolled. He was violence made flesh. Watching him attack and maim demon after demon, I imagined he was invincible. He'd strike, parry, kick, and then heads would roll. Body parts went flying. Dark blood splattered. There was nothing that could stop him.

Envy emerged from the deepest part of the shadows, his eyes glittering like emeralds. "Seize him."

He snapped his fingers once, and I just made out the shadowy forms of the Umbra demons as they swarmed in like a hive of vicious wasps. Wrath fought, thrashed, and managed to take out a few more, but it was no use. Even something as mighty as the demon of war couldn't hold back the tide of invisible bodies that kept coming for him. Not unless he unleashed his full magic.

Strangely enough, not one of them so much as breathed in my direction.

Eventually they held Wrath in place. His power rumbled, rolled through the tunnels, but Envy only laughed as rocks rained down. I managed to dodge out of the way as a large piece crashed where I'd been standing a second before.

"Go on. Use all of that might, brother. You'll bury your witch." The grumbling deep within the earth ceased. Envy cut a glance my way, smiling. "Don't worry. It still has nothing to do with his feelings, pet. You are a means to an end. Isn't that right, brother?"

"If you do this, you'll be damning yourself, too." Even held down, surrounded by enemies, Wrath didn't look cowed. "Is that what you really want?"

"Maybe I like being damned." Envy flicked imaginary dirt from his lapels. "Maybe you ought to remember what it's like, dear brother. To have something you covet taken away. Pity you didn't remember that I, too, am something to be feared. Allow me to remind you."

If it wasn't for the sickening wet *thwack* and Wrath's muffled groan, I might not have known something—aside from being surrounded by invisible mercenary demons—was wrong. I watched in silent horror as Envy's dagger sank deep into Wrath's groin, and he dragged it across his body, opening him from hip to hip. Guts spilled out as Wrath hunched over, his eyes wide.

"Go," he coughed. Blood splattered across his lips.

I stared, unblinking. I think I screamed.

Sounds around me were replaced with a high-pitched keening noise in my head. My face got hot, then cold. Wrath's entire abdomen was flayed open. One second he was standing, fighting, and then... then... there was so much blood. I fell to my knees and retched.

Envy laughed, the sound bouncing off the walls. "I've been wanting to do that for an age, brother. I cannot tell you how good it feels, watching you bleed out." He glanced over at me, his upper lip curling. "Watch closely, pet. This is how I treat family. Imagine what being my enemy is like. Do not think I've forgiven what you and your grandmother did to me."

He twisted the dagger and Wrath coughed dark-colored blood. I forced myself to watch, to stand. I couldn't fall to pieces yet. The Umbra demons holding on to the demon of war must have let go; Wrath slid to the ground, staring down at the brutality of his injury.

Envy lifted his blade again, but I couldn't bear it.

"Stop!" I choked on a scream as Envy ignored my pleas and stabbed him once more for good measure. He stepped back to survey the damage. Wrath struggled to look in my direction, but couldn't quite make it. He never struggled. I didn't think it was in his nature.

"Please... Emilia. I—" He gasped; the sound raspy and labored. He was dying. Truly dying.

Something stirred in me.

I rushed to his side, hands fumbling, and tried to stop the bleeding. "It's all right. It's going to be all right. You just have to heal yourself."

Once again, I had no spell, no magic to call upon to bind his wound together. I was too rattled to think clearly. I only had my two hands, and the hope that he could heal himself quickly enough. He slowly turned to me, the light leaving his eyes before he met my pleading gaze. This couldn't be happening. I needed him.

"No." Now more than ever, he had to get up and be okay. I shook him a little. He was unnaturally still, pupils fixed. I knew what that meant and couldn't... *he* couldn't be dead. This stupid, arrogant demon was supposed to be immortal. "Get up."

He needed to heal. He just needed some time. I could hold his wound for a few more minutes. That's all he needed. A few minutes. I could do that. I could stay there until he stitched himself together again.

I was still kneeling there, hands full of gore, when his body vanished from this realm.

I stared at the wet blood on my palms. There was so much of it. Too much. No mortal would survive those injuries. Wrath had always healed instantaneously before.

He was hurt, but not dead.

Just like Lust when he'd been struck with Wrath's blade. He *couldn't* be dead. That was the point of immortality. But…I'd seen life leave the demon's eyes. Lust hadn't looked like that. He'd still been breathing when he'd vanished back to Hell. *I* suddenly couldn't breathe. Without him, I…

I held out my hands; they were shaking. I glanced down and watched in a strange, detached manner as my whole body violently trembled. Seeing my sister's mutilated body had been horrible, but watching someone get eviscerated…I rubbed my hands down my skirts, but the blood wouldn't come off. I scrubbed and scrubbed and—

"Enough of that." Envy wrapped long fingers around my wrist, grinding the bones together. A little more pressure and he'd fracture something. "All of this unpleasantness could have been avoided if you'd have listened. You have no one to blame but yourself."

"W-will…w-will h-he live?"

Envy knelt beside me, and pressed the flat side of his dagger beneath my chin. The blade was still slick with Wrath's blood. "You ought to pray to your goddess he doesn't. Now give me the Horn of Hades and I might consider ending you swiftly."

I dragged my gaze away from the spot of blood where Wrath

had fallen. He'd fought for me. He put himself between his brother and me, and paid for it. Anger suddenly swept in, cleared my mind of grief. I glared at Envy, and shoved my hand into my skirt pocket. I quickly looped Vittoria's amulet over my head, finally bringing the Horn of Hades together.

A whiplike crack split the silence as the devil's horns were reunited. Power surged through me. "Get out. Get out before I *make* you."

"You're making a terrible mistake." Envy didn't stagger back or run, but he did obey me. "I will not soon forget your disobedience, pet. And neither should you. It is no small thing to have a prince of Hell for an enemy. Come."

He gathered his invisible assassins and left the dank tunnel. I waited until he was gone before I slumped to the ground. After that show of power, I couldn't bring myself to move. I pulled my knees to my chest. Things had gone spectacularly wrong, and this time I had no idea how to move forward. Wrath was gone. My family was in hiding, and winning against the princes of Hell all by myself seemed more impossible than ever. Seeing Wrath ripped open from hip to hip rattled something in me. I'd thought he was invincible, so what chance did *I* really stand?

I wanted to be brave, and bold, and smart, and vanquish my enemies with cunning. Admitting I had much to learn felt like defeat. I had magic, and the Horn of Hades, but no time to learn darker tricks to even the playing field. Nonna said she'd try to slow the gates of Hell from opening, but who knows if she'd succeed before our time was up.

Being a realist didn't mean I was a defeatist. Maybe things *would* be better if I stopped fighting, and waited to see if the devil wanted to claim me.

Or maybe now that I had his horns I should summon him, make a bargain of my own, and stop further destruction. My attention shifted back to where Wrath had fallen. I had a feeling I knew what he'd do. And I knew what Vittoria had chosen. But I still wasn't sure what I wanted.

So I sat there, beside the drying blood of my worst enemy, and wept.

FORTY-FOUR

Resurrection spells are part of both the dark arts and the Forbidden because they go against the natural order. If you attempt to steal back life, Death will take its retribution elsewhere, balancing the scales. As above, so below.

—*Notes from the di Carlo grimoire*

An hour later I found myself outside the ruined palace. I had nowhere else to go that was safe, and hoped Wrath's magic was still somehow protecting the building. I'd made it into the lower level and had just closed the door when a tiny spike of coolness grazed my neck. I went to ignore it when I recalled what Nonna had said about being Marked by a prince of Hell.

Wrath had given me a way to summon him.

I dashed upstairs, and pulled supplies out of an extra bag I'd packed days before. Black candles, a few animal bones from the restaurant, my own personal grimoire I'd started, and…

Blood and bones! Without Wrath's dagger, I didn't have any gold, which was a main ingredient I needed to summon a demon from House Wrath. I paced around the room and cursed.

For one bloody moment I wished something would just go easily.

I shoved the candles out of the way and sank onto my bed, blinking back tears. I'd been so angry with Wrath after our kiss, so devastated by his omission about what he was truly after, that I'd wanted to hurt him back, but never like this.

Watching someone you know die, even if it's someone you *shouldn't* like, was no small thing. Then Envy's threat, the loss of my family…I didn't know how to proceed from here. I lay down and stared at little lines in the ceiling, thinking they were like the small fissures that had cracked my life into a million little parts. Each line represented another path, another choice, another attempt to right the wrongs committed. I mentally retraced my steps over the last several weeks, trying to divine where I may have taken a wrong turn.

When no wise answers were forthcoming, I gave up and rolled onto my side. The little dresser beside the bed had a bottle of prosecco and two glasses. A small bowl of chocolate-covered orange slices was also there. I couldn't recall seeing either of them before, but Wrath might have brought in the treats while we were playing scopa.

I didn't know what to make of that, so I banished those thoughts and popped the cork, watching the bubbles fizz and softly crackle as I filled my glass. If the world as I knew it was ending, I deserved a drink before I made a deal with the devil. I brought the glass to my lips and paused. Wrath had said to look in the dresser if I was bored. I wasn't bored, but I *was* intrigued.

I set my glass down and pulled open the top drawer.

A small gold ring hammered into olive branches sat on a bed of crushed velvet.

It was simple but beautiful. I picked it up and slipped it onto my forefinger. It fit perfectly. My heart twisted. I knew exactly why he'd left it for me. During ancient Roman times, an olive branch was given by an enemy as a gesture of peace. A tear slipped down my cheek as I thought back to him calling it a twig of truth. Wrath, likely surmising I didn't have much gold of my own, had given me the final piece I needed to summon him. He'd prepared for everything. Tactical to his very core.

Feeling hopeful for the first time in what felt like ages, I set the candles up in a circle and lit them, placed freshly cut ferns and bones down, then began the summoning. I used a bit of my own blood in offering, and fed the circle a few drops.

"By earth, blood, and bone. I invite thee. Come, enter this realm of man. Join me. Bound in this circle, until I send thee home."

I knelt there, waiting for the telltale smoke of Wrath's arrival. Seconds passed. I kept my hope in check. Last time, seconds after the incantation was done, the first signs of his arrival had occurred. Maybe, since he was greatly injured, he needed a bigger offering. I squeezed a few more droplets of blood into the circle. Nothing happened.

"Come on, demon."

I went over the ritual again. Adjusting the ferns, bones, and candles until they formed a perfect circle. I set my ring inside the containment area, then dripped more blood.

"By earth, blood, and bone. I invite thee. Come, enter this realm of man. Join me. Bound in this circle, until I send thee home."

I left out the Latin again, seeing as the last time it ended in an unplanned betrothal and Wrath said it wasn't necessary. When all remained silent, I tried one final time, and used the same incantation that would bind us together in unholy matrimony if Wrath accepted it.

"By earth, blood, and bone. I invite thee. Come, enter this realm of man. Join me. Bound in this circle, until I send thee home. *Aevitas ligati in aeternus protego.*"

A stiff breeze blew one of the candles out. I waited, breath held, for the mighty demon of war to rise. Immortal. Furious. Breathtaking. I braced myself for a lecture that was sure to come. Moments came and went, but there was no smoke, or sign I'd summoned anything. I waited and waited. Birds began calling to each other outside; morning wasn't far off. And the spell for Wrath could only be cast at night.

Still, I tried again, hoping this time would do it.

Eventually, the last of my hope was extinguished. Nonna said as long as he lived, Wrath would come. The fact that he didn't appear filled me with dread. I thought back to the very beginning, when I'd prayed to the goddess of death and fury, and couldn't help but wonder if she finally exacted the revenge I no longer wanted against him.

I watched the candles flicker, wishing they'd set the bedding and whole palace on fire. It would only be fitting for the rest of my world to go up in flames. Wrath was really, truly gone. And with him he'd taken the last of my hope.

The Horn of Hades was in my possession, but I wasn't sure how to use it to close the gates of Hell. My family had fled, Antonio was kidnapped by Envy, and my best friend's mind was still trapped between realms. Umbra demons had infiltrated this city, and I had no idea how to get rid of them all.

I blew out the summoning candles one by one until I was left completely in the dark.

FORTY-FIVE

By the time the sun spread its first rays across the sea, I was already dressed for battle. I stood in the mirror and finished braiding half my hair into a coronet, and left the other half down in loose waves. I secured the upper portion with two large diamond-encrusted olive branch clips that—with the exception of the precious stones—matched my new ring. I dabbed my lips with wine-colored stain and swept kohl across my lids.

I stepped back and admired my work; I looked dangerous. My dress was a deep berry with capped sleeves made entirely from gold scales. It was dark enough to hide blood, but wasn't another all-black ensemble. I didn't mind the color—it just felt too much like mourning.

And I was completely through with feeling sad.

Wrath said I had a choice—I could either be a victim or a victor. And, much as I was loath to admit it, he was right. Others would always be out there, trying to knock me down, to tell me who I was or who they thought I should be. People carved words into weapons often, but they only had power if I listened to them instead of trusting in myself.

If my enemies wanted to create doubt in me, I'd believe in my own abilities even more. Even if I had to fake it until it felt real.

I left the Zisa and headed deep into the heart of the city.

I cut a swath around Old Town and headed to Ballarò Market where food stands had been set up around the royal palace. I wasn't surprised to see the Nuccis already had a small gathering of people waiting for their arancini and panelle. Both fried rice balls and fried salted chickpea pancakes were popular street food.

Domenico Senior blotted his brow with a cloth and passed out a bag of food. I was happy to see him away from Greed's gambling den. It made one part of my plan easier.

I watched as his line slowly thinned, and people walked away with their bags of food. My stomach grumbled at the sight and smells, and I decided purchasing something was a good excuse to talk. I needed to eat anyway.

"*Buongiorno,* Signorina di Carlo. What would you like today?"

"Panelle with extra lemon wedges, please."

The elder Nucci fried the flat pancakes to perfection, hit them with some sea salt, then added them to a paper bag with an extra wedge of lemon. I handed my coins over, and drifted to the side where his awning provided a bit of shade. "How is Domenico Junior?"

"He in trouble?"

I wasn't sure how to answer that, so I pulled one of Wrath's favorite tricks and ignored it. "My sister had mentioned him, and I've heard he's been spending a lot of time at the monastery. It must be hard on him, losing someone he cared about."

Domenico Senior's gaze drifted to the person standing behind me before he passed out an order of arancini, and set another few into the fryer basket. "He's all right. He left for Calabria this morning to help his cousin."

I stopped chewing my panelle. Of all times for Domenico Junior to leave home, it was odd that he chose now. I changed tactics. "Have you spent any time in that gambling hall?" I asked, hoping it wasn't too rude. "I need to find it as soon as possible."

He shook his head. "Afraid I can't help you. I heard the guy who runs it left."

Internally I screamed and cursed the goddess of missed opportunities. I was about to leave when I noticed a strange tattoo inked onto his forearm. A pawprint clutching what appeared to be a fennel stalk. My gaze fell to the side of his food cart—the same symbol was painted there. I'd been wrong. I'd never seen it in my sister's diary. I'd seen it the day Wrath and I had tried to get close to investigate the murder of Giulia Santorini. My breath caught as it finally clicked into place. Signore Nucci was a shape-shifter.

I swallowed hard, and slowly dragged my attention up. Domenico Senior noticed me staring at his tattoo, and hastily rolled his sleeve back down despite the heat of the day.

His reaction set off warning bells.

I thought back to my sister's diary. All it had said was Domenico Nucci. There had never been a mention of junior or senior...

"It's you," I said, dropping my bag of panelle. "Vittoria wrote your name in her diary. It's never been Domenico Junior. Did you hurt her? Did she find out what you are?"

"It's not—don't shout those kind of accusations around. Give me a second."

Domenico flipped the stand's sign to CLOSED, and motioned for me to follow him around the corner where there was less foot traffic. I didn't want to leave the crowds, and he seemed to know that. He stopped where we were still surrounded, but couldn't be overheard.

"Your sister passed out drinks at Greed's gambling den."

My heart beat wildly. Finally, after all this time, I had another hint about what Vittoria had been up to right before she was killed. "And? Did she know what you are?" He nodded. "Did you ever see her with Greed?"

"Yeah. She came to him one night with an idea. They were working on a plan they both felt comfortable with."

"How did you get involved in all this?" He didn't seem inclined to respond, so I pulled the knife I'd hidden in my bodice and let the sun glint off the blade. I'd learned a good many tricks from the demon of war. "One way or another I will get my information, signore. The choice is up to you on how we go about it."

"All right, all right." He swallowed hard and glanced around. "You know about the benandanti."

I nodded. Everyone did. "Shape-shifters, in a sense. Their spirits change into animal forms to astral travel four times a year. They also fight in the Night Battles."

"Well, that's what the benandanti are. We're not them, but they have taken on our symbol so we're often confused. We can physically shape-shift whenever we please. We're called Ember Wolves. The benandanti are human, we are not. At least not entirely. Most would say we're werewolves."

"Werewolves," I repeated. "You physically change into a wolf?"

Domenico Senior nodded.

I took a moment to recover. I had never heard of an Ember Wolf, but there were plenty of tales about werewolves. From old stories I'd been told, the wolves stuck with their pack and were loyal only to each other. I didn't understand how or why he'd associate with the demons.

"Why were you with Greed?"

His gaze dropped to the ground. "We made a bargain."

A memory of seeing him with stacks of gambling chips crossed my mind. I had a sinking suspicion I knew where this was going. "Did he promise to forgive your debts if you helped him?"

He nodded. "I thought it was a fool's bargain for him. Then I found out it wasn't his idea to begin with. He said all he wanted was for the wolves to fight on the side of the devil when the time comes. We haven't shifted in nearly two decades, so I didn't think the bargain held value."

"Why haven't you shifted?"

He lifted a shoulder. "No one is sure. One day we could, and the next we couldn't."

"But that changed recently, didn't it?" I asked. "Did someone shift forms?"

"When a boy celebrates his twentieth year, he usually changes for the first time."

And I'd bet anything Domenico had a birthday recently, and was very surprised when he turned into a wolf. "You didn't tell your son what you were?"

He slowly shook his head. "It had been so long...I didn't think it would happen. When Dom shifted, I knew we were in trouble. I told him what I'd promised." He swiped a tear from his cheek. "The disappointment in my son's eyes was enough to end me. The shame I've brought to our legacy, our family. Wolves do not fight for anyone outside of our pack. Now Dom prays at the monastery for me and for himself, hoping everyone will forgive my sins."

"How did my sister figure out what you are?"

He considered that a moment. "I'm not sure. But she was the one who told Greed to bargain with me. When the deal was struck, she made me promise to keep my word to him."

"Vittoria set up the bargain between you and Greed?" I asked, heart hammering. "You're sure that was her idea and not his?"

"Positive," Signore Nucci said. "It was part of her bigger plan. But she never told me what that was, so I'm afraid I can't help you there. I was only told to be ready when they called on us."

I let out a slow breath. Vittoria had found a way to force two enemies to work together. A united front to fight the true enemy. Which was still an unknown. I considered this new information carefully. My sister had believed in Greed. I'd believed in Wrath. And Envy was still the obvious murderer except…he hadn't bragged about ripping hearts from anyone's body, and he didn't have my amulet. Which meant our murderer could still be out there. "Domenico isn't really on the mainland, is he?"

"No," Signore Nucci admitted, sniffling. "He's at the monastery."

All roads kept leading back to the monastery. And I no longer believed in coincidences.

My sister's body was found there.

Claudia's scrying session went horribly wrong there.

Domenico prayed there almost daily, but, according to Claudia, he also spoke with members of the brotherhood. I'd bet anything he may have confided his troubles to the wrong person, especially with how they acted the night I found Claudia.

I bid Signore Nucci good-bye and hurried off to hunt down my next clue.

Before Vittoria was murdered and my world went to Hell, Nonna said there were witch hunters actively seeking prey on the island. I'd ruled them out after I'd summoned Wrath and found three other princes of Hell roaming the earth. But maybe I'd been too hasty.

If someone wanted to kill witches, the holy order was the perfect suspect. Who better to eradicate the world from evil than those ordained by God?

I thought back to the night I'd found Claudia, to Brother Carmine, who'd had a murderous gleam in his eyes. He'd stepped forward, looking hungry for blood. I knew he despised witches, and he hadn't given one of his vitriolic speeches in the marketplace in years. I could only imagine how much he'd love to climb back onto his soapbox and spew more hatred.

His open contempt for magic-users made him a prime suspect for a witch hunter.

Today, one way or another, I'd uncover the secrets the holy brotherhood were keeping.

FORTY-SIX

A group of robed figures was gathered in the courtyard. Tension was as thick as the summer heat among the brotherhood. One of their members was missing, and several young women were dead. I wasn't surprised they were blaming the devil. I hid near the edge of the main building and my gaze swept around the crowd, searching for one member I knew I wouldn't find.

Brother Carmine stood at the center, his hand punching the sky with each impassioned word that left his mouth. Apparently I'd arrived at the apex of his speech.

"Our God is a mighty God, and will not tolerate an infestation of evil," he said. "We must lead by His example in these dark and troubling times. The hour of judgment is upon us. We must stop the devil before he sows the seeds of his wicked ways! Come, let us speak the Good Word to our fellow man. Let us lead them into their Salvation."

"Amen!" they all yelled in unison.

The crowd disbanded toward the city, off to save human souls. I inched around the corner and released a tight breath. Brother Carmine wasn't talking about the devil breaking the curse, but what he said was a little alarming in its accuracy. For once, human souls really were in danger. My suspicion of him deepened. If a mysterious group of witch hunters had formed, it was very, very likely I'd just located them. I was contemplating whether or not I should follow him when I felt the call of magic coming from within the monastery. It was just like the night I'd found Vittoria's body.

If not more powerful.

Maybe I was just better at sensing it now. Or perhaps it had something to do with the full set of horns in my possession. I removed my sister's *cornicello* from where I'd hidden it in my dress and held it up. Even for a non-human witch it seemed sacrilegious to wear the devil's horns into a holy space. But there was no way I'd go inside without protection. I slipped her *cornicello* on along with the one I already wore, feeling a prickle of magic in my veins.

Before I slipped inside, I cast one final look around. All was quiet now. The brotherhood was gone. I crossed the small courtyard and pushed the door open. As I hurried past the mummies in an otherwise empty corridor, I felt . . . something watching.

I turned in place, and scanned the hallway that used to cause my heart to speed and my hands to shake. This time, when my pulse raced, it wasn't because I was afraid of what I'd find. I *wanted* someone to try and attack me.

"Show yourself."

Unlike in the novels Vittoria loved reading, no villain emerged with a dark chuckle to wax poetic over its master's evil plans. No one emerged at all. I was truly alone. I closed my eyes, grabbed the Horn of Hades, breathed in deeply, and centered myself. When I looked down the seemingly empty corridor of the dead again, I heard faint whispers.

They weren't of this world.

I shut out everything else except the sound of hushed voices. I followed it, traveling deeper into the catacombs. I noted each turn and new hallway I entered, hoping I'd find my way back out again if I had to run. I'd never been this far into the monastery before; I didn't even know there *were* so many labyrinthine corridors that twisted and turned deep, deep into the center of the earth.

As I continued on silently, the hum of voices grew louder. My nerves tingled. Something magical was close. And it was powerful. Part of me wanted to ignore it and run. But too much was at stake. I pressed on, forcing myself to face my fears.

Several minutes later, I stopped in a dank hallway carved of limestone with a lone torch set into a sconce. Light flickered menacingly, like an annoyed cat's tail. I didn't need the sign from the goddess to know something dangerous was close by. I couldn't tell if my stomach twisted in trepidation or anticipation. One way or another, something was about to happen.

A door near the end of the hallway was slightly cracked open in invitation. I took the last few steps and paused beside it. It very well could be a trap, but the whispers had turned frantic now.

I needed to see what was in there. I inched closer, pulse pounding, and pushed the door a bit wider. From the outside, the room looked empty. Looks were often deceiving. Before I entered it, I peered around just to be sure it wasn't a trap. Dust motes spun in circles. All was quiet. Illusions were deceptively easy magic—they often projected what you expected to find.

I should have known better.

FORTY-SEVEN

The moment I crossed the threshold, I knew I'd made a mistake. It felt as if the air was a band that snapped out and locked me in place. I pushed back toward the door, but it was no use. I'd stay in this room until whoever had set the containment spell decided to set me free.

The whispers I'd been hearing turned to full-on chatter. There were so many voices, so many conversations, I could hardly hear my own thoughts.

"It's here."

"She's arrived."

"Open the binding."

"Set her free."

I covered my ears, and searched for any possible escape or means to break the spell. I wanted the noise to stop. *Now.* The glamour abruptly dropped away, as if attuned to my desires. My gaze swept around the true version of the room. The walls were covered in Latin. Lines and lines of it—some in larger script, some smaller—filled every inch of the walls from floor to ceiling. Someone had been very busy. I'd never seen magic used like that before.

The letters softly glowed and pulsated like they were part of a living, breathing entity. I wanted to sink to my knees; a spell that powerful wouldn't be easily broken. But I wouldn't give up just yet. I searched for signs of an ambush. I was alone, except for a book.

My heartbeat slowed. This had to be the "it" Vittoria described in her diary.

When I set my attention on the book, the voices started again, softer, more enticing. I tentatively dropped my hands from my ears. I could hardly breathe. This was the secret my sister died to keep. I knew it deep down in my bones.

A single shaft of light illuminated the old, leather-bound tome lying closed on a pedestal carved from a solid chunk of obsidian. I'd never seen a gemstone that large before, and cautiously moved forward until I stood over the mysterious book. The voices quieted.

A triple moon symbol molded from pewter adorned the cover, but there was no title to indicate what it contained. It was definitely magical, given how much power emanated from its pages. Soft lavender light surrounded it. It reminded me of the *luccicare* I saw around humans, and was the same shade of purple as my tattoo. I didn't know what it meant, but I had a very good idea of what it was—the first book of spells. Impossibly, Vittoria *had* found La Prima's grimoire.

It was so plain, so simple. And yet, it had cost my sister so much.

I suddenly wanted to burn it.

It was no larger than any other old book, but the power was unlike anything I'd ever felt. The cover was worn in places where it looked like it had been opened and closed a million times.

Like the night I found my sister's body, there was a silent, insistent tug in my center. This time, it begged me to open the book, to glimpse the spells I felt spilling from it. I slowly reached over, and flipped it open to a place that had been marked with a ribbon.

Familiar black paper with gold roots edged around the sides greeted me. I scanned the page—it was a summoning for the morning star. I shut the book and stepped away.

Someone had summoned the devil. Or wanted to.

I took a few steady breaths, mind racing. This was the mysterious grimoire my sister had torn pages from. Somehow her magic led her to the first book of spells, and then she'd removed spells to summon demons. I knew for a fact she hadn't snuck this text into our tiny room, I would have felt it the moment it entered our home and so would Nonna, which meant Vittoria must have stashed it away here. But why would she think it'd be safe within the brotherhood's walls... there was a connection, I just had to *think*.

"At last."

I jumped back as a hooded figure stepped into the room, and reached for my blessed chalk. This had to be the person the messenger had sold his secrets to. I bet it was Brother Carmine. How ironic that a witch hunter set a trap using magic. The figure tugged the cowl back, and I froze, ready for the witch-hating brother to attack. Instead, Antonio moved more quickly than I'd thought possible and knocked the chalk out of my hands like it might grow talons and hurt me. I watched it shatter on the ground, then snapped into reality. Relief flooded my system.

"Antonio! You're alive. I thought..." I dragged my gaze up and noticed the expression on his face. Concern wasn't present. It was hatred. My heart pounded as I took a step back. "W-what happened? Did Envy hurt you?"

"An angel of God would never hurt me." His lips pulled into a smile that was far from the sweet, shy ones I remembered. "Unlike you."

I could barely breathe as everything fell into place. Envy didn't hurt him, or hold him captive. Quite the contrary. Antonio had willingly delivered Claudia straight into my enemies' hands. He'd known she was a witch and...

"It's you. *You* killed my sister." My voice trembled. "Why?"

"Is it really that hard to believe? That I, a man of God, would wish to rid the world of evil?"

"You sound just like Carmine." I curled my hands into fists, needing to feel the prick of my nails to keep from lashing out. "Murdering innocent women isn't its own act of evil?"

"God's finest angels are fierce warriors, Emilia. Sometimes in order to accomplish the greatest good, we must first become a blade of justice and carve through our enemies. You wouldn't understand. It's not something you'd be capable of doing, *witch*."

What little control I'd managed to hang on to, left me.

"You know *nothing* of what I can do."

"Maybe not. But if you use magic on me now, you'll prove me right." He jerked his chin toward my combined amulets. They were fiercely glowing. "*All* witches are born evil."

My temper and hurt raged around. I stepped forward and unleashed the pent-up wrath I'd been clutching onto since my twin's murder.

"You're wrong. We're not born evil. Some of us become that way. Through hate."

Strands of my hair lifted as if there were suddenly a breeze. A storm was brewing and it wasn't of this world. The glowing words that surrounded us pulsed faster. Magic singed the air, and incantations I didn't know swirled through my mind. Maybe the devil's horns were fueling me, or the first book of spells was feeding me its charms.

Perhaps it was simply my own darkness escaping. I didn't care.

I held the Horn of Hades and whispered a spell so foul, the words burned as they left my lips. I lifted my arm, then slashed down in an arc. Invisible claws cut Antonio's robes to ribbons.

This time I spared his flesh.

Fear entered his eyes. He slowly backed away, hands up. As if that would stop me.

"Frightened?" I stepped toward him. "You should be. I've only just begun."

I lifted my arm and he cringed away. His voice quivered. "M-mercy, Emilia. P-please."

"Now you want mercy?" Pure, white-hot anger burned in my soul. "Tell me, did my sister beg?"

I thought of her chest, the gaping hole where her heart had been. He did that to her. Our friend. I threw my arm back and slashed *his* chest open. An eye for an eye. Justice. He pressed his fingers to his wounds, saw blood, and stumbled away. It was nothing more than a scratch.

Fury propelled me forward. "Did you offer Vittoria mercy when she pleaded for her life? Or Valentina? How many women pleaded with you to spare them? Where was your mercy then?"

He fell to his knees and began praying. I waited. But God didn't show up. The goddess of death and fury did. I knelt down, eyes blazing, and forced him to look at me. I wanted him to see my sister's face, too. Tears slipped down his cheeks. I fought the urge to smash his skull against the floor and watch the life leave those hate-filled eyes.

Death would be a kindness. And I wasn't feeling particularly kind.

"When I finally kill you, you will beg for the sweet release of death, Antonio." I glanced at my finger, concentrated on an invisible blade pricking it. A tiny ruby of blood beaded up. "I swear on my blood, you will never know true happiness again. Your heart will be cursed to be broken each time you forget the sins you've committed. And each time you laugh, I will be there, waiting, to remind you."

I was about to seal the vow with the drop of blood, when the scent of urine filled the space around us, awakening a memory in me. I'd scared the piss out of Antonio. Just like Wrath had done when he'd beaten information from... I startled back and let my hand fall to my side.

Wrath, a prince of Hell, had shown mercy.

Knowing the sort of power he had, I don't know how he'd managed restraint. And I wished I could be a little more like him now. But I wasn't.

"New rules. You will tell me the truth about everything I ask, and only then will I consider sparing your life. Do you understand?"

"Y-yes." He nodded several times and inhaled deeply. "W-what do y-you want to know?"

"Before you met this 'angel of death' something must have prompted this. Tell me what grew so twisted inside you. So foul."

"I—I'm not..." He shook his head. "A-all right. A week before my mother died, I took her to a woman I thought only used folk magic and prayer to heal. Turned out, she was a witch." His laugh was hollow. I gave him a flat look and he choked it off. "She caused my mother's death. I vowed, right then, to make amends to God.

I promised if I ever met another witch, I'd send her straight to the dungeons of Hell where she belongs. That's when my prayers were answered."

"How?"

"An angel came to me, shortly after, telling me about the devil's curse. He said in order to break it, the devil needed to marry a witch. The angel told me that couldn't happen, or else the devil would be set free. He said he'd provide the names of potential brides, and all I had to do to save us from true evil, was kill witches."

My gaze strayed to the first book of spells. I thought about my sister again. "Did this angel give you my sister's name?"

His gaze dropped to the floor. "Your sister's death was... I didn't want to... I even asked the angel to spare her, but he said leaving one seed of evil would cause more to grow. I fought it for a little while. I even argued that she wasn't a witch, he was mistaken. Then she..." He refused to meet my eyes. "Then she started talking about summoning the devil that night in the monastery, and I couldn't deny the truth. She had to be stopped."

I held back my fury. Vittoria always joked about summoning the devil, or hexing someone, or other silly things she'd say in front of humans. They normally laughed, thinking she was kidding. I'd worried one day someone might start questioning her. I never thought it would be someone close to us. "You betrayed her. Me."

"And you didn't do the same to me?" he asked, his voice turning momentarily sharp before he caught himself. "You cast a spell to make me fall in love with you. You lied to my face every day, hiding the truth of what you are." Despite my earlier show of power, his face contorted with rage. "You belong in Hell with the other cursed and damned souls. You're not even human. You disgust me."

"I have *never* used a spell on you for love."

"Can you honestly say—before tonight—that you've never used magic on me without my consent? Are you an exception to the rule?"

"Of course I haven't, I..." I closed my mouth. I'd used a forbidden truth spell on him when we were children. I'd violated his free will. What I'd done was wrong, but it didn't give him the right to murder women in retribution. "How were you planning on stopping the devil from finding a witch in a different city?"

"By summoning him."

"You, a man of God, doing the work of supposed angels, want to summon the devil?"

"Oh, I don't want to do it, Emilia. But I'll do what has to be done. I want him to watch as I destroy his horns."

My hand went to my amulet. "How do—"

"How did I know you're wearing the actual horns of the devil?" he mocked. "My angel of death. You see, first we'd destroy every living witch. Then, we'd summon the devil and put a blade through him."

"What was this angel's name?"

Antonio lifted a shoulder. "He wouldn't tell me. But there was something...powerful about him. I knew he wasn't lying. Only something heaven sent could inspire that much glory."

Whether Antonio knew it or not, I'd bet my soul he'd been influenced by a prince of Hell. And I think I knew exactly who had orchestrated it all: Envy. The traitor demon. I just needed proof, and then I'd destroy him.

"How do the hearts factor in?"

He gave me an odd look. "Hearts?"

Like he didn't know. Clearly, his cooperation was ending. Or maybe there were parts of his beastly acts he couldn't face. I stopped paying attention to Antonio, and started thinking about my next move. I thought about my sister, about her plan to summon the devil. She wanted to bargain with him.

Maybe she knew Envy, or some other prince of Hell had been nudging the hands of fate, and that the only way to stop him was to help Pride break the curse. Which would explain why she wanted the werewolves and Greed to team up. Whatever her reasons, she thought her best course of action was to go to the underworld. Antonio might be the instrument of death, he might have chosen to commit these atrocious acts, but he hadn't acted alone.

Now I wanted to find out who else had helped kill my sister.

An idea, wild and mad, formed in my head. If Antonio actually managed to summon the devil now, I could use it to my advantage. My sister believed that ruling in Hell was her best choice.

Maybe it was mine, too.

"If you're going to summon the devil, why wait?"

"*You're* going to summon him." Antonio smiled. "And I'm going to kill him when you do."

I'd like to see him try. I pointed to the half-finished summoning circle and gripped the amulets in my hand. "Light the candles."

He did as I asked and quickly finished setting up the circle. Instead of using animal bones, he placed flowering wolfsbane between each candle. I stared at the helmet-shaped deep purple and blue petals. It was not at all what I'd think one would use to summon Pride.

When the last piece of wolfsbane was in place, he stepped back and murmured an invitation for me to repeat in Latin. His "angel" had taught him well.

Like the time I summoned Wrath, smoke filled the circle. Lightning whipped around, the atmosphere crackling like we were stuck in the midst of a terrible storm. I expected to see a beautiful man standing before us. I did not expect to see Antonio. His eyes were pools of silvery blue; the only indication he was not the young man who'd grown up next door.

He glanced around, his movements not quite natural. I held my ground as he looked me over. Pride had taken possession of Antonio's body. Before I could force my expression into a mask of boredom, he stepped closer. My breath hitched. His attention lingered on the diamond-encrusted clips in my hair.

"I have a gift for you, *Stella Strega*."

His voice was beautiful. After what I'd recently learned about good and evil, I don't know why I expected it to be multi-tonal and screeching. "And what will this gift cost me?"

His smile was anything but tender. "Only your soul, of course."

I smiled back at him, my new groom. He had no idea a storm would soon be approaching Hell. "You have my attention, Pride. Impress me."

He ran his gaze over me slowly, and snapped his fingers. A charge of magic filled the air. Something crackled and a gown appeared.

It hung from an invisible source, skirts fluttering. The top was a metal corset covered entirely with thorny vines. Layers of black panels gathered at the hips, and flowed to the ground in frothy midnight waves. Every other layer had tiny smoky gems sewn into it, reminding me of crushed hematite. Glittering black snakes twined together in intricate knots at the waist like a belt.

I'd expect nothing less dramatic for the future queen of Hell.

I was pleased my plan was working, and also terrified. There was no turning back now.

The gown swayed and twirled on its own, as if worn by some invisible being, sweeping closer and closer to where I remained motionless. It brushed against me and rushed around my body, spinning wildly until I squeezed my eyes shut. I didn't like how it reminded me of Lust's invisible party. In fact, I hated it.

Everything stopped at once. I glanced down, startled to see my berry-colored dress was gone, and in its place the dark beauty hugged my curves.

I gasped as it squeezed me tighter.

The devil inclined his head. "All hail the new consort."

My heart pounded. "I haven't received a crown yet."

"Oh, but you will." From thin air, he yanked out a dagger with a roaring lion's head and aimed it at his/Antonio's heart. "I've heard of the vengeance you seek. Accept this human sacrifice as a gift from House Pride, your highness."

"No!"

The singular word came out in a strange multi-tonal voice that was at once mine, and completely foreign. The blade hovered against Antonio's skin, but didn't pierce it.

I drew in a shaky breath. "I will meet you, or your representative, in an hour in the cavern where I first summoned Wrath. I have something I need to do before I give my final answer."

The devil's focus shifted to mine. "Done."

"Somnus," I whispered, putting Antonio's body in an enchanted sleep. If anyone exacted revenge on him, it would be my hand that dealt his punishment.

Heart hammering, I glanced toward the first book of spells. I'd wanted a few minutes to read over it, and glean any last-minute magic before hiding it from the Wicked, but it was gone.

No matter. I'd make do in other ways. Without a backward glance, I left the chamber wearing the devil's horns and my sinister new dress, feeling my pulse quicken with each step. Before the night was through, I'd strike a deal with Pride that would hopefully be his realm's undoing.

I silently vowed to my sister I wouldn't rest until *all* those responsible for her death met their end.

FORTY-EIGHT

The devil didn't arrive on the back of a fire-breathing steed, or in the midst of a violent storm. In fact, it wasn't the king of demons who came for me at all.

Wrath stepped into the flickering light, looking ice-cold and dangerous. I unconsciously moved toward him, then froze. A low growl swept through the cave. It didn't come from him, but some animal hidden deep within the shadows. A warning from a goddess, no doubt.

Something was very wrong...

I inspected Wrath from a safe distance. There wasn't anything familiar about this demon. This creature left little doubt as to where he ruled. He was the most wicked of the Malvagi.

A traitorous part of me was relieved he was alive. Even though I knew he was immortal, I hadn't fully believed he'd lived through Envy's brutal attack. Another, wiser part of me reeled with denial that *he* was the one who'd come to collect my soul. Betrayal burned inside me.

I don't know why I expected anything else from a despicable prince of Hell.

Angry tears stung my eyes. Nonna had been right about everything. The Wicked were skilled liars. Wrath had certainly fooled me with his act. He made me think he was dead. And that he'd cared. It must have greatly amused him—watching me fall under his spell. A naïve, lonely witch who'd been desperate enough to seek help from her mortal enemy...

And our kiss. I'd thought I'd felt passion, heat. Another illusion cast by my enemy.

I fought a chill as he ran his gaze over me. Where it once burned with intensity, it was now frosted over. It was impossible to discern any of his thoughts. If I was to be his queen, he didn't seem impressed. I desperately wanted to believe *this* was the act, that he wasn't truly this cold and cruel. He said nothing and expressed even less. Envy, Greed, and Lust seemed downright human compared to this alien before me.

He wore a suit befitting his royal station, hands casually tucked into his pockets. A black crown with ruby-tipped thorns sat upon his head. If turned upside down, it would appear to be dripping blood. His clothing was layered charcoal and obsidian with gold stitching. Silk and velvet. If I didn't look too closely, he appeared more angel than dark prince.

My chin inched higher, giving him a clear view of the amulets around my neck. "Demon."

"Witch."

"I thought you were dead."

"Sorry to disappoint you."

His attention flicked to the containment circle where Antonio floated in a sort of suspended animation. Shadows along the ceiling grew talons. I could almost hear the rough scrape of their nails against stone. Wrath's expression remained blank, but I imagined he didn't expect to find a human magically imprisoned. I didn't bother hiding my taunting smile. Let him see what I could do.

He turned a flat look on me. "Are you ready to sell your soul?"

I stared a moment, taking in this version of him. I hadn't realized how often Wrath gazed upon me with blazing fire until it had been replaced with icy indifference. Whoever stood before me now wasn't the same demon I thought I'd known. I wanted to step away from him, to run.

"Well?" His tone was clipped. There was victory in this demon's gaze. No frustration, or flash of desire, or hard-won respect. I was a means to an end. Another potential witch queen to add to the list of those who'd been slaughtered before ever walking down the aisle. I tried not to think about my own uncertain fate. Even if it boiled down to living out of spite, I vowed to survive no matter who, or what, came for my heart. I had little doubt my life was in jeopardy. Wrath had told me the monsters would come for me, and that I believed. One stood before me now. "Have you decided?"

"Almost."

He appraised me, a small frown forming. Maybe he was disappointed I wasn't cowed by his royal presence and authority. I refused to pretend I understood anything of what he felt, or desired. I wasn't foolish enough to think he'd fallen in love with me, but I could have sworn we'd both shifted from cool animosity to something a bit warmer. I clutched the Horn of Hades as I considered my dwindling options. The slight buzz of magic was comforting—like a hug from my grandmother. If I stayed, the gates of Hell would weaken and open, destroying everything I held dear. I'd already encountered Umbra and Aper demons, the snake-like Viperidae, and four of the terrifying seven princes of Hell.

I was lucky I'd escaped with my life, and I was harder to kill than most. The human world wasn't equipped to deal with the carnage that hordes of demons would bring if the gates opened. I imagined Nonna wearing another ruby red necklace of blood, her eyes milky and lifeless. I saw visions of my mother and father slaughtered in our restaurant. Every innocent human in our city—lying in rotting heaps, stinking in the blazing sun.

I'd already lost my sister; I wouldn't lose anyone else.

"I agree. Under two conditions."

A new spark lit his gaze. Along with anger, intelligence and cunning gleamed out at me. "Very well. Let's hear your counteroffer."

I was proud of how my voice didn't waver. "From this point forward, no other witch will be hunted, no human attacked. I want every prince of Hell to stay out of this world. And Antonio will be my prisoner to do with as I see fit. Otherwise, I will not join myself with House Pride."

"Spoken like a true princess of Hell." His smile was razor sharp. He seemed smug, like he knew a secret. "Are you certain this is what you want? This is what you choose?" I nodded. Wrath stared a moment too long, like he was trying to incinerate me on the spot. "Done."

A scroll materialized along with a raven's quill, the point more blade than pen. When no pot of ink appeared, I immediately realized why. My heart thudded wildly. If I didn't run now, there would be no undoing this. Some bonds could never be broken.

I carefully read over the parchment.

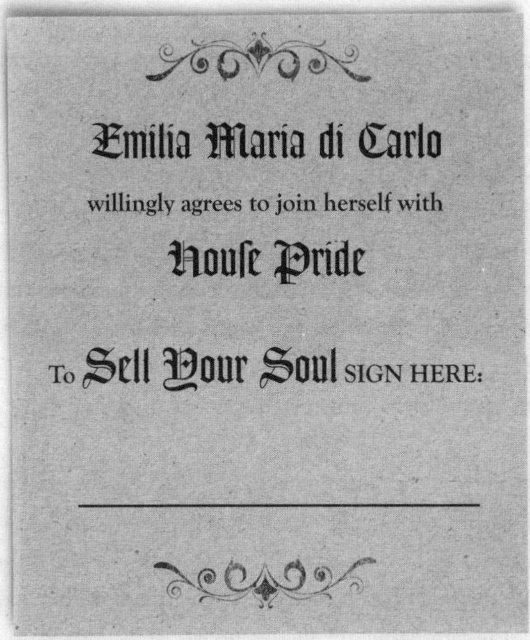

Emilia Maria di Carlo

willingly agrees to join herself with

House Pride

To **Sell Your Soul** SIGN HERE:

It was simple enough. Not much in the way of trickery. Which worried me more. Selling a soul shouldn't be so easy. I had a more difficult time haggling with vendors in the marketplace over clothing. Part of me wanted to laugh. But there was little humor to be found in this cavern.

Before I could run screaming, I pricked my finger and signed my soul away in blood, the magic binding me to the devil for eternity. Once I finished, the scroll disappeared in a wisp of smoke. I stared until the scent of sulfur dissipated, fighting a growing wave of panic.

"Anything else?" I asked as a strange tingling sensation fell around me like a cloak. Wrath nodded to my two amulets. Of course. The devil wanted his horns back. I yanked them from my neck and dropped them on the cavern floor, their absence already a strange sort of torture.

They vanished.

I took a deep breath. I no longer needed to worry about hiding from the Malvagi—the Wicked had found me. But that was all right; I'd found them, too. And I hoped they'd rue the day they came for me and mine. Soon I'd be deep within their realm, and would be perfectly positioned to uncover the true players behind the murders, and what they were really after.

Then I would set about destroying them. If they didn't kill me first.

I brushed past Wrath, walked to the lip of the cave, and glanced down. It might be the last time I saw this world, and I wanted to memorize it. An angry swell crashed against the rocks, spraying upward in harsh whispers. I stared out at the ink-colored waves, trying to calm my racing pulse. They looked like silver blades flashing in the moonlight. Nonna would claim it was a sign of treacherous things to come. This time, I couldn't disagree.

The ground suddenly trembled, pebbles scattered, bats flew out of the cave. I braced myself against the unexpected surge of magic, fearing the cavern would collapse.

I spun around, focus darting to Antonio, or where he'd once been. Vittoria's murderer was gone. In his place, Wrath's power whipped around like the tail of a mighty serpent. He smiled, a quick flash of teeth. We were no longer bound together, and his power was overwhelming, infinite. I refused to let my fear show.

The demon's grin vanished and he silently held out a hand. "Will you come with me?"

I knew he was only asking politely because of the demonic

etiquette. I didn't want to agree, I didn't want to ever touch him again, but I knew I couldn't find my way into the underworld without his dark magic.

"Yes."

I wrapped my fingers around his before my emotions betrayed me. There was crackling power in our connection. Tiny currents sparked over our skin. Before I could think about it, smoke enveloped us. Searing pain followed. It felt like my entire body was burning. I choked on a scream. Wrath's fingers tightened on mine. There was no earth, no connection to the natural world, nothing tangible except my grip on the prince I now hated more than the rest combined.

The pain lasted only a moment before a new sensation stoked even greater fear. We stood on solid ground again. Which meant . . .

Goddess above, I could hardly breathe. I wanted to squeeze my eyes shut forever.

Instead, I stared straight ahead, pulled my shoulders back, and waited for the smoke to clear.

I hoped the kingdom of the wicked was ready for a vengeful queen.

ACKNOWLEDGMENTS

It takes an entire coven of talented individuals to bring a book into the world, and, like Emilia, I have been goddess-blessed to have the following people casting powerful spells for this series:

Stephanie Garber—I'm so incredibly lucky to have a friend like you. This book would not be the same without your constant support, brainstorming sessions, and willingness to hop on the phone and chat about even the smallest details. Our weekly calls about our books (and our favorite TV shows) made drafting so much fun, and I am so happy we get to do it again!

Barbara Poelle, agent goddess extraordinaire, you never cease to amaze me with the many, many hats you wear: agent, friend, fierce business partner, bitmoji queen, and brainstorming champion. Thank you for planting the idea of Princes of Hell in my head way back when I first started kicking this idea around—I can't imagine this story without those sinfully devious demons now!

Maggie Kane and the entire team at the Irene Goodman Literary Agency, Heather Baror-Shapiro (Baror International), and Sean Berard (Grandview) work tirelessly behind the scenes to bring my work to amazing countries and to Hollywood. And I couldn't be more grateful to each of you.

To my brilliant editor, Laura Schreiber, you inherited this book (and me!) and immediately jumped in with unwavering enthusiasm to help find the story that had been in my head. I'm so happy with all of our hard work and cannot wait for what's to come in the next installment!

Liam Donnelly, the cover art and details inside the book make my dark heart sing. A million *thank yous* for the snakes and flowers and skulls—the whole aesthetic is *chef's kiss* fabulous.

Dan Denning, Joshua Johns, Jordan Mondell, Caitlyn Averett, T.S. Ferguson, Erinn McGrath, Charlotte Lamontagne, Maggie Cannon, Ned Rust, Tracy Shaw, Flo Yue, Blue Guess, Alexis Lassiter, the Hachette Sales team, Barbara Blasucci and the Special Sales team, Linda Arends, Virginia Lawther and the production team, and everyone at JIMMY Patterson Books and Little, Brown—your hard work, dedication, creativity, and talent is seriously endless. You have all worked some Wrath-level powerful magic to launch this book during a global pandemic; thank you for everything you do behind the scenes.

James Patterson—none of this would be possible without your constant support. Thank you a million times over.

To my fabulous U.K. crew at Hodder & Stoughton: Molly Powell, Kate Keehan, Maddy Marshall, Oliver Johnson, and the whole team—I still pinch myself when I think about the initial acquisition letter I received and the enthusiasm you all had for this book. I'm still in awe over the incredible edition of *Kingdom* you created.

Jenny Bak, you gave this book a home before you left for new editing adventures, and I am forever grateful for you and our friendship. Much love to you, always.

Julie Guacci, aka "Momma Julie", thank you for all of the fun marketing ideas you passed my way before embarking on your new journey.

Anissa de Gomery—I treasure our friendship and cannot thank you enough for always being there to light up any dark time. Getting to work with you on the special FairyLoot edition—and getting to see all of that fabulous art and the details spring to life was like real life magic.

To my mom and dad, Kelli and Ben, and my whole family—I love you more than words can say. Thank you for always listening to me chatter on about characters and plot points and offering lots of good advice, and for getting just as excited as I do.

There's nothing quite as special as the bond between sisters, so here's a special shout-out to my sister for not only being my best friend but for letting me create *Kingdom of the Wicked* and *Stalking Jack the Ripper* merchandise for her store, Dogwood Lane Boutique. Love you, Kel!

Book bloggers, bookstagrammers, librarians, teachers, booksellers, The Bookish Box, Beacon Book Box, and FairyLoot—your excitement for this book is the stuff dreams are made of. Thank you for all of your support.

And to you, dear reader. Without you, none of this would be possible. I hope this story transported you into a lush new world for a few hours, and I hope you're excited for Emilia and Wrath's next wicked adventure. ☺

ABOUT THE AUTHOR

Kerri Maniscalco grew up in a semi-haunted house outside New York City, where her fascination with gothic settings began. In her spare time she reads everything she can get her hands on, cooks all kinds of food with her family and friends, and drinks entirely too much tea while discussing life's finer points with her cats. Her first novel, *Stalking Jack the Ripper,* debuted at #1 on the *New York Times* bestseller list, and *Hunting Prince Dracula, Escaping From Houdini,* and *Capturing the Devil* were all *New York Times* and *USA Today* bestsellers. She's always excited to talk about fictional crushes on Instagram @KerriManiscalco. For news and updates check out kerrimaniscalco.com.

Turn the page for an extract
from Kerri Mansicalco's new book

One sister. Two sinful princes.
Infinite deception with a side of revenge . . .

Welcome to Hell.

ONE

Hell was not what I expected.

Ignoring the traitorous Prince of Wrath at my side, I took a quiet, shuddering breath as smoke wafted around from the demon magic he'd used to transport us here. To the Seven Circles.

In the brief moments it took us to travel from the cave in Palermo to this realm, I'd concocted various visions of our arrival, each one more terrible than the last. In every nightmare, I'd pictured a cascade of fire and brimstone raining down. Flames burning hot enough to scorch my soul or melt the flesh right off my bones. Instead, I fought a sudden shiver.

Through the lingering smoke and mist I could just make out walls hewn from a strange, opaque gemstone that shot up farther than I could see. They were either deep blue or black, as if the darkest part of the sea had swelled up to an impossible height and had frozen in place.

Chills raced down my spine. I resisted the urge to breathe warmth into my hands or turn to Wrath for comfort. He was not my friend, and he certainly wasn't my protector. He was exactly what his brother Envy had claimed: the worst of the seven demon princes.

A monster among beasts.

I could never allow myself to forget what he was. One of the Wicked. The immortal beings who stole souls for the devil, and the selfish midnight creatures my grandmother warned my twin and me to hide from our whole lives. Now I willingly promised to wed their king, the Prince of Pride, to end a curse. Or so I'd led them to believe.

The metal corset my future husband had given me earlier tonight turned unbearably cold in the frigid air. Layers of my dark, glittering skirts were too light to provide any true protection or warmth, and my slippers were little more than scraps of black silk with thin leather soles.

Ice sluiced through my veins. I couldn't help but think this was yet another wicked scheme designed by my enemy to unsettle me.

Puffs of breath floated like ghosts in front of my face. Haunting, ethereal. Disturbing. Goddess above. I was really *in* Hell. If the demon princes didn't get to me first, Nonna Maria was certainly going to kill me. Especially when my grandmother discovered I'd signed my soul away to Pride. *Blood and bones.* The devil.

An image of the scroll that bound me to House Pride flashed through my mind. I couldn't believe I'd signed the contract in blood. Despite my earlier confidence in my plot to infiltrate this world and avenge my sister's murder, I felt completely unprepared now that I was standing here.

Wherever "here" was, exactly. It didn't appear as if we'd made it inside any of the seven royal demon Houses. I don't know why I thought Wrath would make this journey easy on me.

"Are we waiting for my betrothed to arrive?"

Silence.

I shifted uncomfortably.

Smoke still drifted close enough to obscure my full view, and with my demonic escort refusing to speak, my mind started to taunt me with a wide array of inventive fears. For all I knew, Pride was standing before us, waiting to claim his bride in the flesh.

I listened hard, straining to hear any sound of an approach through the smoke. Of anything. There was nothing aside from the frantic pitter-patter of my heart.

No screams of the eternally tortured and cursed. Absolute, unnerving silence surrounded us. It felt heavy—as if all hope had been abandoned a millennium ago and all that remained was the crushing quiet of despair. It would be so easy to give up, to lie down and let the darkness in. This realm was winter in all its harsh, unforgiving glory.

And we hadn't even passed through the gates yet...

Panic seized me. I wanted to be back in my city—with its sea-kissed air and summery people—so badly, my chest ached. But I'd made my choice, and I'd see it through, no matter what. Vittoria's true murderer was still out there. And I'd walk through the gates of Hell a thousand times over to find him. My location changed, but my ultimate goal did not.

I took a deep breath, my emotions settling with the action.

The smoke finally dissipated, revealing my first unobstructed glimpse of the underworld.

We were alone in a cave, similar to the one we'd left high above the sea in Palermo, the very place I'd set up my bone circle and first summoned Wrath nearly two months before, but also so different my stomach lurched at the alien landscape.

From somewhere above us a few silvery pools of moonlight trickled in. It wasn't much, but offered enough illumination to see the desolate, rock-scattered ground glistening with frost.

Several meters away a towering gate stood tall and menacing, not unlike the silent prince standing beside me. Columns—carved from obsidian and depicting people being tortured and murdered in brutal fashions—bracketed two doors made entirely of skulls. Human. Animal. Demon. Some horned, others fanged. All disturbing. My focus landed on what I assumed was the handle: an elk skull with an enormous set of frost-coated antlers.

Wrath, the mighty demon of war and betrayer of my soul, shifted. A tiny spark of annoyance had me glancing his way. His penetrating gaze was already trained on me. That same cold look on his face. I wanted to claw out his heart and stomp on it to get some *hint* of an emotion. Anything would be better than the icy indifference he now wore so well.

He'd turned on me the second it suited his needs. He was a selfish creature. Just like Nonna had warned. And I'd been a fool to believe otherwise.

We stared at each other for an extended beat.

Here, in the shadows of the underworld, his dark gold eyes glinted like the ruby-tipped crown on his head. My pulse ticked faster the longer our gazes remained locked in battle. His hold on me tightened slightly, and it was only then that I realized I was clasping his hand in a white-knuckled grip. I dropped it and stepped away.

If he was annoyed or amused or even furious, I wouldn't know. His expression still hadn't shifted; he was as remote as he'd been when he offered that contract with Pride a few minutes ago. If that's the way he wanted things to be between us now, fine. I didn't need or want him. In fact, I'd say he could go straight to Hell, but we'd both accomplished that.

He watched as I reined in my thoughts. I forced myself into a frozen calm I was far from feeling. Knowing how well he could sense emotions, it was probably futile. I looked him over.

Doing my best to emulate the demon prince, I mustered up my haughtiest tone. "The infamous gates of Hell, I presume."

He arched a dark brow as if asking if *that* was the best I could come up with.

Anger replaced lingering fear. At least he was still good for something. "Is the devil too high and mighty to meet his future queen here? Or is he afraid of a dank cave?"

Wrath's answering smile was all sharp edges and wicked delight. "This isn't a cave. It's a void outside the Seven Circles."

He placed a hand on the small of my back and guided me forward. I was so shocked by the pleasant feel of him, the tender intimacy of his action, I didn't step away. Pebbles skittered beneath our feet but didn't make a sound. Aside from our voices, the lack of noise was jarring enough that I almost lost my balance. Wrath steadied me before letting go.

"It's the place stars fear to enter," he whispered near my ear, his warm breath a severe contrast against the frosty air. I shuddered. "But *never* the devil. Darkness is seduced by him. As is fear."

He ran bare knuckles down my spine, enticing more goose bumps to rise. My breath hitched. I spun around and knocked his hand away.

"Take me to see Pride. I'm tired of your company."

The ground rumbled below us. "Your pride didn't appear in that bone circle the night you spilled blood and summoned me. It was your wrath. Your fury."

"That may be true, *your highness,* but the scroll I signed said 'House Pride,' didn't it?"

I stepped closer, heart thrashing as I crowded his space. The heat of his body radiated around me like sunshine, warm and enticing. It reminded me of home. The new ache in my chest was acute, consuming. I sharpened my tongue like a blade and aimed straight for his icy heart, hoping to penetrate the wall he'd so expertly erected between us. Wrong or not, I wanted to hurt him the way his deception had gutted me.

"Therefore, I chose the devil, not you. How does that feel? Knowing I'd prefer to bed a monster for eternity rather than subject myself to *you* again, Prince Wrath."

His attention dropped to my lips and lingered. A seductive gleam entered his eyes as I returned the favor. He might not admit it, but he wanted to kiss me. My mouth curved into a vicious grin; finally, he'd lost that cold indifference. Too bad for him I was now forbidden.

He stared a moment longer, then said with lethal quiet, "You choose the devil?"

"Yes."

We stood near enough to share breath now. I refused to back away. And he did, too.

"If that's what you wish, speak it to this realm. As a matter of fact," he yanked his dagger out from inside his suit jacket, "if you're so certain about the devil, swear a blood oath. If pride truly is your sin of choice, I imagine you won't say no."

Challenge burned in his gaze as he handed the blade to me, hilt-first. I snatched his House dagger and pressed the sharp metal to my fingertip. Wrath crossed his arms and gave me a flat look. He didn't think I'd go through with it. Maybe it *was* my cursed pride, but it also felt a little like my temper was raging as I pricked my finger and handed the serpent blade back. I'd already signed Pride's contract; there was no reason to hesitate now. What was done was done.

"I, Emilia Maria di Carlo, freely choose the devil."

A single drop of blood splattered to the ground, sealing the vow. I flicked my attention to Wrath. Something ignited in the depths of his eyes, but he turned away before I could read what it was. He shoved the dagger into his jacket and started making his way toward the gates, leaving me alone at the edge of nothingness.

I thought about running, but there was nowhere to go.

I glanced around once more and hurried after the demon, falling into step beside him. I wrapped my arms around myself, trying desperately to stop the increasing shivers, which only succeeded in making me shudder more. Wrath had taken his warmth with him, and now the metal corset top bit into my skin with renewed vigor. If we stayed out here much longer, I'd freeze to death. I conjured memories of warmth, peace.

I'd only ever felt this cold once—in northern Italy—and I'd been young and thrilled by the snow then. I'd thought it was romantic; now I saw the truth: it was beautifully dangerous.

Much like my current traveling companion.

My teeth chattered like tiny hammers, the only noise in the void. "How can we hear each other?"

"Because I will it."

Arrogant beast. I released a quivering huff. It was meant to come across as exasperated, but I feared it only gave away how cold I was. A heavy velvet cloak appeared from thin air, draping itself around my shoulders. I don't know where Wrath magicked it from and didn't care.

I pulled it tighter, grateful for its warmth. I opened my mouth to thank the demon but stopped myself with a swift internal shake. Wrath hadn't acted out of kindness or even chivalry. I imagined he did it largely to make sure I didn't die this close to accomplishing his mission.

If I recalled correctly, delivery of my soul to Pride granted him freedom from the underworld. Something he once said he prized above all else.

How exceptionally marvelous for him. His stay was over just as mine was beginning. And all he had to do was betray me to secure his heart's greatest desire.

I supposed I understood that well enough.

Wrath continued toward the gate and didn't look in my direction again. He pressed a hand to the column closest to us and whispered a word in a foreign tongue, too low for me to hear. Gold light pulsed from his palm and flowed into the black gemstone.

A moment later, the gates slowly creaked open. I couldn't see what lay beyond and my mind promptly crafted all sorts of terrible things. The demon prince offered no formal invitation; he prowled toward the opening he'd made without bothering to see if I followed.

I took a deep breath and steeled my nerves. No matter what was waiting for us, I'd do what I must to achieve my goals. I nestled into my cloak and started forward.

Wrath paused on the threshold to the underworld and finally deigned to look at me again. His expression was harsher than his tone, which halted me in my tracks.

"A word of caution."

"We're about to enter Hell," I said sardonically. "The caution speech may be a little late."

He was not amused. "In the Seven Circles there are three rules to abide by. First, don't ever reveal your true fears."

I hadn't planned to. "Why?"

"This world will turn itself inside out to torture you." I opened my mouth, but he held up a hand. "Second, control your desires or they will taunt you with illusions easily confused with reality. You had a taste of what that's like when you met Lust. Each of your desires will be magnified tenfold here, particularly when we enter the Sin Corridor."

"The Sin Corridor." I didn't pose it as a question, but Wrath answered anyway.

"New subjects of the realm are tested to see which royal House their dominant sin aligns best with. You will experience a certain . . . prodding . . . of emotions as you pass through it."

"I signed my soul to Pride. Why do I need to see where I'm best suited?"

"Live long enough to find that answer out yourself."

I swallowed my rising discomfort. Nonna always cautioned that bad news came in threes, which meant the worst was yet to come. "The third rule is . . ."

His attention slid to the finger I'd pricked. "Be cautious when making blood bargains with a prince of Hell. And under no circumstances should you ever make one involving the devil. What's his is his. Only a fool would fight or challenge him."

I ground my teeth together. The true games of deception had clearly begun. His warning vaguely reminded me of a note from our family grimoire, and I wondered how we'd come to hold that knowledge. I tucked those thoughts away, focusing instead on my growing anger.

He was no doubt stoking my emotions with his namesake

power. Which enraged me all the more. "Signing my soul away wasn't quite good enough. So you resorted to trickery. At least you're consistent."

"Someday you'll see it as a favor."

Unlikely. I curled my injured hand into a fist. Wrath met my gaze again, and a smile tugged at the corners of his sensuous mouth. He undoubtedly sensed my growing fury.

One day, soon enough, I would make him pay for this.

I gave him a dazzling smile, letting myself imagine how good it would feel when I finally destroyed him. His expression shuttered and he inclined his head—as if reading my every thought and emotion and silently vowed to do the same. In this hatred we were united.

Holding his intense stare, I nodded back, thankful for his treachery. It was the last time I'd fall for his lies. With any luck, though, it would be the start of him and his wicked brothers falling for mine. I'd need to play my role well, or I'd end up dead like the other witch brides.

I brushed past him and strode through the gates of Hell as if I owned them. "Take me to my new home. I'm ready to greet my dear husband."

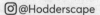